Superi: Revolution
Book III

Clint Thurmon

Christina R. Williams

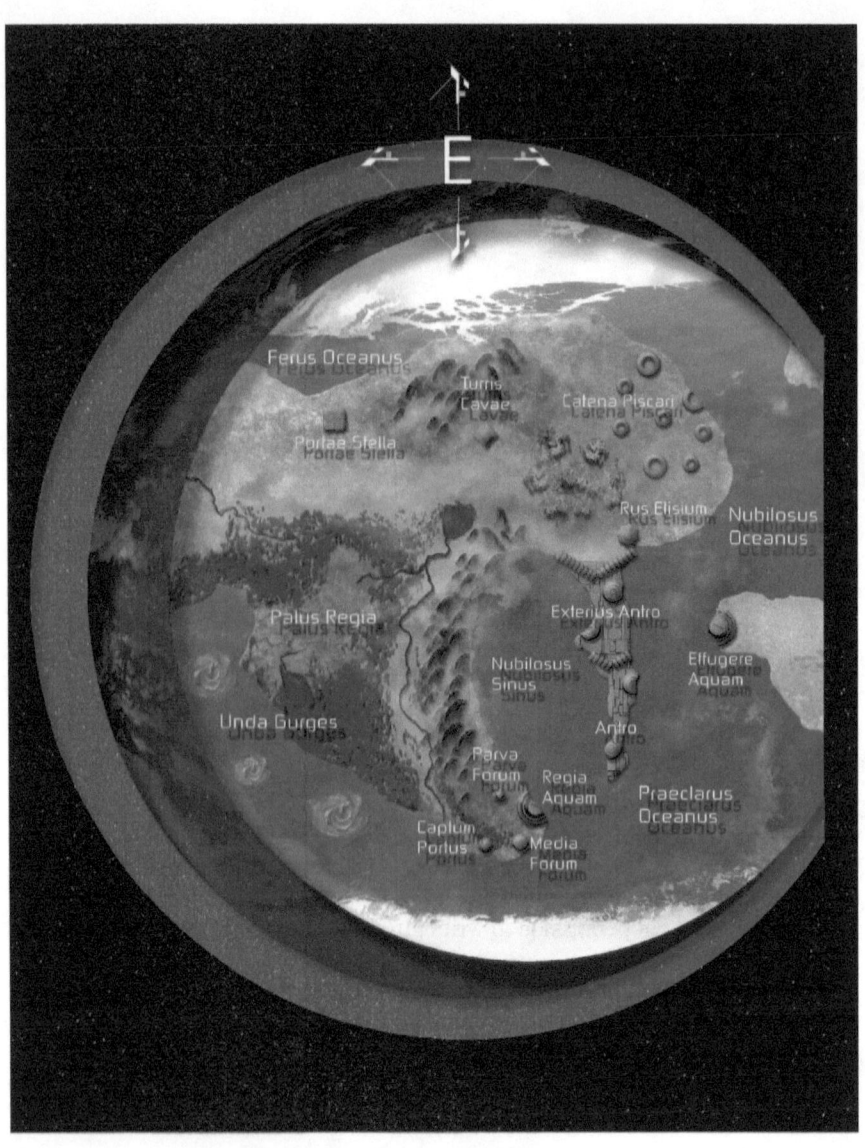

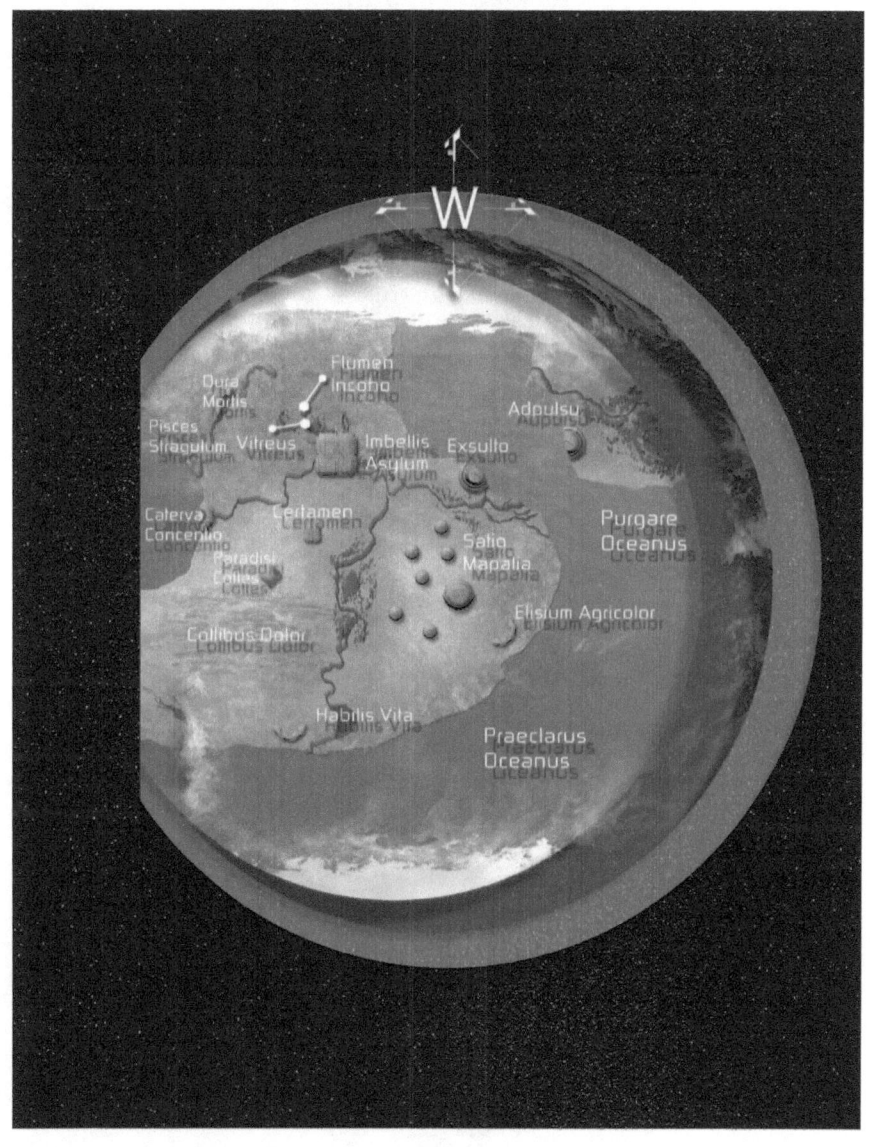

THE BOOKS OF SUPERI

REBORN – BOOK 1

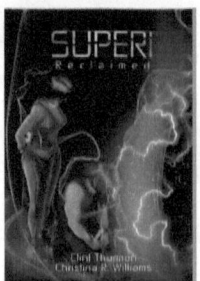

RECLAIMED – BOOK 2

REIGNITED – BOOK 4

RETRIBUTION – BOOK 5

CONTENTS

I

Seeing It Done

The shouting from inside Montilis's home was giving her a headache. Slipping out the backdoor, Shashara, with shoulders slumped, meandered her way towards a meditation pool gracing the House of Aquam's backyard. A peaceful breeze wafted the scent of cherry blossoms over her as songbirds trilled their music from the tree boughs. Nearby, trickling water spilled from a stone statue of a nox aquis wielder's hands. The grass beneath her was lush and green. Her panoramic view was filled with ancient trees and peaceful sand gardens. If she listened hard enough, she could almost hear the oceanus. Beauty surrounded her, and yet, her life was full of ugliness.

The more time that passed, the more her worry grew. She knew firsthand the horrors of the tower. Sorrow for her friends made the heated argument being waged within the house that much harder to bear. They had to find a gate maker willing to get them to Imbellis before Anliac was made like Tristan. They had to save them before Malstar and Calstar's ambitions could further hurt those she loved. Other than reclaiming their property, she couldn't fathom the tower's motive behind taking Tristan and the lack of understanding heightened her dread.

The twin suns poured their red light through a circular window, shining on her brother Davad and tinting his tanned skin with a copper hue. He wore their father's scowl as he faced off against Montilis, showing no fear of the general who wore a mask of aggravation. Davad's shorn, chocolate-brown hair stood up in frazzled disarray. At fifteen, he stood five feet nine, and was quickly fleshing out from boy to man. His temper was growing as well. He did look handsome though in the tailored brown breeches and sleeveless tunic Montilis had given him.

Taking advantage of being alone, she viewed Set unhindered. Covering the left side of his face was the blue teardrop markings of his epoto ability, which was caught within the blue, fine-webbed marking of his newly acquired gate maker one. The contrast against his pale skin was breathtaking. His eyes, like the white blue of frozen water, intrigued her in a way she'd not noticed before he'd kissed her. Her fingers itched to trace the white markings running through his hair. She liked the way his long bangs contrasted with his short hair on the sides and in the back. He was a couple of inches shorter than her five feet seven inches, but what did that matter? *He's younger than you too,* she thought to herself, put off by it.

Though tempted to linger, Shashara returned to the house before the argument could turn to blows—or worse. Not long ago, the sound of Rupert's repetitive clicking had disturbed her. Now she recognized it for what it was: apprehension, concern, and a reflection of Davad's and Set's anger. She laid a calming hand on his large, tanned, furred arm as she passed.

Throwing his hands in the air, Montilis exclaimed. "I've done what you've asked. I sent for the gate maker, but I'm telling you there is no way he will help without Magistrate Rayner's approval." Shaking his finger in their direction, he added. "And glowering at me will not change it."

Hearing this, Shashara asked. "How long before he arrives?"

Set and Davad paused in their ranting to hear Montilis's answer.

As if on cue, a servant entered. "Excuse me, general. Your guest has arrived."

"Thank Superi," Montilis muttered. "Bring him in." To them he said, "Mind your words carefully. He will not be commanded by children. Traydon," he greeted the nox as he entered. Placing a hand over his heart, Montilis bowed slightly, showing more respect than he felt. "Thank you for honoring my request."

"Consider this repayment of my debt to you."

Montilis's eyes narrowed. "Your debt to me is a large one. Coming here is not enough to square us unless you also agree to help us in our endeavor."

In snug fitted, black breeches and a shirt dripping with white lace, Traydon flitted across the polished redwood floor and perched on the edge of a cushioned chair, crossing his legs at the ankle. All but Montilis, who remained standing, moved within the circle of chaise lounges and armchairs to join him. Careful not to knock their shins against the edges of the square, black-marble table at the center, they took their seats. The fireplaces at either end of the spacious sitting room lay cold, leaving the sunlight pouring through a large oval window to draw out the sudden chill that had been projected into the room by Traydon.

Hazel eyes narrowed as, with a petulant mouth, he said. "The reason for this summons was unclear, Montilis. Perhaps you could enlighten me."

Though it was usually difficult to read a nox's mood by their expression alone; their darker skin tone, and sharp facial features, gave them a natural stoicism that was most often coupled with perpetual frowns, but in Traydon's case, his irritation read plainly by his stiff-necked appraisal of them all.

Marveling at the man's androgynous features, Davad cleared his throat, drawing the room's attention. "We need a portal to Imbellis."

Traydon's upper lip furled, his nose wrinkling, "Rumors of three children, and their pet," he said, "have cloaked the city. I am aware of your relationship with General Aquam and the reason for your presence in our city. I will not have my name muddied as the general's has been by associating myself with your ilk."

"Now hold on," Davad said, coming to his feet. "We traveled here—"

"At great risk to ourselves," Shashara interjected.

"To deliver news concerning Montilis's daughter," Davad finished. "All we're asking for is a portal that will get us to where we need to be."

"You mean back to Imbellis where you can stir up trouble and jeopardize crucial dealing between Palus Regia and the Asylum? As General Aquam has petitioned to do on several recent occasions?"

In a uniform decorated with badges of honor and stripes of rank on its sleeves, Montilis's battle scared face was stoic. His eyes were cold and deadly. "They have my daughter. Rayner may be magistrate, but I am the general of Palus Regia, and my standing within this city has not fallen so far that you should forget to mind your words.

"You lead our armies to war on the word of Magistrate Rayner. Without him, you are a mere tool left to gather dust until he calls upon you. Come down from your dais, Montilis, before you are dragged from it."

"Enough," Set said sharply. "The two of you can determine who has the bigger bite later. We're not asking you to go against Rayner's orders. I am a level two gate maker." Beginning strong, his confidence waned under Traydon's dubious smirk. "But I'm untrained. Teach me how to do it. That way, your hands stay clean of the situation, and we can move on."

Sniffing haughtily, Traydon said, "I don't like children." He rose from his seat and made for the exit. "This was a complete waste of my time."

Set darted across the redwood floor; the soles of his boots scuffing the polished wood as he maneuvered himself to block Traydon's route. The warning in his eyes gave Traydon pause. "I'm a newly made gate maker, but I've been an epoto my whole life. I can always take what I want."

2

"Arrogance has felled greater men than you, little boy." Clapping his hands before him, he then spread them apart, effortlessly opening a door-sized, crackling, portal between them. Set stumbled backward as Traydon walked through it, escaping his blockade.

"What was that?" Davad asked turning on Montilis. "How did he make that portal so fast?"

"The shorter the distance a gate maker wishes to travel, the faster the portal can be made. The opening showed the front of Rayner's house. That's where Traydon went." Montilis pinched the bridge of his nose. "Rayner will soon know that we tried to coerce his gate maker."

Throwing her hands wide, Shashara asked. "Well, what do we do now?"

"You will travel with me," he said. "I'll leave now to secure your passage." Montilis stormed out the door without waiting for an answer.

"I'm not waiting another week."

"What choice do we have, Set?" Shashara asked. "It would take us weeks to walk to the coast and we'd still have an oceanus to contend with."

"I need out of this house." Reason abandoned Set as desperation fueled his hasty departure.

"Rupert, follow him," Shashara said. Though the fera complied, the concern tightening her chest did not dissipate.

"Davad, you don't think Set will do something stupid do you?"

"I hope not." Quickly, Davad strode from the sitting room through the expansive foyer to peer through one of the tall, rectangular, panes of colored glass straddling both sides of the large, arched, front door. He saw Rupert fall into step beside Set as they headed into the city.

Set rolled his eyes as Rupert caught up to him. "Shashara sent you, didn't she?"

"She's worried."

Rupert hunched to make himself appear smaller than his eight feet height when their trek through the city's streets began to draw the attention of Palus Regia's citizens. There was nothing he could do to hide his muscular girth, however.

Upon entering the city days ago, he'd conformed to civilized dress as much as he was able. His feet were not made for boots, and nox clothing was not sized for shoulders as wide or for arms as long as his own. Despite the dark brown breeches he wore, and the white linen, unbuttoned shirt tucked into them, people stared.

"Where are we going?" he asked.

Keeping a steady gait, Set warned. "You should go back. Tell Shashara and Davad that you lost track of me."

"No." His sad gray eyes failed to match his adamant tone but managed to make Set feel like a mule for suggesting it.

"Rupert, trust me, you don't want to be with me right now. Char will skin me alive if I get you into trouble, and I'm going to cause a tidal wave of it." He directed his course towards a mounted nox soldier patrolling the outer city area.

"Excuse me," Set called to gain the man's attention.

"What are you doing?" Rupert asked under his breath as he dropped his gaze and tried to appear nonthreatening as the soldier assessed him while speaking to Set.

"What do you want?" the soldier sneered.

Set ignored the man's soured expression. "Could you point us in the direction of the magistrate's house?"

The soldier snorted derisively. "I don't think so, but I'll tell you what I will do," he added nudging his horse forward. "I'll go make sure your fera friend has permission to be here."

Placing his hands on his hips, Rupert shook his head as the soldier hurried his pace.

"What? It was worth a shot," Set said as they continued on.

"It was dumb." Rupert clicked in frustration. "Now every soldier in Palus Regia knows where we're going."

A weak blow landed against the back of Rupert's right thigh. He turned to find a little, brown-eyed nox girl, no more than five or six years old, standing in a bright blue dress with grass stains at the knees, brandishing a wooden sword in her hand. She glared defiantly up at him, refusing to give ground though the enemy she'd chosen stood a half a dozen feet taller.

Seeing her outmatched, three nox boys around her age, in matching trousers and shirts that mimicked the colors of the Regia Aquam Guard, let out a war cry as they joined the battle and attacked.

Their training swords did no damage, so Rupert allowed their game. Falling to his knees, he folded his hands behind his head and accepted his defeat.

They kept the tips of their swords pointed in his direction as they shared startled glances amongst themselves.

"What do we do with him now?" one of the boys asked.

"I was taking him to the magistrate," Set offered. "He's a fera. He can't be allowed to run loose through the city, but seeing as I am a stranger here myself, I'm not sure where the magistrate is. Will you help me?"

The little girl's head tilted to the side, her lips pursing. "He's awful big. What if we can't make him go?"

"I'll help you," Set assured her. "Get up," he barked at Rupert. As he stood, Set shoved him forward. "See. He's big but not very brave."

Letting loose a string of clicks that had the children squeaking and preparing to run, Set shoved him again for good measure. Resigned to playing his part, Rupert hunched his shoulders in mock humiliation and allowed himself to be "taken."

With a patronizing bow that was lost on the younger children, Set said, "Lead the way."

Keeping their prisoner under close guard, the boys stood to the side as the girl took the lead. On occasion, Rupert would glance over his shoulder towards Set, who would wink and duck his head to hide his smile. As luck would have it, the magistrate's house wasn't far.

Rayner's massive two-storied, tan-bricked home with a slanted roof sat a good distance back from the cobble stone street before it. As was common in Palus Regia, the front lawn was landscaped with stone pathways and water features that were both whimsical and daunting. Flower gardens flourished, adding vitality to the venue. Two guards flanked the front door while a handful of others could occasionally be spotted as they made their routes around the perimeter of Rayner's property. There were guards at the ornamental gate as well.

The children stood on weakening knees before the imposing dwelling of their leader.

"My mama says I'm not supposed to bother important people," the little girl whimpered.

Shifting their feet, the boys began to reconsider their actions as well. "Maybe we should let him go," one said. "We can make him swear to leave the city right now and never come back."

Keeping a straight face, Set said, "I'll tell you what. Why don't you leave it to me? I'll make sure our prisoner is brought before the magistrate."

"But you're mortalis," the girl stated. "Why would you help us?"

"I might not be nox, but I'm still a kid...like you. We have to stick together at times like this," Set said. "I'm older, so I can get away with it, and I don't want you to get into any trouble with your mom."

Smiles replaced their worried frowns. "You're very brave for a mortalis," one of the boys praised as they ran off to look for new adventures.

Set and Rupert stood in the street contemplating how to get around the two guards blocking access to the grounds while the guards looked on with amusement.

"Can you smell Traydon?"

Rupert nodded. "He's in there, but we're never getting past those guards without bringing more down on our heads."

"Oh yes we are."

Set's mischievous grin alarmed Rupert. "Set..."

Rupert's call for caution came too late. Storming the guards as if he had an army at his back, Set attacked them head on. Orbs of water formed in their hands as they came forward to meet the inconceivable attack.

"Hold!" the guard on the right said.

Neither Rupert nor Set slowed as the orbs were launched. Set fell into a forward roll dodging one. Coming to his feet, he lunged to the side to avoid another. "Watch out!"

Rupert howled as he took a direct hit to his left shoulder, and then snarled and shook his head as his narrowed eyes pinned his target. The guard's eyes bulged as Rupert's speed ability carried him forward much faster than the other man anticipated. Sheathing his claws to avoid causing serious damage, Rupert slugged the guard's chin, snapping the man's head around and knocking him out cold.

Set grabbed the second guard by the wrist, draining him of his energy and putting him to sleep while Rupert scaled the metal gate and unlatched it from the inside.

The commotion had a crowd of nox forming in the street as their panicked shouts rang out for soldiers' aid.

"That can't be good."

Shoving the gate wide, Rupert shouted. "No time to worry about it now."

"Right," Set agreed. "Let's go."

The ease in which they made it to the front double doors of Rayner's house should have given them warning. They let themselves in and were immediately confronted by three guards standing at the ready. Concentrating on only putting the man to sleep, and hoping he didn't kill him, Set ran forward and grabbed for the closest guard before he could form an aquis weapon. In a burst of speed, Rupert wrapped his hand around the furthest guard's throat. Stepping forward as he lifted the man off his feet, he slammed the guard into the floor, where his head rebounded before he lay still.

"What's the meaning of this!" a nasal voice boomed, echoing between vaulted ceilings and cold, gray and white marble.

"Run, magistrate!" the remaining guard bellowed as he squared off against the two intruders. Water flew from one of a dozen fountains situated along the foyer's dark gray walls, and transformed, mid-flight, into long thin spears.

With Set and Rupert each using their speed, the two ducked and dodged their way to the wielder who, witnessing their advance, formed a double-edged sword in his right hand before creating a shield of water that appeared in his left.

Rupert grinned at the challenge.

Ignoring the child, the guard focused on the fera advancing with a fluid grace that belied his hulking size. With his opponent topping him by several feet and easily twice as wide, the guard broadened his stance and bent his knees. Tucking beneath his shield, he prepared to plunge his blade with an upward thrust into the fera's gut.

Rupert charged as the guard expected but before coming within range of the blade, he leapt over the man's head, his claws scratching the marble as he landed behind him. As quick as thought, he looped one long arm through the crook of the nox's sword arm and pulled up as he planted his other hand on the center of the man's back, forcing him forward to his knees. Rupert clonked him on the top of the head, knocking him senseless and incapacitating him.

A sound of strangled panic reached their ears from above as Rayner, witnessing his man's fall, turned to run.

"Get him!" Set yelled out loud.

Rupert darted up the stairway, with Set following close behind. Reaching the second floor, Rupert grabbed the magistrate's arms and pulled them backward in a vise grip, halting his escape.

"Guards! Guards!" Rayner screeched.

"Shut up," Set warned, planting himself before the magistrate. Ripping the front of Rayner's robe from neck to sternum, he laid his palm flat against the man's hairy chest. "In case my marks are not enough, you should know that I'm an epoto."

Rayner paled; his Adam's apple bobbed as he swallowed. "I know what you are."

"Then you know I'm desperate," Set said. "Call your gate maker."

The magistrate flinched as the front door exploded open and soldiers filed in.

Set ignored them. "Tell them to stay back or you'll be dead before they reach us."

Rupert let go of the man's arms. Unfurling himself to his full height, Rupert drew back his shoulders to expand his broad chest, ripping the white shirt, and loomed large over the soldiers below, deterring rash action.

"Stand down," Rayner said, his voice quivering. In his peripheral vision, he saw the soldiers start forward. "For Superi's sake, hold your positions!"

"Where is Traydon?" Set demanded.

"I left him in my office."

"Get him out here."

Rayner spotted a servant pressed against the wall, peeking from behind a vase of flowers gracing the top of a slender, rectangular hall table. With a frightened visage, the servant was observing the unimaginable scene playing out before her. Rayner gestured with a swift jerk of his head that she should fetch the gate maker. Curtsying on wobbly knees, she obeyed.

Moments later, she returned with a disbelieving Traydon.

"Fools... the both of you. You'll swing from the gallows before the day is out for this." Taking courage from the soldiers' presence, he said, "You have nowhere to go."

"Rupert," Set nodded toward Traydon.

The gate maker found himself wrapped in a bear hug; his arms pinned to his sides as Rupert's superior strength overwhelmed his meager struggles.

"Fine," Traydon scowled, "I'll do it. I can't get you to Imbellis, but I can get you to the coast. I can get you to Exterius Antro."

"Oh no," Set grinned, his visage full of malice. "It's too late for that, Traydon. I can't trust you not to dump us somewhere unpleasant."

The veins in Traydon's temple throbbed as the tendons in his neck protruded with the strain of his words. "Then what do you want?"

"Bring him closer, Rupert." Reaching out his free hand, Set wrapped it around Traydon's wrist. "Take the magistrate."

Rupert released his hold on Traydon to do as Set requested.

Traydon blanched. "What are you going to do to me?"

"As I promised," Set said.

The epoto's touch was like liquid fire inside Traydon's veins. The pain was agonizing as Traydon was brought to his knees by the boy's mere touch. He would have vowed anything to make it stop, but the only sound he was capable of making were screams. His mind opened like a sieve as the epoto stole his knowledge, leaving a vacuous hole behind.

Without pity, Set delved into the gate maker's mind. Seeing that his ability level matched that of Traydon's and that there was no more power to be gleaned, he focused on the nox's knowledge. He didn't bother to block the man's pain and he ignored the piercing screams his touch invoked. Set swayed under the onslaught of information, becoming nauseous as it settled into his mind as his own.

Before his drain could become deadly, Set severed the man from consciousness and watched him fall, drooling, to his side. Glimpsing the seething soldiers from over the balcony, he swallowed hard. The deadly gleams of retribution in their eyes were well matched to those of the men glaring out from the portraits of nox rulers and warriors that hung upon the foyer's walls surrounding them.

"Let's hope this works," Set said as he closed his eyes to focus, bringing forth an image of Montilis's house. Pressing his palms before him as he'd seen other gate makers do, he spread them slowly apart. Peeking at his work, his eyes came fully open as he saw the dark purple shadow of a portal crackling.

"You're doing it," Rupert encouraged.

"You'll never get away with this." Rayner said. "I'll have you hunted down and..."

"Quiet, magistrate, or I'll bring you with us." Set's skin tingled as his webbed mark swam across his forehead and temple, changing in color and shape, to depict the front room of Montilis's home. "Good enough," he said. "Rupert...you have to go first."

"I can't do that." Rupert's eyes flickered to the soldiers.

"I have to hold it open, Rupert." Set's entire body began to tremble slightly under the strain of maintaining the opening. His blood pounded in his temples. The veins in his neck and forearms pulsed, and he could taste bile.

"What about him?" Rupert asked, shaking the magistrate's rotund frame.

"Knock him out."

"No! Please," the terrified nox said. "You're free to leave. I'll issue no orders to see you harmed. Just don't hurt me."

Spinning him around, Rupert bared his spiked teeth. Placing their faces inches apart, Rupert opened his mouth and snarled, his hot breath adding to the sheen of sweat coating Rayner's flesh. The magistrate's eye rolled back in his head as he passed out from fear.

The moment the magistrate crumbled; the soldiers fell into action. A wall of aquis projectiles flew like arrows to the balcony above. Growling his displeasure, Rupert leapt through the small portal, turning sideways to prevent his wide shoulders from being cut on its edges. Set followed, narrowly avoiding disaster.

Davad gaped at the chair he'd just risen from, that was now split in two and charred black where the portal had parted it. Rupert tripped over one section of the chair, his weight shoving it away from the portal as Set tumbled through, crying out in pain as he collided with the marble table. With a resounding boom, the portal imploded, collapsing behind him.

"Blast it all, Set! What have you done?"

"Not now, Davad," Set said. "Where's Montilis?"

"He hasn't made it back yet," Shashara said, pressing a hand to the center of her chest as if it pained her.

"That's good," Set nodded, wide-eyed and panicked. "That means he can't be blamed. Rupert, watch the doors and windows."

"Hurry, Set," Rupert rushed to do as bidden. "We won't have long."

"Have long for what?" Davad asked as he watched Rupert dart from one window to the next.

Feeling the drain on his energy as never before, Set centered himself in order to open another portal. "Exterius. Exterius." He dredged his memory for details of the city's coast, bringing to mind its docks and the clear stretch of land laying off to the side of them, hoping to avoid severing something of more importance than the chair he'd ruined.

"Set, you don't know what you're doing," Shashara cried. "Please, this is too dangerous. Oh!" she gasped, "your marks."

Taking encouragement from his shifting marks, he focused on calling Exterius Antro to him, bending the distance between the two points. With his arms widespread, a growing shadow formed as purple lightning cut through the distance across the eastern continent, seeking the gate maker's destination. Finding it, the image of the coast clarified.

"We've got company," Rupert said. "It appears half the Regia Aquam Guard is at our doorstep." He turned from the window. "Do you want to guess which soldier is leading them?"

"I guess that means we're not supposed to be here." Set grinned despite their dire circumstances. "Time to go home, people. Move."

"Shashara, you first," Davad insisted, positioning her before the portal. "I'll be right behind you."

"But...wait..." she resisted her brother's insistent nudge.

The front door was knocked from its hinges as angry soldiers spilled into the house. Davad scooped his sister up off her feet and jumped through. Rupert snatched Set by the front of his shirt, and launched himself backward through the opening, hauling Set through with him.

II
We Meet Again

Flying through the collapsing gateway, Tristan's impact was cushioned by that of the fera guard holding his leash as their momentum met its match against the stone wall across the tower's prison room. They fell in a tangle of arms and legs as they grappled for dominance. The guard came out on top and slammed his fist into Tristan's face.

Scrambling to her feet, Anliac rushed forward to intervene. "Stop!" she screamed, gagging as a fierce yank tightened the collar around her neck. Her feet flew from beneath her as she landed with a 'humph' on the hard stone floor.

"Enough! We need him alive." Jaydon said. Using the wall for support, he picked himself off the floor, wincing as the blisters Shashara had caused burst open. Cursing, he began to cover his wounds with the bottom of his black tunic but let the bloody, mud caked, material fall. "How on Superi did this happen," he said. "I'm going to kill that incompetent gate maker."

Anliac and Tristan were dragged, thrashing and grasping at their collars, to the center of the room where they were made to kneel.

"I fear the gate maker's failure will be the least of our problems," the guard from behind Tristan spoke. "We may have accomplished our aim, but we lost that battle. Calstar will not be pleased."

Exhaling, Jaydon closed his eyes and pinched the bridge of his nose. "Against children, no less." His head snapped around when Tristan chuckled.

Taking the three strides necessary to breech the distance between them, Jaydon backhanded Tristan across the face, splitting his bottom lip.

"Feel better?" Tristan taunted, tasting copper on his tongue as his blood seeped into his mouth. He could feel the empty scabbard at his waist and wished his sword remained within it and his hands free to wield it. If so, the aer wielder would be dead. As Jaydon pulled back his arm, his fist clenched, Tristan braced himself for a solid blow.

Malstar came through the open door of the prison. "Strike him and answer to me."

Anliac flinched, causing Tristan to glance her way in concern. With a slight shake of her head, she averted her eyes to the floor. She could see the toes of Malstar's black, soft-soled shoes peeking from beneath the hem of his dark purple robe as he circled, inspecting them.

Tristan tracked the fulgo's progress.

"What is your name?" Malstar asked.

With no reply forthcoming, Jaydon supplied the answer. "She calls him Tristan."

"On most occasions, our prison room holds a minimum of four to five slaves. However, after the fiasco that saw my prisoners running rampant through the city streets, this room is empty of all but you." Malstar said.

"I must say," Malstar continued, "Calstar is most anxious to hear your report, Jaydon. His mood is foul. If it were me, I would not keep him waiting."

Offended by Malstar's quick dismissal, yet knowing better than to ignore the warning, he still did not want to be responsible should Calstar's prisoners escape. "I'll send in more guards."

"The two here will suffice." At Jaydon's skeptical visage, he added. "They are bound in arcanite, are they not? The spelled chains have blocked them from their abilities?"

"Yes."

"Then go." Malstar flicked his wrist, forgetting the bounty hunter before he'd disappeared through the door. Squatting down before Tristan, he said, "You and I have never been properly introduced. I am Malstar."

"I know who you are," Tristan sneered.

"Then you know it was I who discovered the secret that was hiding in your blood," Malstar said. "That I am the one that unlocked your true potential, and that between us, the angeli was reborn."

"You should get out of the tower more."

Standing upright, Malstar's shook with silent mirth. "Though this body rarely leaves these walls, I have eyes that travel, as your presence here would suggest."

"Baby snatchers, skin traders, mercenaries." Tristan spat on the floor. "Your eyes are foul and your intent villainous. You make me sick."

"An odd choice of words for one raised by mercenaries."

"Don't you mean betrayed by them?" Tristan surged against his leash, causing the guard at his back to lurch forward. The heavy weight of the fera's hand yanked him back into place. His tether was shortened until he was choked by the arcanite collar around his neck.

"I understand the sentiment." Malstar said. "Truly I do. For they betrayed me as well. I am not the monster you believe me to be, Tristan. I suffer under the weight of my failures and under the pain and sorrow they have wrought, but the endeavor was necessary."

Unable to hold her tongue, Anliac said, "Tell that to those who did the suffering."

Ignoring the scathing remark, Malstar addressed his guards. "Send for a healer to tend their wounds and see them bathed and properly dressed." His nose wrinkled. "They reek of blood and sweat." As an afterthought, he added, "Mind their chains or you'll not live to regret the oversight. When finished, bring them to the room prepared for their arrival, and do not harm them beyond what is necessary to quell errant thoughts of rebellion."

"So, kind of you," Anliac said, "considering our last encounter."

Malstar's brow furrowed as he considered Anliac's words. "How can you say so? Did I not offer you the world in exchange for your help? A life of ease in which you would have been treated as a precious gift? I spared the mortalis girl in case your mind was changed and intended to place her as your maidservant for no other purpose than to please you."

Stiffening her spine, and her resolve, she said, "And when I refused, you turned me over to your men, ordering them to weaken my will," she swallowed back the bile that rose in her throat, "to be more malleable towards your own."

Malstar's face reddened. "A rift maker opened a gateway to another planet, and in ignorance, he trespassed upon land guarded by beings beyond his comprehension. The Superians were beaten back through the gateway, and before the way was closed, one such being cursed us all. They cursed our minds. They cursed our bodies. Tearing us into four races when we were created to be only one. What is to keep them from invading Superi? What would we do in our weakened state if they chose to return?" He did not wait for a reply. "As it stands, like a lit wick on a candle, those born with brilliant minds quickly burn out, leaving only brawn and animals like the fera to rule. Tell me, how long will Superi stand when chaos rules? We must devote ourselves to reestablishing the rightful power we were born with before those who call themselves gods return to finish what they began. I, for one, do not wish to find my death by their hand."

Tristan had listened carefully to Malstar's words, hoping to catch him in a lie, but could find no falsehood passing his lips. The only new information was the fear of the gods returning. "And what part are we to play?"

"The rift maker was an angeli," Malstar replied. "To reopen the gateway, an angeli had to be created. You are that man, and should you fail in your task," his eyes found Anliac, "she will take your place."

"You would ask for our help with one breath and spew threats with the next?" Tristan's eyes narrowed. "Your ambitions would have been better met had you chosen a different tact."

"I'm not asking for your help, Tristan," a cruel grin turned the corners of his mouth, "I am demanding it." Spinning on his heels, Malstar left them as suddenly as he'd appeared.

Tristan tracked the fulgo's departure through the door as images of the recent past bombarded him. The vision of Jacob laying face first in that open doorway, blood seeping from around the arrow protruding through his back; Shashara's screams as her father fell; Davad rushing the guard holding the bow; Set crying out for aid, one that Anliac answered because he'd been too busy mutilating a man on the other side of the door—it all hit him.

He was pulled from the past, and to his feet, as the length of chain running between the shackles encircling his wrists was looped over an iron hook suspended from the earthen ceiling, forcing him onto his toes.

Anliac yelped as she endured the same treatment. Her lesser height left her feet dangling in the air; her arms stretched, and her shoulder sockets voiced their complaint until a stool was placed beneath her.

When the fera bent to remove Tristan's boots, his thigh muscle twitched with the desire to kick the man in his ugly face, but fearing Anliac would suffer for the action, he refrained.

An eight-inch handled blade was pulled from a sheath fastened to his guard's belt, and Tristan's clothes were sliced and torn from his body. His gloves were skinned from his hands and tossed atop the remnants of his other garments, leaving him bared flesh and psyche.

His chore complete, Tristan's guard said, "I'll be back," as he handed the blade to the other fera and left the room.

Anliac's breathing grew ragged; her emerald green eyes went wide as her lips peeled back in a feral snarl. "Keep that blade away from me." She kicked out, knocking over the stool, and caught the fera in his jaw.

The guard rotated his chin and then backhanded her hard.

"Leave her alone!" Tristan shouted as Anliac kicked out again.

"You're not in a position to give orders, boy." As if to prove his point, he grabbed her bound ankles and slung her body backwards. Suspended from her wrists, he waited for her momentum to carry her forward and then he sunk his fist into her gut.

Anliac gagged as her body folded in two from the force of the blow and then went limp.

Grinning, the guard reached for the front of Anliac's tunic with one hand, bearing the knife in his other.

Before the blade touched cloth, Tristan crunched his abdominal muscles, bent his knees to his chest, and kicked out, catching the guard unprepared.

The crushing impact to the guard's chest had air gushing from his lungs as his feet left the floor, and he was tossed into the row of cages lining one of the walls. The wrought iron proved stronger than his spine, which bent backwards unnaturally over the top of the cage. The crack of bone sounded like a lightning strike in the silent moment before his screams pierced their ears. He slid to the ground, his legs, now useless flesh, hanging from his broken, fur-covered body.

Tristan's guard, having returned with servants carrying buckets of sudsy water and fresh

11

garments, stumbled to a stop in the open doorway and appeared poleaxed. "You've got to be kidding me," he said, retaking control of the situation. "You two," he pointed at the men who'd lugged in the water, "see him to the infirmary."

The fulgo servants placed their buckets before the slaves and rushed to aid the felled guard. He lasted as long as it took one to lift him up by his armpits and the other to lift his feet before the pain became unbearable and he passed out.

With slow, decisive steps, the guard picked up the knife that had slid against the base of a cage and handed it to the remaining male servant in the room. Bending to upright the overturned stool, he said, "Place this at her neck, and if she as much as twitches, slit her throat."

The servant's trembling hand had Anliac tilting up her chin while holding very still as a female fera bared her claws and made quick work of removing her clothes. In an effort to retain what dignity remained, Tristan and Anliac kept their eye averted and waited for the ordeal to be over.

No sooner than it was, a beautiful mortalis entered, a heavy braid of blonde hair falling to her waist. Her brown eyes were rich and warm as she approached Anliac. "Oh, you poor thing," she said. "You must be in considerable pain."

Anliac stiffened. "Those you work for are good at inflicting it."

Combining her aquis and healing abilities, the woman pulled water from the buckets and gloved her hands in the cool liquid. She circled behind Anliac, running her hands over the mutilated flesh of her back, and closed the gaping wounds Jaydon's whip had wrought.

Anliac gasped as her flesh knitted itself together.

"I suppose that's true," the woman said as she moved to Tristan, "but we all have our rolls to play." Her nostrils flared and her pupils dilated as her hands slid in a slow caress over the minor scraps he'd sustained, sealing them. "I rather like your eyes on me, angeli, but why do you stare," she asked.

"You remind me of someone," he replied.

Finished with her task, the water splashed to the floor. "I'm intrigued," she smiled. "Who might that be?" When he didn't respond, she traced a slender finger across his jaw. "A mystery for another day then." She turned to the guard. "They're all yours," she said, and left the room.

Hefting the heavy buckets, the servants splashed the cold aquis over them before taking up the lye and scrub brushes. Under the threat of the knife, Tristan and Anliac were cleansed of the battle at the northern gate and then stuffed into plain black robes as they cursed the spelled arcanite that held them prisoner.

Dismissing the servants, the guard shoved Tristan towards the door as the guard yanked Anliac against his chest. Knotting his fist into her hair, the guard placed the tip of his blade against her spine, ensuring Tristan's cooperation. "Walk to the stairwell," he ordered.

His feet did as they were told, but his mouth ran away from him. "I can only imagine how disappointed your Alphas must be," Tristan said.

"Please," the guard sneered. "What would you know about it?"

"What do you think being an angeli means?" Tristan asked. "Fera blood runs through my veins as it does yours, as does the collective dream." He'd no more idea what it meant to be angeli than the disquieted guard, and he'd never experienced the collective dream that his friend Rupert had talked about, but then the guard didn't need to know that.

"I don't answer to the Alphas. I answer to the Asylum," the guard said as they reached the stairwell. "Open it," he ordered. "Up. Two levels."

Tristan obeyed. He followed the winding steps until a sharp inhalation from Anliac faltered his steps "What is it? Are you okay?"

The guard pressed the tip of his blade against Anliac's back, causing her to grunt. "Keep moving," he warned.

"It's okay," she assured him. "I'm okay." As they continued their ascent, she said, "I can feel the flows of the water coursing through the aqueducts around us. I can feel it, but I can't..." her voice wavered. "When I reach for it with my ability, it's like grabbing the wind. There's nothing there."

"I know," Tristan said. "It feels as if my muscles will break my bones. The terra pulls at me as if I'm a meal it would devour. My strength has fled, leaving a weakness in its wake that fills me with pity for those that are born this way and with regret for ever having taken it for granted."

"Save your pity," the guard chuckled. "Your strength has become your curse. I do not envy you, nor would I choose to be as you are."

"It's not as if I chose this," Tristan said between clenched teeth. "Your masters made me what I am."

Reaching the door leading from the stairwell and onto the level just beneath the ground floor, which held the guards' quarters, weapons armory, and storage rooms, Tristan waited for the order before opening it.

"Move," the guard said, reaching past Anliac to shove the back of Tristan's head.

Tristan turned on him with a growl.

Anliac's eyes rounded as her shoulder blades pulled back to avoid the tip of the blade pressed there. "Tristan..." she held her breath in case it was her last.

Turning from the guard, his hands shaking with rage, he slammed his fists into the closed door.

They were directed to a storage room, which had been cleared of its contents and now held two pallets on the floor. Metal rings protruded from the stone wall inches above the bedding.

The guard shoved Tristan forward.

He stumbled but managed not to fall.

"Take it," the guard said, holding out a lock. "I want to hear it click."

Glaring, Tristan squatted down, and connected the spelled shackles around his ankles to the link on the wall.

"Good," the guard nodded, shoving Anliac down onto the pallet. "Don't move," he warned Tristan as he secured Anliac's ankles to the other link. Releasing their wrists from their restraints, he said, "Food will be brought to you shortly. The door will be guarded, so do not waste your time contemplating escape. Behave and your hands will remain free. Choose otherwise and find yourselves back in the prison room. Understood?"

"Yeah," Tristan said. "We get it."

"Then my job is done," the fera said as he closed and locked the door, leaving the two of them alone.

Tristan stretched out on the pallet and then crossed his hands behind his head. He stared at the ceiling. He had no doubt that Set, and the others would be heading to Palus Regia. They would find Montilis, and with the general's help, they would come for them. The question was how long it would take, and would they make it in time. It wasn't likely.

"Can you open the gateway Malstar was talking about?" Anliac asked.

"I'm not a gate maker, Anliac."

"But you are an angeli."

"Not fully," he corrected, thinking back to what Jacob had told them. "From what little I know, the ancient Superians were born with physical abilities like mine. Some greater. Some less, but all possessed more than what we are born with now. The angeli were capable of wielding more than one ability. Jacob said they were like me, if I were to wield aquis and terra as well, or an aether ability along with an elemental one. I can wield nothing. Malstar is wrong. His experiment with me failed, and even had it succeeded, I'm not convinced Malstar has his facts straight. I don't think all angeli could open gateways."

"That means you will fail," Anliac deduced, shivering at the reality his confession painted. "Will it hurt?"

Her fear and disappointment was like acid on his skin. "I have no memory of what was done to me." He couldn't look at her. "I was just a baby. I am so sorry, Anliac." He swallowed, passing a lump in his throat as his chest tightened.

Laying down, she twisted onto her side, propping up on her forearm to face him. "Whatever happens, Tristan, you need to know this is not your fault."

He winced but didn't reply. Instead, he stretched one arm across the floor, his palm open. When he felt the heat of her much smaller hand, he wrapped his fingers around it, savoring the contact.

With his eyes removed from her, Anliac drank in his profile. Though she'd tried not to look, there wasn't an inch of his sculpted body that she hadn't seen. The memory of it heated her flesh in unfamiliar ways. Soft waves of black hair fanned beneath his head and she found herself wondering if it was as soft as it appeared. His unmarred alabaster skin made her conscious of the myriad of scars marking her own.

Seeing him as she had upon their first meeting, his pale skin illuminating the room in brilliant light, his yellow eyes glowing fiercely as he'd ripped the head off the guard dragging her from the prison room, had terrified her. His profound physical abilities had made him a threat. Destiny had made them allies, and though she feared it, her heart was quickly making them more.

Her scent intoxicated him. He was afraid to move lest she take her hand from his. The single peek he'd taken when she'd been most vulnerable ate at his conscience even as the memory stirred his blood. She was breathtakingly beautiful, petite, with voluptuous curves that threatened his sanity. He blamed the fera injection for the overwhelming need to claim her— like a wolf claiming its mate. Though he longed for her, she wasn't someone to be taken.

To try would cheat her of the family she could have one day, for any child they created together wouldn't survive birth. He knew it was ridiculous to contemplate a future when odds were against them surviving the next day, but the thoughts came anyway. He tensed as she wiggled her way across her pallet to curl against his side. When her head came to rest in the hollow beneath his shoulder, he wrapped an arm around her, and pulled her close.

Unsure of her action, her hand eased across his abdomen and wrapped around the side of his waist. "I'm afraid," she whispered.

"I won't let anything happen to you. Chains or no chains, I'll keep you safe."

Lifting her head, she looked into his face, willing him to open his eyes. When he did, she said, "I worry less for myself and more for you. Malstar won't be happy when you fail." Blushing, she forced words past her lips that she feared never having another chance to say. "I don't want to lose this feeling between us before discovering what it means. I don't want to lose you."

Words failing him, he did the next best thing and pressed his lips gently against her own.

***

Days passed, and though their bodily needs were met, it seemed they were all but forgotten by the tower. They were left with too much time. They railed against their restraints, bruising their wrists and breaking the skin, but the locks wouldn't give. They laid futile plans of escape to hold back the despair threatening to break them. They speculated over Calstar and Malstar's plans—plans whose failure or success they feared equally.

With all that was happening, they feared most the emotions that were assaulting them, turning their alliance into friendship, and their friendship into something more. She no longer intimidated him, and she no longer feared him, and in the absence of those emotions, desire bloomed. With every tentative touch, accidental or intentional, they began to explore the new feeling welling up from within them. The fear invoked was not of life and death, but of the unknown, and of daring to hope when the future for them was so unclear.

III

Still Fells Like Home

Davad stepped through the portal with Shashara in his arms. She screeched as they plummeted into the dark gray water of the oceanus off the docks of Exterius Antro. No sooner had their heads cleared the aquis than Rupert, dragging Set with him, landed on top of them.

Shashara was pulled to the surface by Set's frantic hands.

"Crap!" Set shouted as he helped drag her long hair away from her face. "I'm sorry. Are you all right?"

"I'm fine." Kicking her feet to stay afloat, she twisted in the water seeking her brother. "Davad..." she called out until she found him.

"I'm good," he said.

And he was. Rupert had him by the back of his tunic holding him afloat.

Shashara screamed again, climbing her way frantically onto Set's shoulders, dunking him again. "What was that? Ahhh!" She lost her balance as Set surged up and she belly busted onto the oceanus's surface.

Coughing and sputtering, Set wiped the water from his eyes. "What happened?"

"It just a harmless water snake," Davad laughed. "Look, you scared it away."

"Nope," Shashara said, gliding forward in the water. "I'm out of here." She pumped her arms as she made for shore.

"What's your rush, sis?"

"Shut up, Davad," she said between strokes. "I don't like snakes."

Laughter came from the direction of the docks as they became the morning's entertainment. By the time they'd swam to shore, they were laughing themselves. Sloshing onto dry land in their fancy attire, they were a pathetic sight, but one that would not draw attention from the city's guards. They bowed good humoredly to their audience as they accepted applause. Shashara bowed twice since she'd put in the extra work to embarrass herself, before catching up to the boys, who'd started off towards the marketplace.

"Where are we?" Rupert asked. "There are fera here."

"Mortalis and fulgo as well," Shashara said, wringing out her sodden shirt. "Not too many nox settle in Exterius Antro."

Rupert pivoted north. "The Turris region is close then?"

"Not too far." Looping her arm through the fera's, she said, "Come, Rupert. You've shared your home with us. Now let us show you ours." A dark thought stole through her mind. "I suppose by now someone else may live there."

"There's only one way to find out," Set said as they made their way past Clave's forge. The simple, single-storied, white stone building stood as it always had, but Davad's shoulders drooped as he stopped in front of it. "Davad, are you okay?"

"It seems so long ago, doesn't it?" Davad asked, clenching the hilt of Tristan's sword hanging in its scabbard at his waist. "Like another lifetime."

Stepping away from Rupert, Shashara leaned her head against the outside of her brother's shoulder and pried his fingers loose to take his hand. "I've always believed that life was measured by the passing of time," she said, "but it's not." Standing upright, she squeezed Davad's hand before releasing it. "Life is measured by the passing of events. Some can make a grown woman cry for her daddy like a child. Some force boys to face monsters like men. Events age us, regardless of the number of years lived, or yet to be lived."

"Then I am ancient," Set jested as Rupert grinned and rubbed the top of his head. When Davad's steps dragged, Set took the lead. "Look," he grinned, pointing to old lady Moraine working in her garden.

Davad chuckled. "Don't get any ideas. You can pick flowers for my sister somewhere else."

Rupert glanced at Shashara, who shrugged her shoulders as clueless as he was.

Set refused to look at the inn where he'd gotten Tristan hurt and the both of them fired. The ruckus with Sizon and that other guard seemed to be the catalyst that had caused everything to go wrong. Turning onto the familiar street leading to their simple, single-storied, wood home, it was his steps that faltered.

Davad maneuvered around Set and opened the front door. Leaving it open for the others, he found himself standing in the front room staring at the cold hearth, perplexed that he couldn't remember them putting it out before they'd left that night. Somehow, he'd expected it to still be burning.

Shashara brushed past Rupert standing just inside the door and hurried down the hall. "My room!" she bellowed.

Set and Davad appeared in the doorway with Rupert peering over their heads.

She stood in the center of a cluttered floor with rumpled clothes hanging from each hand. She chucked them down. Eyes narrowed, she swore, "If I find out one of you read my journal, the tower will be the least of your problems." She turned her back on them. Rummaging through the mess scattered across her four-post bed, the straw mattress beneath her quilt rustling under the weight of her hand as she leaned across it, she searched for her journal amongst the clutter.

"You need to calm yourself," Davad said, turning towards the room he and his father had shared. A shoe hit him in the back of the head. "Ow...," he paused to rub the back of his head before walking away.

Gesturing with a tilt of his head that Rupert should follow Davad, Set entered Shashara's bedroom. It looked like a tornado had ripped through her private space. "We didn't read it," he said. "We didn't even look for it. Um," he scratched his head, "sorry about the mess. We were kind of in a hurry."

Grief broke through her angry façade. "It still smells like him," she said.

Set's brows bunched.

"The house," she clarified, "it smells like dad; like the leather of his gloves, metallic like the blade at his hip." A sound erupted from the back of her throat that could have been misconstrued as a chuckle had there been any humor in her tearing eyes. "Like the scent of sweat when he'd come home after a job." Her expression crumpled.

"Come here," he coaxed, opening his arms. She came to him easily. He held her, soothing his hand over her shoulder and down her back as she cried. Her sorrow was immense, and it gouged at his psyche.

On a broken sob, she said, "I watched him die, Set."

Her cry carried to Davad and Rupert down the hall.

Davad winced, hanging his head. "Every decision dad made after Shashara was taken," his voice wavered, "everyone, I fought him on. By the time we reached that prison room," he met

Rupert's sad, gray eyes, "I had been angry at him for weeks, and now...I'm angry all the time." He turned his head toward the window. "I know it's messed up, but Tristan's in trouble, and I feel like dad abandoned us."

"Like your mom," Rupert said.

Davad's face scrunched, but he refused to cry. "We're just a bunch of kids, Rupert. How do we take on the tower?"

Shivering from more than mere cold, Davad shrugged out of his wet clothes, and yanked on dry ones. Wrapping his arms around himself, he said, "I have no idea what to do, but" he pointed in the direction of Shashara's cries, "I need her tears to stop. I need the world to stop."

Rupert emerged from the corner of the room, where he'd tucked himself to give Davad a little space, and said, "I'm not so old that I can't remember what is was like to be your age."

Davad sat down on his father's bed and pulled on his boots. "My age was just fine," he said, "until my dad was killed."

Rupert sighed at Davad's dejected slouch. "Char took me in after my parents were killed."

Davad winced. "I'm sorry. I didn't know."

"I was only a whelp when it happened. They left the wilds of Turris to come to this city to defend it during a land attack launched by Certamen. The skirmish turned into a battle and they fell. I survived on my own for a good long while before I found Char and she gave me a pack to call my own. You are fortunate. You have a sister, and two that are like brothers, and I am here to protect you." He rolled his head across the back of his shoulders. "The loss of a parent is great, but to know they died as warriors is great too, in its own way. It means that a warrior's blood courses through our veins, giving us the strength to fight on in their stead."

Davad chuckled and scrubbed at his face. Dropping his arms to his sides, he said, "I don't think I've ever heard you talk so much."

Rupert's pointed ears wiggled. "Shut up."

Shashara peeked into the room. "Are you okay?" Her voice broke on the last word.

"I will be." Davad took a steadying breath. "Where's Set? We need to see if there's anything still edible in the house, and then we need to come up with a plan."

"He's in his room. He...uh...said he needed a moment alone."

Davad stared at his sister. His lips twitched and his brow arched. "Rupert would you mind waiting in the front room? I need to speak to Shashara."

A few swift clicks marked his reply as he exited, sniffling.

Shashara slipped inside and closed the light colored, wooden door behind her, sensing a need for privacy. "Is this about dad? Because honestly, Davad, I don't know how many tears I have left? I'm drained."

"It's not," he said. "Come sit down." He patted the straw mattress beside him as he shifted so they could face each other. "What was the blush about?"

Patting her cheeks, she replied, "I don't know what you're talking about. My face is red from crying, that's all."

"No," Davad objected, "your eyes are red from crying, and your face was pale, up until you mentioned Set." His sister tried to hold her expression blank, but her eyes gave her away. "Out with it, Shashara."

"Davad," she said, caving to the need to tell someone. She grabbed his hands and leaned forward, lowering her voice. "I know Set is younger than I am, and the timing couldn't be worse, but yeah." She smiled. "I think I like him. I mean, I've loved him for years," she rambled, "but I really like him. Is that crazy?"

"For truth, Shashara, I think it's great."

"Really?"

"Yeah," he said. A mischievous grin curled his lips. "It's a lot better than you pinning after Tristan."

She chucked his hands back into his own lap as she lurched from the bed, scowling. "First off, I don't pine, and second," there was a pause during which her temper stuttered, "Tristan's not meant for me. He never was."

Rising from the bed, he joined his sister by the door. "I want to see you happy, sis, but it seems a little fast."

A hint of her earlier happiness returned. "Thank you. And it isn't fast." She paused to collect her thoughts. "It's simply time." She opened the door, ending the conversation.

They left the room together and followed a clanking noise to the kitchen where Rupert was making a mess of things.

"Stop before you hurt yourself." Shashara teased. "Light the stove for me instead."

While she peeled the eyes from the last of the potatoes in the bin, she had Davad open a jar of tomato-based vegetable soup that had been given to them by a lady down the street last year. Adding a bit of water and the chunks of potatoes to the pot that Davad had dumped the soup into, she placed it on the stove to cook. They waited impatiently, with wooden bowls and spoons at the ready, eyeing the hallway for Set to join them.

Just breathe, Set told himself. Feeling the emotions of others as his own had to be the worst part of being an epoto. In fact, it down right sucked. He felt trapped between Davad's and Shashara's grief to the point where there was no room left for his own. Even Rupert had caved under the weight of it and had released more of the sentiment. His ability was absorbing it like a sponge leaving him to drown.

Tristan, I need you. He felt something drip off his chin.

Wiping it away, he realized it was tears. You've got to suck it up, he thought, and pull your crap together. His mind was all for it, but his legs refused to listen. He stood by his bedroom door, with one hand pressed against it, and the other gripping the door lever. "Find your center, Set," he said aloud, "before their emotions rip you apart." He nodded. "Okay, I got this." He left the room and followed the sound of their voices to the kitchen where they sat at the table watching a pot boil on the stove.

"Who did the cooking?" he asked.

"Shashara." Rupert replied.

"Good." He grinned. "As long as it wasn't Davad, it'll be safe to eat."

"Ha, ha, very funny." Changing the subject, Davad said, "So listen. Rupert wants to check in with Char on our way to Catena Piscari."

Rupert's ears wiggled. "I know it's out of the way."

"Not really," Set said. "With my new ability we can make little changes to our plans as we need to. I just wish I would have known sooner that all I had to do to make our lives easier was kill someone."

Shashara looked at him aghast. "Callous much?"

"I'm being realistic. We have to become callous or we won't survive." Taking his place at the table, he said, "Maybe we can find help while we're there."

"Take it back," Shashara said.

"No," he replied. "The truth is all we have, Shashara. My truth may not be yours," he squeezed her hand beneath the table where the others could not see, "but it is the truth."

To break the silence that followed, Davad said, "We still have to figure out how to get to IA,"

"I don't know the city well enough to open a portal there," Set told them, "and opening one inside the tower doesn't seem like the brightest idea. I can take us to Tristan, but whatever trouble he's in, we'll land right in the middle of it."

Shashara left the table to test the readiness of the potatoes with the side of a serving spoon. "So then what do we do?" she asked. "Short of killing someone, that is."

Allowing her sarcasm to roll off him, Set replied, "We'll go see Char, and then we'll see if Triton is in Catena Piscari." He paused before saying, "He should hear about Jacob from us."

"There's no way Triton's had time to make it back to Catena Piscari," Davad said, "but maybe we can leave a message or something with the dock master. So," he leaned back in his seat, "we get to Catena Piscari, and then what?"

"Once we are closer, I can open a portal to the west," Set told him. "I can get us to Pisces Stragulum."

"Are you sure," Shashara asked, "because you don't look sure."

"I'm as sure as I can be," Set admitted. "The guy I took this ability from was able to open a portal back to the tower from the battlefield. If he could cover that kind of distance, then I can too."

"That makes sense," Davad said, "especially if you open the portal from Catena Piscari."

Shashara carried the soup from the stove and sat it down on the table as Davad stood to fill their bowls. "Rupert," she retook her seat, "you haven't said much."

"I am here to protect my littlest pack mates," he said. "I go where you go."

Set reached across the table and patted the back of his hand. "And we are grateful. You are the only one we know we can trust." He made eye contact with the others. "So, then it's settled?"

When no one objected, they ate their fill and then scavenged through the house to gather what supplies they could. Shashara caught Set alone. "You talk about your truth," she said. "Let me tell you the truth I see."

"Okay?" He slung his pack over his shoulder, crossed his arms, and waited.

"You," she shook her head, "are terrified. You are scared of what you are, and you are scared that there is no one to teach you, and you are not okay with taking a life. Set," she took a shaky breath, "there is no shame in doing what must be done, but enjoying it," she looked down, "well, there is shame in that."

"Are you guys ready?" Davad asked, peeking into the kitchen, his stare darting between them.

"Yeah," Shashara said, brushing past Set.

"I locked the doors," Rupert said as they joined him in the front room.

"It looks like we're ready then." Davad smacked Set on the back. "You're up."

"Hey, guys?" Shashara waited for everyone to look at her, "didn't they tell us in Paradisi Colles to not go through so many portals in a day?"

Everyone looked at one another, except for Rupert, as they remembered the warning.

"Well, I guess we are about to figure it out." Davad nodded his head at Set.

"All of you stay back until the portal has stabilized," Set said, glancing at Shashara, who stood with her fingers laced and her head down, "because the truth is, I'm a little scared."

Shashara's head snapped up as a smile spread across her face.

Set closed his eyes, pressed his hands together, and focused.

Rupert and Davad watched as a darkening shadow formed. It was streaked with purple lightning that zigzagged within blurred edges. Holding their breath, they waited.

Shashara couldn't tear her eyes away from Set. The teardrop marking remained solid and still, while the webbed lines threaded their way through Set's skin like strokes of an artist's brush. The colors changed, swirling into the image of a meadow over the left side of his face.

"I think we're good," Set said, his eyes opening. "Rupert, you first."

Anxious to see Char, Rupert didn't hesitate.

Davad followed after him.

Shashara reached for Set's hand and they entered the portal together.

A ferocious roar greeted their exit. Shashara screamed as a massive fera with orange and white fur, marked with horizontal black lines, snatched Davad by the throat and slammed him to the ground.

"Donnin, no!" Char hopped in place as she slapped her hands together. "Rupert, stop."

Rupert couldn't hear her over the growl that ripped out of his throat. Coming in from behind, he wrapped his forearm around the man's throat. Latching onto his wrist with his other hand, he hauled Davad's attacker back. Davad rolled out of the way, drawing Tristan's sword as he came to his feet.

Rupert found himself thrown over the fera's back, costing him his hold. He landed on his feet. Falling forward until his clawed hands hit dirt, spinning a hundred and eighty degrees, he prepared to attack again.

Donnin's split upper lip parted in a snarl, revealing dagger-like canines as he fell into a defensive stance. The terror-filled faces of his prey, ones he recognized, abated his temper. "Easy, friend," Donnin said as he extended one arm towards Rupert without lowering his guard. Glancing past the other fera, he addressed Davad. "Sorry about that, son. You uh…caught us by surprise."

Char covered her white-furred face and button nose with both hands. Peeking between her fingers she said, "Rupert… relax."

Rupert helped Davad to his feet as he glared at the man standing too close to Char. "Are you hurt?" Rupert asked Davad.

Rubbing the back of his head, Davad flinched, but said, "No, I'm fine. What are you doing here, Donnin?" he asked, sheathing the sword.

"I came to see her." He stalked over to his clothes piled beside a blanket spread out over the grass and tugged on his breeches and boots.

"You know him?" Rupert asked.

"He helped us get to Exterius Antro and made sure you and the pack knew we'd need your help at the northern gate. He's one of the good guys, Rupert," Davad said. "You can trust him." Turning on Set, his visage darkened, "Thanks for the help by the way."

"Yeah," Set cringed, "that was my bad."

From the emotions of others, he'd felt anger, grief, and even pain echoed with its own emotion, but by far, emotions from lovers were the most intense. The energy of Donnin and Char's private moment had left him immobile.

"Sorry about the intrusion, you two." Heat creeping up his neck suffused Set's face. "I guess I was more focused on the grassland around the house than the house itself."

"No need to apologize," Char said. "You are all welcome here. Come, the house is not far, and we can talk."

Rupert nudged Donnin aside as he fell into step beside Char. Wrapping his arm around her shoulders, he quickened their pace, walking at a tilt as he brought their heads close together. The sound of his short, irritated clicks wafted back between whispered words.

Respecting the other man's place within the pack, at least for now, Donnin slowed, until his towering bulk walked beside his mortalis comrades. "You've been fortunate to find such loyal friends and protectors."

"Why didn't you tell us you were engaged to Char?" Set asked. "When Sole mentioned your betrothal, we assumed it was with someone from Collibus Dolor."

21

"No one lives in the desert, boy. Best you remember that." Eyeing Rupert askance, he asked, "Did you tell him?"

"About the Alphas?" Shashara pivoted to walk backwards, keeping track of three deer bounding through the meadow away from them, envying their carefree existence. "He's a fera, too."

"About their location," Donnin clarified.

"No," she assured him as she turned back around. "We haven't spoken about it even amongst ourselves until now."

"Good."

"If you're going to marry her, why do you care if she knows?" Shashara asked.

His shoulders stiffened. "She is not the one my father had chosen. She is the one I've chosen and that complicates things."

Set punched him on his shoulder, unable to hide the elation he felt as he picked up on Donnin's emotions. "Good for you. Char's great. I'm sure the Alphas will love her."

"Yes, well," he cleared his throat "I have to tell them first."

Davad chuckled. "Sucks to be you. Your dad is one scary wolf."

Donnin's broad shoulders shook with silent laughter even as his chest expanded full of pride. "That he is."

"Eek!" Shashara exclaimed when they disturbed a pack of boars sleeping in the tall grass. They snorted, freaking her out. Rupert and Char glanced back to check on her as Donnin and the boys began to laugh. She glowered at them. "Bite me," she said.

It was a short walk through the golden, neck-high grass, and then they found themselves in the small clearing around Char's home. The hard-packed mud, sandwiched between haphazardly propped up branches, was camouflaged by bundles of tan grass.

Outside of the house, a group of fera sat in a circle tossing colored stones, howling at their wins and losses. Two of the feras, Laccon and Wills, Rupert recognized, but the cloth-wearing feras must have come with Donnin because he didn't know them. They greeted Rupert with smiles and nods as they stood at Char's approach, but their eyes slid past him to the powerful man coming up from behind.

Addressing them, Donnin ordered. "Scan the area in case the portal was seen."

"On it," came a gruff reply as the men scattered in several directions, leaving the stones as they lay for later.

Ducking inside the house, they found Luce and Dunhold sharpening blades with stones before the fire. With so many bodies in such a small area, they were forced to find space where they could. Char and Donnin sat down on top of the low sitting table. Davad was still standing before the door, the leaves and branches crunching beneath his feet each time his weight shifted. Set and Shashara stood together in the kitchen area, hiding their entwined fingers behind their backs. Rupert had chosen the weapons area, as far from Donnin as he could get and still be in the same house.

"Good to see you again, Rupert. Davad," Dunhold said "you look a sight better than when we parted."

"Thanks," Davad chuckled. "Luce," Davad nodded in greeting. "It's nice to see you again."

"You're missing some of your pack," Luce said. "Why have you returned without them?"

"I meant to ask the same," Donnin said. "What happened?"

The children exchanged pensive glances before Davad spoke. "We were discovered in Effugere Aquam. We left for Exterius Antro by portal a day early. Lunam warned Char and she sent the pack." Hand over his heart, he bowed respectfully to her. "Something for which we owe you and your pack a great debt." To Donnin, he said, "They saved our lives, but IA took Tristan and Anliac."

"Why would you keep this from me?" Donnin asked Char, his gold-flecked eyes reflecting hurt.

Char planted her hands on her furred hips in displeasure. "How was I to know that you were involved in helping the children? And what business is it of yours what dreams Lunam grants me?"

"Secrets cause divides that can be deadly," Davad said. "It's best to choose which ones you keep with care."

"Did you reach Montilis?" Donnin asked, changing the subject.

"They did," Char said. "I sent Rupert to guide them, and Luce and Dunhold to guard them. The others returned, but Rupert stayed. This is the first we've heard, or seen, of them since."

"He should be leaving Palus Regia within the week," Set told them both, "but for now, Rayner has used politics to tie his hands. We couldn't wait."

"So, you made yourself a gate maker." Donnin nodded. "Smart."

"Desperation is a cruel task maker," Set said. "Fortune is a capricious thing. Sometimes it shines on us, and at others, it leaves us in the dark. We do what we must to survive, and to save those who are depending on us."

"You know, sometimes when you talk, I forget you're the youngest of us." Davad said.

Set only smiled at him.

"Can you help us, magistrate?" Shashara asked.

"If he will not," Luce twirled a dagger through her fingers, the polished metal catching and reflecting the flames from the hearth, "we will."

"I didn't think you cared." Shashara smiled, her eyes twinkling. "Thank you."

"Please," her sleek orange tail twitched as she stood to her back paws. "I grow restless, girl, and long for a fight."

"Our place is here, Luce," Char said. "I'm so sorry, Shashara. I've not been given the reason, only the command, and I will follow Lunam's orders."

Collectively, the kids swayed under their disappointment. They turned their eyes on the only one left to offer them hope.

Encircling Char's waist, Donnin pulled her into his lap. Into her ear, he said softly, "I want no secrets between us, but if I speak plainly in front of you and your men and ever find myself betrayed, by fera law, you would die first."

Twisting in his arms, Char cupped his wide face, kissing the corner of his feline mouth, tickling his whiskers. "Be glad we are newly mated and that I am in a forgiving mood, for your doubt offends me."

Turning her sideways so she'd be more comfortable, and so he could keep her profile in his line of sight, he said, "I'll return to Paradisi Colles and send Magistrate Rayner a missive. Let us see if his constitution holds towards the restraints, he's placed on General Aquam when a man of equal rank intercedes. I'll send runners to Imbellis as well and inform our men within the tower that Tristan is under the protection of the Alphas, and that Anliac is the daughter of one we would allay ourselves with. By the time you three reach IA, you will have the support you need to bring them out again."

"Thank you," Set said unable to mask his disappointment. "We appreciate any help we can get."

"You will stay here tonight," Char told them. "The morning will be soon enough to begin the next leg of your journey."

IV
Left Behind

Ambushed at dawn, Rupert was livid. "I'm a grown man, Char. You can't keep me here."

"That's true," Char said, "but I am your alpha, and if you want to remain a member of this pack, you'll do as you're told."

He growled, clenching his fists. "I promised to protect them."

Char crossed her arms beneath her white, fur-dusted chest. Her red eyes full of compassion, but no give. "You'll be protecting them by doing this." Her long, pointed ears stood straight up, parting the flowing white hair that fell to the curve of her back.

"How?" he asked. "Dura Mortis is dangerous. You know what will happen to them if they're seen."

"We have to trust that the Alphas know what they're doing," Char said. Coming forward, she raised up on her toes and took him by the outside of his shoulders. "The dream I had last night was clear. You have to convince them that it's in their best interest to change their course."

Shrugging off her hands, Rupert glared. "I'll tell them the truth and let them decide. If you want them lied to, you'll have to do it yourself."

Char was taken aback. "What does that mean?"

"How much of this is your dream, Char," he met Donnin's hard stare over her head, "and how much of this is his influence?"

Donnin placed his wide frame between them, facing Rupert with a foot separating the difference in their heights. "Not only is she your tribal alpha, but she's now a magistrate's wife. You should watch your tone."

Rupert met the other man's challenge. "You are not my alpha. You are not my magistrate, and you are standing in the wilds of Turris. You should watch yours."

Donnin growled and bared his claws.

"Enough," Char said. "He is of my pack, Donnin." To Rupert, she said, "You tell those children the truth. Tell them your opinion while you're at it. If they doubt my integrity and intent, as you do, then that will be their choice."

"Char," Rupert stepped forward.

She held up her hand. "My mother once said that when our young are small, they often step on our toes, but when they've grown tall, they step on our hearts." She sniffed and jutted her chin. "They can choose to question me, but for you to do so…" she shook her head. "Well, you may not be flesh of my flesh, but my heart doesn't know that." Clearing her throat, she said, "They are waiting outside."

Rupert stood, ridged and stoic. "It's not you," he said. "It's your mate I do not trust." Radiating anger, he ducked out of the door.

Donnin pulled her back against his chest. "Are you okay?" With his hands laced around her abdomen, he gave her a squeeze.

"This is what happens when you send your child off into the world." She pulled away, turning to face him. "They return no longer children."

"Grown men do not show such disrespect," he said, a grin teasing the corners of his mouth. "From what I just witnessed, you have years before he is grown."

She laughed. "Thank you."

"We should go," Donnin suggested, taking her by the hand.

"Char, what's going on?" Set asked. "Rupert is upset, but he's not talking."

"He can't go with you," Char said. "I'm sorry."

"What? Why?" Shashara asked.

"We all have our orders to follow, and we are not always given reasons," Char replied, "but he must stay."

"Great." Davad rubbed his forehead. "We came here looking for help, and we leave weaker than when we arrived."

Donnin stood beside Char with the pack fanned out behind them. "You'll have help. You have my word."

Rupert scoffed, drawing everyone's attention.

"That's enough, Rupert," Char said.

Set recoiled from the fury emanating from Rupert. "I think someone needs to tell us what's going on."

Donnin was the one who answered. "The Alphas want you to approach IA from Dura Mortis."

"It's too dangerous," Rupert said. "The feras of that region do not let outsiders in. Even other feras tread lightly when they travel there." The stare he nailed Donnin with dared him to deny it. "You'll be in as much danger in Dura Mortis as you'll be when you enter the tower."

"Then why would they want us to go that way," Davad asked.

"It doesn't matter," Set said. "I couldn't take us there if I wanted to. I have to know where I'm going for the portal to work."

Rupert stared at his feet. "I've been there."

"But you're not coming with us," Davad said. "So, I don't think that helps."

"It does if Set takes his memory of it."

Silence stretched as Char's meaning sank in.

"You'll reach IA much faster this way," Donnin said, "and you'll be approaching the tower from a direction they won't be expecting."

Set's heart began to race as he made his way to stand before Rupert, ignoring Char and Donnin who tracked his movement. "Pulling memories from someone's mind is not a simple thing, Rupert. There is a lot that can go wrong." As he turned toward Donnin, his expression contorted in anger. "Lunam may have sent the dream to change our course, but Char has no idea how my ability works. So, using Rupert, that's all you, and you don't have the right."

"Duty gives me the right," Donnin replied, "and if you want to save your brother, you'll use him."

Stupefied by Donnin's remark, Set sneered, "And here I was beginning to think the fera were different, but you're not. You all serve your own agenda."

Rupert ruffled Set's hair. "I don't like being forced to stay behind, but I'm not worried about me, and you shouldn't worry about him," his head dipped in Donnin's direction.

Using his epoto ability, he searched through Rupert's emotional grid, and then asked, "Are you sure?" When Rupert nodded, he checked with the others. "What do you guys think?"

"If it gets us to IA any faster, then I think it's a risk worth taking," Davad said.

"We're asking a lot of him." Lines furrowed the delicate skin between Shashara's eyes. "You don't have to do this."

Rupert's head turned to Char, and then back to Shashara. "The Alphas' plan makes sense," he assured her. "It's dangerous, and like I said, I hate that I won't be there to protect you, but it makes sense."

"If we're going to do this," Set announced, "we'll need some privacy."

"You can use the house," Char said. "I'll keep everyone out here until you're finished."

Rupert's glare scorched Char but the tribal alpha held her ground.

"She wouldn't force you to stay behind without cause, Rupert," Shashara told him, laying a hand on his forearm to gain his attention. "Char is a good alpha."

"Thank you," Char sighed, leaning her head against the side of Donnin's shoulder, "but I'm afraid he will be angry at me for some time for keeping him here."

Taking long strides towards the house, Rupert spoke over his shoulder, "I may never forgive you."

The twin suns were directly overhead by the time Set emerged, alone. "He's fine," he said before Char could panic as the rest of the pack came to their feet. "He's weak, and tired, but I believe I managed to get what I needed without striping him of his memory." To Davad and Shashara, he said, "He asked me to tell you both goodbye."

"This stinks," Shashara said.

"That doesn't change what is," Davad said. "Set, are we going straight to Dura Mortis?"

Set shook his head. "I can't. The Nebulosus is too wide. I don't want to risk it. We'll go to Catena Piscari today as we planned and to Dura Mortis tomorrow."

"Are you sure you won't come with us?" Davad asked Donnin. "There's a chance, if you're with us, we won't have to fight our way in."

"The Asylum will not give them up easily," Donnin said. "I'm but one man. You'll need more help than I can give. Your cause, our cause, will be better served by my returning to Paradisi Colles. The Alphas need to be notified of your decision to enter through Dura Mortis."

"You're a long way from home, magistrate," Set pointed out. "Without a gate maker…"

"Don't worry," Donnin replied. "Sammel will be here shortly."

Remembering the gate maker from their travel from Paradisi Colles to Collibus Dolor, Set nodded, "Then I guess it's time." Space opened up around him as he pressed his palms together and visualized his destination.

The portal to Catena Piscari opened in less time than anticipated. The webbed markings on Set's face swirled, bent, and straightened into the image of the town's inn, complete with a miniature peacekeeper, who was propped against the wall beside the bar. A larger image of the same could be seen floating in the midst of the dark portal, its edges crackling as purple lightning streaked across it, reaching for those who would enter it.

"Keep your word, magistrate," Shashara said.

Donnin bowed formally. "It will be done."

They bid the pack a hasty farewell and entered the portal one after another with Set entering last.

An angry innkeeper greeted them on the other side. The edge of the portal had burned a black gouge into the hardwood floor. A table had been slashed in two, and the patrons who'd been seated there were spoiling for a fight.

"You idiot," the tanned mortalis innkeeper growled, wagging his finger. "What kind of gate maker opens a blasted portal in a place of business? You're going to pay for the damage!" His heavy jowls shook as his face reddened. "You'll pay for it or I'll take it out of your hide!"

Set held up his hands in surrender. "Sorry. It was an accident."

"An accident!" The innkeeper slammed the side of his meaty fist down on the polished wooden bar and then stormed from around behind it.

"Hold on there a minute, boss," the fera peacekeeper said, placing a restraining hand against the other man's chest.

"What do you think you're doing?" the innkeeper bellowed, knocking the fera's hand aside.

"You can be mad all you want," the peacekeeper told him. "Sure, as anything I'd be mad, but I can't let you hurt him, and it looks like neither will they."

Shashara and Davad flanked Set on either side, their hands glowing red as they wielded their element in Set's defense.

"Listen to the man and back off," Shashara said when the innkeeper attempted to force his way past. Orange flames flared from her fingertips lending weight to her warning.

"Get out." He pointed to the door. "All of you get out. Now! You too, Tidous," he said to the feline peacekeeper. "You're fired." Pivoting towards the bar, he threw his hands in the air. "Drinks are on the house."

Tidous cursed and followed the three of them outside.

"Thank you for defending us," Shashara said, peeking sideways at him. "But...umm... why did you do it?"

"I'm just following orders." Keeping his eyes straight forward, his vertical pupils dilated as he asked, "Why are the Alphas so interested in you all?" His claws elongated and contracted with the clenching of his hands as he forced down his irritation over losing his job.

Shashara feigned ignorance. "Who?"

Tidous covered his mouth with his fist and cleared his throat, cursing his loose tongue as sweat broke out beneath his brown, shaggy fur.

"Do you have any idea how long it might be before Triton comes back to town?" Davad asked, letting the fera off the hook.

Tidous nodded towards the dock where Triton's schooner sat anchored off the first shoot.

Shielding his eyes with one hand, his weathered face breaking into a grin, Hammy came down the gangplank and made his way over. He shook Davad's hand. "It's good to see you again, boy," he said. "Where's your old man and Tristan? And how are you back in Catena Piscari so soon?" His gaze swung wide to encompass them all.

Set answered. "A lot has happened. Besides, we could ask you the same thing. How are you here?"

"We had a hold full of poisoned casks and a shrewd businessman waiting in Effugere Aquam to pick it up. The captain had us stop off in Caterva Concentio to grab Gunth."

"Who's Gunth?" Davad asked.

"He's an old aer wielder," Hammy replied. "Triton hired him to get us back across the oceanus so we could restock. We only just got here." Scratching his whiskered chin, he added, "The captain nearly killed the man. He pushed him hard to get us back to Effugere Aquam before the sale fell through. With the damage done to the ship by the dracon, we couldn't afford to lose the coin."

"I wish we would have thought of that when we were trying to cross before," Davad said. "We might have caught up to the slave ship before it ever made port."

"If there had been one close, we would have," Hammy assured him. "Triton should be in the tavern. Tidous," Hammy greeted the fera with a stiff nod.

Tidous's eyes hardened before he ignored Hammy's greeting and spoke to the others instead. "It would appear you all know each other. So, if you'll excuse me, I need to gather my things from the inn. I've been fired." Without further explanation, he turned and walked away, his bushy tail swishing back and forth with his steps.

"We're so sorry," Shashara shouted to his back.

"I don't think we've met, miss." Hammy bowed slightly.

"Hammy," Davad said, "this is my sister, Shashara."

"It's a pleasure to meet you."

Shashara smiled, tight lipped. "Likewise."

"I could use a drink," Hammy said. "Come on."

They followed Hammy down the wooden dock to the tavern. Inside, Triton was sitting at the empty bar hovering over his mug of ale.

"Hey, captain," Hammy shouted, "look what the wind blew in."

Triton's barstool swiveled around, and then a solitary sweep of his astute gaze had him coming to his feet. "What's happened? How did you get back here?" he asked, his countenance darkening.

"I remember you," Shashara said, her eyes narrowing. "You're the one who tried to buy Anliac."

He took a closer look at her face. "You're Shashara, Jacob's daughter."

Her chin lifted. "I am."

His eyes drifted to the puckered purple scar running from beneath her left eye to the hollow of her cheek. "I'm glad to see Jacob and the boys were able to get you out of the tower." Checking the empty doorway behind them, he asked, "Where is he?"

Tensions grew as the silence stretched.

Triton scowled. "Someone needs to start talking."

"Dad didn't make it out." Davad's voice was gruff. "He got us into the tower and led us to the prison room where Anliac and Shashara were being held, but" his throat closed off with a lump of emotion.

"He took an arrow to the chest," Set finished for him.

Triton's tree-trunk-sized legs held him steady as his upper body swayed under the impact of Davad's words. Stiffening his spine as his blood ran cold, he asked, "And the boy? Where's Tristan?"

"We were ambushed outside of Exterius Antro. Tristan and Anliac were both taken," Set said. "They're back in the tower, again."

Triton's brow pulled down. "Boy, what happen to your mark? It looks like a gate mark." After a brief pause of no one answering, he planted his fists on his narrow hips and growled, "Someone start talking!"

Set shook his head. "We don't know what to say." His piercing blue eyes clouded as memory took him back. "I figured out that if I kill with my ability, the ability I take is mine to keep." He shook his head to clear his emotions, "I just wanted the man to reopen the portal. When he refused, I drained him. I made sure to kill him, so I could keep the ability. You knew my dad. Why are you so surprised? And don't judge me. I'd do it again if it…"

Astonishment slacked Triton's expression. "Epotos keep what they kill to take?"

"Well…yeah," Set said. "You were friends with my father. How did you not know?"

Startling everyone, the nox threw back his head of long, black, oiled hair, and laughed. "I'd give my ship to have a few words with your father right about now." A thought made him blanch. "That son of a badger…Matthew really got me good." He pinched the bridge of his nose and shook his head. "Oh, that explains so much, boy." He chuckled again. "If you only knew."

Set pressed his lips together as Triton burst into laughter, overloading his epoto ability with mirth. Though he tried to contain it, Set cracked up.

"Would one of you care to explain?" Shashara said with an arched brow.

"No," Triton grinned. "I'd prefer to keep my humiliation private." Getting them back on track, he asked, "So what's the plan, epoto?"

"I'm going to portal us to the southern border of Dura Mortis and then we'll follow the river back to IA."

"Dura Mortis?" Triton snorted. "You're as crazy as the man who raised you, boy." The memory of Jacob softened his face.

"Five days," Davad scowled, having had enough of the lighthearted banter. "It's been five days." With the humor sucked from those in the tavern, he said, "We went to Palus Regia and found Montilis, but Rayner refused to let him leave until he and Imbellis could reach an agreement. Who knows how long that could take, and Tristan and Anliac are out of time?"

"We've talked with Donnin. He was in the Turris region on our way here," Set said. "He's promised to do what he can but…" he shook his head.

"Who is Donnin?" Triton asked.

"The magistrate for Paradisi Colles," Shashara said.

Triton's eyes narrowed. "Paradisi Colles isn't known for being friendly to those not of their race. How did you meet?"

Set's tone brooked no argument. "It's a long story for another time."

Triton's thick, black brows crawled up his forehead. Prepared to tell the boy what he thought of his tone, he was interrupted as the door to the tavern flew open, and a spunky, redheaded, fulgo girl about their age stormed through. Her pale cheeks were blotched with scarlet patches as she confronted Triton, her yellow eyes glowing fiercely.

"Listen here, you chauvinistic cur," she said, waving her finger like a sword, "you have no right to refuse me work simply because I'm a girl."

Triton folded his arms over his chest. "A young thing like you has no business on a ship full of men, and if that's not reason enough, you're too weak to pull your own weight. I'm not having this discussion with you again."

Her eyes swelled with tears. Her voice rose in pitch, becoming a pathetic whine. "I have no one, nowhere to go, please."

"No," Triton said, unmoved by her emotional display.

Her tears dried up as quickly as they'd started, and her visage returned to that of anger. She stomped her foot, pivoted around, and stormed out of the double-sided doors leading to the covered seating area outside. Plopping down at a table, she propped her feet up in a chair, crossed her arms, and glared at him. Her right brow arched; her lips pressed thin. The smirk she gave him said, I'm not going anywhere.

"Stubborn females," Triton said, looking at the fulgo. Turning his attention back to the conversation, he found Shashara glaring as well.

"Men." With an indignant sniff and a fling of her hair, Shashara joined the girl just outside.

"Sassy little thing, isn't she?" Triton said low enough that the girls wouldn't overhear.

"Which one?" Hammy said from the seat he'd taken at the bar, laughing at his own joke.

"Shashara's her father's daughter, that's for sure," Set told him. Taking a deep breath, he braced himself for another refusal and then said, "Triton, we could use your help."

Triton led them to a table and sat down. "Bring us over some drinks, Hammy." Drumming his fingertips on the table, he said, "You both know how long it takes to cross the Nebulosus and with you making yourself a gate maker, Set, I don't see how I can help."

"You can help by setting sail and crossing as quickly as you can," Davad said. "Montilis is compromised by his position, and Donnin has his own agenda. If we fail, or if we're captured...Triton, we're on our own here."

"Boys, the only way I got back here so fast was using my aer wielder, Gunth, and I only did that because I needed to get back here to resupply after that bilge rat poisoned my supplies. By the way," he nodded to Set, "thank you again for that. It took five days to get here and I wrecked the ship doing it. I had to have the aquis wielders level out the oceanus in front of the ship, so we could sail smoother. Though I will admit, I have made it before in three days when your mother was around."

"Hammy told us about the aer wielder," Set said. "And I'm sure you can do it again, just imagine Beth is there snapping a water whip at you." He smiled.

"My father called you friend." Davad focused on the dented copper mug Hammy had placed in front of him to avoid looking up. "Now he's dead, and we don't know who else to trust. There is no one else who cares enough to get us out if we fail."

Razoran barged through the large side doors and bellowed, "Someone better tell me what's going on." He loped over, placed his clawed hands on the table, and leaned forward. "There's a girl outside that claims the mercenary is dead, and that Tristan is trapped in IA."

"It's true," Davad said. "The girl is Shashara. She's my sister."

"Captain," Razoran said taking a seat, "Tristan is my friend, and the mercenary was yours. When are we leaving?"

Triton tapped his finger on the tabletop, thinking. "Send runners to the surrounding fishing villages. Find me another aer wielder and get them back here. We'll keep the ship's sails full with two wielders until we reach Pisces Stragulum. I don't think Gunth is up to the task alone. Tell the aquis wielders we are going to tabletop the oceanus, they should prepare."

Razoran's black lips peeled back in a sharp-toothed grin. "This is why you're the captain." He shoved back his chair and came to his feet. Shaking the boys' shoulders in turn, he said, "Give me a day."

"For all of our sake, good luck," Davad said, "and thank you."

"Wait," Shashara said.

With her arm looped through the redheaded girl's, the two re-entered the tavern through the side door. "Wait," Shashara said again. Having overheard the conversation between the fera that had stopped to ask them questions and his captain, she said, "There's no reason to search. Skylar is a level three aer wielder."

Skylar smirked. "Still think I can't pull my own weight, captain?"

"I think you're a child."

Shashara was riled by his response. "Set turned fourteen the day before my father was killed. Davad's fifteenth birthday past without notice because we were too busy trying to reach Palus Regia. Tristan will turn seventeen tomorrow locked in the tower. I know because his birthday follows mine which is today, which began with me waking from a nightmare about my own time spent there. Age is irrelevant when you're trying to survive, Triton, and we'll take help where we can find it."

Davad's unfocused stare was accompanied by, "I forgot my own birthday," before he shook his head to pay attention.

"One trip across the Nebulosus will either make or break the little fulgo," Razoran smirked. "She wants to sign articles. I say we give her a test run."

Skylar's grin went nowhere near her eyes. "If you weren't helping me get what I want, you and I would have words over the little fulgo bit."

"It's good you have some fight in you," Razoran said. "You'll need it."

After a moment, Triton relented. "Very well. I've no idea how long it will take, but we'll make port in Pisces Stragulum. If you're not there waiting on us when we arrive, then we'll meet you in Imbellis."

"Thank you," Set sighed in relief.

"If Magistrate Donnin is successful, we'll have help from within the tower," Davad said, "and help from General Aquam if Magistrate Rayner keeps his word."

"Who are you people?" Skylar asked wide-eyed. "Magistrates, generals, ship captains; you have friends in very high places."

The explanation would have taken forever, so they ignored it.

"How soon can you leave, Triton?" Set asked.

The front door came open, and Tidous and a young, gangly nox entered. Hammy's eyes zeroed in on the man, but Triton paid them no mind.

"From the look of that incomplete mark crowding your face Set, you're not a level three gate maker. You will need time to recuperate your power and I have preparations to make. We'll sail in the morning after you off." He paused. "I'm assuming you have rooms at the inn."

"Not exactly," Set winced. "There was a bit of damage caused by the portal. I don't think he's interested in renting us a room."

From the table across the tavern, Tidous snorted at Set's comment as he ordered a stiff drink for himself and a glass of goat's milk for the boy that was with him.

"So, you'll sleep in the forecastle." Triton stated and then watched as Set turned green.

"Unless you have a prisoner you want tortured, one that I can drain," Set swallowed, "I don't think the forecastle, or your men, would appreciate that."

Razoran chuckled. "He's got a point, captain."

Leaning back in his chair until it rested against the wall, Tidous chimed in. "They can stay with me." He shifted in his seat when their heads swiveled in his direction.

Distrustful of his motives, Shashara said, "That's very kind of you considering we cost you your job."

The corner of Triton's mouth twitched. "You got him fired? How?"

Davad cleared his throat. "The innkeeper wanted to take the damage to his business out of Set's hide. Tidous helped us out."

Triton turned to Tidous. "Why?"

Tidous crossed his arms over his chest. "We all have our orders," he said, avoiding Shashara's skeptic stare and the questions in it.

"Amazing," Skylar said, dumbfounded. "Help seems to simply fall in your laps."

"Don't be stupid, girl," Tidous snarled, gesturing to the nox that had come in with him. The incomplete yellow diamond design situated between the boy's thick, black brows marked him an aether wielder.

"I have a name," the nox said. "I'm Kervan."

"You're an oracle," Shashara said.

"I'm a level one, which makes me a soothsayer and pretty much useless. I can't see the past, and what I see of the future comes when it wants to, and never when I need or want it to. I see moments that's all."

"Sometimes moments can count for more than years," Triton said. "How old are you boy?"

31

"Thirteen."

Triton drained his mug and set it down as he considered. "Someone like him could come in handy where you're going."

The three of them stilled as Triton's meaning became clear. Without Jacob, they would be entering the tower blind. They would be going where moments could mean the difference between life and death.

"Whatever you're scheming, go ahead and ask," Kervan said. "My ability shows that I'll say yes," his shoulders slumped, "even if it doesn't show me what I'm saying yes to."

Knowing the danger in what they were about to do, Set laid it out plain. "We're going to jump through a portal to Dura Mortis and then break into the Imbellis Asylum, where we plan to rescue two friends. The tower knows we're coming, which means we're all likely to end up prisoners or dead. Do you still want to go?" When Kervan didn't immediately say no, or run screaming from the tavern, he said, "You would be our eyes when we can't see what's coming."

Snatching the mug of ale sitting on the table before Tidous, Kervan chugged the whole thing. "Like I said...I have to say yes."

"The luckiest people I've ever seen," Skylar said in awe.

V

A True Gateway

With heightened awareness of their prisoners' deadly potential, the IA guards kept them moving along the Vitreous River's edge, and towards the Asylum's private grove north of the tower. An unnaturally straight line of ancient oak trees towered over them as they walked a stone path that brought them to a magnificent, square piece of land that was walled off on all four sides from prying eyes by white stone piled fifteen feet high. A handful of guards rushed ahead to open the arched double doors made of aged redwood.

The path grew wider as they entered the gate, affording Tristan and Anliac a clear view of their surroundings. From beneath the northern wall, the river flowed and split into two canals that encircled a piece of land marked with wavering lines gouged into the ground before continuing its journey beneath the northern wall and towards the tower. At the heart of the circle was a stone foundation with runes carved into it. The runes were filled with arcanite. A straight, scorched line ran ten feet beyond a large, grey anchored stone that had two iron rings secured into its sides. At the far ends of the stone foundation, black, wrought-iron fire bowls, representing north, east, south, and west, were sunk into the tops of six-foot-high, square, stone pillars. The bowls lay cold with dry tinder that filled their bellies.

White birds, with long, orange legs and slender, pointed beaks, high stepped across the banks of the river looking at them with curiosity.

Bound in arcanite chains that blocked their abilities and collars around their throats, Tristan and Anliac came to a stop as their tethers were drawn up short.

"Few have been privileged enough to enter here. It has been named Bealson's Grove." Malstar lifted the hem of his dark robe as he crossed a narrow, wooden bridge and stepped within the circle. "Its existence is as miraculous as it is abominable. The man responsible, Nathon Bealson, was both brilliant and deranged."

"Funny, all I see is wasted arcanite and a pathetic rock."

Anliac nudged Tristan in his ribs to quiet him.

Refusing to be baited, Malstar ordered, "Bring them across." He folded his hands before him as he began to lecture. "The flow of the river, the fires when lit, as well as the ground beneath our feet and the air we breathe; the ancient Superians could draw energy from these elements to aid a gate maker in opening a portal."

"Wow," Tristan taunted, "that's fairly pathetic. I've met level ones that could do it all by themselves."

"Tristan, shut up."

"I'm sorry, Anliac. I'm just calling it like I see it." Tristan smirked at Malstar's ire.

"Open your mind, Tristan. Think beyond Superi to other worlds because that was the strength of the gateway, not portal, opened here."

The scorched line on the ground began to take on new meaning. Jacob had told him about this gateway, about the Earth god that had stepped through to curse them. He'd never thought to see it for himself.

The line of stiff-backed guards blocking the exit parted.

Malstar's arms opened wide. "Ah, Xander, as always, your timing is superb."

"I've learned better than to test your patience," Xander said, giving Tristan a pointed look. Tall and willowy, the fulgo lowered the hood of his robe to the back of his shoulders as he approached. A mask of multicolored webbed markings covered his pale face from beneath his hawkish nose to his graying hairline.

Turning to Anliac and Tristan, Malstar boasted, "Xander is a level three gate maker. There are none his equal."

"If he's so great, why are we here?"

"He is indeed a wonder, but" Malstar sighed, "he's not an angeli, Tristan. You, however, are."

The corners of Tristan's square jaw clenched. His nostrils flared.

Malstar nodded towards the guards holding his leash. "Tie him down," he said.

"Wait. What?" Tristan dug in his heels, resisting as four guards dragged him towards the stone. Overpowered, he found himself on his knees. They snapped on iron cuffs and fastened them to the stone anchor before removing the arcanite from around his wrists and ankles.

As soon as the arcanite had been removed, Tristan showed them the angeli. Golden marks poured down the sides of his thick neck, veins bulged as glowing fluid lines spread over his shoulders, running down his arms to his wrists. As his power coalesced, he curled his biceps, and snapped the chains with an upward pull. He swung his fist and spun the guard on his right like a top. With an uppercut of his left fist, he caught the second guard beneath his chin and flipped him off his feet. His image blurred as he pivoted towards Malstar to attack, but what he saw rooted him in place.

Anliac's eyes were peeled wide, her chin tipped back, as Anliac's guard wrapped her tether around his wrist, shortening her leash to hold her in place. Four other guards stood before her with the tips of their short swords pressed into her neck. Scarlet drops of her blood welled to the surface.

"Be easy, Tristan," Malstar said. "Consider this a practice run. Xander will attempt to open the gate to Earth. We are not trying to keep it open. Our goal today is merely getting the gate to respond. All you must do is pull the natural energy from these elements," he gestured to their surroundings, "and feed it to Xander. The energy you provide will boost his ability beyond its natural limitations, allowing us to verify that the gate is still functional."

Tristan brought his ragged breath under control, dulling his marks, as he turned from Anliac to Malstar. "That's all, huh." He shrugged his shoulders. "No big deal."

"Well," Malstar spread his hands as his head tilted to the side, "if you're not up to the task, I can always put Anliac through the transition process. Perhaps she'll succeed where you fail to even try."

Tristan couldn't look at her again. The image of her caramel skin so pale, her chest heaving with erratic breaths, and her full lips pressed into thin lines as she bravely held captive the screams of fear trapped behind them were burned into his brain already.

Turning back to the stone anchor, he held his arms out straight and didn't fight the guards that brought forth new iron chains to bind him again. It didn't matter. He'd proven the chains couldn't hold him, but with Anliac's life on the line, he'd follow their rules.

"Just so we're clear," Tristan said, "what you're asking is impossible."

"Nonsense." Malstar waved away his concern. "All angeli were capable of this, and you are an angeli, Tristan. You can do this. Xander," Malstar said, placing a generous amount of space between himself and the heart of the circle, "let's begin."

Superi's twin suns burned brightly from overhead. When the guards stepped forward and lit the pyres, the added heat made the air oppressive as it shimmered in visible waves.

Anliac and Tristan had seen portals opened before, but never a true gateway, and never by a level three. They missed the initial shadow that had begun to form, since they were focused instead on the webbed mask coloring the gate maker's face. The lines quivered before slithering through his skin. They solidified into a round-shaped symbol with dark patches of midnight blue shadowing its surface. The edges of it appeared smudged.

Everyone turned to look at the gateway when it crackled. A grey shadow began to grow, giving off small bolts of purple lightning in all directions. The shadow turned black, enlarging until it was the height of a man, and doubly as wide. Its circular edge was shattered as the purple lightning ripped through it. At its heart stood vague colors of blue and swirling vortexes of white that failed to complete an image.

"Something is wrong. I can't hold it." The veins in Xander's temples throbbed. Those in his neck were gorged with blood as he struggled to contain the energy, he'd used to initiate the gateway's opening. He turned to Tristan, "Help me, you fool."

Suddenly, like a gaping maw, the white vortexes reached out from the gateway and inhaled. The two guards next to Tristan were sucked through the opening where a streak of purple slashed from the gateway's edge, spearing one of the men before both were lost.

Anchored to the rock, Tristan's body lifted from the ground. Wrapping his hands around the chains, he screamed as a vortex reached for him, stretching his body toward the opening until his joints popped. He tightened his muscles and released his hold on his angelic ability. The illumination on his skin was so great that the brilliance of it could be seen through the black material of his robe. He threw back his head and howled as yellow light flooded from his eyes. Hand over fist, he climbed the iron chains to grab hold of the anchor, desperately hoping the anchor held.

"Help him!" Malstar roared as his feet slipped from beneath him. Arms windmilling, he groped for the guard's hand that reached out to keep him from being sucked away.

"I can't!" Tristan yelled over the whirling wind released from the gateway. The vortex moved away from him, dropping his lower body to the ground. "Close it!" he roared.

"I can't!" Xander shouted, pressing his palms against his temples as he lost all control and began to scream. Blood from his ears seeped between his fingers.

"Tristan!"

Fear seized him as Anliac tumbled across the ground towards the gateway. Leaping to intercept her, his reach fell short as the chains binding him to the stone wrenched him around. "Anliac! No!" he yelled as he snapped the chains around one wrist and began to reach for her again.

Anliac managed to grab hold of Tristan's ankle. She climbed up his leg until she could reach his hand. With the air whipping them around like flags in a storm, they locked eyes and rode it out, ignoring the pain in their limbs as the gateway tried to pry them apart.

A loud boom shook the stone walls. The river jumped within its banks as the ground rippled and the gateway imploded. The vortexes fell apart as the wind quieted.

Xander stumbled forward in a daze, with rivulets of blood seeping from his tear ducts and ears. His webbed markings lay in a tangled knot between his golden-orbed eyes. With blood trailing from his nose and dripping off his chin, he fell to his knees before crumbling to his side, unconscious.

Cupping Anliac cheeks in his palms, Tristan asked, "Are you okay?" Running his free hand down the side of her neck, his eyes scanned her for injury. There were scrapes and bruises, but nothing life threatening.

"I think so."

Relieved, he ran his hand up her back, pulling her against him. The embrace was made awkward with her bound hands trapped between. "Thank Superi," he whispered into the hollow of her neck. "I thought I'd lost you."

"What was that?" she asked.

With the danger past, Malstar became irate. Snatching a cudgel from the nearest guard, he bore down on Tristan.

Knowing what was coming, Tristan shoved Anliac away as the first blow fell across his left bicep.

Enraged, Tristan jumped to his feet, and snatched the cudgel from Malstar's hand. The fulgo stumbled backward in startled fear, his eyes growing wide as Tristan raised the weapon over his head to bludgeon Malstar's skull.

Anliac cried out.

Weapon at the ready, Tristan's gaze swung towards her and he froze. She was on her knees, her hair pulled back in a guard's fist, with a sharp blade at her throat.

"No!" Tristan dropped the cudgel. "Don't hurt her."

"On your knees," Malstar barked, "or she's dead."

Tristan did as he was told, his eyes never leaving Anliac's as Malstar fastened the familiar arcanite collar around his throat.

"You almost got me killed," Malstar stated as he snatched the cudgel from the ground and struck Tristan across the back.

Tristan grunted as his shoulder blades pulled together.

"Stop it!" From her knees, Anliac fell forward onto her hands. "Stop!" she cried out again when Malstar backhanded Tristan across the face.

"Shut up!" a guard growled as he dragged her to her feet by her hair.

She yelped, but the air was knocked from her lungs as her back came up hard against the guard's chest.

Fear for Anliac held him captive in ways the chains never could. He could have ripped the fulgo to shreds. "I told you I couldn't do it," Tristan snarled and then grunted as Malstar stepped into the blow directed across his abdomen. Tired of being hit, he tightened his core and the cudgel rattled out of Malstar's hand.

"Liar! All you had to do was hold the gate open using the energy of the elements. The diary was explicit." He ran his fingers through his hair, shoving it back from his sweat sheened face. "It came naturally to the angeli who did it last. You're," he planted his boot on Tristan's back and shoved him forward, "pathetic." Winded, Malstar stumbled backward. "Do you not understand what is at stake? They took everything from us," he said, jabbing a finger towards where the gateway had opened. "They destroyed the perfection of the Superian race. They reached into our minds and twisted them until we could no longer build upon our civilization, until we could no longer advance in any way that matters. That gate," he snarled, "has to open. This isn't about me. It's not about the tower. It's about our blasted right to reclaim what is ours. All you had to do was channel the energy."

Tristan shoved his upper body off the ground until he was in a kneeling position. "And I told you...I can't." Defeated, he found and held Anliac's woeful eyes. "I'm so sorry."

Anliac sobbed.

Malstar scrubbed at his face with both hands as if wiping away a nightmare. "I don't understand. This should have worked," he mumbled under his breath. He began to pace, talking to himself out loud. "We'd thought all angeli possessed a core set of abilities that allowed them to travel through the aether. Could we have been wrong?"

Tristan wrapped a hand protectively around his busted ribs. "Malstar..."

Malstar spun on his heels to face him. "I have no idea what you're capable of. Ugh, I should have tested your abilities before we tried this." Disgust appeared on his face. "You are a failure."

"Your experiment is flawed," Tristan said. "Your facts are wrong, and what you are trying to do is insanity," Tristan tried to reason. "Let us go."

Malstar's eyes brightened. "You're right. The facts are wrong. Thrasher..."

A short, stout, black and white fera with a barbed tail bounded forward on bowed legs. "Sir."

"I want a list of every ability known on Superi that absorbs, redirects, or drains energy," Malstar ordered.

"Yes, sir." Thrasher dipped his head in respect. By the time he reached the massive double doors leading beyond the stone wall, he was at a steady trot.

Tristan's heart stopped beating. Oh no, he thought. They need an epoto.

"Bring her," Malstar said as he re-crossed the wooden bridge. "Let us see if the next angeli possesses the combination of abilities we need."

When her guard tugged on her leash, Anliac began to struggle. "No. I won't let you do this."

"What about him?" a guard asked, ignoring the girl's hysterics.

Opening his mouth to respond, Malstar spotted the gate maker. Rolling his eyes, he said, "Someone get Xander. The rest of you stay here and watch the angeli."

"No!" Anliac redoubled her struggles, desperate not to be taken back to the tower.

Tristan attempted to run to her, only to have his feet yanked out from beneath him as his own tether was pulled. He hit the ground flat on his back, the air gushing from his lungs, and his head swimming. He lay helpless as Anliac's screams tore at his gut.

"Settle down before you hurt yourself," her guard growled and then grunted as Anliac's elbow connected with his stomach. "Oomph." He shook her violently. "Knock it off," he said, shoving her towards the egress.

Sinking to the ground, Anliac refused to walk. When the guard grabbed a handful of her hair and began to drag her forward, she began to scream.

"Oh, for Superi's sake. Shut her up," Malstar said. "Knock her out if you have to."

"With pleasure, sir."

A solid 'thunk' of the guard's meaty fist caused Anliac's eyes to roll into the back of her head.

Tristan yanked against his chains, dragging the guards holding his tether forward as others rushed to give them aid. Outnumbered, and left with no recourse, he said, "The man who opened this gate was a fool. He broke us, but you, you're going to destroy us. Don't do this, Malstar!"

VI

Transfused

Anliac groaned and reached for her aching head. The rattle of chains accompanied her failed attempted. Dropping her arms back to a solid, cold surface, she moaned. "Tristan?"

"She's waking up."

"I can see that Jaydon," Malstar said as he leaned over the rectangular slab of ebony rock situated in the center of his laboratory's dirt floor to peer down at her. "You should know that there are no water sources here for you to pull from." He looked overhead and then down again. "At least, there are none you can access without flooding the entire tower."

Anliac shook her head to clear it and then wished she hadn't as a wave of nausea washed over her. The stench of the grease lanterns and their sickly, flickering light did nothing to ease her discomfort.

Malstar backed away as she lifted her head and took in her surroundings. Empty shelves lined the stone walls she could see. Clear outlines of differing shapes were encircled by dust where items had been recently removed.

Her eyes were pinched as she gently laid her head back down. Movement from her right side had her turning her head. When she saw Jaydon smirking back at her, she twisted onto her side as far as her chains would allow and vomited.

"It's nice to see you again too, little nox."

"Shut up," she groaned. Rolling flat, she breathed slowly through her nose. Malstar appeared at her feet. "Unless you're willing to release me so I can kill him..." she swallowed the bile rising again in her throat, "what is he doing here?"

"I paid a hefty sum to watch you suffer," Jaydon said.

"Hmm." The right corner of her lips twitched. "You're not very bright, are you? When I come off this table..."

"If...you come off this table," Jaydon interjected.

"Look at what I'll be." Her voice firmed, as did her resolve. "I'm going to kill you."

"I've heard you say as much before and yet here I stand."

"Enough," Malstar said with impatience. "Stretch out her arm. I need to insert the needle."

She tried to resist but Jaydon was stronger. Her breath came in short pants as her heart rate accelerated. She winced as the sharp projectile pierced her skin, entering the thick blue vein in the bend of her arm.

Malstar released a valve clamping closed the thin tube running from the needle into a green vial he held in his hand.

The dark red blood that filled the tube made its way into her body.

Sucking air between clenched teeth, her eye grew wide as fire-like heat burned its way through her veins. Sweat beaded on her skin as her body went rigid. Her mouth flew open as she inhaled on a gasp.

A scream ripped out of her throat, echoing in the enclosed space as her bone structure began to change.

Her joints popped as the ligaments stretched.

Her head was tipped back as her hair, caught beneath her, prevented her from sliding up the stone as her body elongated.

"Would you look at that," Jaydon said, stepping forward for a closer look.

"Stop!" she pleaded. "For mercy's sake! Stop!" Her skin felt as if she'd been submerged in acid. "Please," she cried one last time before her voice failed her completely.

"Amazing, is it not? She's grown nearly a foot and look at her color. It's paling out beautifully," Malstar said, rubbing his hands together. "Grab her other arm."

"No." Frantic, Anliac fought against her restraints.

Her jerking movements made sticking the needle into her arm impossible. "Bring in the guards."

"With pleasure."

Sticking his head out of the door, Jaydon called for two of the four guards waiting outside. Seeing the girl restrained atop the rock, they gaped, surprised by the changes already wrought in her physical appearance by the alchemist.

"What do you need us to do?" one asked.

The guards were strong but not altogether bright. Jaydon gave them simple instructions he hoped they could follow. "Keep her still."

Moving to the center of the room, one fera stretched out his thick frame over the top of Anliac, pressing her down as the other squatted at the head of the stone. He wrapped one thick arm around her neck, holding her head in place, as he pulled down on her right shoulder, preventing it from moving.

She felt the pinch of the needle and then the pain renewed. Blood rushed to her head. "Let me pass out. Let me pass out." Her eyes widened as her mouth rounded into an O of astonished agony. "Son of the damned," she screamed until her lungs had been depleted of air. She refilled them on a loud inhale. "For mercy's sake," she cried. "Let me pass out."

The fera holding her head fell to his backside and skittered away from the stone. "What's wrong with her ears?"

The cartilage softened like wax, held to her head only by the raw skin encasing it, as they began to reform.

"The mortalis blood is taking effect. The points of her ears have dissolved." Malstar said, soothing back her hair. As her screams quieted to whimpering moans, he gestured for the other fera to back away and then whispered into her ear. "Breathe through the pain, Anliac. Soon you will be magnificent." Lifting a handful of her hair, he shifted it to where she could see. Her black hair held streaks of blonde mixed with deep browns.

Her expression crumbled at the evidence of change.

"Please stop. I'm begging you. No more."

"I'm afraid I can't," he said. "We've the blood of the fera to go. Shh," he cooed when she began to cry harder. "It will be over soon."

"Please…"

"I could listen to you beg all day," Jaydon smiled, reveling in her agony.

"Take off her shoe. There's a good vein in the top of her foot that I can use." As one of the fera did as instructed, Malstar said, "The injection of fera blood has a profound impact on the subject's body."

Her mumbled pleas were ignored as Malstar pulled down on her toes, keeping her foot in place as he inserted the third needle into the tender skin at the top.

"Prepare yourselves," Malstar warned, releasing the valve and opening the clamp.

Anliac's body bowed off the rock as the pain shattered her mind and invoked a flight or fight impulse that took control. Unable to flee, she went berserk as the fera blood shredded and tightened her muscles.

Her calves split first. "Take it out," she cried. "I can't…" her head thrashed from side to side. "No more!"

"Try to relax," Malstar suggested. "It might help."

"I hate you!" she shouted. Words failed as her screams took over.

Her thighs hardened, cramping up until she would have gladly cut them off to spare herself the agony. The muscles ripped. Her mind fogged until thought escaped her completely and she was lost to the pain.

Her abdomen went rigid. Her knees, hindered by the chains around her ankles, bent. Her upper torso bowed. Her body, desperate to stop the cruel contraction, outstretched before her back arched.

The tearing of her abdomen was not yet complete when her arms began their transition. Her biceps balled up as new muscle formed on the backsides of her arms.

Her body went cold, draining away some of the heat, giving her a moment to catch her breath. Gasping for air, she began to choke. Blood spewed from her throat, damaged by her screams, and coated her teeth and tongue red. Splatters of it fell on her chin.

"Is it…over? I can't…feel…my body." Her head fell to the side. Staring up at Malstar from beneath lowered lashes, she asked, "Am I…dying?"

Her breathing stuttered and then stopped as her body went limp atop the stone. Her eyes slid closed.

The feras backed towards the wall trying to become invisible as Malstar stood there stupefied. Slowly at first, Jaydon began to laugh.

"Get out," Malstar snarled. "Now."

"Whatever," Jaydon said. "I got to see what I came for."

Malstar moved calmly and slowly to her head, watching her body carefully.

Before Jaydon made it to the door, her left arm twitched. "Get the arcanite chains on her. Quickly!"

The feras searched the floor and the shelves. "Where are they?"

"Find the blasted chains. And summon more guards," Malstar said. He grinned triumphantly. "We're going to need them."

"Yes, you are," she said, coming awake.

With a solitary pull, she broke through her restraints. She rose into a standing position, her feet hovering inches above the stone as she stared at the gawking men through calm, yellow eyes. Skinny slivers of golden marks sinuously wrapped their way around her torso, dipping downward to caress the tops of her thighs. The lines coursed over her shoulders and up the sides of her neck as a pattern of golden stars and swirling crescents wrapped their way around her bare left shoulder, contrasting beautifully with the dark blue aquis marks she bore on her right one.

Her arms snapped downward. Slowly, she clenched her fist.

"Sir," a fera said, staring at the floor.

"I'm aware," Malstar shouted. He lifted the hem of his robe as water began to seep up from the earth beneath them.

Reaching out with her other hand, she wiggled her fingers and the stone walls of the chamber trembled. As chips of rock clattered to the floor, dirt rained down on them from the ceiling above.

The two feras screamed in horror as the water suddenly closed in on them, freezing them in place as it rose up their legs to their waists, leaving the rest of the floor dry. A flick of her wrist ripped two stone rocks from the wall that flew into the ice.

The feras' screams were cut off as shock stole their voices. Their legs and guts shattered. Their upper bodies thudded to the floor. Organs oozed out of their open chest cavities as blood seeped from their eyes and ears, dribbling from the corners of their gaping mouths. They blinked unseeingly until their brains finally realized they were dead.

She turned her attention on Jaydon. "Your turn."

The front of his black trousers darkened as he peed himself. He lunged for the door. The dirt floor rolled beneath his feet, throwing him backward. Scrambling onto his hands and knees, he clawed his way toward the exit. A hole, deep enough to be a grave, opened up, and he fell into it.

"No," he pleaded. "I'm sorry."

The hole around him began to close.

"I love to hear you beg, but I'd love even more to hear you scream." Clenching her fist, the terra closed, leaving only his head above ground level.

And scream he did until his ribs crushed into his lungs. His face turned red and then an angry purple as his eyes bulged from their sockets. They popped free, hanging from strips of pink flesh against his cheeks. His engorged tongue filled the space between his spread jaws.

She turned her head, looking over her shoulder at Malstar. Her body followed. Malstar was on one knee, hunched over with his head down beside the stone over which she hovered.

"I am in awe you," Malstar said. Tentatively, his gaze rose. "You are more than even I could imagine."

The long sleeves of his robe hid his hands as he slowly came to his feet. With a sudden blur of speed that only a level three could possess, his left arm darted forward. A finalistic click sounded as a shackle of arcanite fastened closed around her ankle.

"No," she gasped as her golden marks faded way. The unconquerable power that had raged within her was drained through the metal, leaving her defenseless and exhausted in a way she'd never experienced.

Before her feet could settle onto the black slab of rock, Malstar had the second shackle in place. His image blurred, and then he was at the door, opening it. "Get in here." After the remaining two guards had entered, he slammed the door.

The nox, young and inexperienced, caught one glimpse of Jaydon's head and bent at the waist, losing the contents of his stomach.

"Pansy," the mortalis guard taunted the weaker man before bowing to Malstar.

"Why did the two of you not help?"

"Permission to speak frankly, sir?"

"I would recommend it," Malstar hissed, "if you hope to keep your life."

"The tower doesn't pay well enough to die for it, sir." He shook his head. "A man hears screams like that coming from another man, no blasted way was I coming in here."

Faster than the guard could track, Malstar attacked. Yanking the guard's dagger from his belt, Malstar slashed through the artery at the side of his neck. The guard covered his spurting wound with his hand as he groped for the alchemist.

"The tower no longer requires your services," Malstar sneered as life left the guard's eyes and he fell dead, smacking his head on the slab of stone on his way down.

Anliac stepped backward to avoid the falling body and screamed as she fell off the rock.

Malstar rushed to her aid. "Are you all right?" He kept the blade in clear view to discourage the violence he read in her eyes.

"What do you care?" Her head dropped.

"Oh, Anliac, I care a great deal. Come," he said. "There is no time to rest."

Absent the will to fight, Malstar pulled her to her feet. The ground seemed too far away. When he urged her to walk forward, her legs were unsteady, her gait unfamiliar.

Glancing over her shoulder, she didn't see the bloodbath spilled across the floor. What she saw was the ebony slab of rock upon which she'd died. What had come off the stone was not her, but a weapon created to be wielded by the tower.

"I will not be used," she said.

"You will be used or you and your boyfriend with both die, and I will find others to do what you would not. This is not a game, Anliac. Failure is not an option."

VII
I Am A God

Tristan lay draped over the two-foot, rotund stone anchor before the gateway site. If not for the long black robe and its shielding cowl, he would have been scorched. The water the guards had grudgingly, and sparingly, shared had kept him from dehydrating, but he was weak. Though he couldn't rise from his knees, he pulled his torso from the rock when the doors of Bealson's Grove opened again.

An ignis wielder in chainmail led a group through. He raised his arms to chest level and began flicking his wrists one at a time. With each movement, light flared from atop a pillar as the tinder and wood struck until all four were lit. His job complete, he fell in at the end of the line as ten guards filed through the gates to the left, while ten others filed into the right, taking up positions around the perimeter of the fifteen-foot-high stone wall.

Malstar was easily recognizable from his purple robe and sinuous gait. He made gestures with his hands as he spoke to another fulgo, drenched in the blood red robes of IA, at his side. Four men with silver collars around their necks, symbolic of their station as bodyguards, flanked either side of their wards.

Malstar stopped just before the wooden bridge. Twisting his torso without actually turning, he stretched his arm behind him and beckoned someone forward. A tall, slender, figure appeared with a wall of fera guards at her back.

Tristan's mouth parted in a silent gasp. There was only person it could be, but the changes to Anliac's body were more than his imagination had been able to conjure.

Though her head was down, the difference in her height was obvious. He searched within the deep cowl of her hood, but the view of her face was blocked. The fine, black silk she wore covered the tops of her shoulders, but left her newly defined arms bare, as well as the thin, blue, intertwining marks of her aquis ability. The material ran down her torso in two gathered strips, covering her breasts and ribs, but leaving her exposed from neck to navel. Tight, ripped, abdominal muscles rippled as she came forward. The splits in the sides of her garment, which began at the intricate silver belt at her slender waist, revealed a glimpse of long, shapely legs with each step. Her skin, so rich and dark before, had lightened into a soft olive complexion.

She didn't fight when Calstar grabbed her roughly by the arm and yanked her forward. "Hurry up, girl. I haven't got all day." Dragging her with him across the wooden bridge, he shoved her toward the anchor point, towards Tristan.

From his knees, Tristan could see inside her hood, where he encountered her hollow, golden-eyed stare. Black hair, streaked with strands of blonde and brown, was shoved behind her pointless ears. Her face was as mortalis as Set's— less angular than before, but just as beautiful.

"Are you okay?" he asked coming to his feet.

She was almost eye-to-eye with him as she raised her shackled wrists to cup his face in her palms. "If I don't do what they want, they're going to kill you. I can't let them do that, but I don't think I can do what they want either."

Yanking her backwards to deny them the physical contact, Malstar hissed, "For his sake, I would suggest you try. Keep him shackled in the arcanite," he said to the guards standing over Tristan with cudgels in hand, "but get him out of the circle. If the girl rebels in any way...kill him."

Tristan put up a token struggle as the guards unlatched him from the anchor point, but they had him across the bridge, standing with the tip of a blade pressed into his spine, in moments.

Anliac remained in the exact same position.

Malstar came around to stand before her. Unfastening the arcanite chains, he freed her. Wrapping his fingers around her chin, he forced her head to turn to Tristan. "We are people of our word, Anliac. You vowed to kill Jaydon and you did. I vowed to make you into an angeli, and I did. So, when I vow to kill him if you try and act against my wishes, you know I'll keep my word."

Her eyes flashed a yellow light that caused Malstar to flinch and step away. To cover up his reaction, he turned to Calstar. "Now brother, we will open the ga—"

The site crackled with jagged, white-blue streaks of light.

Calstar gasped as his two bodyguards pulled him back before stepping, shoulder to shoulder, in front of him.

Malstar's face split with a broad grin. "Was that you?" he asked, his neck whipping back and forth as his eyes moved from the angeli to the lightning.

The hair on Anliac's arms rose as the lightning crackled again. Devoid of emotion, she said, "It wasn't me."

"You, then?" Malstar said to Xander. "Wait until you're told to begin."

Xander's face was drained of color. His eyes were glued to the gateway that was beginning to form. He swallowed hard. "I'm not doing that."

Calstar pivoted towards the bridge and hastily crossed it. His men followed with him.

Snatching Anliac's wrist, Malstar moved them away from the oval-shaped shadow looming before them. As its edges smoothed, the lightning quieted and an image formed. A deep-blue sky with a spattering of white clouds became clear as they shielded their eyes against a single, brilliant, yellow sun. A great expanse of lush, green grass rolled out before large desert mountains.

The gateway shimmered. A man, with honeyed, luminescent skin and a golden wreath set atop his long blond hair, clothed in a white toga with a golden belt girded about his waist, began to run towards the opening on brown sandaled feet.

The slew of guards readied their weapons as the powerful man pushed off one foot and launched himself through the gateway to hover over the ground.

As Superi's gravity grabbed hold of him, he was yanked downward. He landed, knees bent, on the balls of his feet and the tips of his fingers.

Low enough that only Anliac could hear, the man cursed the change in his weight as Superi's gravity took hold of him. He rose to his six-and-half-foot height and faced the small army of armed guards staring back at him.

"Pathetic, little men." His voice boomed with authority. "Did you not learn your lesson the last time? You'd think to invade Earth again with this," he waved his hand around the perimeter of Bealson's Grove, "when you brought thousands before and failed?" Throwing his head back, he laughed.

"You're on Superi, now," Malstar said, attempting, and failing, to mimic the intruder's commanding tone. "Who are you?"

The man's chest expanded as he pulled back his shoulders. With an arrogant tilt of his chin, he announced, "I am the god Apollo, master of the sun, of truth and light. Prophecy is born by my words, healing granted at my whim. I am the bringer of plagues that culls weakness from the world of men."

The Superians watched as the glow emanating from the self-proclaimed god began to fade beneath their suns. Apollo, noting his weakened state, conjured from the light a golden curved bow and lifted a feathered arrow from the quill on his back as he scowled and brought it to cheek. Angered, he let the arrow fly.

The Superians stood their ground. As the projectile approached its target, the guard intercepted it with a swipe of his short sword as he deftly stepped aside. The trajectory of the arrow changed, and a second guard, using his shield, slapped it to the ground.

Fury over the god's attack broke the guards from their initial awe. Falling into formation around Malstar, they awaited his instructions. The guards prepared to defend or attack with weapons in hand.

With practiced skill, Apollo notched and loosed a second arrow. It made it as far as the first, but then dropped like a stone a dozen feet short of its target.

Violently, he snapped his bow in half, and tossed the pieces downward where they disappeared before hitting the ground. Chortles sprang up among the IA guards, enraging Apollo. "I do not need a weapon to destroy you! I am Apollo!" The stone walls trembled with his roar.

Malstar gave the order. "Take him." As his men advanced, he said, "And try not to kill him. I have questions, and this god will answer them."

Leaving a dozen guards before the doors, six tramped over the wooden bridge, maneuvering themselves around the semicircle of men guarding Malstar, to face Apollo. Two stood in reserve as the other four took the lead and advanced.

Apollo's left arm snapped out towards the closest advancing guard. Grabbing the man by his throat, Apollo gave a quick twist of his wrist and snapped the fera's black, furry neck. Pivoting to the right, Apollo punched his fist into a second fera's chest. Puncturing through the man's leather uniform, rending muscle and bone, Apollo felt the man's spine settle against the palm of his hand. Closing his fist, he snapped it in two. Balancing on his left foot, Apollo kicked with his right, and sent the dead man barreling into the two remaining guards.

The reserve guards advanced with their swords, the one on the right sliced at the god's abdomen with his long sword.

Apollo tightened his core as he jumped back to avoid the bite of the blade. The guard pulled back his arm to thrust his weapon forward, but instead of retreating, Apollo snarled and attacked. Opening his arms wide, he brought them together in a thunderous clap and crunched the guard's wolf-shaped skull between his hands. Bone shattered and flesh folded like wet pottery as the guard went limp and fell.

Rage filled the last guard, who voiced it with a battle cry as he brought down his blade at Apollo's head. Apollo was too fast.

He pivoted right, swinging around to capture the blade between his palms. "You ignorant beast," Apollo sneered. "I AM A GOD!" Spinning the blade in his hand, he slammed the hilt into the guard's helm, which cracked. The skull beneath it crushed, the man fell.

Three guards from the protective wall in front of Malstar ran towards Apollo, short swords at the ready.

Apollo's image blurred with his speed as he grabbed a long sword from the ground and in one low, horizontal sweep, split the three guards in half at the waist.

"Forget capturing him," Malstar shouted into the silence that followed the unfathomable sight. "Kill him!"

Apollo grinned and fell into action, his every move precise as, one by one and two by two, the IA guards began to fall. His speed was impressive. His efficiency inspiring. Tristan felt no pity. These were his captors, and he found himself rooting for Apollo to win.

A roar ripped from the god's throat as he flung a round shield, like a discus, across the grove. Malstar cursed as one of his guards cowardly slung himself to the side, avoiding the attack. Using his speed, Malstar snatched hold of his remaining guard, and pulled the guard in front of his chest just as the shield struck home. Malstar's grin of triumph became a scream of pain as the edge of the shield cut through the guard and impaled Malstar's own gut.

"No!" Calstar bellowed from across the grove as the guard's torso slid from the shield. His brother stumbled forward, tripping over the guard's lower body, shoving the shield deeper as he made impact with the ground. Calstar watched in helpless fury as Malstar's body stiffened and then went lax as his blood poured from the mortal wound.

One moment Apollo stood before the gateway surrounded by the death he'd delivered, and the next he stood before Anliac. Reaching inside her hood, he grabbed hold of a handful of her hair and forced her head back. "Who are you?"

"No!" Tristan panicked. He turned to his guard. "You have to get me out of these chains."

The guard's fear was palpable, yet he hesitated. "I'm under orders not to release you no matter what happens."

"You'd rather die?"

"Well," the guard pulled a key from his pocket and turned the lock of the first shackle "when you put it that way," he said as he placed the key in the second lock.

Splattered with blood and hands clenched in front of her, Anliac met Apollo's stare without fear. "Will you kill me now?"

His head cocked to the side. "Is that your desire?" Apollo roared as a blade punctured the back of his shoulder. Spinning away from Anliac, he reached with his left hand to pull free the blade as he searched for the one who'd thrown it.

The guilty party revealed himself when Calstar bellowed to the last remaining guard within the circle, "Do something!"

Apollo blurred over to the guard and ripped his head from his shoulders. Pointing a finger at Calstar, he said, "I'll deal with you momentarily." Focusing on Anliac, he made his way back to her. Lifting the hood from her shoulders, he tipped her chin as he studied her features. "You are an angeli. I would know how? Were you born or made this way?"

The arcanite shackles dropped like dead weights from Tristan's wrists as the second lock was turned. He couldn't fight in the robe, so he tore it off over his head, leaving him standing in tight fitted, black trousers, and boots.

When she refused to answer, Apollo wrapped his hands around her slender throat and squeezed.

A burst of light had Apollo turning his head. His hand fell from the woman's throat as his jaw dropped. No longer chained, the black-haired boy revealed himself as an angeli, as sinuous golden lines spread over his pale skin. He blinked when the boy disappeared, and then howled in pain when slashing claws separated the flesh from his bone down his left forearm and across his chest.

Tristan leapt backward as Apollo braced his weight on his left leg to kick out. Pivoting to avoid the god's vicious right kick, he ducked low and swept Apollo's left leg out from under him.

Apollo flipped five times in the air before landing face first on the ground. Growling, he slammed his fists into the terra, causing it to shake before springing to his feet in righteous anger. "You are not stronger than a god!" Gathering energy from the planet's strange light, he conjured it into an orbed ball hovering before him. Tightening his shoulders, he brought back his arms, elbows bent, to launch the weapon. "You are not stronger than me."

"Stop." The single word was so melodically pure it pierced even the god's heart and gained her his attention.

Golden, wavering lines traveled up Anliac's thighs and over the curve of her exposed hips. They caressed their way up her firm stomach; peeking from beneath the black silk hiding her feminine curves as they traveled up her torso to kiss the sides of her neck. Elongated squares, like cut diamonds, separated by small, filled in circles, graced her left shoulder and drifted down to her elbow.

"Dissolve your weapon," she said, her voice calm considering whom she was trying to command.

His countenance stoic, he growled, "There are two of you," and then he launched the light orb.

With a flick of her wrist, a slab of stone was sliced from the surface of the terra. Quick as thought, she lifted the slab into the air, and then shoved with her open palms against invisible space sending the stone to crash into the orb cast by the god. The impact hurled the orb and stone into the air above their heads, where it exploded in a shock wave of reds and yellows.

Two shafts of light poured from her eyes, pinning the god where he stood. "Run," she told the god, "While I still give you the option."

"I'm not afraid of you, girl," he scoffed "I'll run from no one."

Never breaking eye contact, she dipped her chin. Inhaling, she lifted it again, exposing a sardonic grin. Without effort, she pulled whips of water from the river that combined into a massive aquis vortex. Rocks, and large chunks of terra were pulled and ripped out of the river's banks and were sucked into the swirling mass looming ominously behind her.

Distracted by the girl, Apollo never saw the other angeli move, but he felt his strength as a solid blow struck his kidney. He swung a backhand in defense, but the angeli was gone.

Tristan vanished and reappeared in flashes, striking quickly to knock Apollo off balance. Inch by inch, foot by foot, he worked to edge the god back towards the gate.

"Stop moving and fight, you coward" Apollo screamed through gritted teeth.

With both hands forward, Tristan appeared straight in front of the god, shoving him several feet backwards. "Why, so you can embarrass yourself some more?" Tristan taunted.

Apollo struck Tristan's left temple with a thunderous right hook, spinning him around.

Tristan smiled. "I guess I'm even stronger than I thought, or you're much weaker. That didn't even tingle."

Apollo pointed at Tristan, drawing himself up to give a grand speech, but never got the first word out. A drill-shaped cylinder of water and stone hit Apollo square in the chest, driving him closer to the gate's edge. He was overmatched and he knew it.

"I'll return, angeli," he vowed, "and I will not be alone."

He saw the girl rip another section of terra loose and saw her unleash it. His attempt to evade it failed. His feet were lifted from the ground as his body curved around it, whooshing the air from his lungs. Again, and again, the slabs of terra flew against him until the last of it was carried with him back through the gateway.

From the other side, they saw him land flat on his back, buried beneath Superian soil. The rock blasted apart as the god rose to his feet unscathed. He swung his arm in disgust and the gateway closed.

Anliac turned the conjured water into spears of ice and aimed them at the guards flocking to Calstar's side, ringing them in, as Tristan moved to stand beside her.

"You did good, gorgeous," Tristan said, taking her hand.

"He might have killed you." Her voice was achingly sweet and contrasted greatly with her violent words. She turned her head and looked directly at him. "I couldn't let that happen."

"No one else is dying here today," Calstar said with hands raised in surrender. His guards mimicked his posture. "There's no need for this." He gestured to one of the ice spears inching its way beneath his chin.

"Does this mean you're done hunting us," Tristan asked, his golden marks flaring, pulsating over his body, matching Anliac's.

"It does," Calstar said. "It was never my decision to chase you, nor was it my hand that made you both as you are now."

"But you knew what he was doing," Tristan said. "So, don't bother playing the victim here."

"I admit that I'm guilty of indulging my brother. We both know his mind was not right, a side effect of the curse cast by the gods. He spoke of his experiments, but you yourself know that he was anxious to show me what he'd done, which means I had no foreknowledge."

"If you're as ignorant as you claim, then you're of no use to us. I should let her kill you and be done with it."

Calstar pressed his lips together tightly.

Lifting their linked hands, Tristan kissed the back of hers, stealing some of her attention. "It's over, Anliac. Let them go. They can't hurt us anymore."

The spears turned to harmless water and splashed at the guards' feet.

Out of fear, or out of respect, Tristan and Anliac didn't know which, but they watched as the guards took to one knee and left Calstar standing alone.

Anliac shook her head and looked to Tristan as if seeing him for the first time. A tenderness filled newly yellowed eyes. She smiled a tentative curving of her lips, "You have a strength that surpasses a god. Our enemy kneels before us, and you," she shook her head again, "choose to show them mercy."

"I choose not to become what I hate," he said.

VIII

We Are Here To Rescue You?

"Are you certain you want to do this, boy," Tidous asked Kervan as they followed behind the others towards the clearing beside the docks of Catena Piscari. "You've nothing vested, nothing to gain, but a life to lose."

Shoving his hands in his front pockets, Kervan hunched his shoulders. "You're a good man, Tidous, but you tolerate my presence at best."

Tidous didn't contest the statement. "I won't be here when you come back."

"Who said I planned to?" He yanked his hands free to steady himself when he tripped clumsily over his own feet. Hearing Tidous snicker, he said, "It was a hole," as his face flushed.

Triton and Razoran were waiting for them in the clearing.

"Here," Triton said, holding out a coin purse for Set to take. "You'll need it."

Shashara laid her hand on Set's outstretched arm, pushing it down. "We would appreciate it greatly if you'd see to it that the innkeeper's damages are paid."

Tossing the pouch into the air, Triton caught it in his fist. "If that's what you want," he said, passing the coin purse to Razoran. "See it done."

"Aye, captain. Good luck to you all," he said. "We'll see you in Pisces Stragulum." Receiving nods of acknowledgment, the fera loped up the dirt street towards the inn.

Shashara narrowed her eyes at Triton. "You will be kind to Skylar, and you'll make sure your men treat her with respect."

Triton scowled as Set and Davad chuckled.

Scratching behind his ear, Set's expression contorted. "That's a tall order to fill Shashara. You might be asking too much of Triton's men."

"Seriously, Set?"

"Seriously," Davad said grinning. "She'll survive the trip, but if its respect she wants, she'll have to earn it."

Tidous nudged Kervan forward. "He's all yours. Safe trip."

"Thank you again for your help yesterday," Shashara said, "and for your hospitality."

Tidous turned his back. "Don't mention it."

"Real nice guy," Davad quipped.

"Nicer than most, meaner than some," Kervan remarked, "but if not for him, I would have starved. So...umm...watch what you say about him."

Slapping Kervan on the back, Set grinned. "Davad has said the same thing about Triton, here."

Triton crossed his arms over his chest. "Nonsense. There's nothing nice about me." His visage darkened when the kids began to laugh. "Don't you have a portal to open," he asked, which only made them laugh harder.

"He's right," Set said. "We should get going."

The others backed away, including Triton, when Set said, "I wish Rupert were here." Closing his eyes to block out any distraction, he pressed his palms together as he brought forth the image of the Vitreous River where it crossed through the southern border of Dura Mortis into Imbellis.

Peeking over Davad's shoulder as the developing shadow coalesced into an image of grassland, Shashara asked, "See any feras waiting to ambush us?"

"Is she kidding?" Kervan backed further away from the portal just in case.

"I wish," Davad said. "The feras of Dura Mortis are all about segregation from the other races. If they catch us, we're in trouble."

Set's eyes came open. "It's time to go."

"You first," Kervan said, inching backward.

Shashara giggled and took his hand. "It'll be fine," she said, leading him forward. "We'll step through together."

Davad darted around them. "Later, Triton," he said before entering the portal.

"Be nice to Skylar, Triton," Shashara said again, dragging a reluctant Kervan through the portal with her.

"All seems quiet," Davad said as Shashara and Kervan emerged.

Set came through last, the portal collapsing behind him as he scanned the flat wavering grassland. "Rupert's memory is good. He took us straight to the river. Now all we have to do is follow it back to IA."

After a time, they left the grasslands behind and entered a sparse forest. Slowly the trees changed from evergreens and oaks to flowering and fruit-bearing ones.

"We're in the grove," Shashara said. "We have to be getting close."

The suns had passed their zenith when the ground trembled beneath their feet. The river water rippled inside its banks as fruit and leaves were shaken loose from their branches.

"What was that?" Kervan asked, wide-eyed.

"Listen," Davad said, cupping a hand around his ear as he turned his head in the direction of the noise. "Is that screaming?"

Shashara's heart jumped into her throat. "Please don't let that be them," she said as she ran full out, fear bolstering her speed. She could hear the pounding of feet as the others raced to keep up. Their progress stalled as a fifteen-foot stone wall rose up against them.

A loud boom had them covering their ears and ducking for cover. A huge slab of terra with the grass still in place flew into the air, shoving before it a huge golden orb of energy that exploded violently. The ground shook again as a series of smaller explosions sounded in quick succession.

"Blast it," Davad cursed. "There's no way in."

"The gate has to be on another side," Shashara said, wringing her hands and looking to her brother for answers.

"What do we do?"

Kervan tripped.

Set reached out to steady him.

"We don't even know for sure if it's them," Davad growled, running his hands through his hair.

"Yes, we do," Set and Kervan said in unison.

The quiet that had settled on the other side of the wall was disconcerting.

When Davad and Shashara turned to Set for an explanation, he said, "Kervan caught an image of what's on the other side. I was touching him. I...I saw Tristan."

"What about Anliac?" Shashara asked, her voice rising in pitch along with her panic.

"I didn't see her."

"Okay, we need to get in there now," Shashara said on the verge of hysterics.

"We'll go around."

"No," Shashara said. "I have a better idea."

Unclasping her cloak, she let the material fall. Taking a deep breath, she launched herself into the river. They saw her head bob above the water just before she went back under, allowing the current to sweep her beneath the wall barring her path.

"Crap!" Davad tore his cloak from his shoulders, glaring at Set.

"Don't blame me," Set said, removing his own cloak as he approached the river. "She's your sister."

"What about me?" Kervan asked, eyeing the river askance.

"You've no defensive ability, Kervan," Davad said. "Follow the wall until you find the gate. We'll meet you there."

Kervan nodded, relieved, as Set and Davad dove into the river.

Shashara's hands reached for them as they emerged on the other side, dragging them onto the bank of a circular canal. Their appearance drew no attention away from the jaw-dropping scene playing out in the central circle, where bright fires burned from atop stone pillars. The flames reflected off the blue-tinted arcanite runes running through it and the silver lines tracing the ground around it.

IA guards were bowing before Tristan and a tall female that stood at his side. Calstar had his head bowed and his hand covering his heart as if paying homage to his ruler. The sight of it paled in comparison to the blood and carnage that littered the ground. Malstar was slumped over with a shield buried in his gut. A man's head lay several feet from its body, its eyes open.

Everywhere they looked, there was death.

"So, what now?" They heard Tristan ask as the guards came to their feet.

"I need to go back to the tower," Calstar said. "What's happened here concerns the whole of Superi and they will look to IA for answers."

"Tristan," Set called out, drawing his brother's gaze. "Are you okay?"

"Where's Anliac?" Shashara asked as she and the boys made their way over.

The woman stepped behind Tristan's shoulder as he turned towards them. Clasping forearms with Set, he said, "It's good to see you, little brother."

"Oh, Anliac." A sob broke between Shashara's words. "We were too late. I am so...so sorry." She reached for her, but Anliac shied away.

"She's fine," Tristan said. "She just needs a little space."

"What happened here," Set asked, his eyes bouncing from one horrific scene to another. His jaw dropped when he noticed the craters gouged from the terra as if by a giant's hand.

"The very thing Malstar and I feared has come to pass," Calstar said, kneeling down beside his brother. Rolling him onto his back, he removed the shield protruding from his center. "Threats from the gods of Earth have come again." Smoothing his brother's silver-streaked, black hair from his face, he said, "But Malstar gave us hope. He gave us the angeli."

"We can't reopen the gateway," Tristan said.

"Not yet," Calstar stood, glancing at Set's marks.

Tristan stepped in front of Set, blocking Calstar's view. "Head to the city. We'll follow after."

Calstar fidgeted. "You and Anliac are too important to go unguarded."

"No more guards. No more chains," Anliac stated, drawing eyes.

"Whoa," Davad said as Shashara and Set gasped at the golden sinuous lines flaring from the tops of Anliac's thighs to the outsides of her neck.

"Sorry to interrupt," a fera with an eagle's head and white feathers announced, "but who does he belong to?"

The guards reached for the weapons at the unexpected intruder. When they saw who it was, they lowered their defenses.

"Kervan," he said yanking free the scruff of his shirt from the man's hold. "My name is Kervan." Indignant, he made his way over to stand beside Shashara.

"You have no orders to be here, Lan," Calstar said. "Get your men back to the tower."

"No can do." Lan ordered his men to position themselves at the gate. "I've received word from Magistrate Donnin," he directed the statement to Tristan, but his gaze encompassed all of them. "My men and I are at your service."

Calstar grew irate. "You work for the tower."

"Not anymore."

The ground trembled.

"No more guards. No more chains."

"Anliac, calm down," Tristan said. "There's no one here strong enough to hurt you. I won't let anyone hurt you."

"She's doing this?" Shashara asked, flabbergasted.

"You seriously need to calm yourself," Davad suggested as Kervan came to stand beside him.

"Don't take offense, Lan," Set said. "We have trust issues with adults, and more issues with adults carrying weapons and wearing the insignia of IA."

"No offense taken. We're here to help."

"There's a ship headed for Pisces Stragulum," Set said. "If we're not there when it docks, a slew of angry pirates are going to storm the tower."

Calstar's spine stiffened. "Excuse me?"

"And General Aquam should be arriving any day now," Set continued. "It would be best if someone were to meet them, to update them, before more people die."

"Are you sure you don't want me to leave a few of my men with you?" Lan asked.

"Are you people trying to destroy my city?" Calstar shouted.

"Why shouldn't we?" Shashara asked. "Your city has destroyed our lives." She glanced sideways at Tristan and Anliac before refocusing on Calstar.

"The tower is trying to save the life of Superi and all who dwell on her surface." Calstar shook his head. "Ignorance is bliss, little girl, and right now, you are ignorant. Come," he said to his guards. "I have work to do."

"I'll send word to Donnin," Lan said, "and send runners to Pisces Stragulum to intercept the ship. Who is the captain?"

"Triton," Davad told him. "What about General Aquam?"

"He'll be looking for his daughter, but we lost track of her this morning, and so far, my men have been unable to find her." Lan admitted.

Anliac tugged her hood lower, hiding beneath the black cowl. She spoke with her head down. "Tell my father to go home. There's nothing left of me to save."

Lan covered his surprise. "I'm not sure he'll listen, but I'll deliver the message."

Tristan wrapped his hand around her shoulders. "Just find out what you can about his location. It would be better if he spoke to one of us before father and daughter share their reunion."

"Will do," Lan nodded. "Let's move out," he said to his men as they filed back through the gate, at last leaving them alone.

Anliac stepped over bloodied corpses as she made her way to the river's bank. Sinking to her knees, she leaned forward, scooping water with her hands to splash her face and neck, washing away Malstar's blood and the sweat that clung to her skin.

Shashara, drenched from her swim in the river, squatted down beside her. "Anliac," she said. "Look at me."

"I can't."

"You are the same person on the inside, and you're still beautiful on the outside. Anliac," she touched her shoulder, "you're not alone."

"I know I'm not. I have Tristan. We're the same now." Rising, she walked back to Tristan's side. "I want out of these clothes," she said. "I need to be away from this place."

"Then let's go," Tristan took her hand. Once they were through the gate, Tristan leaned over and whispered into Anliac's ear.

She nodded, and then fell back to walk beside Shashara and Davad, allowing Set and Tristan a moment of privacy. She ignored the nox who walked at Davad's other side.

"You've been busy," Tristan said, eyeballing Set's new marks.

"Becoming a gate maker was the only way to get here in time." Shoving his hands into his sodden trouser pockets, Set said, "Guess it wasn't fast enough after all."

"You did in days what it took us weeks to do when we came across for Shashara." He bumped shoulders with his brother. "Jacob would have been proud." Curiosity got the better of him. "How did you do it? How did you become a gate maker?"

Set hunched in on himself. "Apparently, if I kill by draining someone, I keep what I take." He couldn't look at his brother.

"That's going to make fighting pretty interesting, especially with what we just saw."

"Do you want to talk about it?" Set asked.

Tristan shook his. "Not yet. I do have a question though."

"About?" Set asked.

"I thought you couldn't jump through multiple portals in the same day? Didn't the fera tell us that?" Tristan asked in return.

Set shook his head slowly as they walked, "Yeah, we thought the same thing, but I feel fine." He looked over his shoulder at the rest of the group, "No one else has complained either. I guess they were just being paranoid. You know how adults get sometimes."

Tristan only nodded in response, keeping his eyes forward.

Set paused, sensing his brother's introspection, but then had to ask, "When did he change her?"

"We came through a portal into the tower the day we were taken," Tristan replied. "We were locked in a room for days. This morning he brought us here. When I couldn't open the gateway, they knocked Anliac out, leaving me chained in Bealson's Grove while he dragged her back to the tower. You see how she came out."

"Is she okay?"

"She will be," Tristan said. "Everything is new to her. Her body doesn't feel like her own. Her senses are heightened. Her emotions are raw. She's overloaded with power and she has very little control." He cleared his throat. "I've tried to deny it, what I am, but that ship has sailed. Anliac and I are the only two of our kind." He swallowed hard. "I don't want to hurt

Shashara, and I know Davad won't be happy about it, but…"

Set snapped a peach from a tree on the way by. "I kissed her," he said, before biting into the fruit.

Tristan stumbled and glanced back at Shashara, who tilted her head to the side and arched a brow. He turned back around. "Good for you, little brother."

Shrugging off the embarrassment, Set asked, "So are you going to tell me what Calstar was talking about?"

"You need to be careful what you say around him," Tristan said. "Set, the man that came through that gateway, he opened it from the other side, and if there are more like him then Calstar's right. Superi is in trouble."

"He's stronger than you?"

"No. He's no match for me, but he does have skills I don't have," Tristan said, without arrogance. "He can conjure weapons of energy like a wielder calling forth an element. I've never seen anything like it. He ripped through the IA guards like they were nothing."

"Where is he? Obviously, you won?"

"I didn't." He took a deep breath. "Anliac hurt him. She used huge blocks of terra to shove him back through the gateway. It should buy us some time, but he said he'd be back—and that he wouldn't be alone. There are only two of us, Set."

"How many gods are there?"

Tristan shrugged. "I'm hoping Calstar can tell us that. Malstar mentioned a journal. He's going to want to reopen that gateway, and until we're ready, we can't let that happen."

Set's brows bunched. "I thought you said neither of you could open it."

"We can't." He stopped and turned to face his brother, "But as an epoto and a gate maker, you can, and it won't take Calstar long to figure that out."

"Great," Set said, checking to make sure Shashara was okay. "That's just great." Tristan continued to talk to him, but his mind was occupied with what Tristan's words meant.

Davad rolled his eyes over the concerned look Set threw back at Shashara. When Shashara caught Set's look, she blushed.

Anliac looked down at her side, down to the girl she'd looked up to before, and smiled. "You and Set, huh?"

Shashara grinned, blushing a deeper pink. "You and Tristan, huh?"

The mirth drained away. "Does that bother you?"

"It doesn't bother me," Davad said. "I'd prefer my sister to stay away from guys all together, but if she had to choose between the brothers, she chose the better one."

Anliac's eyes began to glow.

"For her," Davad said, holding up his hands in defense. "She chose the better one for her."

"He's right, Anliac," Shashara said. "I never thought twice about Tristan like that until we were captured, and then, I thought of him because I knew if anyone could save me, it would be him. That's not love. That's…holding on to hope when hope feels lost. I'm happy that the two of you have each other. Just don't forget that you have us too."

"Tristan and I barely survived the fight against Apollo," Anliac said.

"Who?" Davad asked.

"The Earthling god that opened the gateway from the other side." Keeping her eyes straight ahead, she said, "If they come in force, Superi will lose. Who is the boy?"

The swift change in topic was jarring. It took a moment for Shashara to answer. "He's a soothsayer we met in Catena Piscari. He offered to be our eyes when we thought we'd have to go into IA to get you guys out. He's name is Kervan."

"What do you see of our future, Kervan," Anliac asked. "Will the gods destroy us?"

"I can't see that far into the future. I'm only a level one."

"But you see something," she said. "Your heart sped up when I asked." At his incredulous expression, she said, "There's water in your blood, and blood in your heart, so I can tell when the beat increases. Besides, there's a tremble to your voice that betrays you."

Shashara was a little creeped out by that but kept it to herself.

"Is she right?" Davad asked. "Did you see something? Because if you did, you need to tell us."

The tower was before them with the white stone city gleaming ahead. Tristan and Set waited for them to catch up before they followed the road around the tower to the plaza.

"Kervan saw something," Davad said.

"What did he see?" Set asked as they walked.

"He was just about to tell us," Shashara said.

Kervan was hesitant to answer. "Part of the city will fall before the suns set. That's all I know."

They were distracted by Calstar's raised voice as he addressed a gathering crowd around the tower's front entrance.

"The sounds coming from our northern border were frightening, I'm sure, but do not fear. The Imbellis Asylum has unfailingly protected Superi and her denizens for generations. Trust that we've done so again today. Let not your hearts be troubled. The threat has been identified and nullified for the time being. We will be ready should the threat rise again."

"What was the threat?" someone shouted from the crowd.

"What caused the ground to shake?" another asked.

"And the explosion that people are claiming they saw, what caused it?"

Calstar raised his hands into the air to quiet them. "All very good questions, and ones you deserve answers too, but…"

"The sound of his voice turns my stomach," Shashara said as they followed the river towards the marketplace, traveling out of hearing range. "The man speaks in circles."

"In this, he's right to," Anliac said. "Individual people can be intelligent creatures, but as a whole, people are stupid. They are panicky and prone to violence. Tristan," she said, pointing to a boutique boasting women's dresses from its front windows.

He turned them towards it and held the door open, allowing them to enter first.

"Can I help you," an elderly nox asked from behind a waist-high counter, tucking her short, silver hair behind her double-pointed ears. "Dear," she said to Shashara, "you're sopping wet. Please don't touch the wares." Worrying her bottom lip, she added, "Perhaps you boys could wait outside for your lady friends?"

"No," Anliac said as she self-consciously traced the smooth rounded edge of her own ear. Dropping her arm, she squared her shoulders. "I need leggings, a corset and tunic, boots, and a cloak to match."

"And socks," Shashara said, showing her support as the boutique owner began to frown.

"I suppose you have coin to purchase these items?"

The boys busied themselves rubbing the back of their heads and surveying the floor as if to find the coin there.

"Should have taken Triton's coin when he offered it," Set said under his breath.

Shashara smacked his shoulder.

"What about your sword?" the nox suggested. "It would bring enough to see you all outfitted."

Davad unfastened the sheath from around his waist.

"This does not belong me to me." He lifted it towards Tristan. "We found it at the northern gate."

Reverently, Tristan fastened the belt around his waist, adjusting the sheath and blade to hang just right down his left thigh. "Thank you for keeping it safe."

"Well, you can't buy something with nothing," the owner said, disappointed in the lost trade.

"We should go now," Kervan said.

He was ignored.

Clutching two handfuls of the black silk she wore, Anliac said, "Surely a set of commoner's clothes costs less than this material. You can have it in trade."

The lady's nose wrinkled in distaste. "I don't have to be a fera to smell the stench of blood and death soaked into your robe."

Kervan tugged on Davad's sleeve.

"What?" Davad snapped.

"We need to leave...now," he said.

"Why?"

The walls of the shop began to shake. Merchandise skittered to the edge of their shelves and toppled to the floor. Glass shattered.

"Not again," the nox cried as she ducked behind the counter.

Anliac leaned over the top and pinned the panicked woman in beams of light that shot out from her eyes. Her voice was piercingly sweet, achingly melodic, and full of power.

"I am of a Ruling House, the daughter of a general, I will not beg for clothes."

"What in Superi are you?" the nox asked, cowering away.

Anliac's angeli marks were fully emerged as were the golden elongated diamonds and interspersed circles that awakened her terra ability. The windows exploded outward. People screamed from the sidewalk outside. The ceiling began raining down on them.

"Anliac, calm yourself before you bring the whole roof down on our heads," Davad shouted above the increasing noise. "Tristan, do something."

Tristan swept Anliac off her feet, threw her over his shoulder, and shouted, "Everyone run."

Restrained, Anliac went wild, forcing Tristan to let her go. Her breathing was erratic as her power overwhelmed her. The ground rolled out from around her like growing waves that crashed into the buildings in their path, leveling them.

Screams of fear and pain echoed back to her. Panic filled her eyes as she sought Tristan. "I can't stop." Her whole body quaked as the ground rolled again. "Make it stop!"

City guards were encircling them, weapons drawn.

"No," she said as the sight of them quelled her fear and reignited her anger. "They will not take me again."

"Stand down," Tristan shouted "before she levels the whole city."

He watched as an arrow was loosed. Intercepting the arrow, he broke its shaft and dropped it then Tristan had the man by the throat before he could notch another. With a twist of his wrist, the man's spine gave way. Before the broken arrow landed, Tristan was back at Anliac's side.

Shashara was doing her best to keep Kervan out of the line of fire as Set and Davad did their best to protect her. "This is bad," she said. "Very, very bad."

"I told you all to get her out of there," Kervan squeaked, his voice breaking, "but would anyone listen? No."

"Shut up, Kervan," Davad said. "You can gripe later."

"Crap! Here they come," Set said.

From the ring of angry citizens shouting encouragement to the city guards, a dozen fera broke through. Recognizing Lan, Tristan wrapped his arms around Anliac and spoke into her ear.

"Breathe, Anliac," he said. "You don't want to be responsible for killing innocent people. Let the fera help."

Forming an outward facing circle around them, Lan spoke up loud enough for the guards to hear. "Lower your weapons and stand down."

"Move aside, traitor," a ranked guard snarled.

"Not going to happen," Lan said with a challenging grin.

The thudding of horses' hooves against the cobble stone street broke the impasse. From atop a brown mare, Calstar waved his arms and bellowed. "Stand down! For Superi's sake, stand down!"

IX

Message For The King

The door to Davimon's room opened. He sat up swiftly and swung his legs off the edge of the bed. Bracing himself with his arms to hold himself upright, he shook his head to clear it and then wished he hadn't. As last night's rum came back to haunt him, he lurched across the scarred wooden floor to the empty water basin placed atop an old chest of drawers and emptied the contents of his stomach.

A mountain of soft, snow-white fur filled the doorway to the room adjacent to his own. Lishous' pointed ears twitched. The front corner of his snout peeled up as his sharp, elongated canines pushed down on his bottom lip revealing a crooked smirk. His piercing blue eyes were full of humor.

"This is what happens when you don't listen to me."

"Shut up." Davimon gagged.

Lishous chuckled. "I told you to eat. A man can't drink his weight in rum on an empty stomach and then expect not to suffer."

Davimon sank to the floor and leaned back against the chest of drawers. He drew his knees up and rested his forearms on top of them. His head hung forward as he reined in his ragged breath. His sun-kissed skin was sheened in sweat and his hands trembled. Shoving back his short-cropped, brown hair, he looked up at his friend through eyes of the same color.

When the pupil of his left eye began to pulsate, Lishous stepped fully into the room and shut the door. "Take it easy, Davimon," he said, squatting down beside him, resting a heavy clawed hand on top of the seer's shoulder. "Tell me what you see." His eyes traced over the yellow and silver, four and five pointed stars that ran from Davimon's left temple to his chin, completely covering that side of his face as he waited for an answer.

"It's not the booze."

"Got it," Lishous said. "So tell me what it is?"

Davimon stare was unfocused. "The guards are dead. Malstar is dead." His eyes widened as they locked onto Lishous'. He scrambled to his feet. "We have to go. I think Imbellis is under attack." In haste, he strapped on this sword belt and bolted for the door.

"By whom?" Lishous asked, coming to his feet.

There was a pause as Davimon searched through the memory of the vision for clues. "I don't know," he said, "but the marketplace is going to be leveled."

As they dashed down the stairs, the innkeeper shouted after them from the common room. "Hey! Where do you two think you're going?"

"Add the charges to my bill, Scotty," Davimon said as he and Lishous rushed out back to where their horses were stabled.

They startled the stable boy. "Sirs, if you'd give me but a moment, I'll have your mounts saddled and ready for you."

"No time, kid," Davimon said, leading his black and white mare out of her stall by a lead rope. "We'll come back later for our tack.

58

Lishous' giant black stallion made Davimon's mare seem like a pony by comparison as the two men led the horses outside of the stables before mounting.

"As you wish, sir," the stable boy said, sighing deeply and wiping his sweaty brow as soon as they'd gone.

Sinking his heels into the horse's flank, Davimon raced towards the marketplace.

"Move you blasted ingrates. Move," Lishous snarled to those too slow in moving aside.

Their horses reared as the ground shook. The sound of splintering wood, shattering glass, and of people screaming wafted to them as a large cloud of dust rose from the direction of the marketplace.

"We're too late," Davimon said, snapping the reins to gain more speed.

"Do you want me to go ahead?"

Cursing, Davimon nodded. "Give me your lead."

Bringing his mount even with Davimon's, he handed over the rope.

"Go!"

With a beastly roar, Lishous leapt from his mount. As soon as his feet made purchase, he tore off for the marketplace, leaving Davimon and the horses behind. Women shrieked, hurting his sensitive ears as he rounded corners. Men shoved their women behind them as they brandished their weapons in preparation for an attack. Lishous ignored them all.

His progress was slowed by the rubble blocking the main thoroughfare to the marketplace. In an outward growing circle from the center of the open plaza, the ground was cracked, and the shops were leveled. Citizens were dragging bodies from the debris, separating the dead from the dying, and the dying from the merely wounded.

A ring of tower guards encircled a group of children as they faced off against those of the city. Riders came up at a gallop from the northern side of the marketplace. Calstar was in the lead with clear panic in his eyes.

"Stand down!" He heard Calstar shout. "For Superi's sake, stand down!"

The crowd parted to allow him access through to the center. The feras surrounding the kids held their ground until a tall boy, with pale fulgo skin, nudged the ranked fera aside. A woman, draped in a black ceremonial robe, stuck close to his side as he confronted Calstar.

"You are responsible for what's happened here," the boy said. "She will not be blamed."

Sliding off his mount, Calstar approached, gesturing for his personal guards to hold their positions. "No one will be punished," he said, "but I need to know what happened."

The citizens voiced their disapproval through jeers and taunts. With their arms raised and fists clenched, they spewed curses and demanded justice.

"She just wanted a change of clothes," a young mortalis girl, with long, wavy, brown hair, said. "You've left us with nothing."

An aether wielder took her hand.

"Lishous!" Davimon spotted his friend, who stood a head taller than those gathered around him and nodded as Lishous waved him over. "Which side do we defend?"

Lishous shook his head as he took back the lead rope to his horse and remounted. "I have no idea."

"You're right," Calstar said. "This is my fault. I should have thought ahead. Come back with me to the tower and I'll ensure that your needs are met."

The robed female stepped to the forefront of their group. Lifting the hood from her head with grace, she let it fall to her back as light flared from her yellow eyes.

"Do you take us for fools?" she asked as golden marks emerged through her olive-toned skin.

The marks on her shoulder marked her as the terra wielder responsible for the destruction around them. The rest of the marks marked her as something more, something that shouldn't still exist.

"I won't be taken into that tower again."

The piercing quality of her voice made Lishous want to howl. "What is she?"

"Malstar was successful," Davimon said stoically. "You're looking at an angeli."

"Superi save us," Lishous said.

"Indeed." He turned to Lishous. "We need to tell the king."

The crowd turned into a mob as they took up weapons and advanced on those who would protect the ones responsible for the deaths of so many.

After a barked order from Calstar, the city guards converged to ring around the tower guards and the kids, including Calstar in their protective circle.

"Look," Lishous said, standing up in the stirrups to see.

Davimon mimicked Lishous' pose. "You've got to be kidding me." He dropped heavily back into his saddle. "Get us to the tower, Lishous, and let us hope our gate maker is there."

With most of the city's populace gathered in the marketplace, they made good time. Stabling their horses, they entered the tower, ignoring the chaos going on inside, and took the winding staircase running against the stone wall to the first upper level. Bursting through the entry door, into the apartments set aside for mortalis representatives, Davimon shouted for Ashuna; the gate maker assigned to them.

"What?" the auburn haired, green-eyed vixen said as she entered from her private room. "What is it?" She paused, placing a hand to her chest at the harried look of the men. "The tower is in a frenzy, and rumor has it that a part of the city has been destroyed. What's going on?"

"I'm sorry, Ashuna, but there's no time to explain," Davimon said. "Open the portal. Once we're gone, stay in your quarters until we return. The Asylum is no longer safe. We must warn the king. Trust no one."

"Come then." Pivoting on light feet, she led them into her quarters, where a large section of marble floor was clear of furniture.

Closing her eyes, she took control of her breathing and centered herself. Pressing her palms together, she called forth the image of the next portal site.

"Go," she said when the portal was stable. "Warn our king."

Lishous, as always, stepped through first to ensure Davimon's safety.

***

"I hate you," Lishous said as they emerged from the last portal beneath the palace of King Normis.

Davimon would have laughed at Lishous' discomfort if he weren't feeling so ill himself. "A body never gets used to going through a half a dozen portals in a row." He grinned. "But you have to admit it's not as bad as it used to be, right?"

"If you say so."

They left the portal room, their steps steadying as their equilibrium caught up to them. Servants paused in their tasks to bow as Davimon passed, warily eyeing the muscle-bound fera at his side.

Having been rescued by the king from the burning house that had taken the lives of both his parents, Davimon had lived for years as a servant before being raised to the position he now held. He nodded at each of the servants in turn to acknowledge their show of respect; one not bestowed upon him by right of birth or blood.

"Where's the king," Davimon asked a passing clerk with the king's signet stitched in large symbols on the back of his light blue robe.

"He's in session, Master Davimon." He bowed slightly. "It's good to have you home. The king has been unsettled."

Davimon's right brow rose. "Is that so?"

The clerk's eyes rounded as he realized the slip of his tongue. "Forgive me. I've spoken out of turn."

"These are unsettling times," Davimon said in his king's defense. "Do not mistake the king's vigilance for disquiet."

"Of course, sir."

"Dismissed."

"Thank you, sir."

Lishous chuckled as the two of them watched from over a balustrade as the clerk skittered down the stairs and across the open main floor to reach the offices on the other side.

"I like it when you make them squirm."

Smacking his friend across the stomach with the back of his hand, Davimon said, "I don't do it for your enjoyment. I do it for mine." He smiled. "Come, you can walk with me as far as the right wing."

Lishous rolled his eyes. "You growl at a man one time, and you can never live it down."

Davimon's booted steps resounded against the marbled floor while Lishous' furred back paws made no sound at all.

"You're fortunate he didn't kill you."

Lishous shrugged. "I knew you had my back."

Reaching the hallway that would lead to the king's office chamber, they were met by two guards crossing their spears to block their path.

Lishous snatched their spears from their grasp and snapped them like toothpicks. He tossed them at their feet.

"Come on, Lishous," one of the guards complained. "We're just doing our job. You know you can't be up here."

Lishous snarled. "Keep your puny little sticks out of Davimon's face next time and maybe I'll let you keep them in one piece, or maybe next time, I'll snap the two of you instead."

"Easy, Lishous," Davimon grinned. "You're going to make them think you're a mean guy."

"I am."

Chuckling, Davimon said, "This shouldn't take long."

"I'll be here," Lishous said. Crossing his ankles and his arms, he leaned back against the wall to wait.

"Seriously," a guard said to Davimon. "Can't you make him wait somewhere else?"

Lishous' lips peeled back in a feral snarl. "Try and make me."

"You boys play nice," Davimon said, walking past them down the hall. "Move," he said to the servant who'd stepped in front of the lavish, ornately etched, metal door.

"You should wait to be announced, Master Davimon. The king has an audience."

Shoving the servant aside with one hand, he opened the door with the other and barged in. Waning sunlight illuminated the chambers through high, arched panes of glass that covered half of the room's wall space. The rest of it was covered, ceiling to floor, with shelves of books.

Three mortalis men stood on chubby legs, their bulbous bellies pressed against the edge of the king's massive, square, stone desk as they peered at the open scroll spread across it. Their heads turned at Davimon's entry, their thick, heavy jowls wobbling before settling into place around their nonexistent necks.

"What's the meaning of this?" King Normis said, slamming his fist down on his desk. Shoving back his chair, he came to his feet like a storm head. "Have you no sense of propriety?" He leaned sideways to peer around Davimon. "Where's your pet?"

Clasping his hands behind his back, he said, "Waiting under guard at the end of the hall, your majesty."

The king bellowed, "Explain your actions before I have you whipped for your insolence."

"Of course, your majesty," he said, bowing formally. He hid his smile before raising his head. "I bring disturbing news from Imbellis. News I felt could not wait." Kicking his head to the side, he addressed the noblemen gathered around King Normis. "News I cannot share unless, you gentlemen, will first excuse us."

"We take no orders from you," Nobleman Chalston said, shaking his sausage-like finger, jostling the rolls of fat that hung from the underside of his arm.

"This is an outrage," Nobleman Gregor said. "I'll not be spoken to in such a fashion. Especially not by the likes of him," he said to the king.

"Careful of your words, Gregor," Normis said. His strong chin jutted as he pushed his head forward on his neck. "His words hold more interest to me than your collective whining. Get control of your districts, gentlemen, or I'll find others to take your places. This meeting is over."

Davimon stepped aside to keep from being trampled as the herd of bovine left in a disgruntled huff. He waited for the metal door to click closed before he approached his king, who came from around his desk to meet him.

Clasping forearms, Davimon grinned. "So, you'd have me whipped, ay?"

The powerful mortalis king stood twice as broad and inches taller than his favored subject whose musculature was cut more lean and more starkly defined.

"You're a pain in my arse, Davimon," Normis said. "Now tell me what was so important that it couldn't wait until the end of my meeting."

"Oh, it could have waited, your majesty, but where would have been the fun in that?"

The king burst out laughing. "Did you see their pompous faces? Priceless."

"I'm glad you approve, your majesty." He cleared his throat. "I'm afraid, however, that the news from Imbellis is not so jovial."

"Out with it then," Normis said. "What have those idiot brothers done now?"

"Malstar has been successful. He's recreated the angeli and has turned them lose in Imbellis. A section of the city has already been destroyed. The citizens have been incited into a mob."

"Superi help us," Normis said, running his fingers down his silver goatee to its point. "We need to send criers into Imbellis." He began to pace. "Our people should exodus the city as quickly as possible. They need to relocate to mortalis territories." He snapped his fingers. "And we'll need a sketch of this angeli. I'll send an artist back with you to see it done." His head whipped around. "Did you see him?" he asked. "What abilities does an angeli have?"

"You misunderstand, my king."

Normis's pacing faltered as the lines around Davimon's eyes and mouth tightened.

"There are two of them," Davimon told his king.

X
Unwanted Friend

The guards were outnumbered, and the mob had grown into a frenzy. Anliac was anxious. The glow emanating from her eyes and the golden lines pulsing beneath the surface of her skin were adding to the citizens' fear.

"We have to do something," Lan said, "before they riot."

"The way to the tower is blocked." Calstar wrung his hands. "These are my people. I've spent the better part of my life protecting them. I don't want them hurt."

"You should have thought of that before you made me," Anliac said.

Taking a deep breath, she pushed her way past their ring of guards until she was standing where the mob could see her. She raised her hands and the mob's forward progress stalled.

"I've had enough," she said, her voice amplified by the power coursing through her veins.

With Anliac exposed and vulnerable, Tristan's own fear set off his angeli abilities. His marks flared as brightly as Anliac's as he came to stand at her side. He scanned the mob for bows and spears that could be launched from a distance as Anliac continued to address the crowd.

"We did not ask for this," she said. "We were hunted. We were tortured." The ground began to tremble. "We were made. Your rulers created us." Lifting her arms high, she said, "Behold the angeli."

"Who among you wishes to challenge us?" Tristan asked, allowing his voice to echo and boom. "For they will die first."

Davad cursed. "What in Superi are you doing, Tristan? We're trying not to get killed here."

"Anliac has the right idea," Tristan said. "We have to back them down."

"I should have stayed in Catena Piscari," Kervan whined from the heart of their group.

"I'll keep you safe, Kervan," Shashara said, patting his arm.

"We're all going to die," Set said.

"That's really not helping," Lan said over his shoulder to Set.

Anliac lifted her chin defiantly. "Thanks to the Asylum, I possess the power to level this city, and you threaten me with mere weapons."

The crowd screamed and then withdrew as a crater sank into the center of the marketplace.

"Disperse," she said, "or step into the grave I've created for you."

"Is she creeping any of you guys out?" Davad asked.

A lift of his brows was Set's only response.

Calstar and the guards exhaled in sharp relief when the citizens lost courage and began to disband. At first a few, and then in droves, as they returned to the colossal chore of sifting through the rumble to salvage what they could.

Climbing into the saddle of his horse, Calstar spoke. "Good people of Imbellis, do not despair. We will rebuild this section of the city, and it will be far grander..." The sound of his voice trailed off when it quickly became clear that his people were not listening. Disgruntled, he said, "Can we just go?"

The city guards stayed to lend what aid they could to the devastated people while Lan and his men closed ranks around the kids. Behind Calstar and his personal guard, and as a unit, they returned to the tower.

"What now," Shashara asked as they came through the front entrance. Her words echoed back to her from the vaulted ceiling of the great hall.

Calstar, flanked by two guards, turned on the dozen feras who'd betrayed the tower. His upper lip furled, "Your actions today have severed your ties with IA. I have no authority over you, but this I can still demand, strip those tabards from your backs before I have them removed."

"You're done making threats," Davad said. "The feras are our people now, and you will watch how you speak to them."

Lan and his men growled their approval.

Panting, his eyes filled with ire, Calstar snapped his fingers. "Have rooms and clothing prepared for them, and tell the kitchen..."

"You still don't get it," Anliac said as she rubbed at the goosebumps that sprung up on her arms. "I can feel the arcanite held in this place. Each piece of it is like a void in the pattern of the tower's architecture. I'm not closing my eyes under this roof."

"The tower is a place of death for us," Set said as his epoto ability absorbed the emotions flooding at him from every direction.

Calstar threw his hands into the air. "What would you have me do? I cannot keep you here against your will, but neither can Superi afford to let you run loose. The two of you are the world's greatest defense against what is coming. Should one of you be killed, all could be lost before the war even begins."

Lan stepped forward and pivoted until he faced the group. Clasping his hands behind his back, he said, "We are prepared to provide for your needs: shelter, clothing, food, and in addition we can provide correspondence between you and the tower, as well as other interested parties."

"If you're referring to the ship merchant, he is but one man," Calstar said, "and easily dealt with. As to General Aquam, he is coming for his daughter, not to destroy the tower."

Set and Davad chuckled.

"We'll be sure to tell Triton you said that" Davad said.

"And the general's daughter is gone," Anliac said, wrapping her arms around herself, as if holding herself together.

"She died on that slab of rock. What shall you tell him that will divert his wrath?"

"Kervan," Shashara said, "this is why you came. This is why you're here. What should we do? Tell us what you see."

Kervan flushed under the sudden attention. "You know my ability doesn't work that way." He squished his eyes closed. The blue lines of his incomplete marking wiggled. "All I can see is a black book."

"The journal." Tristan said, glancing at Anliac before nailing Calstar with a hard stare. "Malstar mentioned a journal in Bealson's Grove. Is it black? Where is it?"

Calstar stood his ground. "I will tell you everything in it. We can sit, and I will read it to you line by line, but I am not giving you the journal."

"Then we have our answer," Shashara said. "Lan, we will be going with you."

"No, we will not," Anliac said. "If we go with the feras, we are essentially aligning ourselves with them." She bit down on her bottom lip as she collected her thoughts. "Until we have all the facts, I believe that would be a mistake."

"We're running out of options here, Anliac," Tristan said.

Calstar placed a hand over the front of his chest. "While what has been done to you was necessary for the defense of Superi, the tower recognizes the suffering its endeavor has caused, and the cost of it to each of you. Allow IA's coin to replace what it can." When Anliac moved to object, he added, "There are no strings attached and no debt will be incurred."

Sensing their concurrence, Set spoke for them. "Agreed."

"Find Shorlynn," Calstar snapped at the servant he'd summoned earlier, who'd stood silently awaiting command.

The servant's white robe flowed behind him as he rushed to do Calstar's bidding.

"There are those who will not be pleased by your choice," Lan said, "but we are at your service none the less."

Aware that Lan was speaking of the Alphas, Shashara said, "We are grateful for your protection, but those who would be displeased are not our masters."

"Uncle Calstar," a dark-haired, fulgo beauty called from the balcony. She descended from the upper levels, down the winding staircase, on long, elegant legs.

A smile broke across Calstar's face. Beaming with pride, he watched his niece approach. Reaching out his hand as she drew near, he pulled her to his side. "Allow me to introduce Shorlynn, my departed sister's daughter."

"He makes me sound like an abandoned waif," she giggled, batting her thick, sooty lashes at Tristan. "Tell someone you're an orphan and they pity you." Gliding forward, she laid her hand on Set's chest. "I am far too beautiful to be pitied. Wouldn't you agree?"

Davad took hold of Shashara as flames ignited from her hands.

"I'm going to slap that pretty right off your face if you don't move that hand," Shashara said.

"Oh," Shorlynn withdrew, "seems I've touched a nerve." Her long black hair sprayed out like a fan, smacking Davad in the face as she twirled around in her curve hugging, dark green, satin dress. "You asked for me, uncle?"

Calstar lifted a heavy silver chain from beneath the neck of his robe. Dangling from the end of it was his personal signet of office. She lowered her head as Calstar slid the chain over it. The signet snuggled between her mounding breasts, drawing not only the boys' stare, but that of the guards as well.

"What shall I do with it, uncle?" she asked, tilting her head to the side, caressing the signet with a single finger and smiling at the jaws that dropped.

"You are to escort our guests around Imbellis," he said. "Whatever they desire, you are to see it done."

Her nose wrinkled as she looked Anliac and Shashara over from head to toe. "I'm assuming new attire is first on your agenda."

"Hey," Tristan said.

Shorlynn traced her fingers down the outside of Tristan's shoulder, pausing to test his bicep before moving on. "Oh, not for you, honey," she said. "It would be a disservice to Imbellis to cover all of this up."

Tristan blushed.

The guards at their back parted as Anliac turned for the door. Shashara hurried to catch up, glancing backward at the boys who'd yet to move. Lan's men split into two groups; half headed for the door while the rest stayed with the boys.

65

"Where are we going?" Shashara asked as they took the stone steps down into the plaza.

"I'm going to kill her."

Shashara blew a wisp of hair from her face. "Can I help?"

Anliac, looked sideways at her friend, and smiled.

"We'd better go after them," Davad said as the others agreed, and they took off at a sprint.

"Wait!"

They turned at the sound of Shorlynn's voice.

"These shoes weren't made to run in. Oh!" she cried, arms windmilling as she tripped on the hem of her glimmering, dark-green dress.

Tristan caught her up in his arms.

Shorlynn squealed in delight as she snuggled against his bared skin. Licking the tip of her pink tongue over her bottom lip, she sucked it into her mouth and moaned. "My hero," she said.

Tristan dropped her legs first and settled her back on her feet as he hurried to Anliac's side. "What?" he asked at Anliac's scowl. "Was I supposed to let her fall?"

Anliac crossed her arms. "Yes."

Set approached Shashara like he was walking up on a cornered wolf. He avoided eye contact though he could sense her seething well enough and laced his fingers through her own. Leaning forward until their foreheads met, he said, "I'm not blinded by things new and shiny, Shashara. Remember? I see only you, and you are the most beautiful creature I've ever laid eyes on."

"Yes, well," Shorlynn said, smoothing her hair into place, "there is no accounting for taste now is there? Shall we go?" she asked, waving a hand in front of her face. "This heat is oppressive."

Shashara's spine stiffened. "Did she just insult me?"

"Let it go, Shashara," Davad said, rolling his eyes. "I'm the best-looking guy of the bunch and she hasn't looked at me twice."

"Maybe she only likes unavailable men," Anliac hissed. "Look at her. If she swings those hips anymore, she'll dislocate them."

Shashara covered her mouth and giggled.

Kervan talked to Shorlynn, walking by her side as they traveled at a snail's pace through to the southern side of the city. She led them to a sprawling two-storied inn and waited for Kervan to open the door.

"Such a gentlemen," she said, tapping the end of his nose. "Very helpful."

"Yes, very helpful, Kervan," Shashara said on her way past. "Will you fetch her meal for her next?"

"Or perhaps rub her feet from her arduous trek across the city," Anliac added, sneering down her nose at him.

Kervan had one brow arched with the other pulled down. His mouth twisted to one side as Set chuckled. "It's going to be a long night for us all." He patted Kervan's shoulder. "Hang in there."

Kervan inhaled and said, "I'll try," on a breathy exhale.

Set paused in the doorway and stared back at the guards that had followed them from the tower. "Are you all coming in?"

"I am," Lan said. "The others will watch the front and back egresses in case trouble starts."

Set shook his head. "Well, don't tell Anliac. She'll take it as you are pinning her in. We'd be fortunate if she doesn't bring the inn down with us still in it."

"I hear that," Lan said, repressing a grin. "That girl is going to be a handful. Is it just me, or has this change affected more than just her abilities?"

"Too early to tell, I think," Set said. "She's been through a lot and it's not over yet. She needs time to grieve."

"Grieve?"

Set nodded. "Anliac died and was reborn into something she didn't want, doesn't know, and is afraid of. She just needs a little time."

Lan took the door after Set entered, allowing Kervan to do the same before he barked orders to his men and went inside himself.

Shorlynn made a showing of pulling the signet from where it lay. Seeing it, the fulgo innkeeper set down the glass he'd been drying and rushed over.

"Welcome," he said, bowing at the waist. His reverent gaze slipped as it slid past Shorlynn to the rest of them, but he quickly had his façade back in place. "It's not often we are graced with the presence of one of your ranking. I am Tahyhill. How may I be of service?"

"I am Shorlynn, Mr. Tahyhill, Master Calstar's niece."

Tahyhill swallowed hard as sweat broke across his fleshy brow.

"He has placed me with the responsibility of seeing to it that his very important guests," she gestured to the others without turning, "receive anything they desire. Can you help me see to it, Mr. Tahyhill?"

The way she said his name made Shashara and Anliac want to gag. The whole display was disgusting and classless.

A man, seated in the common room, fell out of his chair as he leaned it over too far in search of a better view.

Shorlynn giggled as the man scrambled to his feet.

"Ma'am," he said, dipping his head as he sat his chair upright.

Talk sprang up from the half-full common room, which before had contained only silence, as the patrons tried not to embarrass themselves the way the other man had.

"Forgive them, Mistress Shorlynn," Tahyhill said. "They are but common men."

"We will each require private bedchambers," she said, "but first, send for a seamstress with a selection of ready-made dresses that can be altered easily. These young men will require new attire as well."

Tristan's pectoral muscles jumped self-consciously at Shorlynn's disappointed visage as she contemplated the image of them covered up.

"I'm sure we would all appreciate a hot bath before we take our meal as well."

"We have private chambers where you and Master Calstar's guests can dine in quiet."

"That's fine," Shorlynn said, "but I would like for you to arrange for entertainment tonight. They have endured a great deal of late, and I feel it is part of my duty to see their spirits raised. Let there be music, Mr. Tahyhill. Let there be dancing." She lifted her arms until one hand hung delicately in front of her chest and the other floated gracefully above her head as she twirled. She spun herself into Set, who instinctively wrapped his arms around her slender waist.

Their faces were level with one another.

Set froze.

Tilting her head as if to kiss him, she whispered, "Thank you," before giggling and shoving him lightheartedly away. "Can you do that, Mr. Tahyhill?"

"Yes," he said. "Yes, of course." His eyes were open, but his mind was blank.

"Our rooms," she said. "We should start there."

"Rooms!" He snapped his fingers, and two fulgo servants in black and white livery approached. "I'll see to the seamstress myself," he said to Shorlynn, who patted his rounded cheek.

"I'm sure everything will be perfect."

Curtsying, one of the servants said, "I am Seraphina, and this is my sister Thea. If you would care to follow us, we will show you to your rooms."

"I'm afraid we only have six rooms available," Thea said as the two women led them up the red-carpeted stairs. "Would you rather share rooms, or would you prefer a private room below? They are not as opulent as these, but they are more than sufficient."

"I won't be sleeping tonight," Lan said. "The hallway will be sufficient for my needs."

"And Shashara and I can share a room," Anliac said.

"We can bring in another bed if you would like to share their room, Mistress Shorlynn."

"No!" Shashara and Anliac gushed in unison.

XI
Revenge Foiled

Lan intercepted Seraphina at the top of the stairs. "Your reason for being up here?"

"Dinner has been prepared, sir. Mr. Tahyhill has asked that I inform his guests that they may come at their leisure. Their meal will be kept warm for them."

"I'll do it. You can go."

Seraphina sniffed, biting back a sharp retort. "As you wish," she said, flouncing down the stairs in a huff.

Enjoying her sass, Lan toyed with the idea of asking her to dance later as he went down the hall tapping on doors and delivering the message.

The boys emerged in cool cotton pants and loose flowing cotton shirts. They had soft-soled, leather shoes on their feet. The only difference in their clothes was the color.

Set tugged at the off-white material of his shirt. "I thought I would hate these, but man, I don't ever want to wear anything else."

Lan's brows quirked when Tristan jumped, bending his left leg beneath him and kicking out with his right foot.

Landing lithely on the balls of his feet, Tristan said, "Fighting in these would be easy."

"I hope you're right," Davad said, looking down at the dark blue set of clothes he'd been given. "I look like such a pansy in this color; I want to kick my own butt. Others are likely to do it for me when we leave the inn."

"Right," Kervan agreed. "This red isn't working for me either."

Lan burst out laughing. "The boy might have a point, and...umm..." he chuckled, "I think that is pink, not red."

"Of course, it is," whispered Kervan.

The others joined in his mirth until the door to Anliac and Shashara's room opened.

"Now there's a body red looks good on," Tristan said, causing Anliac to blush as he sidled over to her, kissing the corner of her mouth. "You look amazing."

Her dress was a simple, strapless design. The red material hugged her breasts where it gathered below them and flowed to her feet, gently caressing the curves in between.

"I would have filled it out better before the transition," she said, smoothing her hands over the material.

"Are you kidding me?" Tristan teased. "Your butt would have looked huge in this dress before."

Anliac slapped the side of his arm and smiled.

"We match," Shashara giggled as Set swiped over his lips with his thumb and looked at her hungrily.

"I'm glad," he said. "It's a public disservice the way you look in that dress because if I see another guy looking at you, I might pull an Anliac and destroy something."

She gave herself a good once over. The off white, heart shaped top, with gold thread sewn in, hugged her from breast to waist. From there, yards and yards of gathered gossamer silk flowed to the floor, hiding her matching soft-soled boots.

"I do look good," she grinned.

"Yes, you do."

The expression in Set's eyes made it difficult for her to breathe.

"I apologize if I've kept you all waiting," Shorlynn said, joining them.

The back of Kervan's arm smacked Davad across his abdomen.

"Whoa," Davad said. "Shorlynn, you look...um...wow."

The long-sleeved, black, fitted dress she wore left little to the imagination. The essentials were covered, while the rest of the dress was transparent, mimicking the color of her pale skin.

Without acknowledging Davad's compliment, she asked, "And what do you think, Tristan? Set?" She turned slowly, allowing them to see her from every angle. "Does my appearance please you?"

"Your beauty is like a moon," Tristan said. "In your place, you are spectacular, but if you wish to shine, you should avoid standing too close to Anliac, for her beauty is like the suns. She eclipses you."

"I see," Shorlynn said, her eyes narrowing.

Anliac leaned toward Tristan and said, "I thought for a moment I was going to have to hurt you."

Tristan chuckled.

"And what of you, Set? Are you so blinded by your female's beauty that you see no others?"

"I see too much of you," Set said. "I prefer a little mystery in my woman."

Shashara laughed.

"Well, then," she forced herself to smile, "would you care to escort me to dinner, Davad?"

"If a person drops a cookie on the ground and then offers it to you," Davad said, "you might take it. If they put it in their mouth first, you'd have to think about it, but if they chew it up and spit it into your hand, well, a man would have to be starving to want it then."

Lines appeared between her brows as they bunched in confusion.

"Sorry, Shorlynn," Davad said, brushing past her towards where Lan waited at the top of the stairs, "but I'm just not that hungry."

Kervan offered her his arm. "I'd be happy to escort you downstairs."

Shorlynn took it. Shaking off the rejection from Tristan and Set, she was already planning how to regain their interest.

They made their way down the stairs where Thea waited to show them to the private dining area. They passed by the musicians who'd begun to set up on the stage built against one wall of the common room.

Seating themselves around a long rectangular table, Shorlynn laid her cloth napkin in her lap and waited for the server to place their plates and leave the room before saying, "We may be spending a great deal of time together while those in higher positions make necessary decisions."

"Let us hope not," Anliac said. "For your sake."

She took a breath. "Anliac, I fear we've gotten off on the wrong foot. I am" she flitted her wrist "spoiled rotten by my uncles, I admit, but I'm not a terrible person."

Anliac and Tristan exchanged a knowing glance. Neither of them willing to be the one to tell her that Malstar was dead. Apparently, no one else was because they all kept their mouths shut.

"Female fulgos are cloistered. We are pampered and trained to be items of beauty that are brought out for display during ceremonies or called upon to entertain important people. Which is why Uncle Calstar called for me. We are of similar ages and, therefore, likely to have more in common."

"That sounds terrible," Shashara said, slowly lifting a bit of roasted duck, which she popped in her mouth to keep from having to say more when Shorlynn tilted her head sideways.

"How so?" Shorlynn asked. "It is a pampered life of ease and luxury. We leave troublesome things to the men and aid them by being a comfort to them in any way we can."

Fearing the conversation would soon deteriorate into hair pulling and eye gouging, the guys ate their meal of duck and mashed potatoes smothered in thick gravy, with baby carrots and corn drenched in a rich butter sauce as if it would be snatched from them any moment.

"They are from a common house," Anliac said. "But even I, daughter to General Montilis Aquam, of the Regia Aquam Guard, am appalled by the vision your words inspire. Female nox train beside their men. We can lead them into battle. We can rule over our own Houses. We can think for ourselves, and we like it that way."

Shorlynn's smile was patronizing. "That's a fine story," she said. "Very imaginative and something tells me that your knowledge of nox life may be accurate. But if you're a nox, then I'm a fera." Her lips puckered and pinched as her head bobbled on her shoulders, her expression daring Anliac to disagree.

There was a moment of silence during which the five of them peered at each other, trying not to laugh. They failed.

Set, seated next to Kervan, slapped the other boy's back. "Oh, lighten up, Kervan," he chuckled. "If you knew the whole story, you'd find that hilarious."

Kervan jerked away from Set's hand. Shoving back his chair, he came to his feet, the broken lines of his mark quivering.

"What's wrong with you?" Davad asked as they all stared, dumbfounded by his strange behavior.

"You all kept saying the general, or General Aquam, of which there are dozens that could have been raised to that position, but never once did you give his first name."

The hate in his eyes as he turned to Anliac had Tristan coming out of his chair. "Easy, Kervan."

"My aunt was married to Montilis Aquam. Your father had her hung. Our House was broken, brought down to the level of commoner. My mother could not bear the shame of it. So, she drowned herself. I could not bear the shame in that," he snarled. "I left Palus Regia to find you, to kill you for what your family did to mine. You were supposed to be just some stupid girl." He turned and punched the wall. Pivoting back around, he yelled some more. "And yet here you are. The most powerful female on Superi, guarded by the most feared male. You are untouchable and my revenge has been stolen from me just like everything else."

"Inabeth was punished for breaking our laws," Anliac said. "She brought bounty hunters into the city; bounty hunters she sold me to. I was given over to the tower and this," she gestured to her changed face, "is what they did to me. I have as much reason to hate you for sharing her blood as you have to hate me for the blood that was spilled, but I do not. You are not to blame, but neither am I."

Kervan stormed from the room.

Lan wiped his mouth and moved to follow. "I'll see him out and see to it the men know not to let him back in."

"Shorlynn," Shashara said, "see to it that he has coin enough to fill his pockets. He's said too much to stay, but we know what it is to be orphaned, and it takes coin to survive."

"If that is what you wish. Excuse me," she curtsied. "I'll return shortly."

Finding themselves together, and alone, for the first time since the battle at the northern gate, they took a moment to collect their thoughts before the questions began.

"Why are we still here?"

"Where else are we to go, Set?" Shashara asked.

Tristan disentwined Anliac's fingers from the material of her dress that she had bunched in her hand. "What about your father?"

"What about him?"

"Will you return with him to Palus Regia?"

"I'm not a nox anymore."

"Just how bad is the threat?" Davad asked. "How involved should we get in all of this?"

"Can the god you fought open the gateway whenever he wants? Exactly how many of these gods are there supposed to be?" Set added his questions to Davad's as they all looked to Anliac and Tristan for answers.

"We need that journal," Tristan said. "That's the only way we have of finding out for ourselves what's going on. Our only other recourse is to choose who to trust and hope we land on the right side."

Smiling with too many teeth, Shorlynn re-entered. "It would appear your guard has been taken captive by one of the servant girls. Seraphina, I believe. Shall we join them?"

"I don't think we feel up to dancing, Shorlynn," Shashara said, "but please don't let that stop you from enjoying your evening."

"Are you sure?"

"Trust us," Anliac said with a smirk, "we'd much prefer you flirting with the men in there than with those in here."

Giggling, Shorlynn left the room.

No one spoke.

"Just say it, already," Set said, shifting uncomfortably in his seat.

They looked at him askance.

"Oh, come on. I may not be able to read your thoughts, but I can't deal with all of our emotional crap alone. So, spill it, and maybe we can manage it together."

Tristan spoke first. "Does anyone else feel like we're in over our heads?" His broad shoulders slumped with exhaustion. "This whole situation feels bigger than us. I miss the good old days when the biggest worry I had was whether or not I would find work that day."

"Or whether or not today would be the day Clave hired me on as his apprentice," Davad said.

"Whether or not dad would make time for me before he left for work," Shashara said with downcast eyes. "Or sitting around the fire in the front room wondering if he would come home that night, or if he'd be gone for a few days. I hated it when work kept him away."

Set lifted her hand and pressed a kiss to the back of it. "Why don't we try and get some sleep," he said. "We can deal with the grownups tomorrow."

"What are we going to tell them," Tristan asked.

Anliac stood. Pressing her palms flat against the table, she leaned her weight forward, and said, "We will tell them that we stand as one. That we act as one, and that we will remain alone in our stand until trust has been earned."

"They won't like it," Davad said, "but I do."

"There," Set grinned as he and the others rose from their seats, "now we all feel better."

Laughing at the goofy smile on Set's face, they left the room and made their way past the common room before heading up the stairs in search of their beds.

XII
Patience

Shashara sat on the small, cushioned stool before the vanity in the corner. Leaning towards the cloudy mirror, she traced her fingertips down the puckered, purple scar that ran from beneath her left eye to the hollow of her cheek. She turned as Anliac gasped.

"Hey," she said, seeing that Anliac had come awake. "You're okay."

Anliac nodded, her yellow eyes peeled wide. The hands clutching the quilt to her chest were not her own. They were too pale. The long legs jutting down the length of the bed were like phantom limbs that moved at her bidding. She curled her legs beneath her as she scanned the room Shorlynn had obtained for them the night before. The disconnect between her mind and the body she now possessed wreaked havoc on her emotions.

Moving from the vanity to the edge of the bed, Shashara lowered her weight onto the mattress and pried loose Anliac's hands from the quilt she clutched. She then took them into her own. "How can I help?" she asked.

Staring into Shashara's baby blue eyes, Anliac took a deep breath and let it out slowly, her muscles relaxing as she did. "I'm sorry about the way I spoke to you yesterday back at the grove," she said.

Shashara's head tilted in question.

"You said that I was not alone," Anliac winced, "and I said that I knew that because I had Tristan." She squeezed Shashara's hand. "I'm grateful that I have you too. Your friendship means everything to me. I need you to know that." The soft smile Shashara gave her put a lump in her throat.

Shashara's grin became a giggle when Anliac stomach rumbled like thunder, shattering the emotionally charged moment between them.

"Jeez," Anliac said, covering her face in embarrassment.

"Get dressed," Shashara suggested, coming to her feet, "and we'll go feed that beast before it turns ugly."

Tossing back the quilt, Anliac swung her legs off the side of the bed and rose to her full height. She looked down at Shashara, wondering if she'd ever get used to being taller than the girl she'd once looked up to. Shaking her head to clear away the disturbing thought, she pulled on a pair of tight-fitting breeches and a flowing red blouse that fell to mid-thigh.

Shashara handed Anliac a pair of leather-soled boots before plopping onto the floor to lace up her own. "Thank Superi, Shorlynn had them bring us pants instead of dresses."

"Agreed," Anliac replied. "That girl might as well be wearing nothing given the outfits she puts together." With her own boots laced, she reached down to help Shashara from the floor.

"Right," Shashara laughed as Anliac opened the door, and they stepped out into the hall.

Lan was asleep in the hallway. He knees were pulled up and his back was resting against the wall. His beady black eyes popped open as they drew near, nailing them in place. "Going somewhere, ladies?" he asked, grunting as he came to his feet.

Anliac's stomach let out another ferocious growl.

The two girls exchanged a grin as Lan chuckled, "Sounds like someone woke up hungry. Shorlynn and the guys are still asleep."

"Don't wake them," Anliac said. "Sleep is the only escape we have."

When Lan nodded, Shashara patted his shoulder on their way to the stairs. Neither of them was surprised when he fell into step behind them. The foyer was empty, and only a few patrons had found their way into the common room.

Lan found a seat at the bar while Anliac and Shashara took seats at a table close to the wall.

With unsure steps, Thea approached them. "What can I get for you?"

"Coffee," Shashara said.

"And food," Anliac added. "Lots and lots of food."

Shashara covered her mouth with her hand to hide her grin.

"Will the others be joining you?" Thea asked.

Movement in the foyer caught their attention. Lan stood from the bar to intercept the three boys as they came into the common room, prompting Anliac to reply, "I guess so."

"I'll tell the cook to get started," Thea said, walking off as the others joined them.

Set slid into the chair next to Shashara. "Good morning, gorgeous," he said. "How did you sleep?"

"In spurts," Shashara replied as she smiled and nodded at Tristan, who took the chair next to Anliac.

Tristan leaned over to nuzzle Anliac's cheek. "Good morning."

Anliac took his hand and pulled it into her lap beneath the table as Davad and Lan took the remaining seats. "Shorlynn still asleep?" she asked.

"Yeah," Davad smirked. "We could hear her snores through the wall."

"She makes more noise than Hammy," Set grinned.

Tristan laughed as Anliac's brows furrowed. "Who?" she asked.

"He's one of the pirates on Triton's ship," Shashara volunteered. "I met him in Catena Piscari on our way here. Funny guy."

Thea, with Seraphina's help, carted over a carafe of coffee and a jug of fresh milk along with cups for them all. As they poured themselves drinks and waited on breakfast to be prepared, the weight of recent events pressed down on them.

"Have you all discussed what your next move will be?" Lan asked, taking a sip of his coffee.

"Well," Anliac began, "we know we can't stay here."

"The feras' offer stands," Lan told them. "We can offer you a safe haven in Paradisi Colles and can more than match what monetary gain the Asylum has promised."

"We appreciate that," Set said, "but we can't take you up on it." Before Lan could object, he said, "Calstar owes us, Lan. The tower owes us. We are not incurring debt by taking his coin, but whether you will admit as much or not, your offer comes with strings we cannot afford to be tied by."

"Set's right," Davad interjected. "The only advantage we have is our independence from the political stew pot this whole situation has brought to a boil."

Lan leaned back in his chair and tapped his fingers on the tabletop. "Without alliances, you are vulnerable." He shook his head. "Five cannot stand alone against the rulers of Superi as well as the threat from Earth and hope to survive."

"We know we need alliances," Tristan said. "What we don't need is a master. We need to bring the races together, and to do that, we must ensure that they come to us."

The conversation was put on pause as trays of food were placed in front of them. Anliac and Tristan began shoveling scrambled eggs into their mouths with one hand, tearing into fat strips of bacon held in the other while the others watched in amusement.

"What we need," Shashara said between slower bites, "is a place to set up. Somewhere that each of the races will feel comfortable reaching out to us without fear of tripping across some territorial line."

Washing down her food with a drink of milk, Anliac suggested, "What about Caterva Concentio?"

Shashara quirked her right brow. "It's a slave city, Anliac. That's not exactly the kind of the place that says, hey, come join us. Besides, with how populated the place is, we'd never find an abandoned building to claim, and we don't have the coin to build from scratch."

"There is nothing to say we have to stay on this continent is there?" Set asked. "I mean, we could go back to Catena Piscari. The fishing villages there would keep us close to the oceanus and put the Turris region at our backs as well as put a little distance between us and the Asylum."

"Too much distance," Davad rejected the idea out of hand. "Anliac and Tristan have to stay close. The point to all of this is to make sure Superi has her guardians if that god returns, or worse, returns with friends."

"Ugh," Shashara said, "Davad's right."

"May I offer a suggestion?" Lan asked.

"We value your council, Lan," Anliac assured him. "That's why you're sitting at the table with us."

"There are mining villages to the south east of here that reach from below Exsulto to Elisium Agricolor. There, you would be close to the oceanus as well as Imbellis should the gateway open again."

"These villages," Tristan asked, "how populated are they? Wherever we go, we bring danger with us, and I don't want innocent people hurt if we can avoid it."

"The villages have been abandoned for a while," Lan told them, "but, there is one obstacle that would have to be contended with before the villages could be claimed."

"There is always an obstacle to be contended with," Set chuckled without mirth. "Tell us what this one is."

Lan scratched the side of his neck, his fingers disappearing beneath the downward flowing feathers. "There is a terra wielder there by the name of Bengim. He's a level three, mean as a snake, and just as deadly."

Mention of a trained terra wielder grabbed Anliac's full attention.

"What's his story?" Tristan asked, glancing sideways at Anliac before refocusing on Lan.

"They say his family was murdered," Lan said. "The violence that their death inspired; the insanity that gripped him; they say the people of Satio Mapalia abandoned everything to escape it."

The picture his words painted left them speechless.

"There is one pocket of miners, a few low-level terra wielders with a handful of ignis wielders that stuck it out."

Lan's neck twisted a hundred and eighty degrees, though his body remained sitting forward, as the swishing of Shorlynn's skirt announced her arrival.

Shashara swallowed hard at the disconcerting sight and shoved away her plate, her appetite stolen. When Lan was once again facing them, she exhaled in relief that he, in fact, had not broken his own neck.

"There is distance between the miners and the area Bengim holds," Lan continued. "They won't be a problem."

As Shorlynn drew close enough to overhear, the conversation died. Placing a hand on the back of Set's chair, she greeted them. "Good morning. Mind if I join you?"

Reaching backward, Lan dragged a chair from the next table over and placed it next to his own.

"Such a gentlemen," Shorlynn smiled, sitting down.

"No," Lan retorted. "I'm just trying to keep you far enough away from Anliac and Shashara that they don't find another use for their utensils besides stabbing food."

Her spine went ramrod straight. "There is something to be said for honesty, I suppose." The uncomfortable silence that settled had her asking, "Did I disrupt the sharing of secrets?"

Seeing no reason not to tell her, Tristan replied, "We were discussing potential places for us to set up away from Imbellis."

Her eyebrows went up at her inclusion. "Have you thought about Pisces Stragulum?" At their gawked expressions, she added, "It has its own harbor, of sorts, and the ancient dwellings are still sound. It would need work, but it's doable. It's close to Imbellis, and yet, it's unclaimed."

"I was expecting you to say something stupid," Shashara grumbled.

Shorlynn grinned. "I'm sorry to disappoint."

"We need you to do something for us," Tristan told her.

"I'm here to serve," she said.

"Ugh," Anliac groaned, her upper lip furling.

"We need you to set up a meeting with Calstar," Tristan continued. "Before we can decide on anything, we need access to a journal he has in his possession."

"My uncle holds court each morning until midday," she informed them. "I can speak to him after."

"That would be great," Tristan said. "Thank you."

"Tell him we want to see him today, Shorlynn," Anliac demanded. "This city makes my skin crawl."

"I understand," Shorlynn replied. As those gathered around the table continued to stare, she flinched. "You want me to go now?"

"That would be best," Set encouraged.

"Fine," she snapped, coming to her feet. Her fingers were curled into angry fists at her sides as she stormed off in a huff.

Lan cast a leery glance in Anliac's direction. "I need to be going too," he said. "I'm taking my men to see if we can lend a hand with the cleanup in the marketplace. I'll leave enough manpower behind to see to your safety."

"I'll go with you," Tristan volunteered.

"Yeah," Davad said. "Me too."

Set nodded. "Beats being trapped in the inn all day."

Lan was skeptical. "Are you sure that's a good idea?"

"Word will spread from Imbellis into other regions," Tristan said, "about what went down yesterday. The citizens need to see that we are not the enemy. That our actions were about survival."

"There is a lot of hate within the city," Lan pointed out. "There will be some looking for retribution. Shashara," he said, "help me out?"

"Danger lies in equal measure," she said, "whether we stay here or venture out. The only difference would be the strategy used by the one wanting to hurt us. We were not raised to hide, Lan," she smiled, a soft turning at the corners of her mouth, "and we've run as far as we intend to. We truly have no enemies," she said, "and the fact that we are looked upon as an enemy by so many..." her lips pressed into a thin line. "We can't wrap our minds around it."

Davad spoke. "With Malstar dead, and Tristan and Anliac free, if it weren't for the threat to Superi by the Earthling gods, we could fade into anonymity. We just want to go. We want to live our lives separate from the violence of our parents' legacies."

"I have never seen such unlikely rulers," Lan said, "or ones so hesitant to lead." The boys followed suit as he stood from the table. "Yet with every word spoken, each of you prove that you are worthy of the mantle you now wear." Stepping sideways, he gestured towards the exit with an outstretched arm. "Shall we go?"

Set cupped Shashara's chin with his finger and thumb. "Are you coming?"

"No." She glanced over Set's shoulder, up into Tristan's eyes. "Tristan has to do what he thinks is right," she lowered her gaze back to Set, "and it's good that you and Davad will be there to guard his flank, but I think Anliac and I will hang back."

"My men will keep them safe," Lan said as his arm dropped to his side.

Tristan concentrated on Anliac's face, on the beat of her heart that drummed beneath her quiet breathing, measuring the tension around her mouth and eyes.

"Go, Tristan," Anliac said. "I'm not alone. I have Shashara with me."

Lan's men were waiting for them outside.

"Stay close," Lan told them as they made their way north on cobblestoned streets toward the marketplace. "Our orders are to help aid those effected by yesterday's events; however, our main consideration is for the safety of our charges."

Set missed a step. "I've been called many names, but a charge, well, that's a new one."

"I'm choosing to ignore the patronization that name implies," Tristan said, half in jest, half wanting to knock Lan's beak off his feathered face.

From Tristan's tone, Lan inferred his mistake. "I meant no offense."

Davad draped his arm over Lan's shoulders. "Some offense taken," he chuckled, "but we like you anyway."

"Oh, man..." Set's jaw dropped as they cleared the last building that stood between them and their destination. "It looks worse than it did yesterday," he said. "How is that possible?"

Lan led them over the ripples in the terra, around the craters left in the wake of Anliac's desperate fear, to a city guard barking orders from a central location. "Where do you need us?" he asked.

The guard checked out the ignis marks that flowed over Davad's right shoulder and upper arm, and then did a double take at the aether marks on the left side of Set's face. Catching a good look at Tristan, the guard's eyes went wide. "We don't want any trouble."

"And we're not looking to cause any," Tristan said. "We didn't mean for any of this to happen, and we want to help clean it up...if you will let us."

After a long moment of hesitation, the guard said, "Follow me," as the eyes of the people followed them.

When an elderly fulgo woman rushed forward, falling to her knees at Tristan's feet as she reached for his hand, he caught her by her shoulders and gently pulled her upright.

"Ma'am," he asked, "are you okay?"

"Please," she said, her tears washing lines through the dusty grime on her cheeks, "no more. I beg you, show mercy, or if not, tell us our offenses so we do not offend again."

At a loss, Tristan sought Lan to give him council. "What do I do?"

"She believes you to be an all-powerful being, a god," Lan answered. "After witnessing the golden marks that flared from within your and Anliac's skin, after seeing with their own eyes the power possessed by the angeli, many of the citizens here believe it so."

The guard was intrigued. "Do you deny it?" he asked Tristan.

"It's ridiculous," Tristan and Set said together.

"Tristan is simply a guy that had his blood tampered with by the tower," Davad said. "He was just the first not to die."

"Ma'am, I'm no god," Tristan told her, and then, in his peripheral vision, he caught sight of a blur in the aether that led back to a man, half hidden behind a pile of rubble, a crossbow in his hand.

The woman flinched, cringing behind arms thrown up to ward off a blow, as Tristan's hand shot forward, his fingers curled as if to close around her throat. "Please!" she cried, dropping to the ground. "Oh!" Braced on one elbow, her other hand flew to cover a heart she feared would explode.

"Stop him!" Lan bellowed, pointing in the direction the assailant had fled.

Tristan couldn't move. His whole body trembled as he clutched the bolt meant for him— the bolt that would have killed the old woman instead. "Are you okay?" Her frail hand as she reached for his aid to rise broke the ice that had frozen his blood.

"You say you are not a god," she said as she cupped his cheek with tentative hands, "but this day, you were my savior."

"We should head back to the inn," Lan said. "Now."

Tristan opened his mouth to speak but Set said it for him. "No." Of the woman, he asked, "Ma'am, you want to put us to work?" He would soon regret the offer.

As the suns made their downward trek, it was a bedraggled group of men who returned to the inn, filthy and near ready to drop.

Descending the stairs, resplendent after a day of relaxation and a level of pampering they would never confess too, Anliac and Shashara paused at the sight of them. Shashara's lips made a perfect O, which was symmetrical to the rounding of her eyes.

"Rough day," Anliac smirked.

"I need food," Tristan said, angling for the common room.

Darting down the last few stairs, Shashara intercepted him and the men that followed, her hands held up in objection. "You all need baths. You stink." Her nose wrinkled.

"Oh, thank you, Ms. Jacobs," Tahyhill sighed.

Groans of complaint and of grown men whining accompanied their departure. Lan's was as loud as those of his men. Set goosed Shashara's behind before using up the last of his energy to escape up the stairs.

"Really, Set," Davad asked, taking off after him. "You're going to do that right in front of me?"

Tristan turned to look at Anliac and tucked a strand of her multicolored hair behind her ear. "Any word from Shorlynn?"

"No," Anliac said, "and as late as it is, we're not likely to get that meeting with Calstar tonight."

"Yeah," Tristan said. "Did you have a good day?"

She smiled. "I did."

"Oh, for Superi's sake, will you go get cleaned up already," Shashara quipped.

With a wide grin, he asked, "When did she get so bossy?"

Shashara's eyes narrowed as her lips pursed. "Tristan," she said, starting forward.

Tristan's image blurred up the stairway, but his laughter was clear. The girls, hands on hips, shook their heads and then pivoted from the door slamming shut overhead to the one opening behind them. Shashara sighed and Anliac's shoulders slumped at the sight of Shorlynn stepping into the foyer.

"Where is he?" Anliac asked. "You should have been back here a while ago."

"My uncle wasn't in the tower," Shorlynn replied. "I had to wait for his return." Closing the door, she turned towards them and continued, "By then it was too late to schedule anything for today, but not to worry," she added. "He will be here tomorrow."

"What time?" Shashara asked.

"He sent a request that the cook have venison added to tomorrow's lunch menu," Shorlynn replied. "I take that to mean around midday." Addressing the innkeeper, who stood by the entryway between foyer and common room, she asked, "Would you mind having my meal sent to my room? I'm not feeling well."

"Of course, ma'am," Tahyhill rushed off towards the kitchen to see to her request.

Anliac and Shashara watched Shorlynn's slow ascent up the stairs, pulling herself along with a hand upon the rail, until she disappeared around the turn in the hallway.

"What do you think that's about?" Shashara asked.

"I have no idea," Anliac replied.

A short time later, they sat with the guys enjoying the stew the cook had prepared. Davad's elbow was propped on the table, his head propped in his hand as he struggled to remain awake long enough to fill his stomach. Set winced every time he lifted the spoon to his mouth, his shoulders aching.

Shashara ran her hand up and down Set's back. "I guess it's been a while since you boys had to put in a full day's work."

Tristan chuckled, the stew renewing his energy. "Of all the women in Imbellis, we found the one most like Ms. Moraine."

"Once that woman put us to work," Davad said, "we didn't think we'd ever escape."

"It's probably for the best then that Calstar agreed to meet with us tomorrow," Anliac sighed. "You guys are too exhausted to match wits with him tonight."

As soon as the guys laid their spoons aside, Anliac and Shashara ushered them up the stairs. Pushing them into their rooms and demanding that they go straight to bed, the girls followed their own advice and did likewise.

It was nearing midday before Lan woke up. He was stretched out flat on the hallway floor, covered in a blanket someone had tossed over him. Rolling to his stomach, he groaned as sore muscles voiced their complaint. He angered them further by coming to his feet. His night had been longer than the rest. The man with the crossbow was now hogtied and on his way to Paradisi Colles.

The doors to the rooms were closed, so he made his way downstairs to see if he'd missed them. A handful of his men waited in the foyer. Their shifting feet and darting eyes forebode ill news.

"What's happened," he asked.

One of his men found his nerve and spoke. "They're not here."

"Who?"

Lan glanced to the top of the stairs where Tristan stood, flanked by Davad and Set, waiting for an answer. He turned back to his men, wanting answers himself.

"Anliac and Shashara," the man answered. "Tahyhill said they left right after breakfast."

"Did they say where they were going?" Davad demanded to know. "Or when they'll be back?"

"No, sir," the man replied.

Descending the stairs, Tristan brought with him his own light as the golden markings appeared and began to pulsate. "We have to find them."

"We will," Davad said, "but you have to stay here."

"No," Tristan objected.

"Brother, there's no choice," Set told him. "Calstar is due anytime now, and someone has to be here to get those journals."

The front door came open, and the two girls came through. Anliac was holding a stack of rolled scrolls in her arms. They froze in their tracks at all the angry stares boring into them.

Tristan blurred forward, taking Anliac by the outside of her shoulders; the scrolls tumbled to the floor. "Are you okay?" he asked, his yellow eyes casting her in shadow as he searched for injury.

"Calm yourself, Tristan," she said. "I'm fine."

Set's hands trembled as he cupped Shashara's cheek. "You two just aged us a decade." He took several deep breaths before he attempted to speak again. "Where have you been?"

"Doing research," Shashara told him. "Anliac had the idea yesterday. We thought it would help if we had information on the current rulers of each region: who their allies are, how strong their armies are, how much political pull they have. Ignorance is a weakness we can't afford."

"Let me go, Tristan," Anliac said, wrapping her hands around his forearms to urge them down.

He rubbed the outsides of her shoulders as if to soothe any hurt he may have caused and then stepped away. "Please don't disappear like that again."

"I won't," Anliac said.

"You could have just asked me," Lan scowled.

"You are fera," Anliac replied. "Your loyalty extends to us only so far as Donnin and your Alphas dictate."

His scowl deepened as the feathers on his neck ruffled.

"Can you deny it?" she asked. When he could not, she nodded, her point made.

Shashara leaned around Set to see into the common room. "Shorlynn is still asleep?"

The men in the foyer exchanged glances, searching for an answer among them, but it was obvious they didn't know.

Shashara harrumphed. "For Superi's sake, guys." She climbed the stairs one at time and disappeared around the turn that led to the hallway above.

"She said last night that she wasn't feeling well," Anliac told them. "Maybe she was telling the truth."

No one else spoke as they waited on confirmation.

Shashara reappeared at the top of the stairs. With a hand pressed to her stomach, she descended. "Oh, she's in there. She looks awful."

"I'll find Seraphina," Anliac said, "and have her see if she needs anything. Tahyhill!" she called out to the innkeeper.

As Anliac walked into the other room, Tristan walked to the front window and peered up at the positions of the suns. "Calstar should have been here by now."

"Maybe we should drop in on him," Set suggested. "One way or the other, we need at least one journal."

"Agreed," Tristan said. "Lan, are you coming with us?"

"Perhaps I should check in with my Alphas first," Lan snipped.

"Anliac meant no offense," Davad said.

Coming forward, Lan dropped heavy hands atop Davad's shoulders. "Offense was taken, but" he grinned, "I like you anyway."

When Anliac came back in the room, Set said, "We're going to make a trip to the tower."

"I hate that place," she cringed.

"You don't have to go," Tristan told her.

"Shut up." She rolled her eyes and was the first one out the door. Everyone else filed out after her.

Lan chose a circumspect route through the city that led them around the destruction, but there was no way to avoid the people. Women grabbed their children as they passed, tucking them behind their bodies. Men tensed at their approach, their hands hovering over their weapons, watching with wary eyes for the warning that they should draw them.

A sob came from Shashara. "This is sad."

"It has nothing to do with you, Shashara," Anliac whispered. "It's me they fear."

Crossing one of the two bridges that would gain them access to the plaza in front of the tower, they hesitated. Lawyers mulled about, their bright red robes like splatters of blood amongst the commoners. There were so many, and each posed a threat, but as they moved forward, the reaction they received was unexpected.

"What are they doing?" Shashara asked.

The people were taking to their knees, heads bowed, until they'd passed. Words filled with fear and awe carried to them.

"What are they saying," Anliac asked Tristan, whose hearing was better than her own.

"May we find mercy in the angelis' grace," he answered. "Let us be spared their wrath."

Ascending the white stone stairs, Anliac said, "We are nothing like that god."

"I know," Tristan said, taking her hand, "and soon, they will too."

Entering the Asylum, their collective steps created noise enough to draw attention. A clerk in a white robe rushed over, hands clasped in front of himself. "Welcome, allies of Imbellis. How may I serve?"

"We're here to see Calstar," Tristan replied. "He missed an appointment."

"Of course," the clerk said. "If you will follow me, I'll take you to a place where you can wait while I seek out one who can help you." He eyed the slew of men. "Would it be possible for some of you to wait here?"

"You two come with us," Lan said. "The rest of you wait here."

"Yes, sir," his men said.

With reluctance, the rest of them allowed themselves to be led to the far side of the great foyer and to the enclosed stairwell. Entering, the grease lanterns mounted in the stone wall became unnecessary as Anliac's fear and Tristan's anger ignited their angeli markings. The illumination of the markings provided more than enough light to see by.

They exited on an upper floor and into a hallway with a balustrade overlooking the foyer they came through. After bypassing several closed doors, the clerk opened one and bade them to enter. "I will send in refreshments," he said, "and will return shortly."

Time crept by servants came and went with offerings of cheese and wine, with cider when the wine was refused, and with heartier sustenance when lunch became dinner.

"This is ridiculous," Anliac said, wringing her hands. The walls of stone trembled, cascading dust to the grey marbled floor.

Davad, standing close to Tristan, leaned into whisper, "She's losing it. We need to get her out of here."

When the door opened again, a fulgo with silver streaks running through the temples of his long, faded, red hair, offered his apologies. "Please forgive the wait."

"We'll think about it," Lan said, "once you've given the reason for it."

"It would appear, Calstar, has not yet returned from Certamen," the representative said.

"When did he leave," Davad asked.

"Yesterday, young sir," the man replied.

"You're lying to us," Shashara said. "I can't believe this."

"I am neither brave, nor a fool," the fulgo said. "I know who you are, and I would not take such a risk knowing my life hangs in the balance."

"Shorlynn was here yesterday," Set informed him. "She waited on him to return, and then set the meeting we were to have today with Calstar."

"Ms. Shorlynn was indeed here," the man confirmed, "and she did wait until late in the evening expecting his return. When he did not, one of his councilors set the meeting, unaware that Calstar would be held in Certamen for so long."

"Then why didn't someone just tell us that," Tristan snarled, his eyes flashing.

"We feared your reaction," the fulgo admitted.

"We are not monsters," Anliac shouted. The glow of her terra marks seeped through the blouse she wore, as did those of her angeli abilities.

The floor shook, knocking the fulgo off balance. His shoulder slammed into the doorframe. His legs became tangled in his robe, and he fell hard onto his backside.

"Time to go, beautiful," Tristan said. "I'm not in the mood to be buried beneath a pile of stone."

Anliac closed her eyes, dragging in desperate breaths as she tried to regain control. Losing the battle, she cried, "Get me out of here."

Scooping her up in his arms, Tristan ran from the room and leapt over the balustrade to the marble floor below.

"Tristan!" Shashara shouted as she and the others rushed forward, leaning over the rail in fear of what they would find.

They were just in time to see the door swing open. They could see the startled faces of those peeking in to see what commotion may have caused the haste of the angelis' departure. Disappointed, the spectators returned to their own affairs.

"I'm not sure what I fear more," Lan said, heading for the stairwell, "the return of the gods or the angeli already here."

Anliac and Tristan were waiting for them in the common room when they return to the inn. Anliac had her hands wrapped around a cup of hot tea, the strings of the bag dangling over her fingers. Tristan sat with one arm around the back of her chair, the other rested on the tabletop in front of her as he leaned close.

Her face crumpled when she saw them. "I'm so sorry," she said.

Tristan leaned back in his seat. "Tell her to stop apologizing."

Shashara and Set, with Davad and Lan close behind, entered into the common room.

"Tristan is right," Shashara said, taking the chair next to Anliac. "If there is an apology to be made, it should come from us. We never should have put you in that position. You had no business being in the tower."

"You're back," Shorlynn croaked, swaying as she crossed the floor. She chose a table other than theirs and sat down. "I guess you know."

"That you lied to us yesterday?" Shashara snapped. "Yeah. We know."

Shorlynn's face contorted. "The five of you are so selfish. I had plans of my own before being saddled with the chore of playing nurse maid to a bunch of ignorant whelps who think the world revolves around them."

"The world will only continue to revolve," Tristan retorted, "if we're here to see that it's not knocked off its axis by beings your tiny brain cannot fathom."

Shorlynn lurched to her feet. "I am not my uncle's keeper. You told me to go. I went. You told me to wait. I did. You told me to set a meeting. A meeting was set. So, get off my back."

Shashara's chair scraped against the floor as she pushed back from the table. Shoving her sleeves up her arms, she said, "I've got this," as flames erupted from her fingertips, and she advanced on Shorlynn.

"You wouldn't dare," Shorlynn said, bowing up, rather than running away.

"You obviously don't know my sister," Davad smirked, folding his arms across his chest.

Lan intervened. "This action would have serious consequences, Shashara. You should consider them."

Clenching her fists, the flames went out. "Get her out of my sight," Shashara said.

Lan took Shorlynn by the arm.

"Get your hands off of me," Shorlynn snarled, yanking free, and storming from the room.

Servants, holding trays laden with food, waited for direction.

"Everything is fine," Set assured them as he motioned for them to bring the food. Plates clattered and drink spilled over the tops of glasses, and as quickly as the meal was laid out, the servants disappeared.

"This day needs to be over," Davad sighed, picking up his fork.

It seemed he was not alone in his desire. Even the angelis only picked at the food on their plates. There was little in the way of conversation, and soon, they left the common room in search of sleep—and the refuge from reality it offered.

Lan wasn't in his usual spot on the hallway floor as Tristan and Shashara crept from their rooms early the next morning. They exchanged sheepish grins.

"Can't sleep?" Tristan asked, keeping his voice down so as not to wake the others.

Shashara shook her head. "Anliac's having nightmares. I sat up with her all night."

"Set's struggling too," Tristan told her. "Whatever he did to become what he is," he grimaced, "it's getting to him."

Making their way downstairs, Shashara asked, "How is my brother?"

"I think he's struggling to find his place," Tristan admitted. "He hasn't been himself since Jacob..." he let the rest go unsaid.

"Yeah." Shashara tried to smile.

Tristan pointed at some stools and then sat down beside her.

"What can I get for you?" Tahyhill asked, drying his hands on the apron tied around his thick waist.

"Coffee," Shashara said.

"Warm milk if you've got it," Tristan added.

"How about you, Tristan?" she asked. "How are you holding up?"

"I feel numb most of the time. Thank you," he said as Tahyhill sat their drinks down and then discreetly disappeared into the kitchen. "Sometimes I think we should just camp out in front of the gateway and wait for the gods to emerge. We'd lose, but at least our part in all of this would be over."

Shashara looked over at him. "I don't know what lies on the other side of death," she said, "but I don't want to leave this life only to wake up in the next and have my father whip me good for taking the easy way out."

"Good morning," Set said, scratching an itch on his side as he squeezed Shashara's shoulders before pulling himself onto the barstool beside her.

"Good morning," she smiled.

"Morning," Tristan said, unsure of how good it was.

"Davad's on his way down," Set told them. "What's the plan for today?"

"The plan is to keep Anliac from bringing the inn down," Tristan said. "And with a little fortune, prevent your girlfriend from killing the vixen asleep upstairs."

Shashara punched his shoulder.

The brothers grinned at each other from over the top of her head.

Davad stumbled into the common room. "Tell me the cook is making breakfast, or I'm going back to bed."

"Tahyhill is hiding in the kitchen," Shashara told him. "You'll have to find the cook yourself."

"Fine," Davad said, going behind the bar and through the double swinging doors behind it.

"Where is he going?" Anliac asked, making her appearance.

"In search of the cook," Set replied.

"Oh good," Anliac sighed, going behind the counter to find a cup. Picking up the carafe, she poured herself some coffee and then returned to the other side. Sliding into a chair at a table, she rubbed at her eyes.

Exiting the kitchen, holding a piece of cinnamon bread in one hand, Davad said, "The cook is on it."

"I wonder where Lan ran off to." Set said, swiveling the bar stool until it faced the open room.

"He's outside with his men," Tristan answered. "I can hear them talking. He's sending half back to the," he paused, "cleanup site. The others, he's keeping here with us. He doesn't want us out there again after the bolt that nearly took my head off."

"What?" the girls both asked.

"No big deal," Tristan told them. "Lan took care of it."

"Man, we have to get out of here," Davad groaned. "The inn is starting to feel a lot like prison."

"Nowhere near," Anliac refuted, "but I get what you mean."

"I'd prefer to be the last person to give Shorlynn credit," Shashara said, "but her idea about Pisces Stragulum was a good one."

"What do you guys think?" Tristan asked the others.

"I'm curious about Bengim," Anliac said. "He might be the only one who can teach me. If we invade the mining villages of Satio Mapalia, he might not want to share his knowledge. Pisces Stragulum seems like a good alternative."

"I agree," Set said.

"It's fine with me," Davad added. "Should we see if Lan has some horses we can borrow? Ride out and take a look?"

"No," Tristan said. "Calstar's not stupid enough to stand us up again. We need to be here."

"How long before Triton arrives?" Set asked.

"I'm more worried about my father," Anliac sighed.

"If Rayner let Montilis go as promised," Shashara said, "he should be here in the next day or so."

Tristan ran his fingers backwards through his hair, tugging in frustration. "I'm surprised Triton isn't already here."

"Does anyone else feel like events are out pacing us?" Davad asked.

No one answered as Seraphina and Thea came in from the kitchen with glazed cinnamon sweet bread. Laying two of the pastries on a plate and picking up a glass of milk, Shashara made to leave.

"What are you doing?" Set asked with a tilt of his head.

"Shorlynn may not be my favorite person," Shashara said, "but what I did to her yesterday was wrong. She has no abilities of her own and to threaten her with mine made me less of a person for doing so. She was right about what she said. We've been so wrapped up in our own drama that we never considered what her dramas may be."

"She's been a thorn in our side since Calstar stuck us with her," Anliac said.

"That's exactly my point," Shashara replied. "She didn't ask for this job. Calstar gave her no choice."

Disappointed that none of them chose to come with her, Shashara made her way to Shorlynn's room alone. Tapping on the door, she waited for it to open, searching for what she might say to set right the wrong she'd done.

"Come to threaten me again," Shorlynn asked.

"I've come to ask your forgiveness," Shashara replied. Lifting the plate and glass, she said, "Peace offerings."

Shorlynn moved aside, allowing her to come in. "I know you think I lied to you," she shrugged, "and maybe I did, but not on purpose. I'm between a rock and a hard place you know?"

"Yeah," Shashara sat the sweet bread and milk on top of the chest of drawers. "We all are. You don't look sick. Are you feeling better?"

"I was never sick," Shorlynn said, "at least not physically." Perching on the edge of the bed, she said, "A part of being a woman, a fulgo woman, means our destinies are chosen for us. I had just started to accept mine when you all arrived. I see the way Set looks at you, Shashara, and I envy that."

Shashara stiffened. "Well, Set's taken."

Shorlynn huffed. "I don't want him. I don't want Tristan either, and yet, I'm jealous of the bond he and Anliac share. The relationships between each of you are greater than anything I've ever seen, and I want that. I don't know how I'm supposed to settle for less when I'm reminded that others have a choice or that I know what could be."

"So then don't settle," Shashara said. "Not all fulgo women chose to stay on the path others have set for them. I met a fiery red head back in Catena Piscari who would break someone's skull if they tried to dictate her life for her."

"I'd like to meet someone like that," Shorlynn confessed. "Someone that brave. Someone that willing to face the world alone because that's what it takes for one of us to walk away. I'm betrothed to a very dangerous man, one I barely know, and one that would come looking for me if I broke that betrothal."

"I guess we all have our battles to face," Shashara said.

"Yeah, but I will face mine alone." Shorlynn bit down on her lip and fought against the tears that welled in her eyes. "Please leave," she said. "Showing weakness in front of someone like you makes it worse, so please, go."

She did, and nearly bowled Set over, who stood just outside the room. "What is it?" she asked, laying her open palm flat against his chest. "Has something else happened?"

He closed his eyes and breathed deep before reopening them. "It wasn't you."

"I'm sorry?" Shashara asked, the skin between her eyes bunching.

"She's really sad, Shashara," he said, staring at the closed door as if he could see past it. "I've known it since day one, but it's getting worse, and her fear is growing. Is she in danger?"

"I don't think so," Shashara told him. "She's just trapped like the rest of us, between what we are and what we would choose to be."

"Anliac and Tristan have gone for a walk outside of the city," Set told her, "and your brother is cheating Lan out of his coin in a card game." Taking her hand, he led her into the room across the hall. "I'd like to spend some alone time with my girlfriend if that's okay with you?"

Shashara smiled, blushing as he closed the door behind them.

The suns' traveled across the sky, cutting a path through the orange haze, until at last it was time for them to set, and still there was no word from Calstar. Gathered once again in the common room, they discussed over dinner what their recourse would be.

"We'll give him until morning," Tristan said. "If we haven't heard from him by then, we might not have any other choice than to go find him."

"We should go outside of the city," Davad suggested, "I bet he would come find us then."

"Let's hope it doesn't come to that," Shashara said.

Rising from the table, they made their way upstairs. Lan slid with his back against the wall to the floor.

"Why don't you go with your men, Lan," Anliac said. "You could use a night in an actual bed."

"I'm fine where I am," he assured her. "Donnin would have me scalded and plucked if I let something happen to one of you."

"Suit yourself, bird man," Davad teased, opening the door to his room.

"Offense taken," Lan chuckled as each of his charges closed their doors behind them.

XIII
Where Are My Friends?

At the western gate, two city guards, with the traditional red IA insignia on their matching blue uniforms, came to attention at the convoy's approach.

"Hold," the fera guard called out. "State your business."

"Stand down," Sammel ordered, coming to the front of the group and halting Triton's reach for his sword. "I am responsible for these men. I'll see to it they get where they're going."

The second guard, a mortalis with a scarred face, asked, "And where would that be?"

"That's not your concern." Ignoring their outrage, Triton led his men through the gate, forcing the guards to step aside as he stared toward the tower rising from the heart of the white stone city. "Where do we start looking for them?" Triton asked.

"I don't know," Sammel said, tracking Triton's gaze, "but I don't think they'll be in the tower."

"Watch it," Triton growled, stepping back to avoid the wheels of two empty wagons that kicked up a cloud of dust, dulling the shine on his silver tipped boots and adding snickers to the guard's curses coming from behind him.

The four mortalis men, weary and covered with grime and sweat, lowered the long poles protruding from the front end of the wagons. The stench of death marked them as gravediggers as assuredly as the uniforms they wore.

"Sorry, mister," one of the four said. "We've been at it all day." Pausing to wipe away the sweat running into his eyes, he added, "One more load and that should be the last of them."

"I'd rather be finished sooner than later," one of the more contrary men complained. "If you're done chatting, we should go."

Despite their grumbling, the men bent their backs to the task, lifting the long poles and tugging to get the wagons rolling.

"Hey!" Sammel stepped in their path. "What's happened?"

"Where have you been, fera?" the ornery one asked, eyeing the pirates standing a few feet behind their captain. "The marketplace has been leveled. Now move out of our way."

"How?" Sammel's voice rose in pitch and disbelief, but he was ignored as the empty wagons rolled on.

"Let's go see for ourselves." Triton started off in the direction the gravediggers had provided to a devastated section of the city.

A huge crater sat dead center of the open plaza, and from there, the terra rippled outward, leveling the buildings in its path. People were searching through the carnage, salvaging what personal items they could while other wailed over the death of loved ones.

"Whatever happened," Triton said, scanning the rubble, "let's hope it doesn't happen again."

An elderly nox woman straightened from her task, placing a hand on the small of her back as she stretched out the aching muscles there.

"Excuse me, ma'am," Sammel called out to gain her attention. "We've just come in from the coast. Can you tell us what happened here?"

Her steel grey eyes held as much fear as they did awe. "The angeli have returned and they are angry. We didn't know who they were." Her voice quivered. "We didn't know what they were, and in our ignorance, we offended them," she said. "This was our punishment."

The half dozen men Triton had brought with him from the ship shifted their weight from one foot to the other as they looked around. Sammel seemed only slightly less distraught. Triton scowled.

"Are you telling me the kid did this?"

"I wouldn't call the angeli kids to their faces," she warned. "The girl is easily angered."

Triton's head tilted at her words, but he bit off the questions they invoked.

"Do you know where they are," Sammel asked.

"I saw them leaving the tower a couple of days ago, after..." she gestured with her hands to encompass the destruction. "They were headed to the southern part of the city. Whether or not they left Imbellis is beyond my knowledge."

"Thank you."

The woman waved them off and returned to her task, mumbling under her breath, "May we find mercy in the angelis' grace."

Triton chuckled and shook his head "What in Superi has that boy gotten himself into now?"

Forced to take a roundabout route to circumvent the upheaval of the marketplace, they reached the southern side of the city, where a large two-storied inn came into view.

"Sammel," a rough male voice shouted from the boardwalk before it. A thin fera, with feline attributes, stood waving a hand over his head to gain their attention, gesturing them over, before darting inside the inn to tell of their arrival.

"Friend of yours?" Triton asked, with an arch of his bushy brow.

"Yeah, and our friends will be with him." Sammel said, adding emphasis to the word our. "We're on the same side, captain."

"Hmm." Triton harrumphed. "Time will tell."

Rolling his eyes at Triton's skepticism, Sammel greeted the feras in IA uniforms guarding the inn's door. "I see I missed all the excitement."

"We need to talk about your idea of excitement, Sammel, because if leveling cities is in there, don't invite me to any of your parties." The fera laughed, slapping Sammel on the back as he held the door for Triton and his men.

They were greeted inside by a stocky fera who stretched out his hand. The fera's white feathered head punched into broad shoulders with seemingly no neck at all. "You must be Triton," he said. "I'm Lan."

Triton took it, twisting their wrists to look closer at the bloodstained feathers on the back of the fera's hand.

"Hazard of the job, I'm afraid." Lan's smile did nothing to lessen the warning in his beady black eyes.

Triton didn't bother smiling back. "I appreciate you looking after my friends, but I can handle it from here."

"If only it were that simple. Come," he said, walking from the entryway into the common room. "Let's get some coffee while we wait for them to join us." Choosing a table, Lan called out to Tahyhill. "Two cups of coffee over here and give the captain's men whatever they want."

They could hear the cups rattle as Tahyhill set them on the bar. His hands shook so badly that Seraphina took the carafe from him and poured the coffee herself. Thea sashayed her way behind the counter, batting her eyelashes and smiling outrageously as she took the others orders while the rest of the inns' staff flocked together in the back of the common room fretting.

Triton and Lan leaned back in their seats as Seraphina set down their cups, sloshing a goodly portion of the hot, brown liquid onto the tabletop.

"Sorry," she squeaked, before bolting back behind the bar.

Razoran, carrying a cold mug of goat's milk with him, sat down in the chair next to Triton.

"Who are you?" Lan asked.

"My first mate," Triton informed him, "and in a foul temper."

"My temper is fine," Razoran's low rumble disputed his words.

Triton chuckled. "So, who signed you up for guard duty?"

"I take my orders from Magistrate Donnin."

"You're a long way from Paradisi Colles." Triton glanced down at the stitched IA lettering on the man's uniform.

"I was placed in IA," Lan said, "but my loyalty is not there."

"How far does your loyalty extend to those kids?" Triton asked.

"We have stood between them and the entire city more than once."

"That's not loyalty," Razoran piped in. "That's following orders. What we want to know is why? What is your boss's intent?"

Lan cocked his head to the side, his beady eyes unblinking. "We are here to protect the angeli and to aid them in preparing for what's to come."

Razoran leaned back in his seat and spread his hands. "What does that even mean?" Razoran growled. "All you land lovers are the same. You speak in circles."

"Easy, friend," Lan said as his men moved in from the perimeter after taking offense to Razoran's tone. "The last thing we need is for a brawl to break out."

Triton's men were coming out of their seats, rising to the challenge Lan's men were throwing out. "Oh, for peace's sake, calm down," Triton said, rolling his eyes as if bored.

Footsteps coming from the stairway deescalated the tension as Tristan and his group came into the common room.

A smile split Tristan's face wide. "Razoran!" He started forward, blurred out of focus, and reappeared directly in front of the startled fera, who snarled and instinctively swiped out with his claws.

Tristian dodged it easily and laughed. "Man, it's good to see you." He wrapped his arms around Razoran, trapping his arms as he lifted his friend off his feet.

"I see you took my advice and stopped hiding," Razoran said, "but I didn't tell you to go out and rip apart a city."

"Ha!" Tristan cleared his throat, cutting his laugh short when Anliac stiffened at his side. "Yeah…umm…that wasn't me." Tristan turned to Triton with an outstretched hand. "Set told me about finding you in Catena Piscari. You really came through for us, Triton. Thank you."

Triton clasped Tristan's forearm, but his eyes were on the tall female hovering a foot behind him. His eyes rounded as he realized who she was. "What in the world did they do to you, girl?"

Davad came up on Triton's other side, Set and Shashara flanking him, and said, "Don't go there, Triton. Anliac is a bit sensitive, right now."

"Bite me, Davad." Anliac snapped.

Davad's expression skewed. "You sure? Your boyfriend might not like it."

Anliac rolled her eyes.

Triton checked out the completed aquis marks on Anliac's shoulder. There were no other marks to suggest she was capable of such mass destruction. "How does an aquis wielder level a marketplace without using water, regardless of the size of the fit she throws?" Triton asked.

When her yellow eyes flared, he bent his elbows, holding his hands up in surrender. "Don't feel bad, gorgeous. You should see the repairs Razoran has to make on my ship when we get back."

"Aww, captain," Razoran moaned, dropping his forehead onto his crossed arms on the tabletop.

Tristan laughed at Razoran's discomfort. "What happened?"

"Nothing," Razoran said, raising his head and voice simultaneously.

Triton ignored him. "He tore apart my upper cabin when I told him to stay behind with the ship."

"Aww," Tristan teased, "did you miss me that much?"

"Shut up," Razoran said. "I just wanted off that ship. Skylar has been driving us all crazy." He scowled at Triton. "And don't act like all the damage was mine."

Triton cleared his throat. "Yes, well, I suppose I may have pushed the ship's endurance a bit, but I couldn't have Skylar thinking the old girl couldn't hold up her end, and we were in a hurry."

Their comments about the feisty fulgo made Shashara smile. "I'm going to order us breakfast. Who's hungry?"

"I'm starving," Tristan said.

Shashara grinned. "You're always starving."

"I can attest to that," Triton smirked. "I thought the boy would eat the haul empty before we set him on solid ground again."

"Anliac?" Shashara asked, curious as to whether or not the newly made angeli's appetite would match Tristan's.

Anliac's stomach growled, drawing chuckles from friends and strangers alike.

"Order everything," Davad said, his eyebrows wiggling. "It's on the tower's coin; at least they can pay for the food since they won't talk to us."

"We...umm..." Set began taking a seat at the next table over, "all assumed you'd head out after getting our message."

Triton snorted. "I wasn't leaving without seeing that you were good with my own eyes, and from the looks of this city, and you," he lifted his chin in Anliac's direction, "not all is good."

Anliac's eyes flashed gold, brighter than before as her body began to tremble.

Tristan stepped between her and Triton, forcing her to see only him. "You're beautiful and there is nothing wrong with you. Triton simply meant that the state of things is not good. You know that. So...breathe."

The common room was silent and became charged with anxiety as those within held their breath and waited to see if the angeli would destroy them because of Triton's slight.

Triton, undaunted by her glowing, golden stare after seeing Tristan in action, demanded, "I want to know everything that's happened. It's obvious the tower has changed our girl, and she's packing a lot more power than before. The citizens are terrified of you both, and Lan here, says he's under orders to help you prepare for what's coming. He is to protect the angeli." His eyes darted from one of the five to the next. "Someone explain."

"What did I miss?" Shorlynn asked, going into full flirt mode at the sight of a common room full of gawking men. The black skirt she'd chosen had splits in the sides clean up to her hips, and the snow-white blouse tucked into its wide waist was open from collarbone to navel, with her uncle's silver pendant resting between her breasts.

"Well, hello." Triton came to his feet. "And who might you be?"

"I am Shorlynn, Calstar's niece." She dipped her head and smiled, her eyes twinkling with pleasure at the rough man's response to her arrival. "I was asked to look after the angelis' needs. And you are?"

Shashara and Anliac exchanged a pensive glance.

"Did you come in from outside," Shashara asked.

"Because we didn't hear you coming down the stairs," Anliac added.

"Oh," she waved off their concern. "It's noisy in here. Don't be so paranoid."

"Hmm." Anliac glared but held her peace.

Triton had lost interest as soon as she'd mentioned her lineage. He turned his attention back to the five he'd come to aid. "I'm still waiting on one of you to talk."

"Not here," Anliac said. "I want to trust you because of what they've told me about you, but the only thing I know of you myself, is that you tried to buy me off that ship. Very few actually know what's going on. The rest is just people talking. So…not here."

"I see no reason to keep secrets." Shorlynn pressed up next to Razoran after Triton's quick dismissal of her feminine charms and laid a light hand on his furred shoulder. "We're all friends here, right?"

"No." Flabbergasted by the girl's denseness, Shashara all but screamed. "You are not our friend. You're the one sent to keep tabs on us for the tower. You, and those like you, are the reason we can't talk here. Run and tell your uncle that, since he won't talk to us."

"I can't very well keep tabs on you if I'm running off to the tower, and besides, the company here is too intriguing to walk away from."

Anliac's stare snapped to Tristan. "Can I kill her yet?"

The boys chuckled as Tristan replied, "Sorry, beautiful, but no."

"It sounds to me like none of you should be here," Triton said. "A man would starve if he had to feed off of the trust in this room."

"The feras have prepared a safe haven for them," Lan informed him, "but they fear accepting it."

"We will not form an alliance with one race above any other," Anliac confirmed, "and we have good reason for it."

"Care to share that reason?"

"Triton," she stressed, "not here."

"There's an abandoned sawmill southwest of the city," Lan said. "It runs beside the river but is accessible by road. It's neutral ground and private."

Shashara smirked at Shorlynn's disgruntled expression. "What's wrong, Shorlynn?"

"I hate road trips," she pouted. "I don't understand why anyone would want to leave the comforts of the city."

"Don't worry," Shashara said. "You're not coming." She turned to one of Lan's men. "You say you want to help us. Keep her here long enough for us to get out the city and then let her go. She'll run straight to the tower, but it'll buy us some time before Calstar, and his men catch up to us."

The man nodded, "Done."

"Let's fall out," Lan ordered as he and his men exited the inn.

"It's good to have you here, Triton," Set said as he and the others filed out of the door behind Lan, smiling their agreement.

Triton addressed his crew. "His men claim to be allies, but they reek of ulterior motives. Don't offer them your back."

"Aye, aye, captain," they said in unison as they followed Triton and Razoran outside. Lan's guard snorted at Triton's warning and moved to block Shorlynn's stride towards the egress. "Sorry, little lady," he said, "but I have my orders."

Shorlynn stepped close to the guard and trailed the tip of her finger down the center of his gray and green scaled chest. Tipping back her head, she looked coyly into his black eyes. "Oh, I don't mind. My uncle will be along shortly to collect me. He was already on his way when I walked in. I know you can tell me how you're involved with the angeli."

Taking her by the outside of her arms, he set her away from him. "The most venomous creatures are often the most beautiful. They beguile the senses and blind us to the danger they pose. I've been poisoned enough times to build up a resistance to your kind. So, sit yourself down and behave until your uncle gets here."

Undeterred by the fera's resistance, she said, "Whatever your boss is paying you; the tower can offer more; more coin, higher position, and then of course there are the added perks."

Taking the bait, the fera asked, "Such as?"

Shorlynn grinned.

The door to the inn came open causing the fera to whirl around, shoving Shorlynn behind him as he hissed. His forked tongue flicking out to test the threat level.

The tower guard who'd entered sneered at the fera's reaction. "We're here for her." To Shorlynn, he said, "Your uncle is waiting outside. Let's go."

Shorlynn stepped around the fera. "Think on what the tower could offer you," she told him as she slipped out the door. Stepping from the boardwalk, one of Calstar's men reached down his hand and lifted her behind him on his mount. Her uncle was speaking before she'd settled into the saddle.

"Where did they go?" Calstar asked, wild-eyed and disheveled.

"Good morning to you too, uncle," her curt remark drew his scowl. Rolling her eyes, she answered, "They mentioned an old sawmill, but you should have brought more men with you."

This gained his attention. "Why?"

"Because Triton has six with him and Lan has close to a dozen. You're outnumbered."

Wielding their mounts towards the southern gate, Calstar barked over his shoulder, "We're not here to fight them, Shorlynn. Superi help us…we need them."

A cloud of dust billowed behind them as they put their boot heels into their horses' sides and raced out of the gate. Rounding a curve in the road, just beyond the city wall, Calstar saw them.

"Stop!" he shouted over the pounding of hooves. Reaching them, he pulled back on his horse's reins and slid from the saddle. His two personal guards, silver collars around their throats, followed suit while the handful of men he'd brought with him from the tower remained mounted.

"What are you doing, Calstar?" Tristan glowered. "We've already warned you. We're not your prisoners anymore. You can't control us and," he cut his eyes hard to Shorlynn, "you were not invited."

"You can't just leave," Calstar said. "This isn't about controlling you. This is about keeping you safe, about ensuring that you're both prepared for what's coming. Like it or not, your lives are no longer your own. They belong to Superi now."

"They are children," Triton snarled, his hands clenching into fists, "and you've all but destroyed them. For the deaths that you're responsible for, for Davad and Shashara's father, who also happened to be my closest friend, I should slit your throat now and be done with it."

"Don't try it," one of Calstar's guards warned.

Razoran's black lips peeled off his sharp teeth curtailing the guard's aggression.

"Riders…coming in fast from the south," Lan said. "You three, take up position there." He pointed towards the tree line off the right side of the road. "You three, there." His men quickly found their spots and went down on their bellies to use the high grass for cover on the left side. "The rest of you form a line." Lan was the first to stand his ground. Looking to either side at his men, he added, "You'd all better be dead before they break through."

"Fall in with Lan's men," Triton ordered, "and strengthen the line."

Razoran held his place beside his captain while the rest of the crew followed orders. Anliac pressed up against Tristan's back as Set, Shashara, and Davad maneuvered themselves into the familiar defensive formation Jacob had taught them.

"Calstar, get your men on the line," Tristan said.

"They are here to protect me," Calstar objected as his mounted men formed a half moon circle in front of him.

"Coward," Triton cursed as Calstar scrambled back into his saddle. "So much for your concern for the angeli."

The riders slowed as they approached.

"Oh crap!" Anliac muttered when she saw the man in the lead. "It's my dad." She laid her forehead on the back of Tristan's shoulder. "This is going to be bad."

The general's expression was a thundercloud as he held up his hand, drawing the twenty nox soldiers, in uniforms of blended browns and greens, to a halt. Sliding off his horse, he pulled off his black leather gloves and tucked them into the back of his waistband. He pinned Set with a hard stare as his squad sized up the competition.

"You left quite a mess behind in Palus Regia, boy. Traydon is a drooling idiot, and Magistrate Rayner wants your head on a spike." He turned his attention to Tristan. "I'm glad to see that you made it out, but right now, all I care about is finding my daughter. Why is Anliac not with you?"

Anliac nudged Tristan aside. "I'm here, dad."

Montilis's eyes narrowed as he searched the unfamiliar planes of the girl's face for traces of his daughter. Anliac was a petite, voluptuous girl with emerald green eyes, full of sass and life. The woman standing in front of him was as tall as Tristan, with eyes just as yellow. She was feminine, but not curvy, and defined by cut muscle that Anliac never possessed. The husky, breathless tone, Anliac had inherited from her mother was missing, and in its place, was a voice like chimes—piercingly beautiful.

Seeing that her father didn't recognize her, she flung the edge of her white cloak aside, exposing the aquis mark on her right shoulder.

Montilis's face darkened as his body shook with pent-up rage. "Who did this to you?"

"It doesn't matter," she said. "What's done is done."

"The tower did what it had to in order to save Superi," Calstar said, speaking out of turn.

Set grimaced. "You spend days ignoring us and now you choose to speak? You need to learn WHEN to shut up."

When their general moved so did his men. They prodded their mounts forward, shoving a path through the line as the men forming it drew their weapons, but shifted their positions to give the nox soldiers room.

The boggy ground on the right side of the road was more than enough for Montilis to form whips, which he swung in a wide arc over his head before they snapped out with a loud crack. The unyielding aquis whips wrapped around two of Calstar's men, and with a vicious yank, Montilis tossed them through the air towards his waiting soldiers.

The fight broke out as the IA guards were snatched by the eager hands of Montilis's men and dragged across the ground where the other IA guards were being beaten with aquis hammers as well as with the hilts of swords and bare fists until they simply stopped fighting back. They'd never stood a chance against the overwhelming number of trained nox soldiers.

As a unit, Lan's and Triton's men maneuvered themselves to protect the five as Shorlynn, seeing her uncle's men devastated, dove into the protective circle.

"Enough!" Anliac shouted over the clashing of weapons and fists on flesh as horses reared and men screamed.

Lan's men crept forward, eager to join the fray.

"Hold your positions," Lan growled. "This is not our fight."

Calstar gathered the reins in his hands.

"You're not going anywhere," Montilis snarled.

Using a thick stream of water, he propelled himself forward, grabbed the lawyer by the throat, and used his heavier weight to carry them both to the ground. Straddling Calstar's chest, Montilis allowed his rage to manifest. He pounded his fist into Calstar's face again and again but was caught off guard when Calstar struck with surprising force, clipping his jaw and flipping him onto his back.

Calstar was the first to regain his feet, a malevolent grin turning the corners of his mouth. "You'd better come at me with more than brute strength, general. I'm stronger than you are." With purposeful strides, he advanced.

The ground began to shake, causing the battling men to stumble and the horses to rear and bolt. The fighting stopped as they attempted to retain their balance. The men lifted their panicked faces towards the angeli causing the quake.

She rolled the ground on an outward wave shoving the guards, regardless of the insignias they wore, further away. "I said enough." Her piercing tone dropped several men to their knees as they covered their ears while others emptied the contents of their stomachs. Cupping her hand, the terra rose beneath Calstar's and her father's feet, and on a wave of terra, she brought them in. "The fighting stops now." Ignoring the horrific expression on her father's face, she said in a calmer tone, "Triton, Lan, get over here."

"You too, Razoran," Tristan said.

The guards and soldiers, seeing their leaders separated from them, stormed forward. Their progress was stalled by a ten-foot-wide chasm that split the ground in a running circle, barring their way.

"Hold," Triton and Lan ordered simultaneously to prevent their men from jumping into the crater to their own death as their leaders were forced to congregate in the center of the chaos where the five and Shorlynn waited. No such order was necessary for Calstar's men. The fight had been taken out of them.

The Regia Aquam guards didn't give up so easily. It took all of them to pull enough water from the ground to form an ice bridge over the chasm.

"Call them down," Anliac told her father.

"No," Montilis challenged.

Anliac snapped her fingers and the bridge shattered. Montilis cursed as half his men dropped into the twenty-foot crater.

When the remaining nox advanced, Anliac's vow stopped them cold. "One more step and I close the chasm with them still in it."

"What in tarnation do you think you're doing?" Davad snapped as he whirled around to confront her. "You seriously need to calm yourself."

A sword of ice appeared in her hand as she advanced on Davad, dropping the jaws of her friends.

Tristan caught her by the arm and spun her around, catching her wrist when she would have struck out at him as well. "Hey there, gorgeous. Remember me?" he asked, easily holding her in check. When the heat in her eyes faded, he added, "Davad is one of the good guys and your father's men aren't your enemy. Breathe."

The sword turned to water that splashed at their feet.

Anliac blanched as she realized how close she'd come to hurting Davad, and worse, how close she'd come to hurting Tristan. "I'm so sorry."

Davad shrugged his shoulders, tilting his head from side to side, as he tamped down the temper threating to call his ignis ability to his defense. "Don't sweat it," he said. "We all lose control from time to time. You just have to remember that we don't kill unless given no choice. That's what separates us from those like him." He gestured to Calstar.

"It's this heat," Shorlynn said, fanning her face with her hands. "It's making us all a bit crazy."

Shashara chuckled and then blushed as she became the center of attention. "I'm sorry." She bit down on her lip to keep from laughing outright. "This is all a little funny if you think about it. I mean," she closed her eyes to gain composure before opening them and starting again. "Lan acts like we're a bone he's got in his bite and refuses to let go. Calstar is chasing us down and begging us after ignoring us for days." At this, she did laugh. "Who would have thought we'd ever bring the tower to its knees? We came all the way out here to talk to our friend Triton to bring him up to speed, and Montilis chooses now to show up, and then he freaks out like we didn't try and warn him." She covered her mouth with one hand. Her bright blue eyes were alight with humor. "And Anliac," she laughed, pointing at Davad, "just tried to kill you. The whole of Superi is going insane, and we're standing in the middle of the road with this little priss who's complaining about the heat."

"What we need is a little privacy." Davad said.

Shashara burst out laughing again. "There is no privacy, Davad. This is it." She raised her arms, spreading them wide as if in defeat. "This is our future. Rulers and lawyers, masters of men and race, vying for our favor or plotting our demise. This is it," she shrugged.

"Forget privacy," Anliac said, "we need to get Shashara out of the suns. She's lost it."

Using the chasm as a starting point, she first filled it, spitting the trapped guards onto the ground on the outside of the circle, before building upon it. The ground groaned in complaint as the plates beneath the surface shifted and rose to the angeli's call, forming a high wall around them.

Those on the inside cursed, or ducked, as the top of the wall domed over them. A round hole, the size of a house, was left in its peak to provide light as they became trapped.

Shashara noticed the fear-inspired awe on the outsiders' faces. "She has a flare for the dramatic these days," she said.

Set chuckled. "I take it that's a girl thing."

"No," Davad said. "It's an angeli thing."

Tristan pushed against Davad's shoulder, shoving him slightly off balance. "Shut up," he grinned. "I was never this bad."

"And so, I am?" Anliac asked, her fists snapping to her waist as she tapped her foot and awaited his reply.

Tristan cleared his throat. "I've only ever known this life, Anliac. You're doing fine. You'll get control. You just need to give yourself a little time."

She lost some of her bluster when she glanced past Tristan to a traumatized father staring at her. She closed the distance between them slowly, bracing her emotions in case he rejected her.

"I'm glad you came for me," she began. "And I am so very grateful that you had nothing to do with what Inabeth had done to me, but dad, it's too late. I am not nox anymore."

"You should have let me kill him," Montilis said, jabbing a finger towards Calstar.

"Why?" she asked. "He's not the one that did this. Malstar was and Malstar is dead, and life moves on."

"How can you not want justice?"

Set felt Anliac's and Shorlynn's sadness like a physical blow. Shashara, seeing him tense, looked over in concern, but he shook his head to keep her quiet and took her hand instead. Shorlynn's emotions were a scramble as she heard the confirmation of Malstar's death.

"Because I understand desperation," Anliac answered. "The mercenary desperately fought to rescue his daughter, and it cost him his life. These three," she said, gesturing to Set, Shashara, and Davad, "you know firsthand, and probably with more clarity than I, what they've gone through; what they've done to rescue me and Tristan. I know what they sacrificed to try and reach you, and they did that to save me." She swallowed hard as she turned her head to Calstar while continuing to speak to Montilis. "Calstar and his brother took on a heavy burden. They alone knew the danger that Superi was in, and they've desperately fought for her. To prepare to defend and protect Superi, who is mother to us all, from a threat greater than you can image."

"And they've done this how?" Montilis asked. "By turning you into..." he shook his head at a loss for words.

"Into an angeli," she said, filling in the blank as she refocused her eyes on her father. "They took blood from a member of each race and injected me with it in the hope of creating what we Superians use to be—beings strong enough to fight what lay beyond the gateway."

"A gateway that leads where?" Montilis took his daughter by the tops of her arms. "Who are you so afraid of?" he asked. "I will protect you this time."

Anliac pulled away from her father to stand at Tristan's side.

"No, you can't," Tristan said, taking Anliac's hand, "at least not alone. The gateway is to Earth, and now it's been awakened. A single god from their planet took out more than two dozen men at Bealson's Grove. He nearly matched me for strength, and he's faster than any level three I've met."

"He wields an aether ability that controls energy," Anliac interjected. "He can form weapons from it, a bow of light and orbs that explode," her vision hazed as memory took hold. She blinked to clear it.

"It's just one man," Triton quipped. "God or no god, Superi can handle one man."

"I crushed him beneath stone, and he split it in two and rose again," Anliac said. "The threat to Superi is real."

"And it's not just one god," Tristan explained. "Anliac and I were able to force him through the gateway, but he'll be back, and he won't be alone."

"How many gods are we talking about," Montilis asked, "and what do we know about them?"

"We know very little," Tristan nodded to Calstar, "but he has a nifty little journal that should give us all of the information we need."

Calstar stiffened.

"I should have guessed," Montilis said. "Keeping secrets is what the tower does." Snarling at Calstar, he asked, "Did it ever occur to you that the other races might have helped? You've put the whole planet in danger because of your pride."

"The races of Superi were too busy fighting over trade and water rights to take the threat seriously," Calstar said. "The Ruling Houses of the fulgo knew better and did what we had to in order to protect everyone—despite race or territory. Think me vile if that is your desire, but heed what I'm telling you. The gods of Earth will invade Superi, and they," he said, nodding towards Tristan and Anliac, "are literally our only hope of survival."

"Yeah," Triton sniffed as his chin jutted out, "you're a real hero. Just tell us what the journal says."

"I'm not telling you anything," Calstar sneered, his nose wrinkling in distaste. "You are a pirate. You hold no rank and have no right to that kind of knowledge."

"I'm in no mood for this, Calstar," Anliac warned. "As you've said, we are the weapons you would wield against Superi's enemies, but we are not mindless tools to be used."

Calstar's visage was fretful but still he refused.

"You're going to tell us all about the journal," Tristan said, "or Anliac's temper is going to be the last thing on your mind. I saw your little display of strength against Montilis. Would you like to help me demonstrate mine?"

"Ugh," Shorlynn whined, "Is brawling all you people know how to do? There are other ways to handle disputes. There is talking for one."

Set grinned, "Mom always said if you have nothing nice to say, break the other guy's jaw."

"Ha," Triton chortled, "I miss that woman."

"However," Shashara pointed out above Davad's laughter as it joined Triton's, "we can't very well force the man to talk with a broken jaw, now can we?"

Lan cleared his throat, and with hesitation, told them what he knew. "The journal was written by Nathon Bealson. It's a record of his failures and triumphs." Incredulous stares made his heart race. He much preferred battles to speeches, but he pressed on. "He was an angeli, as all were named at the time, with a gift for inspiring others to aid his cause. At his core, he was a good man. He spent most of the journal talking about advancements in technology, such as water wells for the angeli without aquis abilities and building ships so that that gate makers could not take advantage of the people after the continents were split. What?" he demanded at their gawking stares. "I told you that the feras know many things."

"And we should have listened," Shashara soothed. "Please, continue."

"The journal also speaks about his sojourns between Earth and Superi after he learned to harness the river's energy." They looked at him expectantly when he fell silent. "That is all I know."

"We appreciate you volunteering the information," Tristan said. "It goes a long way towards earning our trust." Stalking across the closed interior of the dome, he shoved his finger into Calstar's chest. "Now start where he left off."

Calstar sighed knowing he had no other choice. "Nathon was no mere gate maker. He learned to harness the energy of the river because he was an epoto as well as a gate maker, and that made him a rift maker." He glanced at Set but quickly diverted his eyes. "Epotos can draw on elemental energy and redirect it from one place to another."

Calstar wasn't alone in his appraisal of Set, who nodded once to acknowledge the obvious. "That's good to know," he said, "now continue."

"There was mention of one or two journeys to Earth and then ta…" Calstar was cut short.

"You've a lot to learn about epotos, Calstar," Set said, "they can tell when someone is lying."

Anliac sniffed, "So can I. Your racing heart betrays you."

"I'm not lying," Calstar insisted. "The journals talk about trips to Earth and then a huge battle."

"Journals?" So many said the single word that it was impossible to say who had not spoken.

Calstar threw his hands up in exasperation. "Well, of course there are more than one. Do you have any idea how large the book would have to be to hold that much information? Months of research…"

"Lie," Anliac called out.

"Do it again," Set warned, "and you'll regret it."

"I'm not lying," Calstar whined. "I'm recounting the information as I remember it."

"Tristan, grab him," Set said.

"Curse it all!" Triton bellowed, lifting his foot to back away as Tristan went from normal guy to an angeli before his lifted foot had settled.

Montilis back peddled, knocking into Razoran who shoved him off before he brought himself under control. Slack jawed, Montilis stared as Tristan grabbed Calstar from behind and crushed the man's arms to his sides until his breath came in short panting draws.

Shorlynn screamed.

Shashara turned and slapped her across the face. "Knock it off."

"Thank you," Shorlynn said, wide-eyed and rubbing her cheek. "I think I needed that."

With a slow roll of his shoulders, Set walked over to stand before Calstar. His blue eyes were frigid, unyielding, as he said, "I told you not to lie, but not to worry; we understand it is in your nature. Let me show you what's in mine."

"Do I need to let him go?" Tristan asked, the deep hollow base of his voice causing dirt to shake loose from the walls.

"No, just hold him still," Set said.

Shashara caught his arm. "Set, are you sure?"

"I'm learning to control it, Shashara," he assured her. When she let go of his arm, he placed his fingertips on Calstar's forehead. "What are you hiding?"

The onlookers fell silent as Calstar body grew ridged. He gasped, his mouth gaping, and then he began to scream.

"Uncle!" Shorlynn cried as she attempted to run to his aid. She didn't get far.

Anliac caused the terra to rise and encased Shorlynn's feet, rooting her in place. Her efforts were unnecessary.

Set jerked his fingers from Calstar's flesh, wiping his hand on his pant leg as he turned his back and began talking aloud to himself.

Tristan's hands on Calstar's arms had been all that kept the fulgo on his feet. When he let go, Calstar crumpled. Tristan stepped over him to reach his brother. "Set, are you okay?"

"Yeah." He winced. "Head hurts a little. His thoughts are scattered, chaotic. I'm trying to make sense of it, but it's a lot of information to take in at one time."

"Try and focus on the story he was telling," Anliac suggested.

"I'm trying." Set bent at the waist and gagged. Turning his head, he glared at Calstar. "You and your brother are sick. I understand why your sect has done what they've done, but, man, there had to be another way to go about it."

"Maybe you should sit down," Lan said. "You don't look so great."

Anliac must have agreed. As soon as Set stood, a chair rose from the terra behind him, bumping the back of his knees, buckling them, and dropping him into it.

"There are years of research, not months." He closed his eyes and focused. "Dozens of trips to Earth where he learned about their planet. It's bigger than ours, but the pull on the people is less."

"What does that mean?" Shashara asked, kneeling in front of him.

Set opened his eyes and tried to think of a way to explain. "The force that keeps our feet on the ground, the energy that causes things that go up to come down again, theirs is less. A person that can jump ten feet here could jump forty to fifty feet there."

"That would explain why Apollo stumbled when he came through the gateway," Tristan said.

"Would you mind letting me go?" Shorlynn grumbled.

Anliac glanced from Tristan to Shorlynn's feet and the ground receded. "Are there other differences between their planet and ours?" she asked Set, who sat rubbing his temples.

"They only have one sun and one moon." His expression went slack. "Their people don't have abilities."

"What?" Tristan scoffed. "Tell that to Apollo."

Set stood from the terra chair and began to pace. "Apollo is a god. The denizens of earth are just...human. Those with abilities are gods. They are worshiped by the humans. They draw their strength from that worship. Buildings are erected in their names, where the humans offer gifts and sacrifices to them. We were there for..." he shook his head. "Wait." The skin between his eyes bunched as he reevaluated the information he'd pulled from Calstar. "Their measurement of time is different. Their years are shorter than ours, and they don't live very long."

Calstar wrung his hands. "We are among commoners, epoto. They don't need to know everything. They shouldn't be told anything."

Set ignored him. "Jacob was right. The Superians overstepped. They set themselves up as gods on Earth, and the gods already there took offense. There was a huge battle. The Earthling gods won. We tried to escape back through the gateway, but one god...stronger than the others, came through with us. Calstar memorized the last few lines in the final journal: And the one that followed was righteous in his anger; glorious in his rage, as he cast forth the curses that brought wails of agony to the people of Superi. Chaos ensued as our singular race was physically torn into the four that emerged, even as the second curse implanted itself into our minds, making stupid what once was not. Hope..." He paused. "The journal ends there."

Tristan crossed his arms over his chest. "What about Nathon?"

"He doesn't know," Set said.

"It's more than we knew before, right?" Shashara's optimism fell flat.

"What do you mean by stupid?" Davad bowed up as if Nathon Bealson's insult was freshly given. "I'm not stupid."

Calstar pressed the fingertips of both his hands together. "We understand it to mean the inability to advance technologically. There have been many cases over the decades where denizens from every race found themselves on the verge of a new discovery only to go mad. Their insanity drove them to take their own lives."

"He's telling the truth," Montilis said. "We've seen it happen in Palus Regia."

"In my race as well," Lan admitted.

"So, let me get this straight," Triton said. "A slew of angeli fought the gods on Earth and lost. The first curse made us weaker. The second curse made us dumber. It took two angeli to handle, not kill, one of their gods on Superian soil. Cursed I may be, but I've fought enough wars to know the odds are not in our favor. They are coming in number and only two angeli remain. We are damned."

Davad shivered. "Why couldn't the whole thing have turned out to be the rantings of an old drunk man?"

"That's a common misconception, boy," Triton said. "Lies are conceived by the concealment of a truth we fear. Drunks most often speak the truth because they do not fear it."

"He said hope," Shashara whispered, rubbing the outside of her left arm. "We should look into finding some." Her voice gained strength as she continued. "Perhaps we are not as strong as we once were, but we are stronger in number than apart. An angeli wields two elements. We must use the marks on our skin to recreate an army. Cluster ourselves into units that will level our odds when the time comes."

"Guys," Set attempted to smile and failed. "I want to go. This dome is beginning to feel like a grave."

Gesturing Shorlynn over, Calstar used her outstretched hand to pull himself to his feet. "I can't force you to return with me to the tower, but remember that the offer has been made, and we would appreciate being told where we can find you. The gateway sits at Imbellis's back."

"It's a reasonable request," Tristan agreed. "I think it's fairly simple. Not one of us desires to spend another night in the tower, but neither do we intend to hold the fulgo population accountable for the desperate actions of a few." He turned to Lan. "We've met those you answer to and know from their own mouths where they stand. We offer the fera population a place among us, but it needs to be understood that the feras will stand at our side. We will not stand at theirs."

"Then it is settled," Montilis said. "You will all accompany me back to Palus Regia."

"No, father," Anliac declined. "We may not agree with what Calstar and his brother have done. However, understanding their reasons, they are the most vested in our cause, and that makes them allies whether we like it or not. The feras have aided us countless times, proving their loyalty by action while allowing us the freedom to choose without consequence so long as our actions do not cause harm to them directly." She bit down on her bottom lip, her eyes begging him to understand. "The nox have disappointed and betrayed us at every turn. You said yourself that Magistrate Rayner wants Set dead, and we all know why it took you so long to come. Please," she held up her hand when he would have interrupted, "the nox may send an emissary. We will not exclude any of the races, but we will not return to Palus Regia."

Triton grinned. "This is why I love the oceanus: neutral territory."

Calstar's eyes bulged. "You're going to side with the pirate?"

"No," Davad said. "We are going back to Pisces Stragulum." He glanced at Anliac, and then to Tristan, assuring himself that it was okay for him to speak for them. "It's easily accessible by land or water. It's close to the grove in case Apollo returns and it's been abandoned for generations. Now it has been reclaimed by the angeli."

Grunting in approval, Lan asked, "May we travel with you?"

"Of course," Shashara said. "Twice you've stood to defend us. You've shared your knowledge with us. As long as your actions continue to prove you mean us no harm, you will always be welcome. That goes for all of you."

"Whoa," Set swayed.

"Easy, boy," Triton said as he scooped Set off his feet to Shashara's panicked shout. "He's all right. He just needs air. Girl, bring a wall down and let's go."

"I can walk," Set croaked.

"Sure, you can," Triton said, "but for right now, why don't you hang tight."

Anliac lifted her arms. Her eyes slid closed and she breathed, forcing herself to relax. Her anger had made building the wall the work of a moment. Without it, she needed to concentrate.

"Oh, thank Superi," Shorlynn sighed. Marching up to one of her uncle's men, she stamped her foot and demanded, "Take me home."

"Not so fast," Calstar's words had her spinning around. "As Shashara has so graciously offered, the fulgo race will wish to be represented in Pisces Stragulum, but until the council can convene and emissaries chosen, you will travel with them as our ambassador."

"Uncle Calstar, no." Her eyes welled. "I was to relocate to Certamen after this was over. You promised."

"Things are not yet settled."

Anliac's and Shashara's eyes met with equal parts pity and shame.

"You are welcome among us," Shashara said with as much sincerity as she could muster.

"There will be far too many men for you to choose from for you to bother with ours," Anliac added.

The underlying threat in Anliac's humor was not missed on Shorlynn. She lowered her head and bowed. "Thank you. I…" she swallowed hard. "I will endeavor to be of more help than hindrance."

The men who'd been trapped outside of the wall visibly relaxed as their leaders were revealed once again. They rallied to them, awaiting orders—all but the men, who were held at bay by a sharp look from their general.

"Anliac," he asked, "may we speak?" She smiled and his heart broke, for in it he saw a glimpse of the daughter he'd lost.

"I may look different on the outside." She shrugged. "I may even be different on the inside, but I'm still your daughter. That is the one thing that nothing can change."

"Shashara is fiercely protective of you," he said, a slight, crooked smile appeared and then was gone. "She threatened our entire line of border guards to gain entrance into Palus Regia, and she held nothing back once they'd found me."

"I know her worth," Anliac grinned.

Montilis nodded. "She's offered each of us a place among you, but my question is for you alone. Am I welcome?"

"We both know you have responsibilities in Palus Regia."

His shoulders drooped.

"But for as long as possible," she continued as a single tear escaped, "I would like very much for you to join us."

"What's the hold up?" Davad asked. "Triton and his men have already left. They're taking Set to the ship."

Tristan grinned. "We can't let that happen." He nodded to Montilis and reached for Anliac. "Let's go save him."

XIV
Limitations

Set came awake to Triton's face staring back at him. Squirming, he came out of his cradled position in the gruff captain's arms, twisting himself upright in the saddle. The constant sway of the beast's strides wreaked havoc on his gut. Fearing he would vomit; he slung a leg over the side and landed on wobbly knees.

"Set!" Shashara scrambled from her position behind Razoran before he could draw the horse to a stop. Sliding her shoulder beneath Set's arm to keep him standing, she reprimanded him. "You could have broken your neck."

His blue eyes shot daggers at Triton who came down from his mount. "He was going to take me onto the ship."

Triton chuckled as he handed Razoran the reins.

Tristan and Anliac, riding double, with Montilis and Davad flanking them on either side, joined them as the rest of their convoy converged in the open section of tall grass surrounded by the dilapidated buildings of Pisces Stragulum.

"Your men would have mutinied," Tristan grinned.

"What is their problem with Set," Montilis asked as he and Davad dismounted.

"His weak stomach," Razoran replied. The horses whickered, tugging against his hold as he collected the others' reins.

"Sir," a nox solider bowed. "Where do you want us?"

Razoran handed over the lead ropes. "Thanks for the loan."

"No problem," the soldier nodded, relieving Razoran of his burden. "Sir?"

"We are here as guests," Montilis said. "How can Palus Regia serve the angeli?"

Anliac searched her father's face for signs of sarcasm. Finding only concern and compassion, her gaze swung wide. It wasn't only the nox waiting for orders, but the feras as well, along with the handful of IA guards standing with Shorlynn and the pirates who'd gathered on the docks. The suns had long set and the moons cast an eerie glow over the abandoned town. Exhaustion weighed heavily on the faces looking up at her, but her mind, misfiring, could offer no direction. She swayed in the saddle.

Tristan wrapped his arm around her slender waist and drew her up against his chest. His eyelids were sliding closed despite his effort to keep them open. "She's wiped out." His words were slurred. "She needs rest."

"And so, do you," Davad said. "Lan..."

The white feathered fera stepped forward.

"Have your men set up a perimeter," Davad instructed. "It's not likely we'll be accosted yet but better to see it coming than to be blindsided by what we weren't prepared for. Check inside the buildings. There's at least one man who calls this place home. Don't hurt him."

"Done." Lan gestured that his men should follow. He was issuing orders as they walked

103

out of earshot.

"Triton," Davad ignored the bemused, crooked grin on the captain's face, "tell your cook to recruit help. We all need food."

"And we'll need bandages," Shashara said, "soap, and clean water." Her lips pursed, "and some way to convince the injured to accept my help. What?" she asked. "Men never want to admit they're hurt."

"If you can see what you can do about supplies, Triton," Montilis said, "I'll have a few of my men round up the injured."

Triton nodded stoically and headed for his ship with Razoran at his side.

Davad turned to the IA guards. "Setting up a temporary camp until morning will be your job. We'll need wood to burn. Tear it from the wooden buildings if you have to, but see it done, and let's work on beating down all of this tall grass here in the center of town. We have enough things to worry about without adding snakebites to the list. General," Davad added, "have your men help."

A nod was all it took and Montilis's men were off and running.

"And what are my orders," Shorlynn asked. Her pale skin appeared grey and there were dark circles under her eyes. She held one hand flat against her stomach as she swallowed convulsively.

"You look worse than they do," Shashara said, tilting her head towards Tristan and Anliac.

"I'm fine," Shorlynn sniffed. "I'm just not used to all this physical exertion."

"Right now, you're useless to me," Shashara replied, "and so are you," she grunted to Set as he leaned heavily against her side, threatening to knock them both over. "Catch them!"

Tristan had fallen asleep, and both he and Anliac were on a collision course with the ground. Montilis lurched, arms outstretched to catch his daughter, but her fall was cushioned by Tristan's chest as he landed on his back, the air gushing from his lungs.

"What happened?" Tristan mumbled as Anliac rolled off him.

"General, these four need a bed," Davad said. "Ask Triton if he can make room for them in the forecastle."

"I'm not going onto that ship," Set groaned.

"I get the impression the captain doesn't care for me," Montilis reached down a hand to help Tristan and Anliac to their feet, "but I'll see what I can do. Come on, girl," he barked at Shorlynn. "Help Set. Shashara has work yet to do tonight."

As Shorlynn took her place at Set's other side, Shashara glared. "Don't get any ideas. I'll want him back."

Tears welled in her eyes as Shorlynn whined, "I'm dirty. My feet hurt. I reek of sweat, and I'm more tired than I've been in my whole life. Trust me. I've no interest at the moment in playing with your boyfriend."

As the group walked off towards the docks, Davad came to stand at his sister's side. "Don't worry," he said. "Set's not interested."

"That's so not the point," she scowled. Dropping her hands to her sides, she turned to face Davad. "I guess we're the last ones standing."

"Looks that way," he smiled.

An IA guard came up at trot. "Sir..."

Davad's eyes went wide. "Me?" He pointed at his own chest.

"Yes, sir," the guard replied. "There's a problem."

"What is it?"

"There's a disagreement between the men. It's going to turn to blows if you don't do something about it."

"Miss," an old mortalis with a bent back and a bad limp ambled over with full packs dangling from his shoulders, "my name is Swiney. Triton said you were trying to patch up some of these boys."

Shashara smiled, tightlipped. "I welcome the help. I'm not a healer." To Davad, she said, "The men must forget what uniforms they wear, or we'll never make this work."

"I'll handle them," Davad assured her. "Let's go."

"Yes, sir," the IA guard replied. "This way."

A wide circular trench had been cut to enclose the blazing fire started by the men. A scale-skinned, barrel-chested fera was snarling at a nox solider who was built like a stack of bricks, short and stout.

"That uniform doesn't mean squat here. You don't give orders to me."

"Someone has to," the nox retorted. "Beasts can't think for themselves."

The fera threw the first punch, catching the nox square in the jaw.

The soldier's hand reached for the hilt of his sword.

"Draw your weapon and you'll answer to me," Davad warned. "Infighting will not be tolerated."

"Your threat lacks weight, boy," the nox sneered.

"Your general said something similar once. He now carries the scars of his mistake." It was a stretch of the truth but served his purpose. Davad placed himself between the two men, facing the more aggressive one. "Back off."

"I can't believe you're taking his side." The soldier cursed as he put distance between himself and the fera who'd slugged him.

"I'm not taking sides," Davad said, "but I am drawing a line. There are no nox here. There are no fera, or fulgo, or mortalis for that matter." He raised his voice to be heard by more than the two involved. "We are Superians. It's time we start acting like it." Under his breath, he muttered, "Or there won't be a planet left to fight for."

"What?" the nox asked, leaning forward to better hear.

"Nothing," Davad said. "The point is, we have to learn to work together, and here is where we start, now, in Pisces Stragulum."

"I'm not taking orders from him," the fera said, jabbing his finger in the nox's direction.

"What's going on here?" Lan asked, coming up on the scene.

Davad held out his hand. "Stay out of it, Lan." To the fera, he replied, "You take your orders from Lan, but Lan takes his orders from the angeli. They are of no one race. They are of all races, and if you can't get behind that, then you need to leave."

The nox snickered.

"You are on dangerous ground," Davad snapped. "Your general has yet to earn the respect of the angeli that the feras have long since obtained. If there is a pecking order, you rank lowest. Tomorrow, the two of you will come and find me. Together, we will begin digging the latrine that the town will need as more people come."

The nox shook his head. "That's not going to happen."

"At last, we agree," the fera said.

"Oh, it's going to happen," Davad assured them, "and I'm going to help because, here, no one person is above the other, and if you two insist on stirring crap, we might as well dig a hole for it. Are there any other disputes I need to settle between grown men?" When no one piped up, he said, "Good. You," he pointed to those standing to the right of the fire, "see if Triton's people are ready to start hauling over the food. The rest of you spread out. See if

Shashara needs help tending the wounded. This wood won't last and we've a long night ahead of us. Some of you should talk to Lan. Patrols need to be set up, and the feras shouldn't have to cover them alone. They're as tired as the rest of us." When they just stood there, slack jawed, he shouted, "Move!"

They moved.

"Well done," Lan praised.

Davad shook his head. "These men don't understand why they're here. They are simply following orders and that's not good enough."

"What would you have us tell them?" Lan asked.

Davad sighed. "I wish I knew." Slapping Lan on the side of his arm, he said, "Keep an eye on them for me. I need to find Triton."

"Will do."

Swiney was shoving supplies back into the packs when Davad finally came back. Shashara had her hands on her hips and the toe of her right foot was tapping furiously.

"Cuts and bruises, girl," Swiney said, "nothing to strain my abilities over."

"Some of these men have cracked bones and open gashes."

"We wrapped the bones and cleaned and cauterized the wounds." Swiney grinned. "That ignis ability of yours sure comes in handy."

"They are still in pain," she insisted.

"Better them in pain than me dead," the mortalis stated. "Healing that many would put me down."

"Come on, Shashara," Davad took her hand, "it's time we found a place to crash."

"I can't leave them!"

"Yes, you can. They're fighting men, sis, and their wounds are superficial. Right now, I'm more worried about you."

She glared at Swiney. "Fine, but I don't like it."

Swiney nodded gratefully to Davad. "I'll finish up here and see you back on the boat."

"I wonder where Montilis put Set." Shashara wondered aloud.

"Let's go find out."

Triton stood at the base of the gangplank, laid out at the end of the chute, blocking a furious Montilis. He shoved a blanket into Set's hands and pointed further down the docks. Set stumbled as he made his way down the squeaking boarded path. Spreading the blanket, he lowered himself onto it, rolled it around him, and passed out.

"I want to see that my daughter is settled," Montilis gritted out between clenched teeth. The corners of his jaw were pulsating.

"You'll have to take my word for it," Triton grinned, his eyes were as hard as the onyx they resembled.

"Why is Set sleeping on the dock?" Shashara asked, coming to stand beside Montilis, with Davad on her other side.

"He refused to come on deck," Triton told her without taking his eyes off the general.

"Anliac and Tristan?" Davad inquired.

"Anliac and Shorlynn are using the upper cabin and Tristan crashed in the forecastle."

"Sounds good." Davad looked between the two men. "What seems to be the issue?"

"He's not coming on my ship."

"What is your problem with me?" Montilis asked.

"You're a traitor."

Montilis swung his fist and then cursed when his knuckles cracked against an invisible wall of air. A fulgo with the reddest hair he'd ever seen sashayed down the gangplank. Nudging Triton aside as if he wasn't three times her size, she squared off with Montilis.

"Sorry about the hand," she said, "but, if you would have hit him" her head tilted to one side, "then he would have hit you," her head tilted the other way, "and where would that have gotten us?" She smiled at Shashara. "It's good to see you again, Shash."

Shashara grinned her reply.

"Can we get back on point," Montilis growled.

Triton stepped forward. "You mean the fact that you tried to hit me or that fact that you're a traitorous cur who abandoned your men because both are reason for me to slit your throat."

Montilis's aggression was equal to Triton's own. "She's my daughter."

"There is no one life worth the lives of many. Your actions prove that you cannot be trusted to act in the best interest of the whole and that makes you a liability. If the five of them choose to keep you around, there's not much I can do about it as long as you stand on the soil they've claimed," Triton stated, "but make no mistake, my ship rests on the oceanus. Step foot on her deck and you're mine."

Davad ran his thumb across his forehead, rubbing at his temple before he dropped his hand. "You are both leaders of men, and yet, you bicker like children."

His statement drew two sets of stares as Skylar snickered. She shrugged. "He has a point."

Squeezing Montilis's arm, Shashara offered, "I'll sleep in the upper cabin with Anliac tonight. If there's a problem, I'll come and find you. You have my word."

"Fine. I'll be with my men."

"Which is where you should have been in the first place," Triton goaded.

Montilis's shoulders stiffened at the insult. He stopped, looked over his shoulder at Triton, and then walked away.

Triton's broad shoulders shook. "He looked peeved."

"Enough, Triton," Davad said. "Save it for tomorrow. Sleep well, Shash."

Shashara's brow arched. "Only the redhead gets to call me that," she said, slipping past Triton to loop her arm through Skylar's as they walked up the gangplank onto the deck.

"Where are you going?" Triton asked when Davad turned away.

"I'll be with Set."

"There's room in the forecastle."

Davad sniffed. "Better that I don't leave a man behind, right? Wouldn't want you marking me as traitor and slitting my throat in my sleep."

"Davad..."

Davad waved him off. "Tomorrow, captain."

XV

Who's Running This Place?

An ice-cold splash of water woke Davad with a start. Bolting upright, squinting against the glare of the suns reflected off the surface of the oceanus, he searched the dock for Set. His absence was explained by the string of curses coming from the water. Lurching onto his belly, Davad leaned over the edge and reached for a floundering Set, all the while laughing until tears blurred his vision. Dragging Set up on the dock, Davad rolled to his back and laughed some more.

Set, rattled from his rude awaking, laughed with him. "I kid you not...the oceanus will be the death of me yet."

A shadow fell over them.

"What happened?" Tristan asked, his eyes sparkling with humor.

"Your brother decided to go for a swim." Davad stretched up his hand and had Tristan pull him to his feet.

Set stood as well, and then shivered as a passing aquis wielder glanced his way and pulled the water from his clothes. As the liquid drained through the cracks in the dock's boards, he said, "Thanks," to the man who'd never stopped walking.

"Everyone is waiting," Tristan said. "You did a good job last night. Let's hope you do as well today."

"Why me, and who's everyone?" Davad asked. His eyes widened. "Tell me Montilis isn't on the ship."

"He's not." Tristan told them. "Some of the nox spent the night cleaning out a few of the domed houses. Triton, Razoran, Montilis, Lan, Anliac, and Shashara, they're all waiting." He grinned at Davad. "Last night, you made yourself our spokesmen. We think you should keep the job."

"Well, I don't," Davad squawked.

"Too bad," Tristan chuckled. "The angeli have spoken."

"The angeli can bite me."

Set and Tristan laughed. Davad paled.

As they made their way over, Set asked, "What are they waiting on us for?"

"So, we can tell them what to do," Tristan smirked.

"Who put us in charge?" Davad grumbled.

"Apollo, I think," Tristan replied.

A nox guard stood before the front door of the domed angeli building, squinting against the suns' glare. "Everyone is inside, sir," he said to Davad.

Tristan and Set grinned as Davad missed a step.

"Thank you," Davad replied to the guard as he glared at his friends. "You guys did this to me," he said as he opened the door.

Inside, Montilis and Triton were standing as far apart as space would allow in the empty, spacious sitting room. Shashara and Anliac were in the center of the room wearing matching scowls of irritation. Razoran leaned against the wall with his arms crossed over his chest, shaking his head.

"Thank Superi," Shashara gushed, throwing her hands in the air. "They're driving me nuts." The floor trembled, stone chips dropped from the ceiling. Shashara whirled around. "Anliac, seriously, knock it off."

"I will when they do," Anliac said.

"This is ridiculous." Davad took a seat on the floor. With his back to the wall, he bent his knees and draped his forearms over the top of them. "Here is what we're going to do. Triton, the dock is a wreck. It won't be long before word spreads and ships start coming in. Repairs and expansion to the dock, along with repairs to the buildings running beside it, will need to be made."

"Agreed," Triton nodded. "I've already started making plans."

Montilis snickered. "The captain's interest lies in the lining of his pockets."

"As it should," Set said. "We're going to need the coin, and so far, his holds have supplied us with everything we've used."

"The docks belong to Pisces Stragulum," Davad interjected, "but I agree, recompense is necessary. What do you say, Triton? You take all the coin until the cost to you has been met, and then we split the profit made from there on out?"

"We can discuss percentages later," Triton nodded, "but it sounds fair."

"Good," Davad said. "Unless there's something else you need, why don't you get started?"

"I'll need supplies."

"I'll add it to the list of things we don't have," Davad sighed.

Triton opened the door to leave as Shorlynn entered, dipping into a small curtsy, which Triton ignored. "Well, then," she blew a stray wisp of hair from her check, "that wasn't rude at all."

"He doesn't like you," Razoran said as he left to catch up to his captain.

"What is it you need, Shorlynn?" Anliac asked.

"I'm a little surprised that I wasn't included in this meeting," she said. "I am the fulgo representative."

Anliac opened her mouth but Tristan cut her off. "She's right. Please forgive the oversight. We're all learning here."

Shorlynn's smile was sickeningly sweet. "And for that, I'll remind you that IA's coin is at your disposal. You only get one first impression and with the emissaries and ambassadors that will soon begin arriving, you need better accommodations and something more to feed them than mystery soup and dry biscuits. Oh," she focused on Shashara, "and there is a fera burning up with a fever this morning. He's asking for you."

Davad came to his feet, brushing off the seat of his pants. "Lan, make a list of supplies and see that Shorlynn gets it. Shorlynn, select a few runners from IA and send them to your uncle." He paused. "Thank you."

She nodded.

"I know nothing about trying to organize armies or running cities," Shashara said, "but I do know that injuries are going to keep happening, and with this many people in one place, sicknesses are bound to follow. I'm going to see if one of the buildings can be used for an infirmary."

"That's a good idea," Tristan said. "Shorlynn, go with her and, Lan, make sure tinctures and bandages are on the list."

Shashara cupped Set's cheek. "You scared me yesterday. So, do me a favor and take it easy today."

He pulled her hand from his cheek and kissed her fingertips. "I'm not sick. My mind just needed to reset after the influx of information from Calstar, but I'll do my best not to visit your infirmary for any other reason than to see you."

Uncomfortable throat clearing, and snickers of humor had Set blushing and Shashara smirking. "They're just jealous," she said as she and Shorlynn made their exit.

" We need to call a gathering," Davad said as soon as the door closed. "The Superians need to know why we're all here, what they will face if they stay, and what their responsibilities will be."

"True," Set agreed, "but there are other matters we must address first."

"Such as?" Tristan asked.

"Such as how we are to feed ourselves," Set began. "We need to find those who can hunt and fish. The weather is favorable right now, but the rains will come, and so will the cold. We will need housing. Shashara has the right idea about an infirmary, but an ignis wielder can only do so much. She'll need more help than Swiney alone can give."

"The town won't hold if we can't defend it," Davad interjected. "We need to divide the men into who will work, who will guard, and who will fight."

"They can neither defend nor protect, if they're starving or sick from the elements," Set argued. He spread his glance between Anliac and Tristan. "Where do we start?"

"Why are you asking us?" Tristan rolled his head over the back of his shoulders. "Everything that's been mentioned needs attention."

Davad expression skewed, "Because the two of you are the angeli. Like it or not, it's your call."

Lan's pacing along the interior wall came to a stop. "The burden of leadership can be heavy if the weight of it is carried alone. We are here," he gestured to Montilis who stood with his hands folded behind his back, "to aid the angeli. Use us."

"Father?"

"I will give my opinion if asked, Anliac," Montilis said. "I will do whatever you require, but in this I cannot lead. Commonsense will often carry you through times of indecision. What does your gut tell you?"

"Davad," she began, "since your primary concern is toward the defense of the town, you will use my father's council and see to it. Set, the town itself is now your responsibility." She turned to Lan. "You will help him."

"It is a good beginning," Montilis agreed.

"Spread the word among the men that at midday a gathering will be held," Davad stated. "By then, we should have the details worked out."

Lan cleared his throat. "I would offer caution."

"In what regard?" Tristan asked.

"There is a reason for rank. Tell a man too much, and he will either break under the strain, or turn the knowledge to his own gain."

"We can't leave them ignorant," Davad objected. "The threat from the gods is real, and we are the first line of defense against them."

Tristan grew stoic. "The gateway was reopened because of secrets that were kept. Davad is right. We have to tell them. The choice has to be their own. Anliac?"

"I have my concerns," she said, "but if we are to give Davad control of the town's defenses, then I say the choice is his, and it will be our responsibility to stand behind it."

110

Set chuckled, a sneer flaring his nostrils and curling his upper lip. "The animosity running rampant in this town is a greater threat than what the gods pose at the moment. Even those we turn to for council would rip each other apart if not for our presence here."

Montilis locked his jaw and held Set's stare.

"Are you suggesting we shouldn't tell them?" Davad asked, his breath stolen by the cold blue eyes that turned his way.

"I'm saying it doesn't matter. If they break, we don't need them, and if they turn, I'll feel no guilt when I add their knowledge and abilities to my own."

Silence descended as Set's declaration fell upon stunned ears.

Anliac's eyes flared, chasing the shadows from the dimly lit room as she left without speaking.

Tristan shoved his finger into Set's chest. "You and I are going to have a talk, little brother," he said before following Anliac from the building.

Set rubbed at his chest. It hadn't hurt, but if Tristan knew his true strength, he would keep his hands to himself.

Montilis came forward to stand before the epoto. "Lead through fear, and your back will be perpetually vulnerable to the ones who follow you. Earn their respect, and they will guard your back with their lives."

Lan shook his head. "I'm disappointed. I've come to think better of you five."

Davad nailed Set with a hard stare. "I need a moment alone with our epoto. I have no reason to leave the conversation for later," he snarled. "You and I are going to have a chat right now."

"We'll leave you to it," Montilis said as he and Lan made a quick escape from the mounting tension.

"I've said all I need to," Set stated.

"Who are you," Davad asked, "and what have you done with my friend?"

Set's hard expression never changed. "He's in here, Davad, but so are the others. There is a cost to my ability...and it is myself."

Davad stormed forward. Putting his face inches from Set's he snarled, "Poor you."

"I would suggest you back off."

"And I would suggest you either stop taking abilities or learn to calm yourself," Davad growled. "I don't care how many personalities you have bouncing around in that thick skull of yours. You don't scare me, Set." He shouldered his way passed. "You need to think about what you're doing."

"Where are you going?" Set asked.

"I have a latrine to dig," he replied without turning around.

XVI
Scary Fun

Tristan's long stride made short work of Anliac's head start. "Hey," he said, falling into step beside her, "are you okay?"

Without looking over, she shook her finger at him. "Do not try and defend him, Tristan."

He caught her by the arm, forcing her to stop, and turned her towards him. Her eyes flashed and he grinned. Tucking her calico-colored hair behind her ear, he said, "There is seldom a defense for the things we do when we let the power we possess go to our heads. You should know a little about that by now."

The skin between her eyes furrowed. "What is that supposed to mean?"

Sliding his hands down the outsides of her arms, he laced their fingers together. "You know about the scars Set carries because of me, because of an outburst of anger I couldn't control, and it wasn't long ago that you called me a monster for decapitating a guard in a tower."

She arched her brow. "I seriously doubt you hurt your little brother on purpose," she said, "and what happened in the tower was done to save me and your sister. It's hardly the same thing. The idea of taking more power excited Set." She looked away. "I could feel his heart racing."

"Was it excitement? Or was it fear?" he asked. "Are you an empath now?"

She yanked her hands free. "He's dangerous, Tristan."

"So are you," he replied. He winced as she flinched but continued. "You leveled a city because you wanted a change of clothes."

"That's not fair."

"You threatened to kill half of your father's men when they refused to follow your orders." He took a deep breath, knowing this needed to be said. "You tried to kill Davad, and when I stopped you, you turned your aquis blade on me."

"I had been tortured," she whispered. "I have no control."

He pulled her back against his chest and wrapped her up in his arms. "I know," he shifted to see her face, "but there are things about his ability that we don't understand. You have me to help you learn control. Who is there to help him?"

She held up her arms and stared at the dim yellow light pulsating through the thin sinuous lines tracing up and down her skin. "I have all this energy." She bit down on her bottom lip as she struggled to find her words. "It's like an itch under my skin that drives me insane. Do you feel it too?"

He grinned. "All the time." He looked over her towards a wooden house being torn down, which was a good thing considering it looked ready to crumble on its own. "Come on. I have an idea."

"Where are we going?"

"To expend some of that energy," he said.

The workers paused in their labor at their approach.

"You guys mind if we lend a hand?" Tristan asked.

They kept their eyes averted and went back to work, but at a slower pace than before, distracted by the two angeli.

"Where do we start?" Anliac asked Tristan, irked by the men's rejection but determined to keep her anger in check.

Tristan reached overhead for a loose, low hanging board and ripped it free. "First," he said, "we get rid of the pieces not really attached to anything." He tossed the wood through the front door where it landed in a pile the men had started. "And then the fun starts."

She cocked her head.

His grin was contagious. "We tear the boards off the main studs, and if we're lucky, they'll be stubborn because then we get to tear down the walls and rip the boards apart one by one."

She went up on her toes and latched onto a support beam.

"Whoa!" Tristan laughed. "Not that one!"

It was too late. She tugged, and the ceiling began to fold. The workers ran, covering their heads, spewing curses.

Tristan tossed Anliac over his shoulder and blurred through the doorway. Setting her on her feet, they stood together and watched as the house came down.

Wide-eyed, she said, "That wasn't supposed to happen, was it?"

Tristan shrugged. "No one was hurt, so no big deal." He walked up to the house and dragged a one foot by one-foot support beam from the rubble. "It is our fera blood that makes us so strong. I can't help but wonder though, who is stronger, you or me?"

Intrigued by the challenge, she smiled. "Can you lift it?"

Bracing his feet, he grabbed hold, leaned back, and the beam protruded out like an arm. Seeing her intent, he said, "Strike at the center."

Her fist smashed into the thick wood and it snapped in half. Her arm shot straight up into the air as she shouted, "Yes!" She turned glowing eyes on Tristan. "That felt good!"

"My turn," Tristan said and returned to the rumble to find another piece to play with.

***

Set was alone, really alone, and not just the last one in the domed house they'd used for the meeting. Sitting on the floor with his back against the wall, he thought about what he'd said. He'd meant it, but he hated it, and the internal war being waged in his mind was tearing him apart.

He needed to talk. He needed someone to listen. Leaving the house, he skirted the ancient angeli buildings and bypassed three wooden ones before hearing Shashara's voice coming from a small stone building on the perimeter of the old marketplace.

Taking the four stone steps leading up to the building, he leaned against the doorframe and stared at the beautiful girl who, unbelievably, belonged to him.

Propping her weight on the handle of her broom, she blotted the sweat on her upper lip with the back of her hand as she asked a fulgo coming from the upper floor, "Are all the walls washed down?"

"Yes, ma'am," the fulgo replied.

"And the windows?"

113

"They're going to need to be replaced."

"Crap. Well," she breathed deep and exhaled in a rush, "Let's see if we can find some oiled skin or waxed cloth to put over the openings for now."

"The ship owner might have some we can use," the fulgo replied. "I'll go see."

"His name is Triton," Set volunteered, drawing their attention.

"Thanks," the fulgo said as Set entered and the fulgo exited.

Setting the broom handle against the wall, Shashara dusted her hands on the sides of her skirt and smoothed back the damp tendrils of hair sticking to her face. "How did the meeting go after I left?"

Set shrugged. "Can we talk?"

Something in his tone made her heart catch. His skin, a little on the pale side, was ashen. The whites of his eyes were streaked with red lines, and they were puffy as if he'd been crying. "Are you okay?"

"Physically, I'm fine," he tried to assure her, "but…"

Crossing the floor, she looped her arm through one of his and led them through the door. She sighed as a salty breeze cooled her heated flesh. "The weather is changing. It will be cold soon, but for now, it's nice."

"I hadn't noticed."

"Walk with me," she said, "down by the coast. We can watch the seabirds."

Set took her hand.

She could feel his trembling but held her peace until they were at the end of the docks. Soon they were sitting with their bare feet dangling over the side and minnows nibbling on their toes. "Okay, talk," she said.

"I don't want to scare you," he admitted, "or make you hate me."

"You used to tug my pig tails," she grinned, "and put frogs in my bed. I swore I hated you, but I got over it."

"This isn't exactly the same thing," he smiled, despite his current mood.

"Try me," she said. Folding one leg while leaving the other dangling, she turned sideways to face him.

He focused on the oceanus to avoid looking at her. "When we were leaving Exterius Antro, there was a fera guard. Jacob told me to take care of him, and I did. I wanted him to sleep and so he slept. Later, on the ship, Socmoon told me I severed his body from his mind. I killed him."

"I see." She placed her hand on the top of his leg. "That wasn't your intent, Set. You're an epoto without training. It doesn't make it right, but neither can you blame yourself."

"I wasn't trying to drain anything from him."

"I know."

"In the tower," he paused, "the night your father died, the guard at the desk had an ability. He had a level one agility. When I attacked him, he was trying to use it, and I was focused on killing him and finding a way out."

Shashara's tone was harder. "He deserved death. They all did."

He closed his eyes and shook his head. "I took his ability. The marks appeared on my lower back, but more than that, I took his knowledge of the tower and of the city. Now it's a map in my mind that's always there."

"Set, I don't understand," she said. "This is all old news. What's really bothering you?"

"Just hear me out, okay?"

She nodded. "Okay."

"At the northern gate, there were two men. One had a strength ability. I drained him, but he died by the dagger I put in his neck, and so the strength was temporary, but the one with speed...I drained him. I watched the life leave his eyes, and now I carry his marks from thighs to calves. I wasn't interested in his knowledge, and so, I was spared that part of him."

"Spared? That's an odd choice of words." She held up her hands when his eyes squinted, and his expression pinched. "I'm sorry. I'll be quiet."

"The gate maker," Set started again, "I needed his ability. So, I took it," he traced the smooth skin at his temple knowing the markings where there, "but in my anger, I forgot to take the knowledge of how to use it. When Traydon refused to help...I was focused only on his gate making ability, and on making him suffer, now I have the knowledge of his ability...and I left him with a broken mind."

Shashara opened her mouth to tell him that these were desperate circumstances, but before she could, he spoke again.

"Calstar is in my head."

"You mean his knowledge is in your head?"

"No," he clenched his fists. "His knowledge of Earth, and of the gods; of Nathon Bealson, and of the journals... of Malstar and his experiments, of the sect of people determined to recreate the one race...Shashara, I needed his knowledge, and so I took it."

"But you didn't kill him," she pointed out. "That has to mean you're learning control of it."

"You don't understand," he gritted from between clenched teeth. "I don't feel guilt over the deaths I've caused. I feel no regret for any pain they suffered. I'm terrified..."

"Why?"

"Because!" he shouted. "I can't tell where I end and Calstar begins." He pinned her with his cold stare. "Experiences and memories make us who we are. They change us. Calstar's life is as real to me as my own. I've lived his life, which is longer and more twisted than mine." He chuckled. "I'm just a speck in the midst of his psyche." He turned away. "I'm losing myself."

"Look at me." She cupped his far cheek in her palm and tugged gently. "Look at me," she said with more insistence. "I know who you are. I won't let you lose yourself. I promise."

"Oh yeah? What's my favorite color?"

His question surprised her. "Blue," she said, "like my eyes. You have always said that."

He pulled her hand from his cheek and laced his fingers through her own. "That's funny."

She cocked her head, the skin between her eyes bunching. "How so?"

"Set's favorite color is blue, but mine, I prefer the color yellow. It detracts from the pasty white of my skin."

She smacked his shoulder with her free hand and chuckled. "What are you talking about? You are the same tanned color as me and Davad. Tristan is the pale one." Her smile slipped when Set's countenance fell. "Pale like a fulgo...like Calstar?"

He nodded. "I keep losing my balance when I walk, and I find myself wondering why I can't reach things." He squeezed her hand. "And Renna, when did she get so tall?"

"Who's Renna?"

"Renna is Shorlynn's middle name," Set said. "I called her that to separate myself from my brother Malstar, who used to be her favorite uncle, until I started spoiling her." He smiled. "I even arranged an engagement for her with Maltris Langworth. It's a good match for her. She will never want for anything."

"You mean Calstar did?"

"What? Oh..." Set said as he realized that he'd been speaking from Calstar's memories instead of his own.

"I think I'm starting to understand," she whispered. Taking control of herself, she took a deep breath, squared her shoulders, and said, "Whatever is going on with you, we will figure it out together. I don't care how many people live in your head. I'll be here to remind you of who you are."

"Promise?" he asked as his tears fell.

"You belong to me," she said. "So yeah, I promise."

"Your animus is the purest of anyone's I've ever seen." He raised her hand to his lips and kissed the back of it. "You're my true north moon, Shashara. Without you, I'm lost."

Boot steps coming down the dock had Set clearing his throat and wiping his eyes.

"Sorry to interrupt," Triton said, "but we've been summoned."

"The gathering," Set groaned as he and Shashara slipped on their shoes. "I'd forgotten about it."

Together, they made their way to the southern side of the marketplace where two wooden pavilions miraculously still stood. Davad and Lan stood under the cover of one, deep in conversation as the men congregated, eating a quick midday meal and talking amongst themselves as they waited.

Set approached Davad with an outstretched hand. "I'm sorry about before."

Davad clasped Set's forearm and pulled him close, embracing him briefly before letting him go. "We all have bad days."

"Yeah," Set said. "So, what are we doing?"

"Waiting for Tristan and Anliac." Davad looked away from Shashara's searching gaze. "We have a problem."

"What is it?" Shashara asked.

Lan answered. "Apparently, our angeli had a little extra energy to burn off after the meeting. They...uhh...they decided to lend a hand in tearing down some of the wooden buildings, only, they were having a bit too much fun."

Shashara and Set looked at Davad for clarification.

"They were ripping the house apart with their bare hands." He shrugged. "By itself, that's no big thing, but..."

"But?" Set urged.

"They were breaking support beams one by one across each other's arms; then they decided to see how many pieces of wood they could break in one hit," Lan told them. "According to the men, they ran out of wood before they figured out how many they could shatter at once."

"Hmm," Shashara grunted. "Let me guess, they were glowing."

"Not as brightly as back in Imbellis," Lan said, "but enough to frighten the men."

"Just great, huh," Davad grouched, "now they're afraid of the very people meant to bring us together."

"Where's Montilis?" Shashara asked. "Maybe we can get him to talk to them about showing a little self-control."

Triton chuckled.

"You have something to add, Triton?" Davad asked.

"They were having fun. I say let them be. And as for the general," he sneered, "he has his own problems." He pointed towards the back of the crowd where Montilis stood arguing with two men. "Looks like he's received a summons home."

Their heads turned as the men fell silent and an isle appeared in their midst as Anliac and

Tristan made their way to the pavilion. Their raised spirits dampened as their eyes fell on Set.

"We still need to have that chat, brother," Tristan said, "but for now...are we good?"

"Considering when this is over, I'll be taking my lecture after you take yours," he grinned at the confused look on Tristan's face, "yeah, we're good."

"What's he talking about?" Anliac scowled.

"Later," Davad said, his breathing accelerating as he realized what he was about to do. "Right now, I have a speech to give." He opened his mouth to call everyone's attention but turned to Anliac instead. "I'm going to need you to point out a few of the men who don't want to be here."

Set cleared his throat and spoke under his breath. "It might be easier to pick out the ones who do."

"Very helpful," Davad muttered. "Thanks."

"There," Anliac pointed, "the one by the cast-iron cooking pot. His heart is fluttering like a hummingbird's wings."

"That's because you're pointing and staring at him," Set chuckled.

"Oh..."

Tristan tugged her against his side and whispered into her ear. "Don't worry, beautiful. You make my heartbeat faster too."

She nudged him in the ribs. "Do you ever get used it?" she asked.

"To being the freak and scaring everyone away?"

"Yeah," she said.

"No," he answered, "but after a while, the rejection stings less."

"The nox standing to Montilis's right has hate dripping off of him," Set revealed. "If you need an example, I'd start with him."

"Okay," Davad said, turning to the crowd and raising his voice. "If I could have everyone's attention. Some of you came with us from Imbellis, others have since been called in by your respective leaders, but only a handful of you know why. Though we have been cautioned against telling you the truth, the angeli, and those closest to them, set ourselves to a different standard than what you are accustomed to. Lies and deceit breed more of the same, and there is no place for it here."

Murmurs of approval rippled through the men.

"So here is the truth," Davad began. "Superi is in danger, not from internal strife amongst the different races, but from the old stories that have been reopened. History tells of ancient angeli, of Superians, who went to war with the gods of Earth. The history is true, and now, it is repeating itself."

Chortles of disbelief swept through the crowd, but Davad was not discouraged. He wouldn't have believed him either if he hadn't seen so much with his own eyes.

"A few days ago, our angeli," he gestured toward Anliac and Tristan, "battled a god by the name of Apollo."

Their chortles stopped.

"They were able to send him back through a gateway, but he vowed to return, and when he does...he will not be alone."

"They're about to bolt," Set warned. "You'd better do something."

"I understand the instinct to run," he said, "but trust me when I tell you there is nowhere to hide. You," he pointed to the nox beside Montilis, "your hatred of the angeli runs deep, but they are all that stand between the gods and you."

"Who opened the gateway and let him in?" the nox shouted.

Anliac stepped to the edge of the pavilion's floor. "It was not us," she said. "The gate was opened from the other side. Nor did we ask to be made into what we are. The fight was brought to us. When the gods invade Superi, and they will, our choice will be to fight...and perhaps die, or to die the slow death of slavery. We will not surrender. We will fight. The question is, will you fight by our side or die when the gods find you."

"You're not helping," Davad snapped.

Tristan took her hand and pulled her back. "Easy, gorgeous. He's right."

Shaking off Anliac's interruption, Davad started again, though his nerves made his words seem rushed. "When the last war with the gods took place, we were all angeli. The first curse cast upon us stole that advantage. Our hope now lies in reuniting Superi. To do that, we must set aside our differences, those of region, those of race, and all the prejudices that go with them. There is a planet full of powerful beings that want us destroyed. I choose to stand with my fellow Superians. I choose to face the gods on my terms. I choose to support the angeli. Now you must make the choice for yourself."

Conversation sprang up as the men turned to their own kind to discuss what they'd been told. One voice rose louder than the others.

"How are the angeli different than the gods? Why should we die for them?"

"They are not asking you to die for them," Set stated. "They are saying they are willing to die for you. Battles will come. War will rage, and Pisces Stragulum is where it will begin."

"What do we have to do?" another asked.

"For now," Davad said, "we continue as we've begun. We need workers, soldiers, cooks, healers, fishermen, builders, all the things a town needs to function. The angeli will harbor no ill will towards those who wish to leave, but for those who stay, get used to change. For we will introduce a lot of it. New leaders will be assigned, and the units will be a conglomeration of the races. Segregation will not be tolerated here. You will learn to live and work together, or you will leave. Some ranks of station will continue, some will be dissolved, and some new ranks will be set up."

A fulgo, with a touch of silver at the temples of his shoulder length black hair, stepped to the front of the crowd. His nervous eyes darted behind Davad to Anliac and Tristan. "I mean no offense, but you are a quarter my age. Even the angeli have yet to see the turning of their second decade. By what right do you stand before us? We've felt the heat of battle. We've been to war. We've seen bloodshed and felt the loss of our comrades. You lack experience, and yet bark orders like a general."

Shouts of agreements resounded.

"We don't even know your names," a fera snarled.

"Then let me introduce you to those you will follow. I am Davad. This," he gestured for Shashara to step up, "is my sister, Shashara. We carry the mark of a level two ignis, but that is not our strength. Perhaps you've heard of our father, Jacob Davadson."

The name brought whispers.

"He trained us as he trained these two," Davad said, gesturing to Set on his right and Tristan on his left. "This is Set. He is an epoto, a level three, and the abilities he's obtained have strengthened him, both mentally and physically. His brother, Tristan, was changed as an infant into the first angeli. He's had a lifetime to learn his power, to learn to control it, and to learn to unleash it. Their parents helped our father raise us all until their death. Perhaps you will know their names as well. Matthew Suxson and Beth Mathews."

Silence washed over the crowd at the drop of the names.

"Shall I continue?" Davad asked and then spoke without waiting for an answer. "Anliac, daughter of General Montilis Aquam, has been raised in the art of warfare and stratagem since she was lifted from her cradle. Both she and Tristan have suffered at the hands of IA, their blood altered, so that they could stand before you now and say..."

Tristan's voice boomed with authority. "You speak of battle, of bloodshed and loss, we carry the same scars. You speak of our right to stand before you." His muscles tensed; golden pulsating marks glowed up and down his arms and on the sides of his neck. "The pain we've suffered to be made into your leaders gives us the right. You speak of our youth, and yet it is the ignorance of age that has divided our planet." He relaxed and the light faded with the lines.

"Our path has been chosen," Davad said. "You have until the end of the day to place your feet upon it, or choose another, but know this…If you stay, you will take your orders from the five of us. We will work beside you. We will fight for you, and if it comes to it, we will die for you, but in return…you will follow orders. If you have questions, ask them now."

Silence.

"Seriously?" Set asked when no one spoke. "We've just told you that gods from another planet want to kill us and that you will follow those who've yet to see the turning of a second decade into war—and you've nothing to ask?"

One nox raised his hand.

"There we go," Davad mumbled under his breath, recognizing the man from the night before when he'd faced off with the fera and a different nox beside the fire. "What is your question?"

"Did you three get the latrine finished?" he asked. "If not, I may soil my pants."

There was a moment of silence, and then the whole congregation burst into laughter.

"All right," Davad said, "get something to eat, and then report to your current leader for new assignments."

"Nice job," Set grinned. "Even the nox dripping hate loves you a little. It looks like you won most of them over."

"I can't believe you just gave a speech," Shashara said with rounded eyes and an ear-to-ear grin.

"Let's hope I got through to them," Davad said. "We can't afford to lose many, and thank you, sis. Could you tell I was nervous? It felt like my heart was going to burst out of my chest."

"You think?" Anliac smiled. "I could barely hear your words over the sound of it." Chuckling, she added, "I thought you had swallowed a hummingbird for a while there."

Short of breath, Davad shook out his hands as if that would rid him of the nerves as they all laughed. "It was such a rush," he said.

"Are you hungry?" Tristan asked Anliac.

"Starving," she smiled.

"Good," he grinned back. "See, guys, it's an angeli thing. I'm not so weird after all."

"Just because it's an angeli thing doesn't make it less weird, bro," Set teased.

Triton chortled.

"He does smile," Lan piped in.

Triton's smile disappeared. "Nonsense. Smiling is for softies." He turned to the dock. "Everyone knows I'm stone cold."

The others laughed.

Before Anliac and Tristan could walk off, Davad asked. "Hey, do you two think you could lend a hand down by the dock? The other guys can finish tearing down the old buildings, but Triton could use the help."

"You good with that?" Tristan asked Anliac.

"Sure," she replied, "as long as you feed me first."

"Anliac," Set said, "you should check in with your dad. It looks like he wants to talk to you."

"Will do," she said as she and Tristan took the stairs leading from the pavilion.

"I need to get back to the infirmary," Shashara told him. "You okay?"

"Yeah," Set said. "Thank you for being there."

"Always," she smiled. "What are you going to do?"

"Mingle," he replied. "We need to know how the people are feeling, and I'm the empath."

"Read them," her brow arched, "but don't take."

"Yes, ma'am." His grin was forced, and his eyes were sad, but he hugged her and prodded her with a smack on her backside to get her moving.

"How did I do?" Davad asked Lan as they left the market place to walk the city. "I've never been so nervous in my whole freaking life. I mean... talk about intense. Wow! I guess that's how Triton must feel when he's worried about his men mutinying, right? Was I talking too fast? I felt like I was talking too fast?"

"Breathe, Davad," Lan chuckled, "before you pass out. You did well."

"I did awesome!" He fisted the air, right hook...left hook... "I knocked them out with my amazing speech skills." He lowered his voice, dropping into a low base that mimicked Tristan's when he was all angeli mode. "I am the voice of the angeli."

Lan smacked the back of his head.

"Ow!" Davad laughed. "Too much?"

"You think?" Lan mocked.

"What are those?" Davad pointed to a half dozen, huge vertical circles standing with no apparent purpose in a large open area of field between the southern side of the marketplace and the farmland further down.

"No idea," Lan admitted. "We don't think the wooden buildings and homes are going to be salvageable."

"What about the stone dwellings, especially the larger ones?" Davad asked. "Those vines covering them over are tough, but we're going to need those buildings if we're going to house everyone before the chill sets in."

"The men are pulling the vines down now," Lan stated. "We won't know the extent of the damage until it's done."

Davad came to a stop before a tall, white stoned building with an arched door, and beautiful stained glass in its windows. "They did good work," he said.

"Who?"

"The Superians who built that," he pointed to the building. "It's too bad we have to rip down all the vines. They add an ancient beauty that we can't replicate. The green makes the white stone stand out in comparison. Don't you think?"

Lan shook his head. "I think they're weeds."

Davad chortled. "You're no fun."

A nox soldier came up at a trot. "Sir..."

"Yeah," Lan and Davad said in unison.

"Not you, sir," his mouth twisted as his eyes darted from Lan to Davad. "We've received word from General Aquam that supplies from Palus Regia will be arriving within a few days. The men thought it best to secure a place for it before it gets here. Any suggestions?"

"Walk with us," Davad said. "There are some storage buildings out by the farmland. Let's go see if they are salvageable."

"You want me walk with you, sir?"

Davad slapped him on his back and started them forward. "It's a brand-new world, soldier."

"Yes, sir," the nox replied.

After spending the afternoon looking over the two storage buildings and talking it over with a mortalis who'd been a carpenter before enlisting as a guard for IA, Davad gave them their orders.

"We'll reinforce their walls as best we can and lay some fresh tar over their roofs to repair the leaks as you suggested," he said. "We'll use one for storage. The other we'll fill with bunks for some of the men. Let's see what we can do about repairing those horse stalls while we're at it."

"It wouldn't hurt to plant a late crop," Lan suggested. "We'll lose most of it if the frost falls early, but whatever we glean will be more than we have now."

"Agreed," Davad said. "Although I'm pretty sure this stuff was assigned to Set. I need to find Montilis. He and I have a lot to discuss, especially if he's being called back to Palus Regia."

"Are you sure that's why the two nox are here?" Lan asked.

"No, but if I find Anliac, I can find out."

"I'll stay here," Lan volunteered, "and give the men a hand."

"Thanks, Lan," Davad said. "I'm not sure how we would have done without your council."

XVII

Racism

He was stopped dozens of times between the farmland and dock. People asked him questions that commonsense should have given them the answers too. He was ready to pull his hair out by the time he found Triton barking orders from on deck. He climbed the gangplank to join him.

"Hey, boss," Triton grinned.

"Ugh," Davad groaned. "That's not funny. My brain hurts."

"Not as bad as it's going to," he chortled.

"Why?"

Razoran's head popped through the hatch before the mainmast. "Davad," he climbed through, "we need to talk."

"What?" Davad whined.

"You have to keep Anliac in town, or the crew says they're going on deck and not coming off again."

Davad scanned the buildings lining the dock. "It doesn't look like they destroyed anything here."

"No," Razoran glared, "but every time that girl gets riled, those eyes of hers light up, every time she gets excited too, and every time her yellow-eyed counterpart looks her way…"

"I get it," Davad grumbled.

"Good," Razoran nodded. "I'm glad we understand each other."

A bell tolled.

"What in tarnation is that?" Davad asked, searching the perimeter of the town for signs of attack.

"Dinner," Triton stated. "The crew and I will be dining in tonight."

"If my evening proves as trying as my day," Davad said, "I'll join you."

"I encourage it." Triton's obsidian eyes narrowed. "You and I have a conversation to finish."

Davad cocked his head, his brows furrowing, and then nodded when he recalled what Triton was talking about. "Yeah, I guess we do." His steps were slow as he found the dock and then the path that led from the dock to the marketplace. He made it to the giant gazebo that served as a station for the cooks.

The men's hunger gave way to their uncertainty of Anliac as she stepped onto the gazebo, and asked, "Can I help?"

The two cooks averted their eyes. "We've got it under control, but thanks," one of them said.

Davad stood back to see how she would respond. In retrospect, perhaps he should have acted instead.

The fera cook scooped into the cast iron pot and lifted a ladle full of stew. It stopped, hovering over a nox soldier's empty bowl. "You've been through the line once already," the cook grouched, dropping the stew back into the pot.

"You gave me a bowl full of juice, you stupid beast, without a piece of meat to float in it."

"Beast, huh," the fera snarled. "That insult is as old and used up as your darkling mother."

The nox threw down his bowl and, grabbing the fera by the front of his shirt, dragged him across the cast iron pot, overturning it. "At least I came from a single birth and not a cursed litter."

The nox ducked as Travus, the second cook, took the ladle to the side of the nox's head.

"Enough!" Anliac shouted, the high-pitch ring to her voice causing the gazebo to empty out in a hurry, leaving only those involved to face her wrath. Anger had her fully angeli as she raged at the two fera cooks. "You will not use the word darkling in my presence."

"Sure," Travus shouted, beyond caring if the angeli squished him, "take his side. I guess once a nox always a nox despite the pretty speech we heard this morning."

"We didn't start this!" the first cook growled. "He did by calling me a beast."

"Well then, stop acting like one," Anliac snarled back.

"You first," he challenged.

The ground quaked to match Anliac's trembling. Heads spun towards the coast as shouts of alarm sounded. Waves rolled and crashed, slamming the ship into the dock and sending the crew into a riotous frenzy as they searched for the one responsible.

"Did you call me a beast?" Her marks pulsed. Her eyes, like brilliant suns, blinded them.

No one saw from where Tristan came, but they were thankful for his appearance when he grabbed Anliac by the shoulders and spun her to face him. "Knock it off!" he roared.

"I can't!" she bellowed back at him. She glared at her marks as if they were attacking her. "Set!"

"I'm here," he came at a run from the back of the crowd, leaving Shashara, with her hand covering her mouth, at the base of the steps to the gazebo.

"Help me," Anliac cried. "It hurts."

Set reached out his arm.

Tristan caught it. "Careful, little brother."

"Let me go, Tristan," he said. "I've got this." He laid a single finger against Anliac's temple. Her eyes slid closed and her muscles went lax.

Tristan caught her, scooped her up in his arms, and turned on Set. "What did you do?"

"Nothing," Set assured him. "She's just sleeping."

The crowd stared in fear and awe at the power possessed by the three before them. The crew, having converged with the others, waited to see what would happen next.

"What happened?" Tristan demanded.

Travus's voice was far from steady. "The...the nox... called me a beast."

"The fera called me darkling," the nox defended.

Montilis walked up. "Give her to me," he said, "and deal with this."

Reluctantly, Tristan did so. Facing the men, he released his hold on his abilities and let them rush forth. His muscles gorged themselves with blood, doubling his size. His eyes shot out beams of yellow that mirrored what Anliac's had done. The golden marks slithering over his skin produced a halo of light around him. His voice, deeper and more thunderous than it had ever been, washed over the men until they feared the sound alone would end them.

"Words," he shouted, his angeli voice booming with vibrating power. "Racial slurs that have been wielded more often than any sword or weapon formed by man or given by nature. Words! That have caused more wars and death than any cause worth dying for. It is pathetic! You," he pointed to the nox, "you think him a beast?" He pointed to the offended fera. "If so, call me a beast, for fera blood courses through my veins." He yanked off his leather gloves and held his narrowed claws up for all to see. "You think me a darkling, fera?" he turned on Travus, shoving his wavy black hair behind his double-pointed ears. "Call me a darkling. I dare you." He focused on the crowd. "Look at my skin. Behold my glowing yellow eyes and call me a lighten. I was born mortalis. Perhaps tiny is a more fitting title? Stupid...igno-rant...words."

"Perhaps you should tell that to your girlfriend," someone shouted from the back.

Tristan blurred so fast that the people caught in his tailwind stumbled backward. His image solidified directly in front of the one who'd spoken. His hand went around the fulgo's throat. "Careful," he said, so quietly that the warning had greater impact than his rage. He let the man go and pivoted in a circle to look out at those gathered.

"There is an entire planet of gods waiting for the opportunity to rip our heads off," he said, "and you people want to fight each other over insults that should carry no weight. How many times must I say it? The racism stops here, now, and that goes for everyone. And for the record," he added as his marks faded and his voice returned to normal, "I'm more disappointed in Anliac than I am in the likes of you all."

Silence fell as his words ceased.

Davad rested a hand on Tristan's back. "Go see to our girl," he said. "I'll finish up here."

Tristan's head nodded. His shoulders slumped. Walking away, he looked more defeated than Davad had ever seen him.

"Tristan is right," he said. "You're grown men for Superi's sake. Stop the petty fighting and remember why you're here." Exhausted, he said, "Refill this pot and bring out others. There is enough to go around, and if not, we'll make more. No one is going hungry. At least not yet."

A string of yes sirs was heard as the men went back to their business.

Set and Shashara, along with Lan and Davad, walked to where Triton stood with arms folded and fury written outright on his face.

"You need to handle Anliac." Triton barked.

"How bad is the damage to your ship?" Davad asked.

"Less than the damage to the dock," Triton said. "Be glad the water didn't rise high enough to damage the buildings."

"Add what you need to repair your ship to the list," Set told him.

"Shorlynn left right after talking to Lan this morning," Triton scowled, "so I guess we have to hope she brings back what I need from Imbellis."

Davad winced. "Curse it all."

"Indeed," Triton said, spinning on his heels as he and his men headed back to the ship.

"We have to do something," Shashara said, "or Anliac's actions are going to cost us everything."

Lan opened his mouth as to speak, but then closed it and shook his head.

Davad sighed. "Let's go find them."

"No offense," Lan said, "but I think I'll sit this one out."

"We'll see you later then," Set said.

It wasn't difficult to find out where Montilis took her. She was sitting on a pile of blankets in the sitting room of the large, angeli dwelling where their day had begun. Her father was crouched beside her, scowling, as Tristan gave her a piece of his mind causing sobs and a torrent of tears.

"You should have known better. Anliac, what were you thinking?" Tristan snapped.

Set and Shashara slid inside as Davad entered after and shut the door.

"You are not nox!" Tristan roared.

"I know!" she shouted back. "I'm ssss…I'm sorry."

"So am I," Tristan said. "How are we supposed to teach them that prejudice is ignorance when you are as guilty of it as they are?"

Montilis came to his feet. "Take it easy."

Tristan's eyes flared. "Get out."

"Excuse me?"

"She's not under your protection, general," Tristan stated. "She's under ours. We are her family now. Go home. Deal with Rayner. Do your job and let us help her."

"By scolding her?" Montilis shouted. "How does that help her?"

"By helping her gain control," Tristan replied.

The veins in Montilis's temples throbbed. Returning to Anliac's side, he asked, "What do you want me to do?"

"I made a horrible mistake," she said. "The men were already afraid of me. Now they will hate me. I'm losing control. I lost control." She breathed deep as she fought back a fresh wave of tears. "We will need the nox race to stand with us if we are to succeed. You are the be…" she hiccupped, "best chance we have of obtaining it. Ho…hopefully, when you return, I will be the leader you raised me to be," she sobbed. "The disappointment on Tristan's face is bad enough. Seeing yours is more than I can take."

Montilis stood, rigid, unable to look at her. "You fought your first battle trying to enter the world. The healers said you would not survive, but you were born with clenched fists and a fighter's will. You bear the scars of battle on your flesh and wear the mantle of leadership upon your shoulders. I could not be prouder." He cleared his throat. "I'll return."

Anliac flinched when the door slammed shut behind him.

The silence in the room was thick enough to taste.

Pensively, Davad began. "I'm going to suggest something that you're not going to like, Anliac, but at this point it needs to be said."

She bit down on her bottom lip, nodding her head, and braced for another admonishment.

"I'm no expert," he said, "but it's safe to say that your angeli ability is tied to your emotions." He nodded toward Tristan. "His are. The difference is he's had time to learn how to control it. You haven't. There are no gods for you to rage against, which means your allies are the ones in danger. I think you need to leave."

Tristan's growl vibrated in their chests.

Davad rolled his eyes. "You need to calm yourself. Seriously, I've taken about all the aggression I'm going to today. I'm not saying she needs to leave permanently, and I'm not suggesting she leave alone. I'm suggesting the two of you take a little vacation. She has to learn control, Tristan, and you're the only one who can teach her. You are strong. You're fast, but she," he pointed to Anliac, who ducked her head, "is deadly."

"He's right," Shashara crossed the floor, knelt on her knees, and scooped up Anliac's hand into her own. "Between your aquis ability this close to the oceanus, your terra ability that you can't control, and all the rest of it that comes with being an angeli…You're a liability we can't afford, and we need you to get control of it because we can't fight what's coming through that gateway without you."

"How can we leave?" Tristan asked, throwing his hands into the air. "The town is in shambles. We've been here less than a day. Triton would slit Montilis's throat if given the chance, and the men are ready to kill each other. And now this with Anliac…Hmm," he grumbled. "If we leave now…"

"There might be a town left standing to rebuild," Set interjected. "You and Anliac have only one responsibility, and that is to face the gods. Triton will ready the docks. I will see to the needs of the people who are here to aid us, and Davad will see to our defenses."

"I'll make sure to keep them on task," Shashara said with a half-hearted grin. "You two are going to have to trust us to do our part in this."

"What do you think?" Tristan asked Anliac as he reached down and pulled her to her feet.

"You know what I think."

Tristan nodded. "Then it's settled. Set, I need you to still be my brother when I return."

Set tugged Shashara backward until she rested against his chest.

"I've got the epoto," Shashara grinned. "You rein in our angeli."

Davad chuckled, "And I'll do everything else."

XVIII
Control

With packs of supplies on their shoulders, Anliac and Tristan left Pisces Stragulum before the suns had a chance to rise. By the light of the moons, they traveled north, hugging the coastline, and headed into the region of Dura Mortis with every intention of avoiding the fera city.

"It's beautiful up here," Tristan said as he stopped to inhale the salty breeze coming in off the oceanus and grinned as it blew his hair away from his face in an invigorating rush. "Almost as beautiful as you."

Anliac had continued walking. He caught up to her, and she said, "I can understand the feras' desire to live here." Her lips, curved in a heavy frown, quivered.

Off to the right, Tristan pointed to the sparse forest of evergreen trees, where the grass had turned from green to yellow with the changing of the seasons. "The woods aren't thick, but the hunting would be good. Or not..." he said, when Anliac, shoulders slumped and head down, angled left towards the coast.

Tristan tried again to snap her out of her dark mood. "Davad still hasn't stopped talking about your amazing fishing skills," he said. "You could show me?"

Anliac stopped. Her hands covered her face as her slender shoulders shook with the silent tears cascading down her pale cheeks. She flinched when his arms came around her from behind. Turning in his embrace, she tucked herself against him, and sobbed.

"Don't cry," he said, sliding his hands up and down her back. "Everything's going to be okay." When she only cried harder, he cupped her cheeks and tilted her head, so she had to look at him. "Anliac, talk to me."

"They hate me," she whispered.

"Aww." He pulled her to his chest. "No one hates you. They fear you. There is a difference."

"Not in the result," she said, laying her head against his shoulder. "They sent me away." Her voice broke and she turned from him.

He caught her hand and brought it to his mouth where he kissed the back of her fingers. "They sent us out here to gain control, and I promise you, Anliac, they all want us to come back."

"They don't know what they're asking," she said.

"What do you mean?"

"We don't even know what happens to us when our angeli abilities take over," she said. "How can you learn to control something you don't understand? Look at you. You've been this way your whole life, and still, you cannot fully control when the glowing marks appear."

Tristan's lips pulled to one side as his brows furrowed. "We need a name for it," he said.

"For what?" she asked.

"For the change, I like saying, going Super Superian." He shrugged as his head wobbled on his shoulders. "It's kind of catchy."

Anliac snickered. "It sounds ridiculous," but she found herself smiling anyway.

"Okay," he chuckled. "What about transcending? We are changing from who we are to what the power makes us."

"It fits." Poking her finger into his chest, she teased. "It's much better than saying we're going Super Superian." Her smile slipped. "I don't feel super anything when I transcend."

"Well," his smile stretched the corners of his mouth until the edges threatened to reach his double-pointed ears, "you look superhot when you do. You're like a radiating yellow sun."

"A yellow sun?" Her right brow arched as she gave him a crooked grin. "That just sounds weird," she said, wiping away her tears with the heel of her palms. "Suns are red."

He leaned in and kissed her forehead. "Feel better?"

"Not really." Her stomach growled. "Food might help."

His stomach rumbled. "I'd say my gut agrees. Are we going fishing?"

Walking out on the white sand, she pulled her boots and stockings off one at a time and hopped towards the water. "Just remember," she said, "if I catch them, you have to clean them."

Tristan, boots off, rolled his pant legs up to his knees and waded in. He followed behind her as she moved slowly up the coast peering into the grey water."

"What are you looking for?" he asked. When she suddenly stopped, he walked right into her. He wrapped his arms around her waist to keep her from pitching forward.

She leaned back against him, and with a flick of her wrist, deposited a fat solea fish onto the shore.

"Nice," he said, "but watch this." He kissed her cheek. Walking out ahead of her, he slammed his open palms against the surface of the water. Four, unconscious, scaled bellies popped up. "Eh?" he grinned. "Pretty good, right?"

Shoulders stiff, and fighting a smile, she said, "I'm not cleaning them," as she walked past him and out of the oceanus.

His laughter carried for miles.

While Tristan moved further up the shoreline to gut their catch, she found firewood. The aged wood had been soaked through with salt water and baked beneath their two suns. He returned with the fish skewered on a long stick about twice the circumference of his thumb and scowled at the unlit mound of driftwood.

"You have my pack," she said. "Can you get out the flint and stone?"

"Yeah, sure." He dropped the packs off his shoulders and knelt down. "Jeez, how many packs does one woman need?"

"Three apparently," Anliac snipped, dusting her hands off as she stood. "I'm going to wash up. Sand, salty though it may be, does not go well with fresh solea. Look in this one." She nudged the smallest of the packs with her toes and walked off.

"I don't see a flint."

"Then use a blade," she replied.

Leaning over to scoop up sand with which to scrub her hands clean, she plunged them into the water, her eyes on Tristan. She winced as he held the stone in his hand, and in a furious motion, scraped the blade against it. The sparks landed on his flesh and he threw the stone. On his knees, pouting and sucking a tender spot on the outside of hand, she'd never found him more adorable. That didn't stop her from laughing at him.

Walking back over, she said, "Don't tell me you don't know how to start a fire?"

"Hey, don't judge." He plopped onto his butt. "I grew up with two ignis wielders."

Picking up the blade, she reached for the flint. "Well, it's past time that you learn. Come here." As he moved to her side, she demonstrated. "Okay, first you put the blade into the tinder, and then," she struck the flat side of the blade with the rock. "Aim the sparks down into the tinder." She handed the two items over. "Your turn."

His first attempt got them nowhere. "Man, this is rough on the ego," he said as he tried again.

"Get used to it," Anliac teased. "There are going to be a lot of things I'm better at than you."

The blade slipped from his hand. "Oh really?" he laughed, repositioning the blade. "We'll see about that." The third try was golden. Tendrils of smoke heralded his victory.

Together, they leaned forward on their hands and knees and blew against it, grinning at each other as blue flames flickered to life.

He was so close. She could count his sooty eyelashes and see the deeper colors of orange and brown that made his eyes so golden. She stopped breathing as a dim burn entered those piercing orbs. Before she could stop herself, she leaned forward and brushed a kissed against his cheek. Blushing, she snatched the stick, stuck upright in the ground to keep the fish from the sand, and handed it to him.

Holding their catch over the flames, his arm propped on his knee, he said, "You know, your skill with water is flawless. I'm willing to wager your terra ability will come as naturally. All we really need to do is teach you how to handle the transcending."

"I wish I felt as confident as you," she said with a twist of her lips. "Terra wielding is nothing like aquis wielding."

"Jacob wasn't an ignis wielder, but as a telepath, he helped Davad and Shashara with the basics. I used to watch them practice. I figure," he said, turning the fish over, "if Jacob could do it, I should be able to help you too."

"Did you ever consider he might have stolen the information from someone's mind, and that's how he knew how to help them?" Anliac asked.

"Does it matter?" Tristan countered. "They learned, right? And I've watched you wield. Despite your element being different, you do the same things as Shashara and Davad. You decide on what you want the element to do, and then," he snapped his free hand forward, "you release it." Pulling the stick from the fire, he divided the fish by shoving them towards the two ends. After breaking the stick in the middle, he gave Anliac her part. "You know how to wield, Anliac. We just have to work on your control while transcended."

"I guess, but I have to transcend to use the terra ability."

"So, then it's settled," Tristan said. "We'll spend the rest of the day trying to transcend on command." Without thought, he bit into the skewered fish he held, his brows furrowed.

"If you think any harder, you'll have smoke coming out of your ears," she grinned. "What's on your mind?"

Tristan felt his face heat. Anliac filled him with a hunger food couldn't touch. Her black leggings hugged her like a second skin, and while the double layered, brown, cotton shirt she wore hid everything, he knew what lay beneath it.

She laughed. "Tristan, you're staring."

"This is the first time we've been alone without eyes or chains upon us," he blurted. "It's nice."

"True," she said, tucking her hair behind one ear. "This is the most peace I've felt since leaving Palus Regia on the run. Perhaps we belong in the wilds." Her smile slipped. "At least, I do."

There was a moment of pause, and then he threw back his head and laughed.

Her eyes flared.

"You shake the ground and cause a few waves and you think you've gone feral," he said. "Wait until you've ripped a man's head from his shoulders, or shredded your enemy's body with your bare hands, and then we can talk."

Fear flashed across her face. "I don't want that to happen."

"And that's why we're here, beautiful, to make sure that if it does happen, it's to our enemies and not our allies."

Anliac tossed the stick, the last fish still dangling to the end, out towards the oceanus. Unable to sit with all the emotions rampaging through her, she stood and began to pace. "I don't want it to happen it all."

Tristan dusted off the seat of his pants as he stood. Cutting off her pacing, he captured the sides of her neck in his hands. "The transcending happens when we are overcome with emotion. So, let's start there. What emotions drive us?" When she didn't respond, he said, "Fear, anger, self-preservation, come on, Anliac, what else?"

She turned her head away from him and folded her arms beneath her breasts. "I don't see the point in this."

Placing his hands on either side of her waist, he tried again. "What about excitement, desire, need?"

"I suppose so." Her mouth went dry as something in his eyes made her tremble. "Emotions are not my friends." Unfolding her arms, she placed her palms on his chest to push him away, but he leaned in. She felt the tip of his tongue at the corner of her mouth and gasped. When he spoke, his breath was warm against her skin.

"Do you think I'm immune to my emotions, Anliac?"

"You seem to be," she was breathless, "most of the time."

"You have no idea how hard I have to try to control myself around you," he admitted. "I could face a thousand gods and stay in control, but one moment alone with you and..." he held up his shaking hands. "I'm waiting for you, but it's the hardest thing I've ever done."

Her words were whispered. "Waiting for what?"

"For you." He closed the distance between them.

His muscles played beneath her palms. Her breathing was labored and stopped altogether when he leaned in to kiss her. His lips were soft. She could feel his restraint when she deepened the kiss and was overwhelmed with feminine power when her action made him groan. Except then, the tables turned. She opened her eyes, and Tristan was bathed in a yellow light, light that emanated from her own.

"Oh no," she said, staring down at her arms where her angeli marks pulsed in quick chaotic spurts.

Tristan's pride was tangible as was his inflated ego. "You're not ready, but not to worry, beautiful, I can wait." He started to move away.

She caught him by the scruff of his shirt. "I thought we were going to spend the day trying to transcend on command?" Grinning, she added, "Maybe we should start with trying to stop the transcending," and then she kissed him again.

In the days that followed, Anliac would recall that first day on the beach and remind herself why she couldn't kill him. Tristan was worse than her father when it came to barking orders and it was getting under her skin. The irritation in his voice sparked her own.

He threw his hands into the air. "You're not doing it right. Your marks are flickering on and off like a dying star."

Drenched in sweat, Anliac glared. "It's not like I'm not trying, Tristan. It's just a little hard to hold onto my happy place with your growling."

"Ugh," he pulled at his hair. "The only time you can hold the transcending is when you're mad. You can't stay mad all the time."

"As long as you keep talking to me like I'm a child, trust me, I'll have no issues holding onto my mad. I swear, Tristan, if you don't stop it, I'm going to rip your head off."

"Learn to control your emotions like an adult, and maybe I'll talk to you like one."

Her blood ran cold. "What did you just say to me?"

"Oh, you heard me loud and clear," Tristan retorted. "There are other things we could be learning about our abilities, but no, instead I've spent days watching you throw tantrums!" His face was red; his golden marks pulsed with a dim glow that mimicked his frustration. "At least a few days ago, you could hold the transcendence. Now….now you keep…flashing!" He threw his hands over his head again. "I'm running out of ideas here, beautiful."

Anliac held herself rigid against Tristan's onslaught as her angeli marks solidified and she breathed through the rush of power.

"See, you can do it when you try," he said. "What are you thinking about now?"

"I'll show you, child."

"Ahh, crap," was all he had time to say before Anliac blurred. She reappeared right next to him, swinging a fast right cross that had him stepping back to avoid taking the hit to his face. He countered by shoving with both hands against her shoulders, sending her into a controlled back flip.

She landed twenty feet away on the balls of her feet. Flipping her hair out of her face, she glared.

"Glare all you want," he said, "but this isn't helping. You have to control the transcendence without anger. Curse it all, Anliac. Is ticked off the only emotion you know?"

Anliac turned her head towards the snow-covered hills they'd seen from the coast. The lake where they'd made camp was surrounded by open grassland and seemed like a painting—serene and still, with sparse patches of evergreen trees that added a sharp, crisp scent.

"Should I add pouting to anger?" he asked. "You seem to have it down too."

Her head snapped around as her eyes narrowed. "You should run."

"Is that a threat, my little angeli?" His chest swelled as he stood taller. The pulsing of his marks stopped, but the glow remained. "You can't hurt me, but if you're in a mood to run, let's see just how fast you are."

Tristan blurred out of focus as she did the same and the chase was on. The hills became their arena. Their speed cut trenches into the white fluffy powder until Tristan launched himself into a tree forty feet off the ground, jerking Anliac to a stop.

"Bad idea," she stated, as she pointed her open palms at the base of the tree, and the terra sucked inward at her command.

"Whoa!" Tristan shouted, floating in midair as the limb he'd been standing on left him hanging. When gravity returned, he bounced off the first branch he came to, carving a path in the snow when he landed as he took off again.

Fully transcended at a bright glow, she gave chase as Tristan's course carried them closer to the hills. The snow atop them shook with the piercing energy her voice emitted as she called out, "You're making this too easy, Tristan!"

"Hardly," he said from behind her, smacking her playfully on the bottom.

Whirling around, she struck first with her elbow and missed. She struck with her right fist. He caught it, so her left fist flew faster and harder. He caught that one as well. Infuriated, her pupils dilated to the point that most of her yellow irises were hidden. She threw back her head…and wailed.

Like blades being driven into his brain, or standing too close to an angry dracon, the pain of her scream dropped him to his knees. He didn't see it in time.

With a flick of her wrist, a boulder flew. Her fury fled as fear took over, yet she could not recall her action. She saw his eyes widen just as the rock slammed against his side. The skin at his temple split where a jagged edge had struck and bright red blood ran in rivulets down his cheek as he shook his head and then tumbled sideways unconscious.

Anliac lost it. The geography of Dura Mortis was changed as the hills quaked and then fractured, forming valleys where none were before. The courses of small rivers were altered, and the snow on one peak tumbled into a massive ball that leveled the trees in its path. Drained of strength, her power abandoned her as she collapsed in tears at his side.

"What have I done?" She cupped the side of his face as she caressed his bloodied flesh with the side of her thumb.

His eyes flickered open.

"Tristan! You're okay?"

He grunted as he pushed himself upright, leaning on the hip and arm that hadn't been slammed with a boulder, and said, "Now, you know."

She sat back, wrapping her hands around her knees as she pulled them against her chest. "Know what?"

"Just how bad it can get when we allow anger to blind us or fear to rule us." With effort, he raised his bruised arm and with his fingertips, lifted her chin until she was forced to look at him. "Stop worrying, Anliac," he teased. "You throw like Set, slow and underhanded."

"I thought I'd killed you," she scowled. "Why didn't you move?"

"Honestly? I was…distracted, but I'm not sorry I got slammed. The only way to teach you to control your abilities is to show you the consequences of their misuse. No matter how many enemies we slay, if we're not in control, it's those standing with us that are in the most danger. It will be those we love who are hurt by it."

Her visage softened. "You're referring to your brother."

Tristan nodded, "and Jacob. The day he died; it was me that inflicted his first wound. I weakened him. I left him vulnerable to the arrow that pierced his heart."

"Tristan…" she reached for his hand.

"Every day, I am forced to look at Davad and Shashara and know that it was my loss of control that took their father from them. I would spare you from having to conquer the emotion that comes with that kind of guilt because there's no getting over it. There is only the hope of surviving it."

She shivered.

"You're cold," he said. "It will be night soon, and we'll freeze if we stay here." He came to his feet, swaying until he found his balance.

She rose slower, exhausted from the energy she'd expended. "You're hurt," she said. "You should rest."

"I need to clean up," he grinned. "There are plenty of new rivers for me to choose from."

"That's not funny," she said, but giggled.

"You should head back to camp," he suggested. "I won't be long."

"Actually," she winced, "that mud hut I made is too small, and it's so damp I wake up feeling wrinkled. I'd like to find something else. There's bound to be cave or something we can use."

"Alright, but I would suggest you use your terra ability to find it," he grinned. "You'll have more luck than just using your eyes, beautiful as they are."

"Uh huh," she shook her head.

He chuckled. "I'll grab our packs on my way back up here."

She crossed her arms and cocked her head to the side. "How are you even standing?"

His eyes flashed. "I thought you would have understood by now. You have elemental abilities that I don't have," he said, "but I have one that you don't. A little food, a little rest, and by the time the suns rise tomorrow you will never have known it happened. Haven't you ever wondered why I don't have scars?"

Her arms dropped as realization struck. "Because you heal."

He nodded his head with a smile, turned his back, and walked away.

"How fast are we talking?" her curiosity peaked.

"Fast enough, I suppose." He called over his shoulder.

"Wait!" she called out. "How do I use my terra ability without transcending completely?" She heard him laugh. "Great," she said. "Very helpful."

As the realization of Tristan's ability sank in, she paced back and forth and then began thinking of her own.

Focusing hard, she closed her eyes, and tried to feel the terra beneath her feet.

Nothing happens.

"Come on!" she growled beneath her breath, stomping her foot.

Her marks began to glow, a slight illumination beneath her skin that had her closing her eyes again. She took a deep breath, and let it out slow, demanding her heart rate to steady.

It was then that it happened. Beneath her feet, she could feel huge, irregular shaped slabs of rock, made up of shifting grains with stone mixed in. The grains varied in density between that of dirt and that of clay. The stone, most without value, held within it precious gems and pockets of metals, such as iron and silver.

Like a curtain pulled back from a window, her terra ability revealed a world that her eyes alone could not fathom. It was both breathtaking and scary. She sensed areas with voids, some connecting with the surface. She walked cautiously to the closest one.

When she opened her eyes, she was standing before the mouth of a cave; its height was enough to allow her to walk in upright. She did not make it far before a menacing growl stopped her in her tracks. A she-wolf, white fur raised, and black lips pulled back over sharp pointed teeth, advanced. Her angeli marks went dark as fear pooled in her gut. Instinct had her calling on her aquis ability. A water whip, made from the snow, appeared in her hand. With a sharp snap directed behind the wolf, the animal yipped and fled the cave. Her legs went to jelly, and she sank to the hard stone ground.

On shaky limbs, she forced herself to emerge from the cave and began gathering the firewood they would need to stay warm through the night. Using the dagger at her waist and the flint in her pocket, she started a small fire. A breeze caused her to tremble and her nose to wrinkle. Lifting her hand, she stared at Tristan's blood and grimaced at the scent of sweat that clung to her grime-caked clothes.

"I might be part fera," she said aloud, "but that is no excuse for smelling like one." She felt her conscience twinge. Though no one was around to hear the racial insult, she knew it was wrong and vowed to do better. She had no issues with the fera. In fact, so far, they had proven to be their greatest allies.

She left the cave in search of a hot spring, keeping careful watch on the golden marks to assure herself they were not pulsating. After making sure neither Tristan, nor the she-wolf, had returned, she disrobed, teeth chattering, and slid into the spring's welcoming heat with a sigh.

Soap would have been lovely, but sand from around the spring did the job of scrubbing clean her skin. She rinsed her once black, and now streaked with color, hair as best she could. Though darker than Tristan, she would never get used to the pale body she now controlled. Long limbed and slender, she was grateful for the curves that had remained after her transformation.

More than the water's heat warmed her flesh as she thought of the one, she'd be spending the night with. So far, each night had proven the same—with her unable to control the transcending that came with his close proximity, but perhaps tonight would be different. Without Tristan harping in her ear, she'd managed to control the transcending enough to find the cave and the spring without destroying anything; and at night, Tristan never harped.

Though Set, Davad, and Shashara were still young, she and Tristan were of age. What the two of them did in the hills was of no one else's concern. A sound, a mix between a growl and a moan, had her fearing the she wolf had returned. It had not.

Tristan stood, his back laden with their packs, a string of fish dangling from one hand, staring. His thick, corded muscles strained to be released from his hold. Light flared from his eyes, pinning her in the water as he transcended into an angeli. The wavering lines exposed on his flesh pulsed with his heartbeat.

Naked and vulnerable, Anliac felt empowered. "How's that control working for you," she grinned.

He swallowed hard. "I'm hungry," he replied. The fish in hand long forgotten.

Her eyes widened. "The fire! Shoot. I left it burning." She scrambled from the spring and snatched up her clothes.

He dug the fingers of his free hand into a tree standing to his left. "Superi help me," he said, sounding strangled. When he released the tree to pinch the bridge of his nose, he left the imprint of his grasp behind.

She froze with one leg in her pants and one leg out. "It's nothing you haven't seen before," she reminded him as she continued dressing, but it was different, and she knew it. When she was finished, she said, "Okay, let's go."

He caught her on her way by and kissed her hard. She was breathless and weakened when he released her lips from his own. "You are my greatest weakness, Ms. Aquam."

She took his hand. "Then I will also be your greatest strength. Now feed me. I'm starving."

The walk back to the cave was not a long one, and soon the fish were ready. Tristan, still not used to her appetite, laughed at the amount of food it took to satisfy her.

"Leave me alone," she laughed with him. "You are a bottomless pit yourself."

Huddled before the fire with a blanket wrapping their shoulders, Tristan said, "You never talk about your family. I know Inabeth was your stepmom, but what about your birth mother? Or siblings?"

"I had a brother." She smiled though it didn't reach her eyes. "His name was Jagarid. I didn't get to know him, but his drawings and medals of honor are all over the house."

"Why haven't I heard of him before now?"

"He died defending me and my mother," she answered.

"Against what?"

"I was a couple of months old," she said. "It was during one of the last skirmishes, in the last war, the mortalis soldiers had flanked the Regia Aquam Guard, and had forced their way into Palus Regia. I was told that Jagarid, and his closest comrade, saw it happen. They broke rank to tell our father, and then ran home to protect me and our mom."

Her voice quivered, and Tristan didn't need to see the tears to know they were falling.

"Father says that he found Jagarid and my mother slain, back-to-back, with two dozen dead enemy soldiers, and me, crying in my crib."

"That's true love, Anliac." He's voice was as unsteady as her own.

"I know." She smiled through her tears. "He was thirty-seven years older than me, a level two aquis wielder like our mom," she told him, "conceived right after she and my father had wedded. They say Jagarid was the spitting image of father, but then father always tells me that I'm a mirror image of mom." She shrugged her shoulders, "Or at least I was until the transformation."

"What was her name?" Tristan asked.

"Clois Aquam," Anliac replied. "She was only forty-eight when she died. People still talk about the rare marking of the aquis element she bore on her forearm instead of her shoulder."

"Hmm," the corners of her mouth turned up in a soft smile. "Father says they tried for another child, but it wasn't until they'd given up that I surprised them. They used to tell me that I was the best accident they had ever had. Enough," she said, drying her eyes on the edge of the blanket. "What about you? You were adamant with the Alphas that you don't care to learn about your birth parents. Why?"

"Family is not about blood," he said. "It's about love, loyalty, and trust. My parents were amazing." He nudged her shoulder with his own. "You would have loved my mom. She was feisty and beautiful like you. She led Jacob and my dad around by the nose and they adored her for it."

"I wish I could have met her."

They sat for a time in silence as memories swept them away. A huge yawn from Tristan broke the moment. Rising, he took her hand and pulled her to her feet. "It's really cold tonight. Perhaps we should share our blanket rolls for heat."

"That sounds reasonable," she said, blushing scarlet to the roots of her hair. "I've heard people say that flesh on flesh warms faster than with clothes in between."

"I'm willing to try it if you are," he said, with a voice like rough gravel.

In darkness, they entered the cave. Once inside, their angeli abilities gave all the light they needed to find their way. When at last their energy was exhausted, they succumbed to restful slumber, knowing a peace they'd never felt before.

XIX
Anger Management

In the days that followed, they fell into an easy routine. They took turns doing the hunting, and although she still refused to clean the animals caught, they shared in all the other chores. Their nights they spent learning about each other and talking about the future; the one that would come after the gods of Earth had been handled. Their days, while exhausting, were proving very productive.

"Okay," Tristan nodded with a jut of his chin, "I think it's safe to say you can lift the medium-sized rocks, and no doubt, you are a master at dropping them." He knelt between chunks of shattered rock, chest heaving for breath as he grinned up at her.

Anliac, dripping sweat, stood in the center of what she called her stone island; the crater that had formed as she'd pulled up stones of all sizes. She tossed her hands into the air. "Are you kidding me? That last one flew at least ten feet before it dropped."

"A whole ten feet, huh?" he teased. "I didn't know you preferred close combat."

Just as her temper flared, he grinned.

Spotting the perfect stone in her peripheral, she lifted it, slowly.

Tristan watched it rise. "What's on your mind there, angeli?"

"I finally found a stone big enough to match the size of your smart mouth," she grinned. "Then again, there's no way I can miss a target that size."

Tristan laughed. Then his eyes widened as the stone was tossed. Throwing himself onto his back, he covered his head and rolled. His eyes were golden hot when he came to his feet. "And here I thought we were having a good day. What is your issue?"

"I've been trying it your way," she said, "but it doesn't matter how well I do. You always expect more."

He rolled his neck across the back of his shoulders and forced his eyes to cool. "I'm not trying to hurt your feelings."

"You're not," Anliac snapped. "You're making me mad."

"You're not mad yet," he challenged. "Do you want to know how I know?" Walking forward, he swiped a fist-sized stone from the ground and held it up for her to see. "When you're mad, you can rip apart hills. I've spent all day catching these." He held up the rock.

"Excuse me?" Her voice rose as fast as the brows crawling up her forehead.

"All I've said, is that if you don't push yourself, you're not going to advance. That's not rude. It's just stating facts." He tossed the stone to the side. "Once I said it, we started getting somewhere. Look at the size of that stone." He gestured to the boulder she'd tried to flatten him with, and the mound of smaller stones crushed beneath it, and shook his head. "But it doesn't count, Anliac, because you weren't in control."

Anger gone, mostly because he had a point and she knew it, she said, "You should have seen the look on your face." Her lips twitched as she fought through the urge to grin.

"You...uh...moved pretty fast there." She lifted a jagged boulder that doubled Tristan for size.

Watching her wrist for any sudden movements, he said, "Yeah well, I noticed you throw faster when you're riled. Anliac," he swallowed hard, "that thing is bigger than me."

"Tristan..."

"What?"

She smiled, her angeli marks glowing with a steady even pulse. "I'm not mad."

The bolder came at him fast and it wasn't going to miss. Tristan ignited his angeli abilities and dove out of its path. He fell into a forward roll that carried him to his feet right at the edge of her island. Using his legs, he pushed off the terra with all he had. He sprang across the thirty-foot chasm and aimed himself right at her—and left himself wide open. Just as his feet touched the ground, a rock the size of his head nailed him in his chest, and he went airborne again. He landed back where he started. The breath knocked from his lungs.

Anliac launched herself over the chasm landing next to him on her knees. "Hey, you okay?"

Groaning, he pulled her down onto his chest. "That was perfect timing." He leaned up to kiss the tip of her nose before dropping his head back down, "And this time you weren't mad." He chuckled.

She beamed but punched him in the front of his shoulder for good measure. "I thought I told you not to scare me like that," she said as she rolled off him.

"I'll make it up to you later," he grinned, sitting up.

"Promises, promises," she replied, reaching for his hand. "I've decided to end this day on a victory." Grunting at the effort of pulling him to his feet, she said, "You still have clothes to wash this evening, and I...need a bath."

"Fine, but that means you're doing the hunting." He held up his finger, "but no more of those large, rat-looking things. Their meat is stringy."

"And greasy," Anliac agreed. "What do you think they are?"

Tristan grinned. "Hey, as long as what is in Dura Mortis stays in Dura Mortis, I don't care. As long as I don't have to eat it." He looked around at the mess they'd made. "I'm glad you're the one that has to clean this up."

Standing beside him, she smacked his stomach with the back of her hand and then focused. Shattered stones put their pieces together again as the larger ones rolled themselves down the sides of the crater and waited for the rest to join them. The terra trembled as it swallowed up the stones and boulders until every grain of sand had found its place. When she opened her eyes, it was as if nature had never been disturbed.

Tristan shook his head. "I am in awe of your housekeeping."

She turned her head and stuck out her tongue.

He scooped her off her feet, kissed the side of her neck as she settled in his arms, and carried her back to camp. By the times the clothes had been washed and hung to dry, dinner caught, cleaned, and cooked, Tristan failed to keep his promise, but Anliac couldn't complain. They were beyond exhausted and fell asleep as soon as their heads found their makeshift pillows.

Anliac groaned as the suns' light breeched their hideaway. The cave had proven much better than the mud hut by the lake, and as time to return to Pisces Stragulum drew nearer, they'd spent a little less time training, and a little more on the two of them. That wasn't to say Tristan didn't make them work.

Noting his absence, she pulled her clothes inside her blanket roll to warm before she dressed. No doubt, he was out looking for some small furry creature...or four...to feed their never-ending hunger, and then he would turn into her father. Tristan in training mode was a pain her...

"You up?"

She rolled her eyes. "I'm up." Twisting and flopping, she managed to dress without exposing herself to the cold morning air.

"Good," he grinned. "Do you want to start the fire and the coffee or gut the three fat hares I caught for breakfast?"

Crawling out of the covers, she stood upright and stretched until her bones popped. "Do you even have to ask?"

"Do you know how adorable you look?"

Her eyes narrowed. "Why am I suddenly worried?"

Tristan grinned, showing too many teeth. "I have something for you." He blurred out of the cave and returned with his hands behind his back. With a shrug, he said, "I couldn't sleep," and held out a bundle of purple, night-blooming roses.

Smiling, she drew the bundle to her chest and leaned forward to kiss the tip of his nose. "Thank you," she said. "Tell me what it is you did or what you plan to do so that I'll know whether or not to be mad or forgive you."

"Today, we are going to try target practice."

"What is the target?"

"Later," he teased, "after we eat."

Later came all too soon. Tristan, armed with a pack full of apple-sized stones, had spent the day tossing them into the air. He gave her until her arm moved to wield her terra ability and then the race was on. While she yanked rocks from the hills, or ripped terra from the ground, Tristan bounced from boulder to tree, like a wild beast at play, trying to snatch them from the air before she could knock the smaller stones down.

The fact that he succeeded so often was frustrating, but his instruction and stern critiques was enough to drive her mad.

"You're still pulling the wrong-sized stones, Anliac," he said. "What we do uses a lot of energy. You could strike it with a pebble and win the toss. Not to mention that the last one you threw nearly took my head off."

"Hey," she bent her elbows and held her hands up, "this was your idea. Suck it up. You heal."

His eyes flared as they fell to her lips. "Stop trying to distract me," he grinned. "Your smart mouth makes me forget we are here to practice."

"That's the plan," she grinned. "Okay, I'm glad you're having fun, but I'm done with this."

"Fine," he said. "What haven't we tried?"

"Ugh, seriously, Tristan? Every muscle in my body hurts." She plopped onto the ground and braced her forearms over the tops of her knees. "I have moved boulders, tossed boulders, and crushed BOULDERS. I can make the terra wave like a troubled oceanus without knocking down a single tree. I can find my way blindfolded by the feel of the terra around me. I can find more wealth in these hills than we five could ever need. I can open a hole large enough to bury a single man, or I can open a chasm too great to cross. I choose when to transcend, and how much power I infuse myself with. You even made me hover over the ground after we figured out I could, and you know how much that took out of me." She tossed her hands into the air, and falling backward, said, "You've done it. The wild angeli has been tamed." She pulled herself upright. "I want to go back."

"You're not ready."

"Tristan…"

He came at her fast and she responded by rote. A shield of terra, a foot thick and five feet high, rose between them. Tristan slammed into it hard. The shield cracked, falling in two different directions, but he was knocked on his butt. He pounded the side of his fist into the ground. "I'm not ready! Okay? Me!"

"What?"

"I will fight, Anliac," he said, his tone altering from anger to defeat. "Whatever god, however many gods, they send," he jutted his chin and nodded, "I'll stand against them. Ask me to lead men into a battle," he nodded again, "okay, I can do that, but I don't know how to run a town preparing for war. My whole life, people have turned from me, either in fear or in disgust, and now they look to me to save them. I am used to the shadows, Anliac, but now..." With deliberate control, he stretched out his arms, and played with the light flow of his marks, "there is no hiding."

Rolling to her hands and knees, she crawled over to him. "Then we will return to Pisces Stragulum and make it official. We will name you our general. Davad, we will make our magistrate, and Set, we will name our advisor. You can torture, I mean train," she grinned, "all the men and women who have rallied behind us, but I..." she crawled closer, "... am done." She leaned forward and puckered her lips for a kiss.

He gave it with a growl and then, with a sudden grin, agreed. "That sounds like a plan." Jumping to his feet, he dragged her up with him. "I want to go down to the coast on the way back. The oceanus will be a nice change of view."

"That was way too easy, Tristan Matthewson." She planted her hands on her hips. "I'm serious. I'm done with the training."

"Okay," his smile grew. "Let's go get our things."

"What? Now?" Her arms dropped to her sides. "Like, right now?"

He wrapped his arm around the small of her back and pulled her flush against him. "Not quite ready to leave, my little angeli?"

Placing her hands on the outsides of his shoulders, she said, "In the morning will be soon enough."

"How would you like to spend our last evening alone?" He wiggled his eyebrows.

She tossed back her head and laughed. "I was thinking of going treasure hunting."

His face fell. "Really?"

"Yeah," she said. "I have an idea."

They scoured the hills, up and over its peaks, but they hit the sweet spot when Tristan convinced her to enter one of valleys, she had made during one of her tantrums.

"Look!" she said, holding aloft her prize. "It's the same color as Set's eyes."

The gem was dull, but after they had it cut and polished, it would be a beauty. She placed it in the small brown leather bag attached to the wide belt around her waist. The blue gem joined the ruby Tristan had claimed as his color.

"What about for Shashara?" Tristan asked.

She wanted to use some of the stones and some of the metal they'd collected to make personalized gifts for the five of them. They'd all missed birthdays, and they'd prevailed over so many obstacles that they deserved to have something to show for it.

Finding a plain black rock, about the size of her palm, she placed it with Set's and Tristan's stones. "I found mine," she told him, "and I'll get Shashara's from the coast."

"That just leaves Davad then. Hey," he held up a clear stone that had emerald green streaks running through it, "how about this one?"

Anliac smiled. Pushing off with her thighs, she stood from her squatted position. "It's perfect, but too large to carry. Break a piece off for me."

"Can we go back now?" Tristan asked, sliding the fragment of the gem into her bag.

She winced. "Actually, I was thinking of getting a few more stones. We can use them to pay off what we owe Triton. Until we break even, he's going to kill us on his percentage of the trade profit coming in at the docks, and it wouldn't hurt for the town to have a little coin of its own. What do you think?"

"I think that's a great idea," Tristan said. He opened his arms when she walked up.

She opened her arms as if to embrace him, and then laughed as she darted behind him.

"Cute," he snipped, turning to see what she was doing.

Kneeling own, she parted her hands as if opening a book, and terra split just large enough for her to reach the chunks of clear gems she'd wanted. There were two dozen of them, each the size of her fist. Placing them in the larger pack on her back, she stood. "You can hug me now," she said.

He pulled her in, laying his forehead against her own. "How did you know that was there, and does this mean we can go now?"

His hopeful expression made her laugh. "I know all things," she teased, "and I thought we'd stay here for the night."

Centering herself, she reached for more power, transcended further, and the terra responded to her need by raising walls to shelter them. As the terra folded to create a roof over her head, she said, "Isn't it amazing? Think about it, Tristan. This is what all Superians used to feel. The power and control...this sense of completeness." Stepping through the opening she'd left in one side, she told him, "I could almost forgive Malstar for what he did to me."

"Yeah, well," Tristan shuffled his fingers through his hair, "that makes one of us."

The dwelling Anliac had made for them was far nicer than the cave, and when morning came, they were sad to leave it behind. They took their time traveling from the valley to the coast knowing this was likely the last time they would truly be alone until after the gods of Earth had been dealt with.

The breeze wafting in over the grey waters lapping at the coastline was warm compared to the cold wind that had blown down from the hills. The grass and wildflowers were vibrant arrays of color. Like jewels cast out across the shore, small stones decorated oceanus's border, creating a picturesque skyline.

Anliac, so close to her natural element, felt invigorated. She sighed with a lopsided smile.

"You seem happy," Tristan said with a grin of his own.

"I feel at peace with myself for the first time since my transition." Bending, she picked up a stone and skipped it across the water. The waves kept it from going far.

"We spent so much time working with your terra ability and teaching you to control the transcendence that we did little with your aquis ability."

She rolled her eyes. "Tristan, please don't start. There is nothing you can teach me about my aquis ability that I don't already know."

"Anliac, you think I'm pushing you too hard," he said, "but when we face the gods you need to have full control. You need to be able to fight hand to hand, wield your aquis and terra abilities at the same time, and control the transcending so you don't rip Superi in half by mistake."

Her face flushed. "You act as if you have such control, but the truth is, you know as little about what we are as I do. Before we came out here, it was all or nothing with me, but you, you hold back. You do that when the gods appear, and you'll lose the battle for us before we even begin."

"Is that what you think?"

"It's what I know," she replied. "You bark orders at me, but you are the one that needs to heed them. You are bossy and arrogant, and Superi help me, Tristan, I am done with it."

"I'm arrogant?" he huffed. "I know my potential and my limitations. You..." he pointed his finger, "are so busy wielding that you haven't even touched upon your physical abilities. I'm not arrogant. I am confident. I'd rather be that than be like you...scared."

Anliac's golden marks flared to life and the ground between where they stood and the oceanus trembled.

"What?" Tristan taunted. "Have I made you mad? Are you going to actually do something? Or are you going to simply play with your wielding like you did in the hills?"

Not as fast as Tristan, but fast enough, her image blurred. She appeared in front of him and swung a right hook. Her fist flew through the space where he had been.

From eighty feet away, he said, "You're going to need to be faster than that if you intend to land that punch."

She gave chase and he ran up and down the coast and through the trees that lined it. Seeing she wasn't fast enough, she changed tact. "Stop running, you coward, and face me! You're good at telling people what to do, Tristan. Too bad you don't practice what you teach. You should man up or shut up!" She got her desire.

His image solidified two feet in front of her. His angeli marks running wild over his flesh.

Anliac swung her fist with every ounce of strength she had and connected solidly with his jaw.

He laughed at her. "Your elemental abilities are not enough. Without transcending completely, your fists are ineffectual." He cupped his hands and slammed them together. The energy created was like a typhoon.

She flew twenty feet and landed hard, tumbling and rolling to a stop. Dragging herself to her feet, she glared as light shot out of her eyes. "Oh, I know you did not."

"You're mad," he said, "but not mad enough. I know feras that hit harder than you. I thought you were trained by the best. Looks like daddy needs a few pointers on how to get results."

Her steps towards him were slow. Each footfall created a roll in the terra that pushed against the coastline, causing the waves to rise and break over the small seawall to wash under their feet. Her image was a mere shadow enveloped in brilliant light. From within it, her voice was like liquid pain pouring into his brain. "Is this what you wanted? As I am now...I can take you."

"Bring it on, little nox," he replied without fear as he opened himself up, filling himself with the power his blood gave him. "You will learn to control it..."

Expecting a frontal attack, he was surprised when she blurred so much faster than before and disappeared. He closed his eyes and breathed deep to track her scent—and felt his feet leave the ground as a huge rock slammed into his side shoving him towards the seawall.

He grunted. "Still throwing stones, I see. Ugh..." A large slab of terra caught him at the waist, doubling him over, and throwing him closer to the water's edge. He heard the wind of the third object thrown—a boulder large enough to crack his bones. With a roar, he pivoted, bringing round his elbow, the collision between flesh and stone boomed like thunder.

Taking advantage of his distraction, Anliac charged toward him.

Tristan stepped to the side and stuck out his foot.

She flipped head over feet, but landed upright, breathing heavily. The light around her did not dim, but pulled in on itself, revealing an angeli in perfect form. The marks covering her flesh had deepened into a rich gold, and her eyes glimmered like polished gems.

"What is happening to me?" The sound of her voice was pure power, beautiful and terrible. "What have you turned me into?"

He stepped towards her.

"No," she said, raising her palms up as the water from the sodden ground encased his feet. It traveled up his body, trapping his arms at his sides.

Though he was looking right at her, he never saw her move, but he felt the uppercut to his chin. The force of it flipped him backward where he landed on his feet a hundred paces away, only to see Anliac's right hook flying. He caught it in his palm and clamped his fingers around her fist as his feet slid backward, digging into the ground that had caved beneath them.

Her left hook was empowered by rage.

He ducked but was distracted by Anliac's feet hovering above the ground. It did, however, allow him to dodge the knee and the chunk of ground that came up with it. The downside was he'd lost his grip on her hand.

Rearing back her arm, she slung it forward and a whip of aquis reached for him.

He blurred into position behind her. "You don't really want to hurt me, Anliac."

Spinning, she dropped to the ground, opened her mouth, and screamed.

The wail dropped him to his knees. Blood seeped between his fingers as he cupped his ears to shield them. Pain ignited and unleashed more of the angeli ability he'd been holding back. "Not again," he said. Cupping his hands, he slammed them together as before. The energy force countered her wail, throwing it back at her.

The agony of it clenched her teeth and stole her breath, shutting off the wail, but her anger was far from spent. With his eyes on his bloodied fingers, she stood as he did and struck hard and fast. The blow to his gut found its mark.

The left hook he saw coming. He stepped around it, but as his foot came down, the terra gave way, closing over the top of it. Infused with his own power, he ripped himself free and dodged the right cross she threw at his face.

"Stop moving!"

A stiff nod followed his, "Fine," as he stood upright, prepared to give her what she wanted.

She landed blow after blow, lefts, rights, and even an elbow to the temple. When he didn't move, she screamed through clenched teeth and swung harder.

Capturing her furious fist in both hands as she attempted to punch his nose, he kissed her knuckles. In one flowing motion, he maneuvered himself behind her and pulled her against his chest, trapping her arms at her sides.

"I'm sorry I had to make you mad," he said into the hollow of her neck, "but if I lose control, Superi will survive. If you do…there may not be a Superi left for us to save."

Her body trembled in his embrace, but she did not fight his hold. Her head fell forward, as her breathing slowed. "After all of that, you were still holding back?"

"You'll never match my strength or speed," he said, "but in other physical ways, you are my equal, and when it comes to being an angeli, you have accomplished what I have yet to realize."

"Which is?"

He turned her to face him. "You've controlled it."

The pride on his face stole her breath. "I could do that before we left the hills."

He smiled and shook his head. "No. In the hills, you were like me. We either opened ourselves up to the power or we held it leashed inside of us. Look at yourself."

She caressed her shoulder where the blue aquis marks of her birth reminded her of her origin and then traced the golden terra marks that should have faded along with her anger, but it was the angeli marks that dominated her attention. The emanating light that had turned inward had yet to dim. The thin golden lines were like runes in her skin now. She raised her shirt to expose her stomach, and there too, the marks remained.

"Tristan, I feel amazing, but why aren't they fading?" she asked, scanning his arms and neck for signs of the mark. "Yours have."

"Because I have yet to fully accept what I am, I think," he replied, "and you have embraced it. I think the angeli marks are permanent for you. Remember the picture in the Alphas' home?"

"The one of the angeli?"

"Yeah," Tristan said. "He wasn't glowing like I do. He was colored the way you are now." His eyes grew focused as he searched his mind for the words he needed. "When we were at the northern gate outside of Exterius Antro, I was blind with rage, and I felt...it."

"It?" Anliac's head twitched as her right brow darted downward.

"Mmm...another depth to what I was," he said, "what I could do, but I couldn't reach it through the anger. When that leash," he cupped his hands an inch away from his own throat, "was locked around my neck, I couldn't reach my ability at all, but I could see the...it, clearly." His breathing accelerated as his pupils dilated. "I thought if I learned to control my anger, I could grab hold of it. That's why I pushed you too far because I thought anger was the key, but I was wrong. Acceptance is the key." He moved the tendrils of hair blowing across her face and tucked it behind her ear. "I think you are a true angeli."

She looked towards Pisces Stragulum. "If they didn't fear me before, they will now." Her lips pressed into thin lines and then she asked, "How long exactly have we been gone?"

"Three, maybe four weeks," he told her. "Why?" His heart stopped when she stepped close and laid her forehead against his shoulder, just as he'd seen his mother do with his dad countless times. He responded as his father had, soothing his hands over her back, without trying to pull her in. Her whispered thoughts mirrored his own.

"I feel as if I'm standing on the edge of forever waiting on the one stiff breeze that will carry me over. Nothing will ever be the same."

Washed onto dry land over the seawall, a closed shell lay between their feet. Anliac knelt, and with trembling fingers pried it open. Laying inside was a perfect pink pearl. "I guess that means it's time for us to go home."

XX
Vantage Point

"If not for the consequences," Nunbia stated, "I would have had you killed by now."

Montilis leaned forward in his seat and clasped his hands until his fingers turned white as he stared at the much older nox. It was either that or knock the man's head off his shoulders. "Your daughter already tried, Nunbia. We both know how that turned out."

His spine stiffened. "Speaking of daughters," Nunbia sneered, "what was left of yours when IA was finished with her?"

The two men came to their feet; Nunbia backing against the wooden wall of the conference waiting room as Montilis stalked forward. He knew better than to put his hands on another member of a Ruling House, but Montilis needed this man to be blinded by hate.

The heavy wooden door to Rayner's audience chamber came open. "General Aquam," Riker's voice boomed, "Do not make your untenable situation more so. Step...Off."

Nunbia smiled. "It looks like you're outranked."

Montilis backed away, retaining eye contact with his father-in-law until he pivoted towards the door and stormed past Riker into the mediocre audience chamber. Two of the four chairs situated behind the crescent-shaped table were occupied. He took the third and glared up at the man seated behind the small desk placed on the raised platform at the back of the audience chamber; its edges bejeweled with red sapphire and its legs gilded in gold.

"You had me summoned weeks ago, Rayner," Montilis stated. "So why the wait?"

With his attention focused on the two men standing in the doorway, Rayner replied, "You come when I call and wait when I tell you too. I thought we'd established this after your last return home."

Montilis bit back a sharp retort and forced himself not to turn around as Riker's threat reached the ears of those gathered in the audience chamber.

With Nunbia's arm in a vise grip, Riker looked at the man and said, "Goad Montilis again and when this is over, you and I will have a private meeting."

"Do not...threaten me."

"I don't make threats."

Nunbia jerked free of the older man's hold and entered the room. "I guess we know where our senior general's allegiance lies. Yongur, Sinpine," he greeted them in turn as he lowered himself into the last open chair.

"We weren't sure if you would come," Yongur said. "Being in the same room with the man responsible for your daughter's death cannot be easy."

Montilis slammed the side of his fist against the tabletop. "Inabeth tried to have me killed, after she had my daughter captured by those in IA." Leaning forward, he looked down the table, spreading his glare among the men. "If you have something to say...find your manhood and say it to me."

"Take it easy, general," Riker said from his standing position beside Rayner's desk. "We're not here to fight."

144

"Indeed," Magistrate Rayner said. "Let us omit the formalities. We all know why we're here. The gateway at Bealson's Grove has reopened. Two angeli walk Superi again, and the gods of Earth have vowed to return in force. The nox must decide what course of action to take."

Montilis opened his mouth to speak, but Nunbia cut him off.

Jabbing a finger in Montilis's direction, he snarled, "He should not get to speak. His daughter is one of them. He'll say whatever he thinks we want to hear to save her."

"It's obvious General Aquam has found disfavor amongst his peers," Rayner stated. "I, myself, have reason to despise him, but that does not change his rank. He is both a general in the Regia Aquam Guard and a member of a Ruling House. He will have his turn but let us begin with you."

Nunbia stood from the table. "I have secured a firsthand witness of the acts committed by the angeli." He gestured to the mute, nox servant standing beside the door. "Let him in."

With a slight bow, the nox opened the door and gestured for the man waiting to enter. When a brown-scaled fera with green eyes and vertical pupils crossed the threshold, the members were as put off by his presence as the magistrate. Flicking his long, pointed tail out of the way of the door as it was closed, he moved to the side of the room where he waited to be addressed.

"He has asked not to be named," Nunbia began, "but he has been in my service for some time. The information he has gathered will be pivotal in determining our course of action."

Montilis's upper lip curled. "He's a spy."

"He's my spy," Nunbia replied.

"He's fera," Yongur spat. "He cannot be trusted."

"Any information is more than we currently have," Sinpine said. "He should be allowed to speak. Hearing him does not necessarily mean we trust him."

"I agree." Rayner folded his hands atop his desk. "What information do you bring us?"

"The angeli and their entourage cannot be trusted," the fera began. "They've been bought by fulgo coin and have an arrangement with the feras for protection. They've secluded themselves in the abandoned town of Pisces Stragulum. A ship full of pirates, many of them aquis wielders, is tied at the dock, and they have at least one aer wielder at the ready should they need to make a quick escape."

Montilis chuckled. "Is that how you see it?"

"You would deny his claims, cousin?" Sinpine asked.

"Leave the family lineage at home, Sinpine," Montilis countered. "There is no place for it here, and no, his information is correct. It is the implied assumption in his delivery of the information that I disagree with it."

"What of the angeli themselves," Yongur questioned. "What are they like?"

"Tristan Matthewson is strong," the fera said. "You've none that can match him head-on and his speed, when he moves, he's impossible to track. He's arrogant but shows no real desire to lead. Be warned of his heightened senses. He sees what others do not. He hears what others cannot, and his sense of smell alone will make it difficult to get close without him knowing. He is fiercely protective of the female angeli. Threaten her, and he will kill you."

"Do you concur with his assessment of the boy?" Rayner asked.

"Yeah," Montilis said, "but I'd be careful not to make the boy comment in his presence. The five have issues with being referred to as children."

"What of the general's daughter," Sinpine asked. "Does she possess the same qualities?"

"She is strong," the fera said, "but not as strong. She is fast, but not as fast. As to heightened senses, I would equate them to that possessed by all feras, but no greater. Her power lies in her elemental abilities, so does her vulnerability, for she has little, if no, control."

"Nonsense," Montilis challenged. "She's trained with her aquis ability since her birth, and I can attest to what she can do with her terra ability."

"Her terra ability leveled a section of IA," the fera said. "It destroyed the road from Certamen to Imbellis, and a quake resulted in the flooding of the coast off of Pisces Stragulum. Is that your idea of control?" He addressed the magistrate. "Her abilities are now tied to her emotions. She is extremely dangerous. The last I saw her, before traveling to Palus Regia, one of the five had to intervene when she turned on those gathered to aid the angeli."

Yongur twisted in his chair to face the fera. "What do you mean, she turned on them?"

"The five have passed down a decree. Segregation of the races is not tolerated in Pisces Stragulum, but when a fera called a nox a darkling, the female angeli rose to his defense. In her anger, she lost control of her ability, and that was what caused the flooding at the coast. The one called Set intervened."

"Is there anything you would like to add," Rayner asked.

"Both possess the markings of the angeli, but until the power is triggered, and the energy of light released, there is but one warning to the temperamental state of their minds."

When the fera failed to complete his statement, Yongur asked, "Well, what is it?"

"Their voices. His voice becomes like thunder, a force of energy in and of itself that can shake the ground and bring down walls. Her voice," he winced in recollection. "It is as beautiful as it is terrible. Like a dracon's wail, it pierces the mind. The pain is overwhelming."

"Do the members of the Ruling Houses have any questions for the fera before he is dismissed?" Rayner asked.

Yongur's head titled. "How was General Aquam received among them? And what of any other men of rank they surround themselves with?"

"Why would you ask him? I'm sitting here." Montilis tensed. "Are you suggesting I can't be trusted?"

"Of course, you can't," Yongur stated. "She's your daughter. We've seen the lengths you'll go to in her name, and as a result, you are of very little value to us. You are here because protocol demands it."

"Answer his question," Rayner stated.

"There are three men the five looked to for council: General Aquam; Lan from Paradisi Colles under the command of Donnin, son of Sole; and Triton, a pirate."

Rayner's brow arched and the men at the table stiffened at the mention of Sole, including Montilis.

"Sole and Lunam," Rayner smirked, "bedtime stories told to fera to keep them from turning feral. Are you suggesting they are more than that?"

"Most stories are rooted in truth, though it be only a nugget of truth that inspires the story to be told."

"Impossible," Sinpine snapped. "There isn't a scrap of evidence to suggest that Alphas of that caliber exist."

The fera grinned. "Which is why they still do. I think Donnin is keeping his distance. I think Lan is being kept very close, and that the five favor the fera for reasons beyond what we see."

"How do we find the Alphas?" Montilis demanded. "If what you say it true, then the nox are at a serious disadvantage."

"I have no problem spying for the nox," the fera admitted without shame. "It sees my family well cared for, but even if I knew where to find the Alphas," he shook his head, "I'd not tell you."

"Your loyalty seems a bit skewed, fera," Rayner stated. "Care to share your reasoning?"

"It's simple," the fera replied. "I fear them more than I fear you."

"Get out," Rayner said. "Your usefulness has found its end."

"As you wish," he said, doing an about face and showing himself out.

"You're an idiot," Riker growled at Nunbia.

"Quickly! Take the side exit," Rayner said. "Have the beast followed."

"On it," Riker said, slipping through the adjacent door to Rayner's private quarters.

"What's going on here?" Nunbia shouted. "He's one of mine."

"He's also one of the feras," Montilis grinned. "You screwed up, Nunbia. He's playing both sides."

Nunbia paled. "Son of a lighten." He smacked his forehead with the heel of his palm. "How was I to know the feras were that organized? Even you didn't believe in the existence of Ruling Alphas."

"General Aquam, do you vow before this council that you knew nothing of the angeli's ties to these…Alphas?" the magistrate asked.

Montilis stood, overturning his chair. "It is clear that the five are more capable of deception than I've given them credence for. You want my strategic opinion? Here it is. The angeli are too dangerous to go unchecked and pose as great a threat to us as the gods. I say we kill the boy and use my relationship with Anliac to trap her. When the gods return, we will have a bargaining tool. Let them have her. Vow to destroy the gateway at Bealson's Grove and let us be done with this."

"You can't be serious," Sinpine said. "After all you've done for her, now you expect us to believe that you would utterly betray her?"

"My actions were to prevent her from becoming what she has. I failed. As always, my loyalties are to my men, to my house, and to my race."

Sinpine grinned. "I say we kill them both."

"And I think there is something depraved about the entire Aquam line," Yongur said. "Magistrate, General Aquam makes destroying the gateway sound simple. In truth, we have no idea of the complexities involved in destroying something created by a Superian rift maker. We know it has to be tied to multiple natural elements, but we've never seen it. If Nathon Bealson used arcanite to power the gateway site, we could potentially destroy the planet by our endeavor, and we would be fools to assume their gods could not access Superi without it. They are not hindered by our curse."

"Continue," Rayner said.

"We are Superians, and the thought of bargaining with a foreign power rankles. IA will answer for the secrets they've hidden, but the weapons have been forged. The angeli are reborn." He shrugged. "Calstar and his brother were able to reclaim them with less than a hundred men. It is my opinion, magistrate, that we use them. When this matter with the gods is at its end, we can collar them ourselves, unless our general would tell us that the tower is stronger than the Regia Aquam Guard, in which case, we can always kill them."

Nunbia's chest swelled with his intake of breath. "I say we end Anliac, who is the greater threat, and capture the boy. We can release him when the time comes to face their gods."

"Then it is a good thing your opinion doesn't weigh in here," Rayner said, gathering scrolls from atop the desk as he came to his feet.

"Who will you send?" Montilis asked.

"The one man capable of doing his job," Rayner replied.

The door to the chamber swung open. "Sir," Riker had sweat on his brow and his uniform was askew, "the fera had a rendezvous with a pack from the Turris region." His gaze slid to

Montilis. "Care to guess which one?"

Montilis's eyes rounded. "Rupert's."

Riker, tight lipped and with a creased brow, nodded.

"Ready your things, senior general," the magistrate said, heading for the side door to his private chambers. "You are now the official nox representative between Palus Regia and the angeli."

"What about me?" Montilis said, his fists clenched at his sides.

"Your loyalty is to your men, to your House, and to your race," Rayner sneered. "It's time you got back to that."

The sound of Nunbia's laughter followed him from the room.

Montilis couldn't go home, not yet. Bursting from the magistrate's house, he turned toward the marketplace intent on remedying the problem. He'd start with a bottle of rum. After that, the absences of his family wouldn't resound so loudly when at last he found his bed.

"Welcome back, general!"

He nodded by rote without seeing the man's face. The soldier was neither the first, nor the last to greet him, but they were all a haze. Anliac would accuse him of abandoning her again. This time he really would lose her.

The sign swinging from above the door read Dracon's Brew. The light inside was dim, the shutters pulled tight. Drunkards found it easier to consume their vice in shadows while the suns remained aloft. Today, it served him. He smacked the top of the circular bar on his way past it to a table in the back corner. "Rum," he told the barkeeper, "and leave the bottle."

Several shots later, Riker found him.

"Better Rayner sends me than Nunbia," the senior general said, sliding into the seat across from him. The glass he'd swiped from the bar clicked on the polished wooden table as he sat it down and poured himself a shot from Montilis's bottle.

Throwing back his head, Montilis poured the liquor down his throat. He hissed as it landed like lead in his empty gut. "I told the council to kill Tristan. I told them to use me to capture Anliac and to use her as a bargaining tool with the gods."

"And you thought Nunbia would counter by suggesting we cooperate with the angeli instead," Riker deduced. "I guess it worked."

"Nope," Montilis said, pouring himself another shot. "He suggested we kill my daughter and use the boy." He drained his glass. "Sinpine suggested we kill them both. You know…" he poured another glass for himself and refilled Riker's "that I lost my son. If I lose Anliac too, well, my House is without an heir. Sinpine's line will then carry the Aquam signet that has been handed down through my line for hundreds of years."

"I trained Jagarid, remember?" Riker said. "I trained you as well. Tell me what I need to know, Montilis."

"Are you asking as my friend, or as Rayner's right hand?"

"Both."

"They are taking fulgo coin because they have no choice," Montilis stated. "After what happened in IA, they washed up on the bank of the Vitreous with nothing. They hate the tower, but they fought what came through that gateway, and they know that if they turn their back, Superi will fall."

"What about the feras?"

"Lan was with them when I met them on the road from Certamen to Imbellis," he shook his head. "They've never men…mentioned Alphas to me. I can tell you that whatever angle the feras are playing, Rupert is their friend."

"What about Donnin?" Riker questioned.

"Donnin has helped them in the past. As to his linea... lineag... lineage, or the five's knowledge of it, I cannot speak. I don't know."

Riker tossed back his drink. "Can the five be trusted?"

"To do what?" Montilis asked. "They're kids. Their parents are either dead or have abandoned them. Their lives have been turned upside down. They've been chased, captured, tortured...changed, and are now being told that they are to face beings that killed their betters by the hundreds. They did not choose to lead, Riker. They are not jaded by politics. They are not after more power. They're simply trying to survive."

Pulling a handful of coins from his pocket, he laid them on the table without counting them and then stumbled, bottle in hand, towards the exit.

"I'm not their enemy," Riker called out.

Montilis turned back to say, "Then prove it. Forget that you are nox. Go to Pisces Stragulum as a Superian."

The sky had faded to grey as he stumbled into the street. His feet carried him home while his mind took a different course. Yongur waited for him on the front steps. His vision was blurred by the rum as was his speech, when he said, "Have you forgotten how to knock or has my house refused you entrance?"

"You're drunk."

"Yeah," Montilis chuckled, "and you're ugly, but what's that have to do with anything?"

Yongur stood. "Did you love her? Inabeth..."

"What does it matter to you?" Montilis swayed on his feet. He stumbled up the steps, passed Yongur, and caught himself on the exterior wall beside the door.

"I thought perhaps you'd like to know why she did it," Yongur said, turning to face him.

Resting his forehead against the wood, Montilis reached for the door lever, and replied, "Not really, but I have the feeling you're going to tell me anyway."

"It was never about Anliac," Yongur said. "Inabeth craved adoration, and Sinpine gave it to her. His plan was to do away with you and your daughter, marry your wife, and claim your signet for his House."

The lever snapped in Montilis's hand. "We all have our ambitions." He shoved open the door, stumbled inside, and ignored the servants that came at a run. Brushing off their attempted aid, his wavering eyes met the faces of his forefathers staring down at him from their portraits hanging on the walls of his foyer. Their disappointment and disgust were like physical blows.

Dragging himself up the stairs by the railing, the image of his daughter swam in his mind's eye, flickering between the nox he'd given life to and the angeli given life by the tower. Finding his bedchamber, he staggered to the porcelain water basin sitting on top of a chest of drawers and emptied his stomach.

Reaching for the small painted portrait of his son on the bedside table, he flopped, fully dressed, onto the mattress. The moons' light shining through the windows of his room offered little illumination, but he didn't need to see it to recall in vivid detail the image that was on it. His son had died with honor. His daughter, after facing Earth's gods, would die with unmatched prowess. He, on the other hand, would die as a traitor, as the man who deserted his men, hung his wife, abandoned his daughter, and drowned at the bottom of a bottle.

The portrait fell from his hands, the glass covering it shattered as it hit the floor, and from beyond the doorway, he heard voices speak his name.

"Montilis will need your help in the days to come. His enemies are many and his allies are few. Stay close to him."

"I'll do my part, Riker. I'll keep him safe. You just make sure Sinpine doesn't get his wish. Protect that girl."

"What do you get out of it?" Riker asked.

"We all have our ambitions."

Darkness overcame him. Sweet unconsciousness claimed him, pulling him down to where nightmares could not find him, at least not until morning.

XXI
The Chains Of Power

"Davimon," Shirman said, exiting his seat to join the other mortalis at the back of Calstar's audience chamber. "I hadn't thought to see you here. Where is your pet?"

Shaking Shirman's proffered hand, Davimon replied, "Lishous is readying the men to travel to Pisces Stragulum...and he is not my pet."

Shirman smacked Davimon's shoulder and grinned. "Yes, yes, we all know. Lishous is your friend; surly beast that he is."

Davimon looked past the lawyer standing before him, across the room of red-robed idiots, to the platform at the front of the room. The seat behind the bejeweled and gilded desk was empty. "Calstar has chosen to be fashionably late to his own meeting, I take it."

"Arrogant fool," Shirman replied, glancing over his shoulder to see who may have overheard and lowered his voice. "Rumor has it, Nutrine is none too pleased with the tower."

"Really?"

"It's about time," Blisham, a nox representative, grumbled as the side door in the front of the room opened and Calstar entered.

"Find me after the meeting, Davimon," Shirman said, moving to retake his seat, "and I'll catch you up on the local gossip."

Davimon nodded and took a seat in the back of the multi-rowed room. His intent was not to participate, but to observe, and he did not need Shirman to tell him that relations between the fulgo of Certamen and IA were souring. What he needed to know was just how far Calstar had slipped from his lofty perch. It would be a great victory for the mortalis if the king were to claim the city of peace.

Imbellis was ripe for the taking. It was fracturing as its citizens abandoned it to return to their home regions. Those who had remained had broken into factions; those who thought the angeli were gods to be worshipped, and those who felt they belonged in chains.

The crack of the gavel focused the men's attention. Though afterward, Calstar took his sweet time in straightening the stack of petitions laying atop his desk. Lifting the first one, he said, "Boloferd, speak your peace."

A red-robed fulgo stood. "Reports from the treasury department are disconcerting, Calstar. The tower's coffers cannot support the angelis' efforts and repair the damage they've caused to our city. As it is, with the exodus of so many, work has all but ceased for the lack of laborers. Not to mention, that as of this morning, after the wagonloads of supplies we just sent to Pisces Stragulum, the city has denied us any more credit. Magistrate Cloemen feels insecure about the tower's ability to pay its tally."

Across the room from the fulgo, Shirman spoke up. "Loss of laborers and debt will soon be the least of our problems," he said. "Looting has begun. They are scavenging the deserted homes, but it will not be long before they start on the ones still occupied. There are not enough city guards. As the people grow more frightened, their morale will begin to fall and that, gentlemen, we cannot allow."

Blisham came to his feet and shoved a pointed finger towards Calstar. "It is your personal ties to these children, and your overindulgent financial support of them, that has caused the dissent. The nox may agree with your decision to ally yourself with them, but this, it is too much, Calstar."

With that statement, the dozen lawyers present lurched to their feet, overturning chairs, as voices raised to be heard over the others. Forgetting that they were lawyers, and not representatives of their individual races, the meeting fell into chaos. The few representatives that were present fell in with the cause of their own kind.

Davimon remained focused on Calstar, whose reaction resembled only boredom. Leaning sideways in his throne-like seat, his elbow propped on the chair's arm and his cheek resting against the backs of his fingers, he listened to the whining of his councilors as they argued amongst themselves.

"Enough," he finally said, slamming down his gavel when his word was ignored.

Grumbles of complaint and whispers of displeasure could be heard as the men returned to their seats.

"The tower supports the angeli because it knows what the general populace does not," Calstar said. "The gateway has opened. The gods of Earth will come, and the angeli are our only real defense against them. So, yes, if Imbellis must fall...if the tower must fall...so that the angeli can rise, then so be it."

The room exploded into an uproar. When Calstar sat upright, clutching both arms of his chair until his knuckles paled whiter than his flesh, Davimon twisted in his seat towards the doors that had swung wide.

"Is that so, Calstar?"

The ranting of the men was silenced by the authoritative tone of the one who'd spoken. The blue robe emblazoned with a hammer and lightning bolt, the golden insignia of Certamen that he, and the fulgo he stood beside, wore brought the meeting to its conclusion.

"This is tower business," Calstar said. "You are here without invitation."

"You hold that seat by the will of Nutrine," the fulgo speaker said, holding up his right hand for all to see the red spiraling marks that covered his flesh from mid-arm to the start of his fingers. "Though after reading the minds of those gathered here, I doubt you will hold it for long."

Calstar shoved back his chair as he slammed his palms down upon his desk's top. "You will not come into my house," he bellowed, "and threaten me!"

The other fulgo, a gate maker by the markings on his face, said, "Do not make your situation worse, Calstar. Disperse these men. You'll be accompanying us to Certamen."

"Get out!" Calstar waved his arm. "All of you! Get out!"

Davimon stood and looked down with raised brows and pressed lips at the telepath's sudden grip on his arm. He was knocked sideways by Blisham in his haste to leave.

The telepath ushered him to the side to avoid the foot traffic.

"You would be wise to remove your hand from my person," Davimon warned. "I speak for King Normis, and he holds no affection for Certamen."

Without speaking, the telepath pushed his thoughts into Davimon's mind. There is a girl in Pisces Stragulum. Her name is Shorlynn. She belongs to Maltris Langworth. If you desire to gain favor with Nutrine, bring her to Certamen."

Davimon yanked his arm free. "The fulgos' treatment of its women turns my stomach. If one has escaped Certamen's clutches, more power to her."

From outside of the room, Shirman called out. "Hey, Davimon, are you coming?"

"Yeah," Davimon replied. "I could use a drink." The last to leave the room, Davimon turned and caught Calstar's stare. With a miniscule dip of his chin, he closed the door. From the crack beneath it, flashes of light emerged as a portal was opened within.

"Shall we go?" the telepath asked Calstar. "You know how much Nutrine hates being kept waiting."

The gate maker stood with his eyes closed. He pressed together the thumb and pinky of each hand as he concentrated on maintaining the portal. The green cresting waves across the fulgo's forehead had transformed into that of Nutrine's private gardens but, like the image shown through the portal, the picture was hazy.

"A level one is the best Nutrine had to send?" The side of Calstar's upper lip furled. "We'll be fortunate if we make it to Certamen in one piece."

The gate maker's eyes came open and then narrowed. "If you are so concerned with my ability perhaps you should stop running your mouth and hurry things along."

"So be it," Calstar sighed. He approached the portal and stepped through.

One step in, one step out, and a moment later, the telepath and gate maker joined him inside Nutrine's gardens, which were surrounded by thirty-foot walls of colored stone. The stones were arranged to depict ancient Superians, with wings that could fly, and fierce beasts that had become extinct when the curse of dividing had struck.

The grass seemed greener here than anywhere else in the region. The trees were as beautiful as those of the grove, but it was for his collection of rare flowers that Nutrine prided himself most. From all over Superi, he had harvested them, including some he vowed came from Earth, and others, he swore came from several of Superi's moons. The fountains interspersed amongst them had been crafted by the most skilled hands, regardless of the race who wielded them, as were the marble statues and stone benches tucked within the gardens' nooks.

Calstar followed the two men as they led the way to the center of the main garden where Nutrine sat in his blue silk robe beneath a stone canopy at a table set for tea. The heavy gold chain around his long neck held the insignia of his wealth and vaulted position.

"At last," the fulgo's equivalent to a king, said. "Come, Calstar. Join me."

The telepath waited to be acknowledged before he nearly folded himself in half in a revolting display of subservience and then dropped to one knee. He held out his red-marked hand for Nutrine to take at his leisure.

Nutrine reached for it and asked, "What news do you have for me, Mirran?"

His eyes, held open, quivered in their sockets as the telepath delivered the information he'd gathered into his leader's mind. His purpose fulfilled, Mirran stood and stepped away without turning his back.

"Thank you, Mirran," Nutrine said. "You never disappoint." He nodded towards the gate maker. "You have done well, Ashtrick. The task I burdened you with was not an easy one, and yet you have surpassed my expectations. Your services will be gifted to a lower House, and within that position, you will find the prestige you so desire."

Calstar snorted when Ashtrick's attempt to bow carried him so far forward he had to catch his balance with his hands to keep from eating dirt. "Do I need to be here for this?" he asked.

His pale cheeks heightened with color, Nutrine flicked his wrist and dismissed the two men, but that far from left them alone. The guards, in blue breeches and tunics overlaid with light chainmail, made no secret of their positions. The long, yellow sashes hanging at their right hips, opposite their swords and scabbards, whipped in the breeze.

Nutrine snapped his fingers and then pointed to the chair across the small circular table from him. "Sit." As Calstar did, he said, "You are forever testing my patience, as did your brother before his most untimely death." From a delicate porcelain pot, he filled the two teacups sitting upon miniature plates, and slid one to Calstar. Tiny, pink and white cherry blossoms, like those found so abundantly in Palus Regia, adorned the set.

Calstar dropped two cubes of sugar into the steaming brown liquid and swirled it round before taking a sip. The imported tea from Portae Stella was delicious, made more so by the cost of it.

"It seems you have forgotten your place," Nutrine said from over the rim of his cup as he watched for Calstar's reaction to his claim.

"You placed me over IA for a reason, Nutrine," Calstar said, cursing inwardly when the cup rattled against the plate as he set it down. "You said it was because I did not succumb to the will of others easily."

"When did I ever give the impression that my own will was included?" Nutrine asked. "I loathe the tower." He leaned back in his seat and crossed his legs, his hands resting in his lap. "Lawyers are bottom feeders, worms who survive off the successes and failures of others. They cry," he threw his hands up, "Peace! Peace! And all the while they sew the very discord it is their purpose to prevent."

"Without the Imbellis Asylum, Superi would unravel. The days of war would return, and as you and I both recall, the fulgo did not fare well when blade was set against blade."

Nutrine tucked his silver-streaked, red hair behind his ear. "It's true we lost territory. We are not fighters by nature, but you must also recall that we accrued wealth beyond imagining, which is why you are here."

"The tower's treasury, or that of Imbellis's, is not your concern," Calstar said as he leaned back in seat and mimicked Nutrine's nonchalant repose.

The corners of Nutrine's mouth twitched. "Is that so? Is it not Certamen's coin that sees your coffers full?"

"Is it not also Certamen that sees them depleted?" Calstar countered. "Let us not pretend that you were unaware of the tower's endeavor to recreate the angeli."

Nutrine's eyes dilated. "Yes. Let us talk about the angeli. What has Certamen's decades of financial and political support gained us?"

"We are not in their highest favor," Calstar admitted, "but neither are we ostracized. They take our coin readily enough."

Nutrine's face reddened. "You are a fool. It will not take that foul pirate long to have coin flowing into Pisces Stragulum, and then we will have lost the only string you've managed to tie to them." He leaned forward in his seat. "We need to ally ourselves to them more firmly. We need," he pressed his thumb and first finger together, "to ingrain ourselves so deep that the five cannot tell where they end, and we begin."

Calstar's brows furrowed as his head jutted forward on his neck. "You are concerned about the pirate?" He couldn't suppress his grin. "He is...a pirate."

"Triton," Nutrine strained to control his tone, "has survived the worst of the major wars. He fought beside Jacob Davadson and the boy angeli's adoptive parents. Their loyalty to him will be far greater than any allegiance we can form. That makes him dangerous."

"Trust me, Nutrine, those children care nothing for coin or political gain. Their focus is on preparing to face the Earthling gods."

"Perhaps so," Nutrine said, "but their followers grow by the day as the races scramble to gain their favor. The profits to be gained in reopening the trade routes from Pisces Stragulum are enormous, and the race that controls the angeli will also control that wealth."

"Where does your ambition stop?" Calstar asked.

Nutrine closed his eyes and inhaled as if he could smell the ultimate victory. "With the combined power of the angeli, one could rule the whole of Superi."

Calstar shook his head. "There is danger in overreaching. The five will not be so easily manipulated. They are not driven by greed or thirst for power, and yours will be your undoing."

With an indignant sniff, Nutrine gestured forward a member of his guard as he replied, "I thought to send you to Pisces Stragulum to speak on behalf of the fulgo. I see now that I was much too hasty in that decision. You lack the foresight and ambition to see our goals realized. Go back to Imbellis, Calstar, save the city from ruination if you can, but leave the dealings with the angeli to your betters."

Calstar was dragged from his chair by the arm.

"Oh, and Calstar," Nutrine added, "I want Shorlynn brought to me. Her betrothed is anxious to be wed."

"She is in Pisces Stragulum," Calstar sneered. "Collect her yourself."

Nutrine grinned. "See that he is properly reminded of his place," he said to the guard, "before Ashtrick sends him on his way."

"Yes, sir," the guard replied.

***

"Sir!" The two guards flanking the outside double doors of the tower rushed down the white stone steps to reach Calstar as he tumbled through the portal to land on his hands and knees.

Seeing the blood, "Sir, how bad are you hurt?" one guard asked as the other helped him to his feet.

Calstar scanned the open plaza with the one eye that wasn't swollen shut and cursed the pockets of citizens who had witnessed his humiliating return. His left cheek was now on level with the bridge of his nose. The dark purple blocked his downward view. Unsure of where to place his feet, he leaned heavily on the guard's arm as he stood. He opened his mouth, and his fingers touched the split in his bottom lip, which his action had torn wide.

"I'm fine," he said. "Believe me," he coughed and tasted blood, "I gave as good as I got, and I've only just begun."

XXII

Mark Match?

Shashara, armed with a wicker basket stuffed full of Set's favorite foods, left the ancient Superian home she, Set, and Davad had agreed to claim for the five of them.

"Good morning, ma'am."

"Hey, Jonas." she smiled as she gave the personal guard Davad had assigned her a once over. "The new uniform looks great." The silver tunic flashing from beneath his black hooded cloak was the uniform's only color. They were worn by those who'd broken ties with their home regions to join the first Superian Guard.

"You...ah..." Jonas cleared his throat, "you look nice too, ma'am."

"Thank you," she bumped the older nox male's shoulder. "I just hope Set agrees with you."

She had played a hand in the design. Though the boys wore tunics, black instead of silver, like the Guard, she'd opted for fitted black shirts with wide straps to attach the fasteners for the silver hooded cloaks she'd had made for the five of them. With any luck, Anliac and Tristan would find the uniform agreeable.

"Where are we headed, ma'am?"

"Jonas, if you don't stop calling me that I'm going to hit you with my basket," Shashara sighed. "I'm sixteen, not sixty. No offense."

"None taken," Jonas chuckled.

"Please," she touched his forearm, "call me Shashara."

"Yes, ma'am."

She shook her head. "I packed an early dinner for me and Set. Well," she shrugged, "I asked Sophie to make it."

"That's what she's here for, ma'am," Jonas said.

Taking a huge breath, she let it out on a long sigh. "Honestly, Jonas, I've never lived in such luxury. It's...a little embarrassing."

"Nonsense," Jonas objected. "The five have risked more than anyone to bring us together, to offer us the opportunity to fight as one against a common enemy. You deserve the perks of your station."

Looking past the town, towards the hills she could barely see in the far distance, she said, "Anliac and Tristan should have been back by now."

"They had already departed before I arrived," Jonas said, "but I will admit to being curious. If they are half the leaders you three have proven to be, who in Superi would dare challenge you?"

"We have no desire to fight against our own kind," Shashara said. "We are here to defend Superi against the beings of Earth, god or otherwise, and then the five of us intend to find less hazardous and less time-consuming aspirations… like becoming mercenaries, or pirates."

Jonas laughed. "Yes, ma'am."

Shashara fanned the sawdust away from her face as they passed the site of heavy construction on a group of wood framed houses. New homes were popping up all over the town.

They had saved as many of the stone buildings around the old marketplace as they could. The stained-glass windows, and antique archways, covered over with thick, green-leafed vines were too charming to tear down. Most of the wooden homes were too far gone to save, but the rubble had been moved away, and new buildings had started going up.

They'd decided to use the bigger stone buildings in the center of town as a type of council district. Her infirmary was there as was the building where Davad and Set handled town affairs. Lan was in another building in the old marketplace where he handled the directors, they'd appointed a few weeks ago.

The new marketplace was her favorite part of town. They'd started a trading post instead of a mercantile considering coin was scarce for everyone. They had a thatcher, a stonemason, two blacksmiths, and a jeweler.

With Set coordinating the town's affairs, and Davad taking control of the political nonsense forced upon them, Jonas was right. They hadn't done half bad. The storage buildings were filling up nicely as more people joined them, and they would get at least one good crop in before the terra grew too cold. Business at the docks, thanks mostly to Triton and his men, was booming. Their first inn was being built there, with talk of a smaller dock for fishing vessels being added as the main chute already had a merchant ship docked in it. Since they had little coin to put down on the ledger, some construction had been slowed.

"You have got to be kidding me," Shashara said scowling. "They've had him in there all day." There was a line of people running clear out of the door to Set's office building. Marching towards it, she said, "They've already made him miss lunch. They will not make him miss dinner as well." She waved her free hand and used the wicker basket on her arm as a shield. "Move, people, out of my way."

Jonas did his best to maneuver around her to force a path open, but she barreled through on her own.

"Hey, you," Shashara said, plopping the basket down on Set's simple wooden desk. "I thought you might be hungry." She glanced over her shoulder to where Jonas had become a one-man wall between her and the people in line.

"I'm starving, actually," Set grinned, "but they're not likely to let me out of here any time soon."

"You have to learn to delegate," she said, giving him her best stern mother look, and then she turned on the people. "May I have everyone's attention, please?" She raised her voice to be heard outside the door. "If you are here because of a housing issue, you need to see Nezra. If you are here because you are sick, you should be at the infirmary speaking to Swiney. If you are looking for work, you'll find Nikolus down by the docks..." she paused, "I'd check the tavern too. For everything else, see Lan and he will give you the name of the director you're looking for. Once you have done this, and only once you have done this, if you feel your grievance, need, or opinion has not been heard, you may come back in the morning. He will be no good to any of us if he grows sick due to lack of food, sleep, or exercise. You have to let him out of here."

There were a few grumbles and complaints, but the people of Pisces Stragulum knew her well enough by now not to push their luck.

Shashara went up on her toes. "Thank you, everyone," she said to their backs before turning to grin at Set. "Are you ready to go?"

"Absolutely," he replied. He slid one arm beneath the basket's handle and took Shashara's hand with the other.

Set's guard, a mortalis with a perpetual scowl, fell into step beside Jonas.

Shashara glanced over her shoulder at him. "Smile, Travain," she said. "I brought enough for you guys as well." The corner of his lip twitched but that was all she got.

They made their way south past the giant stone ovals that had been part of some game the ancient Superians used to play and entered the line of sprawling oak trees bordering the coast. After spreading the quilt out over the short grass and making sure Jonas and Travain would not starve, she handed Set the flatbread wraps stuffed with roasted potatoes and red peppers.

"They're not as good as Char's," Shashara shrugged, "but they aren't half bad. I asked Sophie to make them for us."

"You're too good to me," Set said, leaning in for a kiss.

Shashara blushed, ducked her head and pushed him back. "Set...they're watching us."

"Who?"

"You know who," she said, glancing at Travain and Jonas.

"So, let them watch," Set chuckled, reaching up with his free hand to snag the back of her neck and pulling her in for a quick kiss.

Travain rolled his eyes as Jonas covered his mouth with a closed fist to hide his grin.

"I'm never going to get used to this," Shashara complained. "It's weird having someone follow you wherever you go."

Set scarfed down his second wrap and reached for a third after taking a long pull from the flask of apple cider Shashara had asked Sophie to pack. "Your brother is right though. The five of us are vulnerable. The extra eyes help."

Despite the chill in the stiff breeze, in no time, the direct heat from the suns had their guards flipping their cloaks off their shoulders to hang down their backs.

"Well, that's interesting," Shashara said.

"What is?" Set asked.

"Look at their marks." Shashara cocked her head to the side as Jonas and Travain, shifted their feet under her scrutiny.

"What about them?" Set asked.

Jonas, a level two aquis wielder, had bulbous waves of thin red marks flowing sideways from the top, front, and side of his left shoulder towards the back. Beneath the lines, lay a crescent moon shape that appeared to rock on its rounded side. Travain, a level two ignis wielder, had thick blue rolling marks that flowed from back to front at the lower, outside of his right arm. Above the thick marks were tendrils with sparks that could have been stars. Standing side by side as they were, their opposite shoulders inches apart, the two designs completed each other perfectly.

"How can you not see it," Shashara asked. "Aquis above and ignis below, with the moon's belly full of fiery stars. The two marks look made for each other."

"I suppose..." Set's brow furrowed.

A bell tolled. Shashara and Set locked stares before Set grinned. "Shorlynn's back."

Shashara was less enthused. "So much for our meal."

"What are you talking about?" Set asked. "I'm stuffed," he grinned, "but then I didn't spend my time staring at the guards."

"Ha, ha," Shashara quipped as she and Set gathered their things.

The bell tolled again.

"Another representative, maybe?" Shashara asked.

"I'm not sure," Set replied. "The last rider that came in said King Normis was sending a representative to Pisces Stragulum, but he shouldn't be here for another few days."

Again, the bell tolled.

"Seriously..." Shashara said.

"Come on," Set took her hand. "Davad's going to need to help."

XXIII

A Little Different Here

Wagonloads of goods cluttered the open square of the new marketplace. People, buzzing like bees, pitched in to help empty them. Shorlynn, ashen faced and picking at her nails, was the unmoving island surrounded by whirling chaos.

When she spotted them, she lifted up her skirt and all but ran to reach them.

"Shorlynn, what's wrong?" Set asked, sensing her unease.

"My uncle," she said. "Apparently there was a disagreement between Imbellis and Certamen, and I have been caught in the middle. Maltris Langworth, my betrothed, wants me returned to Certamen, and Uncle Calstar has decided against the union."

"What is it you want?" Shashara asked.

"She wants to be free to make her own choice," Set answered for her, "and Renna, you do have the right. You will not be forced to wed anyone."

Shorlynn's brows crawled up her forehead as a smile stole across her face. She hadn't been called by that name in ages. "Thank you, Set," she said. Tucking her hair behind her ear, she added, "You two should find Davad. King Normis sent Davimon to speak to Tristan and Anliac. Oh," she snapped her fingers, "and it looks like Palus Regia sent Senior General Riker as their representative."

"What about Montilis?" Set asked.

"I don't know," Shorlynn said. "You'll have to ask Riker, but since we are asking questions, how do you know to call me Renna?"

"It's what your parents called you, right?" Set asked.

"Yes, but…"

Shashara shook her head. "Let it go, Shorlynn."

"For now," she agreed with a slow nod, "and don't worry, Shashara," Shorlynn offered, taking the basket and quilt from her, "I'll see to it everything gets where it's going."

"I'll send you some help," Shashara promised.

Set and Shashara picked up their pace, bypassing the office building in the old marketplace when they found it deserted, and hurried towards the docks. Triton stood with his arms crossed beside Davad, whose jaw was working overtime as he clenched his teeth and waited for the nox general to finish speaking. He glanced over at their approach but didn't address them.

"Magistrate Rayner sent me in General Aquam's stead," Riker was saying. "He apologizes for any inconvenience or confusion, but Montilis has been away from his post far too long, and his first responsibility is to his men."

"What?" Shashara snapped. "Anliac is going to be furious."

"That man is constantly getting in our way," Set said, shaking his head.

A brown haired, brown eyed, mortalis man with yellow and silver four and five pointed stars covering his left eye and the entire left side of his face, standing next to a gorgeous, white-furred fera with canine attributes, said, "Forgive the interruption." His formal bow was a grand gesture that brought smirks to their faces. "I was sent by King Normis to speak to the angeli."

"Representative Davimon," Davad said, "allow me to properly introduce myself." He held out his hand. "I'm Davad Jacobson. This is my sister, Shashara Jacobs, and Set Matthewson. We are as close to the angeli as you're going to get this evening."

Davimon shook Davad's and Set's hand in turn, and then bowed slightly as he kissed the back of Shashara's hand before introducing his companion. "This is Lishous, my personal guard."

"You are quite beautiful," Shashara said before she could recall the words.

Lishous' ears twitched. "A man isn't called beautiful."

Shashara turned scarlet. "Of course not, forgive me. Oh! Skylar!" She waved the fierce, fiery, redhead over. "Would you mind doing us a favor? Shorlynn could use a hand."

Skylar grinned. "I've waited weeks to see if she's the beauty the men around here claim her to be."

"She's pretty enough, I suppose," Shashara mouth pinched.

Set chuckled and squeezed her hand.

"She's in the new marketplace, Skylar," Shashara said.

"I'll take care of her." Skylar sauntered off with a crooked smile and an excited gleam in her eyes.

Davimon wasted no time getting them back to the topic at hand. "Are the angeli not here?"

Davad spoke as if the question hadn't been asked. "We appreciate King Normis sending you as a representative," he said. "We haven't heard much from the mortalis regions, and we are very interested in discussing the intent of your king."

"Don't you mean our king?" Davimon asked.

"I am a Superian," Davad replied. "I answer to no king." His eyes darted to Riker, "And Rayner has not helped his cause by separating Anliac from her father for a second time."

Riker dipped his head in acknowledgment.

"How long before the angeli are due to return," Davimon asked.

"I speak for the angeli," Davad told him.

"You're a child," Davimon stated.

"I am the one who says whether you stay or go," Davad said, squaring his shoulders as his spine stiffened.

"Listen, kid…" Davimon took one step forward before Lishous pulled him back.

"I think we found the purpose of the pirates," the fera said as the men on the main deck of Triton's ship, those along the dock, and those who stood as guards, stopped in their tasks to take up defensive stances.

Triton's, "Indeed," rumbled from his barrel chest. "The odds are not in your favor."

"Our age has yet to hinder our progress," a beautiful, piercing, voice from behind them said.

When they turned to see who'd spoken, they saw that Tristan and Anliac had picked up an entourage of Superian Guards on their way through the town.

"Anliac!" Shashara rushed forward, brought up short as her eyes widened. "Your marks…they're…beautiful. But you're not pulsing." Closing the gap between them, she embraced her friend.

"I don't have to transition anymore." Anliac told her.

"They're permanent?" Shashara asked.

"Apparently," Anliac grinned.

"Hmm," Shashara said when words failed her. She turned to Tristan. "Hey, you!" She slugged him on the shoulder. "Welcome back."

"It's good to be back," Tristan said.

"Riker," Anliac's eyes narrowed, "where is my father?"

Riker bowed at the waist. Caught off guard by the changes in Anliac, he used the time to compose himself. "Magistrate Rayner sends his apologies, but if there is talk of war to come, your father belongs with his men."

"I see." Anliac turned to the other men. "You are?"

Davimon dipped his head. "Davimon from Regia Aquam, and this is Lishous. We are here to discuss terms on behalf of King Normis."

"There are no terms to discuss," Tristan said. "You are either here to help build the army that will face what comes through the gateway from Earth, or you are in our way and should return to your king."

"Rumor has it there have been terms laid," Davimon stated, "such as an alliance with the fera, and coin passed from fulgo hands to your own, not to mention what is being said about your..." he paused as he took in the hulking pirate looming like a dark cloud beside Davad, "nautical companions."

Davad took the lead in responding. "The fera have proven our greatest allies, and have asked nothing of us in return, other than our help in facing the gods of Earth. As to the fulgo coin, it is recompense for what the Imbellis Asylum has taken from us. We owe them nothing."

"And Triton is our friend," Shashara interjected, "as he was our father's friend."

"Should your king desire to align with us," Tristan said, "you should begin by not referring to us as children. It's patronizing and we take offense."

"Davad is the magistrate for Pisces Stragulum," Anliac informed Davimon and Riker. "Set is our advisor. The rules here are different, gentlemen. I would suggest you catch up quickly. Shashara..."

"Yeah?"

"Care to catch me up on what I've missed?"

Shashara grinned, reaching for Anliac's hand. "Come on. We'll let them talk, and I'll show you the house we commandeered while you tell me more about these beautiful golden marks."

"What rules?" Davimon asked to the girls' departing back, but it was Davad who answered.

"There are no racial lines here," he said. "Prejudices are to be left at the edge of town. The only dividing line is between those who have sworn loyalty to the Superian Guard, and those who still wear the insignias of other regions. We live and work as one. We all have a voice here."

"It sounds ideal, but unrealistic," Davimon said. He blinked as his left pupil dilated.

"What images have come into your mind, seer?" Set asked.

"I see Magistrate Nutrine of Certamen, and Calstar, upset by a sudden turn of events." He shook his head to clear it. "Forgive me. The foresight has nothing to do with our current conversation. Lishous," he said, "tell the men to fall in and help."

"They can report to Lan," Set said. "He'll tell them where they are needed."

"On it," Lishous said.

"I was told to take command of the Regia Aquam Guard stationed here," Riker added. "I'd like to inform them of the change in leadership as soon as possible."

"I'll show you to your housing," Set offered, "and then I'll take you to Lan. He can tell you where your men are."

"King Normis has questions," Davimon addressed Tristan.

"As does Magistrate Rayner," Riker added.

"And we will see them addressed," Davad said, "but for now you should see yourselves settled. Dinner will be served in the new marketplace soon. Take the time to acclimate yourselves to your new environment, gentlemen, and we will speak tomorrow of expectations. Set…"

With Lishous' return, Set offered, "If the four of you would care to follow me."

Riker and Davimon flanked Set to either side as Lishous and Riker's guard fell in behind. Leading them away from the dock, north towards the white stone and red domed houses in the old section of Pisces Stragulum, Set said, "I apologize if your arrival was not what you were expecting. We don't stand on formality here. It's a waste of time."

"I fear I've gotten off on the wrong foot with Magistrate Jacobson," Davimon said.

"Call him Davad," Set told him, "and don't worry about it. You're not the first representative to come through here questioning our ability to lead. What you all fail to understand is that we did not ask for this. However, we have been burned too many times to allow others to direct our course. Trust…does not come easily to us."

"Did you trust Montilis?" Riker asked.

"More than most, and less than some," Set replied. "Here we are," he said, opening the front door of the stone house. "Lan's room is up the stairs at the far-right end of the hallway. Shorlynn is the current representative for the fulgo, but she's been in Imbellis, so I'm not sure if she will be joining you, or if Anliac and Shashara will put her with us. There are two rooms available upstairs, and one large room with double beds on the first floor."

"I'm sorry," Riker said. "If the fera have already chosen this place, should we not choose another?"

"This house has been designated for representatives," Set informed him. "We meant what we said, gentlemen, there are no racial lines here."

"What about our men?" Davimon questioned.

"The soldiers are housed together in units placed all over the city," Set told him, "but your guard, and…Lishous, right?" When the fera nodded, he continued, "Are more than welcome to join you here, or they can join your men."

"I could learn to like this place," Lishous said, the first to enter the house.

At Set's inquisitive expression, Davimon explained. "Lishous and I come from very different backgrounds. He is my closest friend, but most often, he is excluded from the circles I run in."

"Because you are mortalis and he is fera," Set ascertained.

"Yes."

"It is the way of it," Riker stated. "Very little is known of the fera race, and with the whispers of ruling Alphas rising, all the other races are taking precautions. You wouldn't happen to know anything about that would you?" he asked Set, who grinned.

"Feel free to wander around," Set said. "With the fresh supplies Shorlynn brought in, there is bound to be a celebration tonight. Come and see for yourself what happens when the people of Superi forget what they are, and remember, who they are—Superians."

As Riker gestured that Davimon should enter first, and his guard took up position outside the front door, Set left them to rejoin Davad, Tristan, and Triton, grateful to find them at the half-finished tavern instead of on the dock.

Triton sat at a table with a mug of ale in one hand, and his other riffling through the uncut gems poured out before him. "I suppose this puts us even."

"And Pisces Stragulum with more than fuzz in its pockets," Tristan agreed.

"What's up with Anliac's marks?" Set asked as he joined them. "I thought she went to Dura Mortis to find some control."

Tristan grinned. "Anliac has fully transcended. Her angeli abilities are ready and waiting."

"You mean the marks are permanent?" Triton asked. "Then what's wrong with yours?"

Pouring a shot of whiskey down his throat, Tristan slammed his glass down on the table, and said, "I'm just not that evolved yet."

Taking the pressure off his brother, Set changed the subject. "What do we think of our two new arrivals?"

"According to Anliac, you're our advisor," Tristan said. "What was your take on them?"

"Thank you," Set said to the fulgo bartender who placed a drink before him. "I think Riker's loyalties are torn between Rayner and Montilis, which means he can go either way. Davimon is arrogant. Without formality and ceremony, he feels off balance. His loyalty is firmly with King Normis, but Lishous is intrigued by what we're trying to do here. Regardless, the bond between Davimon and Lishous is as strong as the one between us. The fera will follow the mortalis's lead."

"I'll dispatch a missive to Palus Regia informing Rayner of our displeasure at Montilis's absence," Davad said, "and let's keep Riker out the loop until Set has a chance to get a better read on him. Davimon warrants a little extra attention. We know he'll report everything he sees and hears to King Normis. Let's make sure we know what he is delivering."

"And you," Triton said to Tristan, "need to be wearing your new uniform before dinner tonight. The people of Pisces Stragulum need to see the five of you together. You and Anliac were gone far longer than we anticipated."

"I can't believe all the changes in the town. We are going to have to start calling it a city soon." Tristan said, focusing on the tabletop.

Set's eyes widened. "So...umm...looks like Shorlynn can bunk in the house with us?"

"There are only five rooms," Davad said. "Where will she sleep?"

"In what was supposed to be Anliac's room," Set snickered.

Triton cleared his throat. "If you will excuse me. This conversation just became awkward." He took his drink with him as he sauntered back outside.

"Am I missing something?" Davad asked.

"All I'm going to say is it's a good thing I wasn't made magistrate," Set teased. "There will be a hand-fasting soon."

Tristan, red faced, stood. "I'm going to check on the girls and get changed."

Davad shook his head. "Wait! I'm the magistrate," he said. "Ugh. I'm so confused."

XXIV
New Choices

The moons over Superi bathed the old marketplace in a soothing blue light. A half dozen bonfires offered warmth to those who'd chosen to take their meal amongst the others instead of returning to their homes.

Davimon and Lishous were at a loss.

"Is that Anliac?" Lishous asked.

"Where?"

"There..." he pointed to a serving station where Anliac spooned a hearty stew into a bowl held out before her. They watched her smile as the man moved on and a woman and child stepped up. "I thought they were here to lead these people, not serve them."

Raucous laughter drew their attention to a group of men squatted in a circle tossing dice.

A fulgo guard, wearing the insignia of IA, punched a nox of the Superian Guard, on his shoulder. "That's what I'm talking about, partner," he said. "We are kicking Regia Aquam's arse tonight."

"The night is young," a mortalis said. "Do not count Regia Aquam, or Palus Regia, out just yet." He bumped knuckles with a nox, who was apparently teamed up with him.

A hodgepodge band of musicians struck up a lively tune from a gazebo in the center of the marketplace. Lishous snarled when he felt his hand taken and looked to see who dared to touch him. He found a silver-furred fera with deep green eyes and a tantalizing tail staring coyly back at him.

"Save the teeth for someone it frightens and come dance with me."

"I don't dance."

"You do now," she said, dragging Lishous into the circle of dancers.

Davimon didn't stand alone for long.

"Care to dance with me?" a lovely mortalis woman, peach skinned, and doe eyed with golden hair flowing to the backs of her knees, asked.

"It would be my pleasure, ma'am," he said, taking her by the hand. He nodded to Riker on his way past.

The clash of metal on metal had Riker cutting a path around the merrymakers to where Davad and Tristan were sparing while a group of men and women in varying uniforms cheered for their chosen champion.

Tristan's sword, one of the finest he'd ever seen, was held at a defensive low guard as Davad took the offensive high stance with the blade held over one shoulder and the hilt at eye level. Each time Davad struck, Tristan countered, until their blades whirled, and their feet carried them round in and altogether different type of dance.

Riker glanced sideways as Triton joined him.

"What do you think?" Triton asked.

"Neither are master swordsmen," Riker grinned, "but they don't stink."

The flat side of Davad's blade caught Tristan against his side.

"Ha! I win," Davad said, raising his sword high as he turned in a slow circle to accept his accolades.

Tristan chuckled. "I was distracted." Tapping Davad on the shoulder, he said," I'll be back."

Davad nodded. "Okay, who's next?" he asked the crowd.

"I am," a short, stocky nox said as he unsheathed a broadsword with a defensive hilt and squared off.

Tristan held out his hand. "I'm glad you decided to join us tonight, General Riker."

"It's just Riker," he said, taking a firm grip on Tristan's offered handshake. "Your sword is impressive," he grinned, "perhaps one day your skill will be worthy of it."

Tristan laughed. "It's not likely." He clenched his fist, turning his wrist inward, as the golden lines appeared, pulsed, and then faded. "My skills do not require a blade."

Riker cleared his throat. "I meant no offense."

Head cocked to the side, Tristan said, "None taken."

"Speaking of blades and where they belong," Triton said, "I come bearing a gift." Pulling his hands from behind his back, he revealed a pair of silver-clawed gauntlets bound in black leather with a pale blue depiction of a dracon stitched into them. "Why not give the dracon blade to one with the potential to master it, and you try these on for size?"

Tristan grinned. "Trying to keep me in your debt, old man?" he chuckled as he took them, running his fingers over the dracon, feeling the smooth leather slide beneath them. Rotating the gauntlets, the flame caught within the silver of the claws. "They are spectacular."

"They are yours." Triton laid his hand on top of Tristan's shoulder. "You may not carry Matthew's blood, boy, but seeing you as you stand now," his head jerked in a stiff nod, "you look every inch his son. He would be proud."

From the corner of his eye, Triton watched as Skylar, with a dangerous sway to her shapely hips, stalked Shorlynn from the shadows.

"Thank you, Triton," Tristan said. "If Davad ever tires, I'll see to it he gets the sword."

"Good," Triton replied. "If you will excuse me." He turned away to do a little stalking of his own.

"If I may be so bold as to ask," Riker said, "how did you come by the sword?"

"I slayed a dracon with it," Tristan smiled. "So much for your theory about my skill," he smacked the general on the shoulder, "wouldn't you say, Riker? Excuse me." He turned and shouted, "Davad, catch!"

His opponent had forced Davad onto his heels. He held his broadsword at mid-guard in a purely defensive move and was losing ground. With his left hand, he caught the hilt of the thrown sword and let the heavy broadsword thud to the ground.

"It's yours," Tristan said, laughing as Davad whirled the light, dracon's sword and stepped forward to reclaim his offensive stance.

Tristan found Anliac still holding a ladle in her hand, although everyone had been served. "Beautiful," he chuckled, "what are you doing?" Her smile, timid and completely unlike her, made his heart squeeze.

"Not all of the people talked to me," she said, hanging the ladle over the edge of the stewpot, "but most of them did. Some of them even welcomed me home." She beamed.

"I haven't seen you light up once, kid," he teased, pulling her against him. "I'm proud of you." Pulling the gauntlets from where he'd tied them at his belt, he said, "A gift from Triton, although they cost me the sword." At her bunched brows, he explained, "Triton asked that I give it to Davad. Apparently," he said, leaning forward to kiss her forehead, "the guy has more potential than I do."

"The gauntlets will serve you better," she said. "It was a good trade. I hope you thanked him."

He nodded. "Have you seen Set or Shashara?" Tristan asked.

"Not since she shoved this outfit at me and told me to put it on," Anliac said. "I'm not sure what I think of it. I mean, the pants are great, and the cloak is nice, but these straps," she tugged at them, "they dig a little, and it's a lot of black." She laid her open palm against his chest. "Though I must say," a smile turned the corners of her lips, "I do like you in yours."

Tristan nibbled at her neck, and whispered, "Seeing you in this getup makes me wish we were back in Dura Mortis."

"Behave," Anliac said giving him a gentle shove. "Dance with me."

"Let me take you home," Tristan grinned, "and we'll dance all you want."

"Promises, promises," Anliac said, her pupils dilating as she took his hand. "Well, come on then. Let's go home."

***

"Whoa!" Set yelped as two streaks of golden light zoomed past the docks where he and Shashara had escaped to and headed towards the domed houses on this side of the town.

Shashara laughed. "It's a good thing no one else is home." Her eyes rounded. "Oh no! Poor Sophie!" She grabbed Set's arm and started to rise.

He tugged her back down.

"We have to warn her," Shashara giggled. "It might not be safe for her in the house," and the two of them fell into a fit of laughter.

"Shh," Set said, putting a finger over her lips. "They'll hear us."

***

"Are you gentlemen having a nice time?" Shorlynn asked, tracing a slender finger down a soldier's cheek. "You boys work so hard; it's the least Pisces Stragulum can do to see a smile on your faces at the end of the day."

"Our day got better, Ms. Shorlynn, with your return," a nox in a Superian Guard uniform said, raising his pewter cup.

"Here, here..." the rest of the men toasted as Shorlynn smiled and sashayed her way toward the next cluster of eagerly waiting eyes.

Skylar intercepted her. "Why do you do that?"

"Excuse me?" Shorlynn asked. "I'm afraid I don't know what you mean."

When Shorlynn tried to step aside, Skylar moved with her. When Shorlynn's forward momentum brought them close, Skylar took full advantage. "I've watched you since Shashara asked me to give you a hand. You don't have to do that, you know? Flirt with every man you see. Not here. That's what make Pisces Stragulum different and worth defending. We are not bound by tradition, or race, or even ability for that matter. We can be who we really are. So, tell me, little vixen, why do you throw yourself at men when you desire the attention of a woman?"

"I am betrothed to Maltris Langworth," Shorlynn said. "I have no interest in another, be it man or woman, and my behavior is as it should be for a woman of my station." She flinched when Skylar raised her hand and traced her cheek with the back of her fingers.

"Will you honestly deny it," Skylar asked, "or is it that you do not know?"

Shorlynn placed a fist over her heart. "Forgive me," she said, "but I suddenly find it difficult to breathe." Skylar laced their fingers together, and all she could do was stare, her mind blank.

"Come with me," Skylar said, snatching a blanket off some guy's shoulder as she urged Shorlynn away from the crowd towards the coast. She led her down an easy slope of terra where a small fishing dock floated out over the aquis. The moons of Superi adorned the grey sky from horizon to horizon, with nothing before them but the gentle lapping waves of the oceanus.

"Sit with me?" Skylar asked.

Shorlynn sat slowly, unsure of the wooden board that was shifting beneath her feet. She arranged her skirt over her bent knees before wrapping her arms around them.

Skylar laid a portion of the blanket around Shorlynn's shoulders, and the rest around her own. As she got comfortable, she asked, "Can you keep a secret?"

"When I try," Shorlynn replied. Her lips trembled when she tried to smile, so she looked away.

"I am the daughter of Magistrate Nutrine of Certamen."

Shorlynn snorted. The flash of anger across Skylar's face made her rethink her opinion. "What? You're serious?"

"Nutrine and my mother were to be wed," Skylar said, "but then he found her in a compromising situation that led to doubts concerning my lineage. Vows were never spoken, and my mother and I were cast out. She told me what it was like coming up in a Ruling House. I wouldn't wish that life on any female."

"It's not like we are passed out as offerings," Shorlynn told her. "Our value comes from our innocence."

"You are dressed and jeweled as dolls, and then used in whatever means the fulgo men decide. It's not okay," Skylar's boot toe tapped against the wood.

Shorlynn chucked. "Is that your way of putting your foot down?"

Skylar nudged her shoulder with her own. "Can you be serious?"

"I don't know what your mother's life was like in Certamen," Shorlynn sighed, "but I loved my life in Imbellis. The tower was my palace. I was treated like glass with the most wealthy and powerful men coming to gain my affections." Taking a deep breath, Shorlynn took a moment to collect her thoughts. "Before being tasked with entertaining and spying," she admitted with a shrug, "on the five of them, I was making arrangements for my move to Certamen where I would have wed into the second most influential Fulgo House in the region."

"You're not being held here against your will," Skylar said. "So, why are you still here? If that is the life waiting for you, and that's the life you want…"

"It is. It…was," Shorlynn winced, "but then I met them, and everything started to change."

"You mean the Five?"

"Is that what you call them?" Shorlynn asked.

Skylar nodded, "Everyone does. I don't know who started it, but it was right after you left."

It was Shorlynn's turn to nod. "I've seen Anliac and Shashara around Tristan and Set. Two sets of equals are all I see, and, I think, I want that." She held up her hand. "In no way does that mean I think the fulgo way of doing things is wrong, but maybe it is wrong for me."

"So then chose a different path," Skylar told her. "I did."

"That's right," Shorlynn grinned. "You became a pirate."

Skylar laughed. "If you weren't so beautiful, I'd make you pay for that remark."

"Skylar..." she blushed. "You can't say things like that. I'm betrothed."

"Betrothed is not wed." Skylar lay her fingers along the far side of Shorlynn's jaw and urged her to turn. "Kiss me, Shorlynn," she said, tilting her head. "Let me show you who you are."

Shorlynn's lips parted as she closed her eyes. She knew when Skylar braced her opened palm flat against the dock, when her weight shifted forward, and still she gasped when Skylar's warm breath mixed with her own. She jumped and pulled away when the bell tolled from the marketplace.

"We should go," Shorlynn said, wide-eyed and flushed.

Skylar checked the position of the stars. "It's growing late. The angeli are supposed to address the people tonight."

Standing, Shorlynn asked, "Will you escort me back?"

Taking the blanket that had fallen to the dock, Skylar laid it over Shorlynn's shoulders; holding it in place as Shorlynn freed her hair from beneath it. "Will you let me walk you home later?"

Shorlynn's eyes shot to her shoes, the toe of one swaying from side to side, as she said, "Maybe," and reached for Skylar's hand.

XXV
A Symbol

The old marketplace was full. People found themselves pooling between the stone buildings and small, wooden homes to hear what the five young people, drenched in black and cloaked in silver, had to say.

"That's almost too much pretty to look at," Skylar said, smacking the back of two guards' heads until they gave up their seats at a table set up for dice.

"They are beautiful," Shorlynn agreed, and then in a timid voice added, "The boys aren't bad looking either."

"Hmm," Skylar grinned. "I knew it."

They fell silent as Davad, standing with the others up on the covered platform from which he'd delivered his first speech, raised his hand to gain the crowd's attention.

"Our town is filling out to be a grand city," he said, stretching his arms wide with an even wider grin splitting his face.

The crowd laughed at his ambitious claim.

"As you can see," he continued, "our champions have returned. Let us show them welcome."

Shouted greeting and bellowed cheers followed.

Davad raised his voice. "It has not been easy, but with the lines of race removed, look what we, the Superians, can do!"

The cheers became a roar as civilians and soldiers raised their fists and voices high.

"What is our motto?" he asked.

"Lead to serve!" the crowd bellowed. "Serve to lead!"

"That's right," Davad said. "We are gathered tonight for more than celebration. We have brought together all of the representatives from the regions of Superi; to hear their questions and to give answers, not only to those who hold positions of authority, but to those like you, who are effected most by the words spoken here."

Davad turned to the left side of the podium. "Gentlemen," he gave a half bow to Lan, Riker, and Davimon, who sat behind him in wooden, straight-backed chairs, and then turned to the right, "and lady," he said, bowing to Shorlynn, who sat beside Skylar out in the crowd, "As representatives of those who are considering joining the Superians, those who stand guard over Superi, we welcome your questions. Senior General Riker, representative for Magistrate Rayner of Palus Regia," with his back to the crowd, Davad let slip a grin, "would you care to speak?"

Riker's brows shot up, but Davad's grin told him he got him. He stood, tugging the hem of his shirt until the brass buttons were correctly aligned, and then said, "Thank you, Magistrate Jacobson." Shoulders back, arms at his sides, he addressed those gathered. "The welcome here has been generous. The social structure of Pisces Stragulum is inspiring and should it one day be held as the example for Superians, it will rival the great cities of peace and diplomacy. I am privileged by the opportunity to witness such an endeavor."

"Thank you," Davad said as Riker retook his seat. "Lan, spokesman for Donnin of Paradisi Colles, you have been with us since before our arrival in Pisces Stragulum and have proven you are an ally to our cause. Would you like to speak?"

Lan, his white feathers taking on a blue cast beneath Superi's moons, stood. "Those who know me, know my thoughts, and those who do not, do not yet matter. Should the gods of Earth return, the fera will stand with the Five."

Applause went up from the crowd.

Davad raised his hand to calm them. "From Regia Aquam, representative of King Normis, Davimon, the floor is yours."

"Thank you, Magistrate Jacobson," Davimon said. "Having newly arrived, I would request a measure of time before attempting to articulate any queries if it would not offend." He bowed as if before his king and sat back down.

"Last, but certainly not least," Davad said, "Shorlynn, representative of Imbellis and of the Asylum, would you care to join us?"

Shorlynn peeked at the woman sitting beside her, tucked her hair behind her ear, and shook her head.

Set walked forward until he stood shoulder to shoulder with Davad. "As Magistrate Jacobson has said, this gathering is for more than celebration, it is about the ability to raise our voices and speak our minds. Are there those among you who have questions or that wish to speak?"

There were murmurs, and foot shuffling, but no one spoke out.

A brown-furred fera, with large black spots, sat on the ground towards the front of the crowd in a Superian Guard uniform.

"You there," Set said, when he and fera made eye contact, "ask anything you'd like."

She stood, wringing her hands. "I…umm…I suppose I do have a question."

"Speak up," someone further back shouted.

She cleared her throat. "All Ruling Houses have an insignia, or a symbol, that allows those who serve to identify those they follow."

"Oh," Shashara said, "we are not from Ruling Houses." She blushed when the crowd chuckled.

"You rule this town," the fera said. "We are your people."

The crowd cheered the fera's words as Davad turned to Tristan and Anliac for help.

"Very well," Tristan said as he and Anliac stepped forward to join the other three, "if the people of Pisces Stragulum desire to place their own mark upon us, we will gladly bear it. For our pride in this town, and in the Superians that reside in it, could not be greater."

"It should be a symbol that represents the Five," a gruff voice in the back called out.

"Stand and be recognized," Set encouraged.

"Sorry, sir," a nox soldier replied coming forward as the crowd parted to make way for him, "but speaking in front of people gives me the bubble guts."

The crowd laughed with him, as did Davad, who said, "I understand," with a broad grin.

Anliac, dressed in black, with her silver cloak hanging down her back, the golden marks on her shoulders and neck exposed along with that of her aquis marks, addressed the people. "This insignia will not be ours alone," she said. "It will brand us as one. Therefore, it is my opinion, that the Superians should have a say in its creation."

Tristan, Davad, Shashara, and Set clapped their hands with the rest of the crowd, nodding their heads in agreement.

"Then it is settled," Davad said over the roar. "The people of Pisces Stragulum will determine the insignia for the first House of the Angeli!"

The Five stood as one, and in one voice said, "We lead to serve. We serve to lead."

XXVI
I Want Her Dead

Zadyst tied his horse's reins to a pole outside the raggedy wooden building and barged through the double swinging doors of another dusty, dilapidated, tavern. Rickety tables were clustered with men in course linen, with unkempt hair and beards and dirt covering their hands and faces as if aquis frightened them. The women were equally disheveled.

His upper lip furled as his nose wrinkled at the unpleasant scent of unwashed bodies. He made his way to a table in the back where he leaned his chair against the wall and propped his booted feet on another.

A mortalis, with knotted blonde hair and a dirty apron tied about her full waist, sauntered over. Her hazel stare soaked up his fine, brown leather clothes, and fur-lined cloak, pausing on the heavy gold chain suspended from his neck before catching on the bulging coin pouch dangling from the belt at his waist.

"Pick your poison, stranger," she said.

"Rum, if you have it," Zadyst replied, "whiskey, if you don't, but for Superi's sake, try to find a clean glass."

The waitress's eyes narrowed as she sniffed. "I'll spit shine it myself."

She went to turn, but Zadyst grabbed her by the wrist. "If you wish to keep that sassy tongue, I suggest you keep it still."

The tension in the tavern grew intense as chair legs scrapped against the wooden floor, and a bear of a man rose to her defense.

"What is your problem?"

Zadyst laced his fingers across his chest as he sneered back at the barrel-chested nox. "I have spent months and an obscene amount of coin chasing a rumor that brought me to this…" he flicked his wrist, "wasteland of villages. I was promised a legendary terra wielder, and what do I find instead? Pathetic level one and two wielders that are of no value to me."

The volatile scowl dropped from the nox's face. There was a moment of suspended silence followed by a burst of boisterous laughter from the patrons. The legs of Zadyst's chair slammed against the floor.

"Care to let me in on the joke?" he asked.

"Renda bring us the bottle," the nox said as he spun a chair at Zadyst's table around backwards and sat. "We're going to need it."

Renda slammed the bottle and glasses down. "I say we send him off on his fancy horse, in his fancy clothes to go see old Bengim. It would serve him right."

Zadyst scowled. "Who is Bengim?"

"I'm Quinten, by the way," the nox said, pouring an inch of liquor into each of the glasses, "and Bengim is the wielder you're looking for."

"How do I find him?"

"You don't," Quinten told him. "Not unless he wants to be found."

"But you know where he lives?" Zadyst asked, his body tense.

"Why are you looking for him?" Renda piped in from behind the crude bar.

"That's not your concern," Zadyst sneered.

Quinten chuckled. "It is if you want our help."

Zadyst tossed back his drink and picked up the bottle to refill it. "I was taken prisoner by IA, along with a wagonload of others."

"And you think you'll get old Bengim to help you get your revenge against the tower?" Quinten chuckled. "Bengim doesn't involve himself in politics."

"One of the women taken captive was Anliac Aquam, daughter of General Montilis Aquam of Palus Regia, who made friends with Shashara Jacobs, daughter of Jacob Davadson."

At the mention of the mercenary, Quinten's humor evaporated.

"The mercenary broke into the tower with three others; Davad Jacobson, Set Matthewson, and Tristan Matthewson. The mercenary took an arrow to his heart, but the two girls were freed. Anliac found the keys and opened the cages to release the other prisoners...all but mine."

"You're talking about the five young rulers of Pisces Stragulum," Quinten said. "Two of which are rumored to be angeli."

"The day the prisoners made their escape, I alone was left alive to tell the tale," Zadyst sneered, "and I fed every crumb of information I had to the brothers of the tower. They vowed to bring her back. She was supposed to suffer, but when they finally recaptured her, they turned her into an angeli and then set her free."

"So, you want revenge for her leaving you behind," Quinten ascertained.

"I wanted revenge for that, yes," Zadyst replied, "but my hatred of her has been fueled by the events that followed her transition. She is responsible for the gateway at Bealson's Grove reopening. She is responsible for the threat of the Earthling gods returning to Superi. She and the one called Tristan are gaining power as we speak. If allowed to go unchallenged, they will be the first gods of Superi, and I will die before I submit to their rule. The whole of Superi is in danger because of her, and I intend to do whatever is necessary to stop her. I will lay her cold and rotting corpse before the gateway to appease the gods of Earth, and then I will be known as the savior of Superi."

With an arched brow, the corner of his mouth twitching, Quinten replied, "It sounds like you have it all figured out."

"Anliac is an aquis wielder by birth," Zadyst said, "but whatever IA did to her, she emerged not only an angeli, but a terra wielder. She has another angeli by her side, along with an epoto who is said to be as dangerous as his father, Matthew Suxson. Perhaps you've heard of him as well?"

Quinten's eyes narrowed. "You may think us ignorant of worldly affairs and crude by your standards but let me enlighten you. Jacob Davadson, Matthew Suxson, as well as Beth Mathews, their stories...," he shook his head, "...they are epic. The brutality they showed during the war put fear in the hearts of those who faced them on the field of battle, and as for General Aquam, his prowess during the aquis war made him a titan among men. Bengim fought against him, as did many of us sitting here. You will be hard pressed to find anyone willing to stand against the progeny of these people, so tell me, how do you intend to enlist Bengim's aid?"

Zadyst smiled. "I have information that Bengim will want."

"There isn't a nugget of truth on Superi that Bengim could not dig up on his own," Quinten said. "You are playing a dangerous game, and those you would bet against have the upper hand."

"Bengim will be the weapon I wield. Anliac will never see it coming." Zadyst upended the bottle forgoing the use of a glass and grinned. "I've told you my story. Now tell me where I can find him."

Quinten drummed his fingers on the table. It was a moment before he spoke. "There are seven villages that make up Satio Mapalia. You'll find him in the largest of the seven. The one that's been abandoned since Bengim lost his family. He turned his back on civilization a long time ago, and of those who've sought him out in the past, few return. The caverns beneath the village he's claimed holds more than riches. They hold the bones of those who've taken the path you're on."

Rising from his seat, Zadyst tossed a few silver coins onto the table. "I'd rather be entombed in caverns of riches than live in submission to self-proclaimed gods."

No one tried to stop him as he exited the tavern. Swinging into his saddle, he tugged the reins and spurred the horse into a gallop. The closer he drew to the abandoned village, the more tenuous his trek became until he was forced to abandon his horse and make his way on foot.

The cracked, rough terra appeared more or less flat, but a myriad of chasms opening down into a labyrinth of pathways endangered his every step. He could see the entranceways into the mining shafts branching from the paths, but he found no way down into them.

He cursed the time it took him to circumvent the obstacles as he made his way towards the ramshackle wooden buildings and decrepit stone houses sporadically placed around an old trading post in the center of the village.

When the ground trembled, Zadyst grinned. "I know you're here, old man," he said. "Show yourself." A loud boom had him pivoting around, his eyes popping wide, as a jagged split in the terra raced towards him. He lunged to the side, rolling as he came to his feet.

From the rip rose the terra wielder. He hovered two feet above the rift, walking on air, until he was again over solid ground. Shirtless, he settled on bare feet, clothed in tattered grey trousers. Short for a fulgo, the man's physique was toned and muscled. Bald, except for the white pointed goatee spearing from his chin, his matching bushy brows were pulled down in a menacing scowl.

"You have nerve, boy," Bengim said.

Two orbs of fire appeared in Zadyst's hands. He tossed them up, juggling them before he clenched his fists and they dissolved. "Our elements may vary, but we are equals, you and I."

Bengim snapped his fingers, and the terra opened up, swallowing Zadyst whole, leaving only his neck and head above ground. "You were saying?"

Zadyst took shallow breaths as the terra around him drew tighter. "I have a proposition for you."

"I'm not interested." Bengim turned as if to leave him there to rot.

"You will be," Zadyst replied. "I have information you want."

"Doubtful," Bengim sneered.

Zadyst clenched his teeth as the pressure of the terra increased. His eyes bulged as blood was squeezed up from his body to pool in his head. "I know who killed your family."

Bengim's long legs picked up speed as he charged toward Zadyst and gave a solid kick to the side of his face. "You will die painfully for mentioning them."

The ability to draw breath was lost as the terra became a vise, slowly tightening until Zadyst's ribs began to snap. Though he viewed Bengim through a haze of pain, his stare was unwavering.

With a growl, Bengim waved his hand and the terra spewed Zadyst out like regurgitated bile. "Speak," he said, "while you still live to do so"

Grunting as he sat upright, his arms wrapped around his ribs, Zadyst shook his head. "It

173

doesn't work that way. I need your help."

Bengim's feet rose from the terra as his eyes narrowed. "I will bury you," he swore. "I will crush every bone in your arrogant body. I will drink to the music of your screams."

"Do it," Zadyst retorted with a crooked grin, "and I'll take what I know to the grave."

"I've broken greater men than you," Bengim snarled.

"No, you haven't," Zadyst stated as fact. "Brave men have lost their courage, warriors have become traitors, ideals have been abandoned, and loyalties have been forgotten when the cost of their stance was pain. A desperate man, however, whose purpose is fueled by hate, is not so easily swayed by torture. I choose death above submission," Zadyst said, "and for the record…" a rolling ball of fire shot forth from one extended hand, blocked by a shield of terra, just as the ignis would have struck, "you are not the only wielder here capable of delivering death."

"What is it you want from me?"

"I want you to create a diversion of chaos and carnage," Zadyst replied. "My enemy is the heart of Pisces Stragulum, an angeli by the name of Anliac Aquam. I want her dead, and if her four companions are casualties of our assault against her, so much the better."

"Do you think me stupid?" Bengim snarled. "Do you think me so far detached from the world that I am unaware of the threat from the gods? You would ask me to destroy Superi's only defense?" Bengim shook his head. "It would lead to my demise and Superi would be lost."

"If you were so concerned with Superi, you would be in Pisces Stragulum adding your strength to the causes of the angeli, but here you sit."

"Perhaps I do not wish to die for any cause but my own," Bengim countered.

"Which is why I came armed with the knowledge of who murdered your family," Zadyst said with a smirk. "For as long as Anliac lives, your enemy lives as well."

"Why should I trust you?" Bengim asked. "What proof do you have?"

Zadyst reached into his pocket and withdrew a tarnished silver chain. A heart-shaped locket was suspended from it. Inside was a tendril of dark brown hair tied with a thin, blue ribbon. "I believe the last time you saw this," Zadyst said, "it hung from the neck of your wife."

"Give that to me." The silver chain, beckoned by the terra wielder, heeded his call. It flew from Zadyst hand into his own.

"Give me your word." Zadyst said, unfazed by the loss of the locket. Knowledge of the one who'd taken it was of far greater use.

"I will split the world and swallow Pisces Stragulum whole," Bengim vowed, "You have your assassin, and I will have my revenge."

XXVII
We Have A Problem

The ascending stone stairway breeched the bank of clouds, which concealed the palace of the Greek gods from the humans below. Apollo raced towards the top of the mountain in long strides, infused with power from the sun. Shirtless, with leather girded about his waist and thighs, his bronze skin played over his muscular physique.

The screech of a large hawk gave warning as it dove into his path. He plucked a feather from its tail and then dodged a swinging fist as the creature of flight transformed into an angry goddess.

"Was that necessary?" Nike asked, rubbing her tender bottom with one hand while snatching for her feather with the other.

Apollo, laughing, held it out of her reach. "You should watch where you fly."

Her white wings folded, cascading down her back like a floor length cloak, as she stood before Apollo in a silver tunic and war skirt with a long, red sash whipping around the sword and scabbard at her hip. Brushing away the wisps of honey-brown hair fluttering over her face, she asked, "Why are you running?"

"It helps me think," he said, continuing his upward trek.

Taking two strides to every one of his to keep up, she asked, "What are you thinking about? Does it have something to do with the secrets you've been keeping?"

"I'm not keeping secrets, Nike," he grinned, "but if I were, you would be the last deity I'd share it with. You are far too capricious to be trusted with knowledge of any importance."

Nike drew up short. Planting her hands on her tiny waist, she said, "Well, that was rude," as she darted forward on armored boots that climbed her long shapely legs before wrapping her thighs in silver wings. "I can keep a secret."

Apollo glanced sideways and arched a brow.

Nike chuckled. "I can," she said, "when the mood strikes me." When Apollo sniffed, she sighed. "Oh, come on. You can't still be angry."

He stopped cold and turned to glare. "I...destroyed the dragon of Delphi." He slammed his closed fist against his chest. "I claimed the Pytho and with it the power of prophecy created by Gaia herself. And what did the goddess of victory have to say about it? Nothing."

"Apollo," she laid her hand on his broad shoulder, "in the eyes of the humans, your triumph was legendary, but it was a long time ago, and by the standards of the gods, it was no great feat."

He jerked his flesh from beneath her palm.

"You," he pointed his finger in her face as his muscles twitched with restraint, "irritate me." He stalked off.

Nike would not be shaken. "What would you have had me do? You killed the Python, but at the time, Ares was unleashing hell on earth." She shrugged. "He overshadowed you. Get over it."

"What about during the Pythian?" he asked. "Even by the gods' standards, it was I, not Ares, who reigned over the games."

"And everyone knows it," she said. "Why do you need me to herald your victories?"

"I don't," he said from between clenched teeth.

"There has been talk amongst the gods, Apollo," she said. "Whatever it is your hiding, I'm going to find out."

"I'm sure you will," he concurred, "but not from me."

She cocked her head to the side. "Ares is with Zeus," she said. "Perhaps he will have looser lips."

"Nike," Apollo began.

The goddess transformed and flew upwards towards the gates.

"Curse it all," Apollo snarled. Like a sunbeam, moving from here to there faster than thought, Apollo reached the gates at the top of the mountain just as she did. "Mind your own business," he shouted as she once again took on her human form.

She inhaled deeply as together they passed through the gates. "Can't you smell it, Apollo? Battle is coming. A battle greater than the wars fought by humans over politics and religion, greater than the wars fought over tragic loves, the aether is charged with energy like in the days when once we ruled this world."

Apollo pivoted towards her. He cupped her cheeks in his palms and forced her to look at him. As his hard stare bore into her own, he said, "What is it about death and bloodshed that calls to you so? Why does Ares alone hold your esteem?"

Wrapping her hands around his wrists to tug them away, she answered, "It is not Ares, but the wars he incites that appeal to me. For it is in those desperate moments, when life hangs by a thread, a choice, a decisive slash of a blade, that heroes are made. To watch them rise, to see them victorious, to have my name on their lips when the heat of battle consumes them; this is what I desire."

Stoic, he stared at the white stoned palace and ascending stairs that led to a golden arched door. Its columned wings, the interconnecting structures raised to honor the gods, were brocaded in gold. The beauty of the palace rivaled the wonders of the world, and yet it sat forgotten, lost in time, as were the gods themselves.

He weighed his words. "We look down upon the humans of Earth. We watch their battles, their ceaseless desire for confrontation, and grow nostalgic for the wars in which we were the heroes. We are not what we once were, and now," he mounted the steps and grabbed hold of the bar that would open the door, "war comes."

Apollo left Nike behind as he entered the palace. His boot steps echoed in the cavernous environs in which marble statues stood, fountains bubbled, and where portraits and busts immortalized all the great gods of the Greeks. They had survived for thousands of years on the reminiscence of their glory. It wasn't enough.

"Brother," Artemis said, "where have you been?"

Apollo turned and watched his sister's approach. As he is like the sun, she is the vessel of the moon. Her long silver hair and cream-colored skin, lips like berry wine, deceived the eyes. The armor and silver bow slung across her back spoke with truer words. The maiden goddess, the huntress, was a warrior.

"You have not answered any of my calls," she said when he didn't reply.

"It is good to see you, Artemis," he embraced her before setting her back, "but now is not the time. I must speak to Zeus."

When he would have walked off, she caught him by the arm. "Brother, Zeus has been in a dark mood of late." She stepped closer and whispered, "There was a ripple in the aether. The Korean god, Munsin, sent a Seonnyeo to tell Zeus of it. None of us knows what it means."

176

He covered the fingers digging into his arm with his hand. "That's why I am here."

Her gold-flecked brown eyes grew round. "What do you know?"

His smile fell flat. "Not now," he said, and turned away.

The sweet smell of incense ticked Apollo's nose as he crossed the threshold of the inner sanctum, which was illuminated by braziers of fire. Its ceilings were vaulted, held

Revolution

aloft by pillars too great to embrace, and its floor was a window to the world below.

Zeus sat upon his throne, a golden wreath about his head, with six empty seats spread out to either side in a crescent formation. His bronze skin was stark against the white toga he wore, but it was the intensity of his azure eyes that gave Apollo pause.

Ares, in black fitted leather, wore a scowl as he stood before the sundial placed at the heart of the circular chamber. Arms crossed, he insisted, "I'm telling you, Zeus, Russia is the key and religion is the hand that will turn it." He rubbed his hands together. "It will ensure that the conflict continues for generations."

"Enough!" Zeus tapped his staff against the floor and the room quaked. "There has been fighting in that region since it was named Kievan Rus. The humans are not our primary concern. I want to know about Munsin's claims."

Ares's arms dropped to his sides as his spine stiffened. "Do you have something to say, Apollo," he spun to face the other god at the back of the room, "or did you simply come to bask in the glory of your betters?"

"I have the knowledge Zeus seeks," Apollo replied. "So why don't you go play war with your human soldiers in Russia, Ares, and leave the larger concern to me."

Ares drew his sword, but before he could bring it to bear, Zeus's thunderous voice boomed.

"Go, Ares," Zeus said, "before it is lightning, instead of your feet, that sends you on your way."

Pointing with the tip of his sword, Ares vowed, "This is not over between us. I assure you."

"Something to look forward to then," Apollo grinned as Ares disappeared.

Zeus chuckled. "Why must you rile him so?"

"We all have ways to pass the time," Apollo said.

"Indeed," Zeus agreed. "I have such a pastime awaiting me in my private chamber, and Hera is otherwise occupied on earth." He rose from his throne. "Tell me quickly what you know of the disturbance in the aether so that I may take advantage of my wife's absence." The corners of his mouth turned down at the visage Apollo wore.

Brows pulled low, lips pressed them, the skin around Apollo's eyes crinkled. "It was the angeli, Zeus."

"The Superians?" Zeus asked, sighing in relief. "They are weak and still cursed." He patted Apollo's shoulder. "Easily handled," he said as he made his way towards the door.

"Zeus!" Apollo shouted. "I faced two of them on Superi...and lost."

The god of the sky turned. "You have my attention."

"Call a summit," Apollo said. "We're going to need everyone..."

Pronunciations:

Tristan Matthewson.... (Tris-tan Matthew-son)
Anliac Aquam.... (An-li-ac A-quam)
Shashara Jacobs.... (Sha-sha-ra Jacobs)
Davad Jacobson.... (Da-vad Jacob-son)
Montilis Aquam.... (Monti-lis A-quam)
Triton.... (Tri-ton)
Razoran.... (Ra-zor-an)
Socmoon.... (Soc-moon)
Inabeth Aquam.... (In-a-beth A-quam)
Malstar Luxson.... (Mal-Star Lux-son)
Calstar Luxson.... (Cal-Star Lux-son)
Inabeth Aquam.... (In-a-Beth Aquam)

Superi.... (Sup-ery)
Imbellis Asylum.... (Im-bell-is Asi-lum)
Pieces Stragulum.... (Pi-sces Strag-u-lum)
Exterius Antro.... (Exter-ius Ant-ro)
Catena Piscari.... (Cat-er-va Pis-cary)
Caterva Concentio.... (Cat-er-va Con-cen-tio)
Certamen.... (Cert-a-men)
Exsulto Adpulsu.... (Ex-sul-to Ad-pulsu)
Vitreus.... (Vi-tre-us)
Antro.... (Ant-ro)
Paradisi Colles.... (Para-di-sy Col-les)
Palus Regia.... (Pa-lus Re-gia)
Nubilosus.... (Nub-i-Losus)
Turris Cavae.... (Tur-ris Ca-vae)

ABOUT THE AUTHOR

Clint Thurmon: is a native Texan. He lives in Southeast Texas with his wife Crystal, and has an adopted daughter, four sons, and a baby girl. Clint works as the director of projects of high voltage construction. He enjoys an active lifestyle involving several forms of martial arts, as well as physical training and weightlifting.

Christina Ranae Williams: was born in Claremore, Oklahoma. She currently resides in Southeast Texas with her husband and three children; where she's spent the last thirteen years focusing on her family. At thirty-five, she's made the decision to turn to the next chapter of her life, by embracing her passion for writing; reaching for her dream with the help of Superi's creator Clint Thurmon.

www.ingramcontent.com/pod-product-compliance
Lightning Source LLC
Chambersburg PA
CBHW021101130626
46554CB00002B/478